Praise for Tricia Stringer

'A witty, warm and wise story of how embracing the new with an open heart can transform your life.'

—*Herald Sun* on *Table for Eight*

'...a moving, feel-good read...a warm and uplifting novel of second chances and love old and new in a story of unlikely dining companions thrown together.'

—*Sunday Mail*, Adelaide, on *Table for Eight*

'Delivers a gentle satisfaction that makes it a great choice for a lazy Sunday afternoon read.'

—*Books + Publishing* on *Table for Eight*

'A wonderful story of friendships, heartbreak and second chances that may change your life.'

—Beauty and Lace on *Table for Eight*

'Stringer's inviting new novel is sprinkled with moments of self reflection, relationship building, friendships and love.'

—Mrs B's Book Reviews on *Table for Eight*

'...a really moving tale...This truly was a delightful read that left me with that feel-good happy sigh...be enticed by this tale of love and laughter, trauma and tears, reflection and resolution.'

—The Royal Reviews on *Table for Eight*

'This winner from Tricia Stringer...is a light-hearted and easy-to-read novel with twists and turns along the way...enjoyable and fun.'

—The Black and White Guide on *Table for Eight*

'Tricia has no trouble juggling a large cast and ensuring we get to know and connect with them…captivated me start to finish; if it wasn't the wishing myself on … a relaxing and pampered break from reality, it was connecting with the characters and hoping they managed to find what they were looking for. Definitely a book I didn't want to put down!'

—Beauty & Lace blog on *Table for Eight*

'A heart-warming novel that celebrates friendships old and new, reminding us that it's never too late to try again…If you enjoy stories that explore connections between people and pay tribute to the endurance of love and friendship, you will love Stringer's new novel. *Table for Eight* is a beautiful book…If you're looking for a get-away but don't quite have the time or funds, look no further – this book is your next holiday. Pull up a deck chair and enjoy.'

—Better Reading on *Table for Eight*

'Tricia Stringer has written a gorgeous book...The pages are filled with wonderful characters, each with their own well-crafted arc and polished prose. This book is the equivalent of a hot bath or a box of chocolates, it's comforting and an absolute pleasure to immerse yourself in. It's realistically romantic, filled with hope, a tale of second chances. If you enjoy well-written family sagas, look no further. *The Model Wife* is perfect.'

—*Better Reading*

'[A] heartfelt saga.'

—*Herald Sun* on *The Model Wife*

'Tricia Stringer excels at two things: strong, empathetic characters; and finding an experience or emotion shared by many, then spinning that small kernel of commonality into an engaging novel. *The Model Wife* is no exception...Stringer's prose is warm and friendly. She pulls you in with an easy and flowing writing style that quickly has you absorbed by the action. It's easy to read, but that doesn't mean it's shallow.'

—Other Dreams Other Lives

'I would highly recommend this novel and hope that readers will gain what I have from it. *The Model Wife* is a beautiful story with familiar challenges and a strength of a family who are connected via their life experiences together.'

—*Chapter Ichi*

'A well-written, engaging story of the everyday challenges of life and love…a wise, warm, and wonderful story.'

—Book'd Out on *The Model Wife*

About the Author

Tricia Stringer is a bestselling and multiple award-winning author. Her books include *The Family Inheritance* and *The Model Wife*, and the rural romances *Queen of the Road*, *Right as Rain*, *Riverboat Point*, *Between the Vines*, *A Chance of Stormy Weather*, *Come Rain or Shine* and *Something in the Wine*. She has also published a historical saga; *Heart of the Country*, *Dust on the Horizon* and *Jewel in the North* are set in the unforgiving landscape of nineteenth-century Flinders Ranges. Tricia grew up on a farm in country South Australia and has spent most of her life in rural communities, as owner of a post office and bookshop, as a teacher and librarian, and now as a full-time writer. She lives in the beautiful Copper Coast region with her husband Daryl, travelling and exploring Australia's diverse communities and landscapes, and sharing her passion for the country and its people through her authentic stories and their vivid characters.

For further information go to triciastringer.com or connect with Tricia on Facebook, Instagram @triciastringerauthor or Twitter @tricia_stringer

Also by Tricia Stringer

The Model Wife
The Family Inheritance

Queen of the Road
Right as Rain
Riverboat Point
Between the Vines
A Chance of Stormy Weather
Come Rain or Shine

The Flinders Ranges Series
Heart of the Country
Dust on the Horizon
Jewel in the North

TRICIA STRINGER

Table for Eight

First Published 2018
Second Australian Paperback Edition 2020
ISBN 9781489280954

Published by
HQ Fiction
An imprint of Harlequin Enterprises (Australia) Pty Ltd.
Level 13, 201 Elizabeth St
SYDNEY NSW 2000
AUSTRALIA

A catalogue record for this book is available from the National Library of Australia
www.librariesaustralia.nla.gov.au

Printed and bound in Australia by McPherson's Printing Group

For Sian

One

Paddington, Sydney, 2018

The rain stopped as quickly as it had begun. A sudden thunderstorm in January wasn't unusual, and Sydneysiders were used to it. On the corner of Mayfair and Third streets the white facade of number one gleamed in the sunshine, a beacon of brightness among the dull greys and terracotta colours of the old terrace houses stretching away on either side. Shoppers were out again, stepping over the puddles, and two joggers pounded around the corner, nearly colliding with a delivery woman who pushed open the door to number one.

A bell tinkled, and the courier paused to take in the decor. The room's discreet lighting added to the sunshine coming in through the large plate-glass windows. The walls were lined with racks of chic dresses, tailored jackets and stylish skirts, perhaps a little too crowded to show off their quality. Another circular rack in the middle of the room drooped under the weight of formal wear – long dresses, silk creations, laces and chiffons in colours from the brightest scarlet to the softest blue. The delivery woman strode forward.

The young assistant at the counter looked up expectantly, her ready smile creasing into a frown as she noted the wet footprints being left across the whitewashed wooden floor of the main entrance to Ketty Clift Couture.

"Deliveries at the side entrance."

The courier plonked a small box on the counter. "I was told this was urgent."

The assistant's eyes widened when she saw the name of the sender. She signed for the package, scooped it up and, with only a quick thought to retrieving the mop on her way back, she hurried past the heavy linen drapes of the fitting rooms, through the client lounge and out into the brightly lit work area.

Neither the woman bent over the large cutting table nor the other two focused on their sewing machines paid her any attention. The warm tones of jazz could be heard each time the machines paused. Six women worked here and they took turns to select the background music of the day. Today it was Miss Ketty's choice and she always went for jazz.

In the back corner of the workshop she caught a glimpse of her employer's now chin-length grey hair. It was swept back from her forehead in a look that might be harsh on some but was softened by the waves of hair that curled back and around to her cheeks. It was a crowning glory above the elegant but simple black shirt and pants the older woman favoured. She was bent over a drafting table with her manager, both engrossed in what they were doing. The assistant hurried in their direction.

Ketty Clift adjusted her reading glasses on her nose with one hand while the pencil in her other swept over the paper, adding lines to the sketch. She was acutely aware of Judith Pettigrew's sharp gaze following every mark.

"Just another tuck here below the bust and slightly more fullness over the hips…and the hem sitting just at the knee."

"You don't think it a little over the top for a woman in her seventies?"

Ketty added a few finishing touches. Judith was an excellent dressmaker and more than capable in her role as Ketty's second in command, but she sometimes lacked that little extra creativity to translate the customer's design into a sketch that could then be drafted to a pattern. Her eagerness to get the job done sometimes made her seem brusque but beneath her stiff exterior Ketty knew Judith to be kind-hearted. Ketty also knew the woman who had ordered this dress very well. It would be the fifteenth special outfit she'd made for Enid Hanson and she understood what suited the tall but curvy body of her long-time customer.

"Our work is to make our client look exquisite but also to feel special. Enid still has great legs." Ketty's hand swished lower down the paper. "The eggplant shantung will complement her complexion and provide a soft rustle as she moves." She could picture Enid in the outfit that, as yet, was still a sketch created from the magazine pictures she had provided at her first appointment.

Ketty looked up at the sound of hurried footsteps across the polished cement floor of the workroom.

"Miss Carslake, we do not run in this establishment." Judith's clipped voice brought a glow to the younger woman's cheeks and she slowed her approach.

Ketty smiled at the young assistant. Her dark brown hair, straight with a fringe sitting just above her eyebrows, created a frame for her pale face. She wore a dress of sheer black fabric she'd designed herself. It was skilfully cut so that it floated around her small frame without bulk and stopped well above her knees showing off her shapely legs, which disappeared into the black leather of her Doc Marten boots. A heavy silver chain hung around her neck, the cross it supported resting just above her waist and giving her the look of an angelic but slightly underdressed nun.

"What is it, Lacey?"

"This box arrived by courier. I think it's the buttons you were waiting on for Miss Davidson's wedding dress." The assistant's look shifted to the orchid chiffon and lace garment on a nearby dressmaker's dummy.

"Thank you, Lacey." Ketty took the box and hugged it to her. "What a relief."

"The dress is looking beautiful, Miss Ketty." Lacey turned back. "You can rest easy on your cruise now. It will be finished in time." She stayed where she was.

"Is there something else?"

"I also wanted to let you know my IT friend has your new website ready. I'd love to show it to you before you go."

Ketty glanced at her watch. "I don't think I have time, Lacey." The internet was of little interest to Ketty when it came to her business, which had been founded on the belief that it was the personal touch that mattered to her customers, and she couldn't equate that with the online world. She'd had a young lad create a website several years earlier and had done nothing to it since. Lacey had convinced her to update it. A friend would do it for a small cost. Ketty had been pleased by Lacey's enthusiasm but it was low on her list of priorities. "It's your baby. I'm happy to trust you with it and I'll have a look when I return."

Lacey hesitated, a flicker of concern crossing her face.

"Hurry along, Miss Carslake." Judith drew herself up. She had a similar angular frame to Ketty's but she was almost a head taller and towered over petite Lacey. "I assume the front counter is unattended while you are out here."

"On my way back now, Mrs Pettigrew."

"I'll look at it as soon as I return." Ketty smiled. "And don't forget to help yourself to my cherry tomatoes when you water the garden, will you? I can't bear to think of them going to waste and I know how much you love them."

"Thank you, Miss Ketty." Lacey's look was earnest. "And don't you worry about your garden, or your cat, or the office, or the website. I'll take good care of it all."

"I know you will." The thing was, changes would have to be made to the business. Ketty's recent trip to the accountant had made that quite clear and a website was the least of her concerns.

Lacey gave a brief nod then strode briskly back across the workshop. Beside Ketty there was a sniff, a soft but censorial sound.

"You won't be too tough on her while I'm gone, will you, Judith?"

Judith flung out her hands. "She finds any excuse to desert her post. You know if she's not checking the internet, she'll be out in the yard every five minutes while you're gone, on the pretext of looking after your garden."

Ketty met her manager's glare. "I like her spunk."

Judith sniffed again. "I like her but I'd prefer she spent more time on her actual duties. Mail, banking, accounts, answering the phone and greeting customers." Judith ticked off her fingers as she spoke. "And I still can't get used to those boots."

"Every day is a new surprise when she comes to work." Ketty smiled. "It was high cork wedges yesterday. We need someone with some style to be the face of the shop."

"There's style and there's style."

Like Ketty, Judith wore plain skirts or trousers to work. It was the job of the dressmaker to blend in and not outshine the customer but the front of house should have glamour and Lacey had that in spades.

Ketty looked back at her sketch. She had great faith in all her employees, Judith included. She had come to Ketty twenty-five years ago as a young dressmaker, painfully shy with a terminally ill mother-in-law to care for and a useless husband. She had been desperate to find work but had lost previous jobs because of her poor attendance. Ketty had instantly recognised her excellent tailoring skills. She had employed her and allowed her to work from home when necessary. Her trust in Judith had been rewarded over and over again; with her hard work and clever cutting, she had proven herself one of the best dressmakers Ketty had ever had. Once the poor mother-in-law finally died Judith somehow found the courage to leave her husband and start afresh. It may have been partly due to Ketty's offer to subsidise the rent in a nearby flat. Nonetheless the confident woman beside her had long since come to stand on her own two feet and had well and truly left behind the downtrodden girl who had first arrived at her door.

"You got the real pearl buttons then?"

Ketty didn't have to look at Judith to know her expression was disapproving. "I did."

"We quoted reproductions."

"I know."

"Then you'd like me to amend Miss Davidson's account?"

Ketty once more locked eyes with Judith. "No. It's my wedding gift to the bride."

"It's no wonder you're barely making a profit, Ketty." Judith tutted. "Have you heard back from the accountant yet?"

Ketty looked down at the package she gripped in her hands. She had confided in the other woman in a weak moment over their regular Friday evening glass of wine a month or so ago. Now Ketty wished she hadn't. The accountant had made it quite clear she was losing ground and had to make changes. Given her age he'd suggested she sell or simply close her doors but Ketty couldn't imagine giving up work yet. It was her life, and not only that; her staff depended on their jobs. His next suggestion, that she cut back on staff, had been equally unpalatable, and yet she had to do something. Her cruise had been booked long ago and in the light of the current situation she regretted it but she'd lose her money if she didn't go. No point in that. And then there was the thought that getting away would give her some breathing space and, she hoped, a clear enough head to see what was best for the future of her staff and her business. She lifted her shoulders and fixed Judith with her most confident smile.

"Please don't worry, Judith. I have it all in hand." She opened the package, dismissing the subject. "Just make sure the buttons are sewn on before Miss Davidson arrives for her final fitting this afternoon." The bride-to-be had declared the replica pearl buttons perfect on her first visit to plan the style and the fabric, but at her last fitting she had declared she'd asked for the real thing. She'd lost three more kilos requiring extensive remodelling, and had swapped her extremely high heels for a lower pair. Bridezillas were one of the reasons Ketty avoided bridal gown work as much as possible but lately she'd accepted any business that came their way. When Miss Davidson had made a fuss Ketty hadn't argued but had agreed to change the buttons. Judith was a stickler for the rules and didn't understand the importance of small acts of benevolence to customers, which not only made them happy but brought return business and recommendations, something that was more important than ever in this online shopping world.

"Very well. I will do it myself." Judith's stiff face softened into a smile. "Now please go and gather your things. The taxi will be here soon."

"You're sure you're clear about this design?"

"Very."

"And you'll see to the buttons?"

"As soon as you leave."

"You will remember our job—"

"Is to make the client feel special. Of course." Judith held out her hands for the package.

Ketty handed it over. With a sharp nod of her head, she turned and made her way through the staff kitchenette and beyond to the stairs leading up to her flat.

The bright and airy rooms above the shop were her haven. The layout was simple: an open plan living, dining, kitchen, with two bedrooms at the front, both with double doors opening onto the balcony which wrapped around the sides of the building with iron lace balustrades. She went to the second bedroom now to close her case and paused to take in the large ball of fluff settled right in the middle of it.

"I wish I could take you, Patch," she crooned as she scooped up the black and white cat. "But you'll be much happier here with Lacey fussing over you."

Patch's look was one of disdain. She blew him a kiss anyway, set him on the floor and shut her case. It took some force to keep the lid down so she could tug the zip closed.

She substituted her plain work clothes for a pair of wide-legged white linen pants and a turquoise three-quarter-sleeved soft knit that finished at her hips. She clinched a wide belt at her waist then sat on the bed to swap her flat black shoes for a pair of blue espadrilles. The woven white handbag with its blue leather trim lay on the bed beside her, already packed with her tickets, passport and wallet.

Her parents had taken her on her first cruise when she was five. The coastal vessel that had travelled between Adelaide and Port Lincoln in faraway South Australia could hardly be called a cruise but she counted it regardless. It had been a rough trip and Ketty hadn't left the cabin. She could still picture the yellow light bulb swaying above her bunk and feel the lurching roll of the ship beneath her. She had been terribly seasick. It hadn't deterred her. At twenty-one she had gone on a cruise with three girlfriends. They had all worked together at the John Martins' costume department in Adelaide and had saved hard to be able to travel together. Once again she had been sick, but that had been more to do with alcohol consumption than rough seas.

Her next cruise hadn't been until she was twenty-nine, and she'd gone with only one girlfriend that trip. Ketty had been sick on board that time too – but it had had nothing to do with the cruise. She sighed. She no longer probed the wound of that terrible time, when she had come home and her world had turned upside down. It was more a scar now; a notch in life's interesting journey and the reason for her move to Sydney. It hadn't happened overnight but Ketty Clift Couture had been catering for special birthdays, weddings and glamour events for nearly thirty years. And when she got the chance, and money allowed, she kept taking cruises.

She glanced at her watch, surprised she'd wasted so much time daydreaming. She did a final check around her flat. Patch had settled on his cushion in a shaft of sunshine from the kitchen window.

"Be good," she said. He barely twitched a whisker.

Ketty bent to give him one last pat, gathered her things and made her way downstairs, throwing a scarf around her neck as she went. Each of the women in the workroom stopped what they were doing to hug her farewell.

"Safe travels, Miss Ketty." Ning, whose name in Chinese meant tranquillity, gave Ketty a gentle squeeze. Ketty always felt like a giant compared to her long-serving seamstress. Nothing ever fazed Ning. Her family had been babies when she had started with Ketty and now she worked to put them through university.

Tien was next, with a similar small frame to Ning's but not so calm in manner. "Don't carry anything from strangers." She wagged her finger and Ketty agreed she wouldn't. Tien's favourite television show was *Border Security* and she often regaled them with stories of ill-fated international travellers.

Ketty moved on to Birgit.

"And no playing up." She grinned at Ketty. "Unless he's a good-looking lad and then it will be all right."

Ketty chuckled. Birgit was half her age and sounded more Irish than the Irish even though she'd been born in Australia.

"Thank you all for keeping on while I'm away. You know I appreciate it and I'm sure Judith will have everything in hand."

Birgit gave an eye roll. "She will. Now don't be worrying about us. You head off and God bless."

For a moment Ketty hesitated but Birgit shooed her towards the door and she was sent on her way to the chorus of their goodbyes. The weight of the decisions she had to make made their farewells all the more poignant. By the time she had trundled her case and overnight bag out to the front room of the shop she felt as if she'd been through the wringer.

Lacey was talking on the phone. Ketty gave her a wave and looked out the window; no sign of the taxi yet. Judith opened the front door for her.

"Miss Ketty?"

She turned back. Lacey had put down the phone, her brown eyes dark circles in her pale face. "That was the customer who came two weeks ago and wanted the six bridesmaids' dresses and the two flower girls'."

Ketty held her breath.

"She's cancelled."

"Why?" Judith asked before Ketty could, her tone much sharper than Ketty's would have been.

"She's seen what she wanted on the internet."

"She'll lose her deposit." Judith shut the door firmly, bringing a harsh rattle from the bell.

"We don't have it."

"Why ever not? It's your job to make sure we've received deposits before we order fabric and the fabric has already arrived. I shelved it myself."

"It's not Lacey's fault." Both employees turned to Ketty. "I ordered the fabric. I thought it would create work that could be done while I was gone. Perhaps you can see about returning it, Judith."

"The hot pink shantung for the flower girls perhaps, but not the bolts of bridesmaids' fabric. That was from Delia's Designs and they don't take returns."

Ketty sighed. The last of her pre-holiday excitement whooshed away like air from a deflating balloon. She had been secretly appalled by the bride's choice of fabric for her attendants and she shouldn't have ordered without the deposit but she'd been so desperate to leave work for her employees in her absence she'd taken the risk. "Perhaps we can use it for something else?"

Judith's eyebrows raised. "Multicoloured retro stretch jersey – and a paisley design to boot! – hasn't ever been used here before and I cannot possibly imagine who would want it."

Ketty's heart sank even further. What would they do with two full bolts of that?

A car horn tooted outside.

"That's the taxi." Judith pulled Ketty into a stiff hug.

Ketty hesitated. "I can't leave you with this mess."

"Of course you can." Judith put a guiding hand on Ketty's back and opened the door again. "We'll sort it."

"You have a fab holiday, Miss Ketty, and don't worry about anything. We will make sure every client feels special in your absence." Lacey gave an emphatic nod of her head then collected Ketty's overnight bag and followed them outside. "Mrs Pettigrew and I will hold the fort."

Ketty smiled as Judith's eyebrows shot even higher. She turned away quickly, overwhelmed by their generosity.

The bags were loaded and Judith had bundled her into the taxi before she had time to draw breath. She lowered the window. "I can keep my phone on if you need to ring or email."

"Don't bother," Judith said. "We won't."

The taxi driver became animated over her destination.

"White Bay? You are going on a cruise?"

"Yes."

As the taxi pulled away she twisted in her seat for one last glimpse of her two employees, one tall, one petite, hands raised in farewell. The ornate facade of Ketty Clift Couture shone brightly against a blue Sydney sky and then it was gone. She would like to be a fly on the wall and watch over them all while she was away. This was the first time she'd left for longer than a day since Lacey had joined them a year ago. Her predecessor had been in awe of Judith Pettigrew. Not so Lacey.

A design student, she had turned up in a long lace dress and knee-high boots, wanting to learn the trade from Ketty. Business had been in decline for a while and Ketty knew now she should never have employed her. Ketty and Judith would have absorbed the duties somehow but something about the young woman had appealed. Lacey's clothes were a little alternative for a couture dressmaking establishment but she was smart and enthusiastic, qualities Ketty admired. Ketty also loved to know that each time a customer rang they were greeted by 'Ketty Clift Couture, Lacey speaking' in the young woman's melodic tone, a perfect welcome.

Ketty sighed. She'd been careful with her money but she hadn't imagined her business would be struggling at this stage of her life. She'd had to dip into her savings to help pay wages twice in the last few months. Over her lifetime she had made adjustments, planned for a future that perhaps hadn't worked out the way she had envisaged in her twenties. She had few regrets but if she had to lay off staff or, worse, close her doors altogether, she would be heartbroken. Now she felt torn by her longing to escape her troubles for a short time and indulge herself in her holiday. Only once in her life had she run away from something and she'd vowed never to do it again and yet now that's exactly what she was doing, prolonging the inevitable.

"You are so lucky to be going on a cruise."

Ketty's eyes met the smiling look of the driver in the rear-view mirror.

"Yes." Ketty knew she was, but everyone's definition of lucky was different. She snuggled back into the seat. The business was out of her control for the moment. The future would be waiting for her when the cruise was over and she would deal with it then. There would be answers, she just hadn't found them yet.

"There she is." The driver gave a low whistle. "Magnificent."

Ketty took in her first glimpse of the *Diamond Duchess* between the giant diagonal struts of Anzac Bridge as they flashed by. The driver's enthusiasm was infectious. She felt the weight begin to ease on her shoulders. If she was going to run away she was certainly going to do it in style.

"You are lucky to be going on this ship," he said again.

"I am."

"Have you been on a cruise before?"

"Yes, I have, many times."

He let out a low whistle. "Very lucky."

The ship was lost from her view now as they wound their way off the bridge and down to harbour level. Ketty put away her phone, dug in her bag for her mirror and checked her lipstick; she dragged her hair back from her forehead and patted the waves that bounced around her ears. Her hair had been long enough to roll up into a chignon until her visit to the hairdresser yesterday. She always had something different done to it before she cruised; it was a small gesture, part of her transformation from everyday dressmaker Ketty to the more adventurous, glamorous shipboard Ketty. A gleam in her eyes reflected back from the mirror. She closed the lid with a smile and added mischievous to her list.

The driver manoeuvred seamlessly through the traffic and came to a stop in front of the terminal. She paid him and bid him farewell, then paused to take in the grand outline of the *Diamond Duchess*. The clouds were disappearing and there was nothing but blue sky beyond the ship berthed on the edge of the harbour. Ketty stared at the white monolith and felt her heart beat faster, just as thrilled to see it as she had been the first time. Like her, the *Duchess* had aged and this was to be her final voyage. Perhaps mine too if the accountant has his way, Ketty thought.

Her gaze swept the rows of windows above the line of the wharf and then on up to the yawning openings of the promenade deck with life boats suspended in each. Higher again were row after row of balconies like hundreds of open eyes, some with people already leaning on their rails, and then on higher – she craned her neck to see the top – gleaming white and sparkling glass against a brilliant blue sky. It never looked real to her, a giant Gulliver and she part of the Lilliput world it was tethered to. Her home for the next ten days. A fizz of joy bubbled inside her and she recalled the taxi driver's words. Yes, she was very lucky.

Ketty made her way across the cement apron to the terminal, towing her cases behind.

"Kathy?"

Ketty tried to turn but she was swept along with the surge of excited people around her. None were paying her particular attention. No one had called her Kathy for years. She was hearing things. There was bound to be someone else by that name in this huge crowd. She hesitated. It had been more about the tone of the voice than the name itself.

She gave a small shake of her head, gripped the handles of her cases tighter and moved on into the cavernous space of the terminal. There she merged with the crowd, already transforming herself as she took her place among the two thousand passengers making their way through the protracted customs, security and myriad of embarkation procedures to enable them to board ship for a cruising holiday in the South Pacific.

Two

Day One – White Bay Cruise Terminal, Sydney

The sun sparkled off the many windows of the gantry that stretched from the terminal building to the ship, a temporary connection allowing passengers entry to cruise paradise. An hour had passed since she'd arrived at the terminal but now the last of the red tape and security checks were done and Ketty was on her way. Excitement escalated with every one of her echoing footsteps, taking her to the top of the gentle incline.

"Welcome aboard, Miss Clift." The purser's smile was wide.

"Thank you," she said and moved on and around the photographers capturing passengers' happy smiles as they embarked. Ketty had so many cruise photos, she didn't need another.

Only a few steps along a short passage and she reached the atrium. She stopped. There was no movement and yet an imperceptible beat pulsed here. To her it was the heart of the ship, stretching up four floors like a mini shopping mall. It housed boutiques, cafes, bars and restaurants all overflowing with food and items to tempt. Everything gleamed, from the polished wood handrails, to the glass balustrades and marble floor. Potted palms towered up into the open spaces, glass lifts travelled up and down and music mingled with the hum of happy voices. Ketty inhaled the fresh smell she liked to call ocean breeze, a hint of vanilla and something else. She never tired of her first minutes aboard ship, absorbing the atmosphere, remodelling herself. Here no one knew her as Ketty Clift Couture. A delicious ripple of delight swept through her as she indulged herself in the anonymity of being simply Ketty Clift.

"Ketty?"

She spun at the sound of her name.

"Ketty Clift, it is you!"

Ketty took in the tall, good-looking woman walking towards her, hand luggage in tow. Her thick blonde hair was beautifully coiffured and her clothes were well cut and stylish. A softly draped scarf picked out the pink in her patterned blouse. Ketty hadn't seen Josie Keller for two years but it seemed only a short time since they'd cruised together.

"Josie, how marvellous to see you."

They drew each other into a hug then stepped apart.

"It's good to see you too, Ketty."

Ketty looked over Josie's shoulder. "Is your friend Pam with you again?"

"No." Josie leaned closer. "I've brought my brother with me this time. He was a bit down in the dumps. Work not going well, relationship over, the usual lows. I decided he needed cheering up. I should introduce you." She glanced around. "He was here a minute ago."

"Well, a cruise is certainly the place to forget all your troubles."

"And have some fun. Didn't we enjoy ourselves last time?"

"We did."

"He and I could both do with someone new in our lives." Josie began to sing 'Love is in the Air'. She laughed. "Remember our theme song?"

Ketty chuckled. The tune was played regularly aboard ship. "But what happened to the man you met last cruise? You caught up with him while you were in Sydney having your dress fitting, didn't you?"

"I did." Josie wrinkled her nose. "It fizzled out. I live in Brisbane, he's in Sydney. He found someone closer to home. I wasn't heartbroken. It was fun while it lasted."

Ketty admired the way Josie looked at life. If something wasn't working she didn't dwell on it but picked up and moved on. They'd met on a cruise to Papua New Guinea, two years prior.

"You're looking splendid as ever."

"Thanks to you." Josie's smile was wide. "The makeover you did for me on that cruise was such a turning point. It changed the way I looked for clothes."

Ketty had made a few style suggestions for Josie, who was tall with a rounded but still trim figure, and she'd ended up having a dress made at Ketty's shop after the cruise.

"I only suggested minor variations."

"Minor! I had a wardrobe full of crop pants and leggings that I donated to Vinnies. Now it's only ever seven-eighths length tailored pants for me. And I wear more styles that define my waist rather than try to hide it, as you suggested." Her phone pinged and she glanced at the screen. "Excuse me, Ketty. It's my brother."

Ketty watched the passing passengers, some strolling by as if they'd been here before, and others looking a little overwhelmed.

"Sorry about that. He's gone up to our suite already." Josie dropped her phone back in her bag. "You and I will have to meet up for a coffee or a cocktail or two."

"I'll look forward to it."

Josie strode away humming 'Love is in the Air' again. Ketty smiled. It was going to be a happy voyage, she was sure of it.

She grasped the handle of her cabin bag and made her way out of the busy hub and on to a flight of carpeted stairs that led all the way to the top of the ship. There was also a bank of lifts but Ketty preferred the stairs; that way she never had to use a gym. She paused for a breath when she reached her deck level.

"Are we at the back of the boat or the front?" A woman stood nearby, peering at the large ship plan on the wall. Her companion leaned over her shoulder and jabbed his finger at the diagram.

"It says we're here."

"Can I help?" Ketty couldn't resist.

"We're trying to find the buffet." The woman gave her a harried look.

"Keep going up these stairs. Three more flights and you can't miss it."

The man groaned. "Let's take the lift."

"They're always busy at boarding time," Ketty said. "The stairs are probably quicker."

"Thank you." The woman gave a grateful smile. "We've been busy all day and we're starving."

They set off and Ketty turned left into the corridor, anticipation speeding her footsteps. She found her cabin number.

"Hello ma'am, welcome aboard." The smiling steward paused beside her. "I am Peter, your room steward. Please let me know if I can assist you in any way."

"Thank you, Peter. I'll be sure to." Being spoiled was another part of Ketty's joy. She'd hardly have to lift a finger for the next week and a half.

She inserted her card, the lock light went green and she pushed open the door. It was a balcony room. In the past, she'd travelled with friends but in more recent times she'd more often cruised alone and usually she had an interior room. Rarely could she afford a balcony. This was an indulgence. She wouldn't have come on this cruise at all but she had elite passenger status with the Diamond line and her trip had been a lucky deal paid for several months ago, a birthday gift to herself. Ketty found it hard to think of herself as turning sixty-five when in her head she still felt forty. Where had the time gone? She'd certainly never imagined when she embarked on her first *Diamond Duchess* cruise that she'd become a frequent traveller. It felt rather odd to be offered special rates and priority check-in, as well as all the other perks, like access to the Diamond Lounge. And here she was in a balcony room. Ketty felt like a duchess herself.

She took a deep breath, let it out slowly and looked around the room. Her case was already on the queen bed, a mat below it to protect the bed cover. She opened every cupboard and drawer, inspected the bathroom, ran her hand over the silky soft pillows, sat on the padded lounge chair, then she rolled open the heavy glass door leading to the balcony and sat in one of the two deckchairs using the little table as a foot stool. She was port side and high above the gantry that had led her aboard. She stood and leaned out over the rail. Workers in high-vis vests were busy on the wharf below her and, in the distance, she could see the familiar shape of the Harbour Bridge. Ketty stepped back inside and swept another look around the room. It was all perfect.

Her phone pinged. She removed it from her bag to discover a text from her nephew, Greg, wishing her bon voyage. She smiled. He was such a thoughtful young man. Her brother's only child, she regarded Greg as her nearest and dearest. Just a shame he lived interstate. She didn't see him all that often but he stayed with her whenever he came to Sydney. She tapped a quick reply and checked her phone again. No other messages or missed calls. Judith wouldn't disturb her holiday if her life depended on it. Ketty turned the phone off and tucked it into the side pocket of her handbag. Neither would be needed again until her return to Sydney.

She threw open her case, her bulging overnight bag, the wardrobe doors and all the drawers then began to unpack. She smoothed each garment as she hung it, savouring the different textures of the fabrics, turning down a collar, fluffing a skirt. It was such a thrill to have the opportunity to wear some of the clothes she had delicately restored or remodelled and of course she was always hopeful the extras she brought might suit someone else in need of a wardrobe addition. Running into Josie again had been a delight. Ketty pondered who else was aboard she might know. She hung the special necklace bag bulging with more jewellery than she would need for herself, then plucked up a black lace wrap and draped it around her shoulders. Perhaps, once again, she would find someone in need of its sensual luxury.

Drawing the lace partly over her face she peered at her reflection.

"Mirror, mirror on the wall, who will be seated at my table in the grand hall?" She laughed at her silly rhyme. "And what intrigue will shipboard life provide this time?"

Bernard Langdon strode purposefully up and back in an empty corner of the deck, a mobile phone pressed to his ear. The pool deck was almost empty. Only a few passengers were wandering among the neatly lined-up deckchairs, peering into the spas or checking out the bars. He assumed most of the early birds already aboard were settling into their rooms or indulging in the buffet dining rather than taking in the sunny delights of the pool deck. Bernard was tall and, he liked to think, still buff for his sixty-nine years. He liked the ladies and they liked him. It was the main reason he'd come on this cruise, but business was getting in the way of him beginning to enjoy himself.

"Sell it, Jack," he barked into the phone.

He groaned inwardly as his broker made excuses from his office back in Brisbane. Bernard had been buying and selling property all his life. He'd employed Jack ten years ago when the time looked right to take a back seat and enjoy the fruits of his smart investor's brain. Jack did the paperwork for him, kept an eye on things. He crossed the t's and dotted the i's that Bernard sometimes overlooked. They made a good team and Bernard had grown to trust him, but Jack was conservative. Bernard got that, even found it useful, but sometimes Jack was downright pig-headed.

"I don't want to hold off any longer." Bernard clapped a hand to his free ear as he wandered too close to the giant music speakers blaring out eighties music. "I should have sold a week ago. I'm losing ground."

Jack's voice whined in his ear again.

"I don't care, Jack, I'm not prepared to wait. Sell, damn it! Or do I have to do it myself? I'm supposed to be on holiday. I'm on a cruise ship, for fuck's sake."

A woman walking past glared at him and ushered her child away.

"Sorry." Bernard called. "What?" He scowled at his phone then pressed it back to his ear. "No, I'm not saying sorry to you, Jack. Just sell the damned property, will you? At least we'll make a bit of money. If we wait till I get back that window will be gone."

He jabbed end call with his finger and shoved the phone into his pocket. He'd had this conversation with Jack only yesterday.

The younger man thought this particular block of flats close to the river and the city of Brisbane would make them a fortune. Bernard had let him buy it three years ago. The market for such a block had shown promise then but they'd done nothing, in fact the tenancy rate was way down. People were opting for the sleek modern apartments going up all around them. Bernard had made his money on quick decisions. If you let emotion come in to play when dealing with property it could be your downfall. He'd seen it happen to others. Jack had fallen for the old-world charm of this particular building but it wasn't paying returns. The good news was he'd had an offer to buy. It was an older building and in the current market in that part of town he thought it better to sell while he could still make a profit. Jack wanted to wait, Bernard didn't, and it was Bernard's money.

He took a long deep breath then turned as he slowly let it out. The pool sparkled in the brilliant sunshine. When he'd flown in earlier today there'd been rain but now the deck and everything on it was bathed in brilliance, including the bar. That's where he should be, perched at a bar, cocktail in hand, waiting for the inevitable arrival of the ladies.

"Would you look at this!" Maude bounced onto the bed. Her broad backside sank into the neatly made covers as she reached for the plate that sat on the cupboard beside her. "Chocolate-coated strawberries with compliments of our travel agent. I knew he fancied me."

Celia watched from her position just inside the cabin door as Maude lifted the clear lid from the strawberries and stuffed one in her mouth. The agent was at least twenty years younger than their slightly-over-fifty and had responded politely to Maude's many questions. Celia had seen no sign, on their several visits to finalise their cruise booking, that the poor fellow had any more interest in them than any other paying customers. However that hadn't stopped Maude from playing up to him, and that was the reason Celia had asked her to come along on this cruise in the first place. Maude was a flirt and Celia needed to learn how to be.

"This is going to be great, don't you think?" Maude didn't wait for an answer but rose to her feet and strode two steps to the bathroom. "Not a lot of room but we should be fine."

Celia took in the space that was grandly called a stateroom. It had two single beds, one pushed against each side wall, and a gap between the two that was big enough for Maude or Celia but not both at the same time. She was surprised by her reflection in the mirror over the bed. She still wasn't used to the spray tan and lighter hair colour, all part of her pre-cruise final makeover, but she was happy with what she saw all the same. Turning sideways she took in the bathroom where Maude was now reapplying her lipstick. It was a tiny box with barely enough room for Maude. Beside it there was a wardrobe that they would both have to share and that was it for their holiday home.

"I wonder where we'll put our cases?" Celia opened a wardrobe door. There was more space than she'd thought but she couldn't see two cases and their hand luggage fitting in there. She glanced back at the compact room.

The thing that bothered her more than the small space was the complete absence of light when they'd entered. They had an interior room almost in the middle of the ship and even with the door open to the passage behind them it had been dark, until Maude had found the light switch.

Maude stepped out of the bathroom and grinned at Celia. "I'm sure they'll fit somewhere. Don't worry about the little things." She patted Celia's shoulder in a condescending manner. "Think about the adventures we're going to have. Are you ready? We've a whole ship to explore."

Celia flattened herself against the wall as Maude reached for the door handle. The other woman squeezed her buxom frame past Celia and let out a small belch as she passed.

"Ooops!" Maude giggled. "Better out than in."

Celia wrinkled her nose at the smell of garlic and hoped she wouldn't regret her decision to ask Maude to come on the cruise with her.

Maude looked back. "Come on, let's go and check out the talent." She gave a laugh that was more like a series of snorts. Celia took a deep breath and followed her out into the passage. After all that's what she'd come for. Her ex-husband was somewhere on this ship with his new wife and she was going to make sure he knew exactly how well Celia was doing without him.

The corridor ran from one end of the ship to the other, so that from the middle it gave the appearance of stretching on forever. Broken at regular intervals on either side by cabin doors and the occasional service door, and the only landmarks were the room numbers.

Christine Romano staggered forward under the weight of a bag over each shoulder and trundled another beside her. Her husband, Frank, walked two steps behind as usual, a backpack slung over his arm. She stopped to look at the number and name by the nearest door and groaned.

"I think we've come too far. The numbers are getting bigger."

"I thought you were checking as we went?"

"I haven't looked at every door," she snapped. Frank had been acting clueless all day, right from when they caught the taxi to the airport, checking in to their flight and all through the various stages of customs and boarding the ship. His reluctance to take some initiative was wearing her down even more than usual.

A steward appeared from behind them. "Can I help, ma'am?"

Christine peered at her name badge. "Yes, Maria, we are lost. We were told to come along this corridor." She held up the card with the room number on it.

"You are in the right place, ma'am. You've come a little too far, that's all."

"The directions we were given were not very clear then." Christine hoisted the bags higher on her shoulders. "I need to sit down."

"Please come this way." Maria set off back along the corridor.

"Let me take one for you." Frank slid a backpack from his wife's arm. The bag dragged heavily on his shoulder. "No wonder you were struggling, what's in this?"

"My laptop, iPad, books."

"Why have you brought all that on a cruise?"

"Here we are, ma'am, sir." Maria smiled broadly at them from a few doors away. "I will be your steward for the cruise. Please ask if you need any other assistance."

Frank strode off, inserted his card and entered, propping the door open with Christine's bag. Maria remained in the corridor.

"Thanks," Christine sniffed. "We'll let you know." She paused inside the door. "It's not very big, is it? I thought a stateroom would be large."

"It's bigger than that cabin we shared with the kids at the beach last holidays." Frank opened the fridge. "Not stocked like a hotel bar though."

"I told you, Frank, we had to organise a drinks package. It was something I thought you might have done before we left." She glanced around again. "Where are our cases?"

"Maybe they're lost." He unlocked the large glass door and stepped out onto the balcony and into the glare of the afternoon sunshine. The heat from outside did battle with the cool from the air conditioner.

"Close the door, Frank."

"You can see the Harbour Bridge from out there." He stepped back inside and slid the door shut. "I'm starving. You said there'd be food once we got here."

"We've only just found our room." Christine brushed back the tendrils of hair that had escaped her ponytail. "We've been travelling all day."

"A swim first then, that will freshen us up, and we can find some food."

"Let's catch our breath. Anyway, my bathers are in my case and my case isn't here."

Frank shook his head. "I told you to pack them in your carry-on luggage."

Christine moved her bag and pushed the door, which shut with a heavy thud. "I forgot."

They locked looks for a moment, then Frank smiled and Christine glimpsed a younger Frank; the carefree man of their pre-children days.

He flopped onto the bed and flung out his arms. "This is a bit of all right, babe. Top shelf stuff, good furniture, our own bathroom and a balcony to boot."

She eyed her husband spread-eagled on the bed as if he had not a care in the world. He probably didn't. Other than what was to eat or how he could fit in a swim or a run, little seemed to worry Frank. He was long and lean and not a grey hair to show for his forty-five years. Christine had been hiding the grey since the birth of their first child and had gone up two dress sizes since then. He hadn't called her babe in a long time. "Thanks to Dad."

Frank's smile disappeared. She wished she hadn't uttered the words. It had taken her months to convince him to come on this cruise. Besides giving her an opportunity to work on her father it was meant to be fun and a chance to spend quality time together. Their lives were so busy at home.

She had been the one to suggest a cruise. Frank hadn't wanted to come. It had taken a lot of work to get him to agree. Then they'd only had enough money for an interior cabin. After several hints to her father that he'd enjoy cruising as well, he'd agreed to come too and pay the extra so they could have a balcony.

"I was happy with an interior room." Frank rolled away from her and rose to his feet. He barely glanced her way as he headed for the door. "I'm going to find some food."

She nodded, a fresh wave of misery flooding through her.

"Are you coming up on deck?" he asked from the door.

"I'll wait for our cases."

He pulled the door closed gently behind him. Christine held her breath. Would he come back? Throw open the door and drag her along with him? She willed him to make a joke of it like he used to but the door remained firmly closed. She let out a long slow sigh. How had it come to this?

It was the first time they'd holidayed alone since before they'd had children. This cruise had to make a difference, surely. She had her sights set on rekindling some romance with her husband. She drew herself up straight and lifted her chin. First, she'd sort her father and then she could focus on Frank. Neither of them could make excuses or avoid her here. She would make sure this cruise worked out perfectly.

Jim Fraser sank lower in his chair. The mobile phone he'd been talking on minutes before slowly slipped from his grip and landed with a soft thud on the carpeted floor of his suite. There was a pounding in his ears and a tightness in his chest. He closed his eyes and forced his breathing to slow. This couldn't be happening. He'd taken his medication and yet the gnawing pain of panic that had been with him for days now deepened and gripped him like a vice.

"I'm sorry, Dad, I'm not coming." Anthony's words echoed in his head. Jim couldn't remember the reason his son had given. A wave of dread had drowned out further conversation. Anthony was supposed to be accompanying him on this cruise and now he wasn't coming. Jim grasped the wooden arms of the chair, closed his eyes and took in a long slow breath. In his head, he could hear the therapist's words. "A long slow breath in, Mr Fraser. Now blow out gently through the mouth and visualise the anxiety flowing out with it."

Jim concentrated on his breathing and gradually the tension eased. He opened his eyes and looked around the suite. Anthony had asked him what the upgraded cabin was like but Jim's reply had been brief. It had a couch and contemporary wooden furnishings with a television and sliding doors out to a corner balcony. The bedroom opened off the small sitting room and was made up with two single beds; one for him and one for Anthony. Jim gripped the chair arms tighter. He would never have come on this cruise by himself.

His daughter, Tamara, had suggested the idea several months ago. Jim had said no but she had kept on at him and her brother until they'd agreed. With Anthony along for company, Jim had felt brave enough to face the holiday. Now here he was alone on a ship about to sail out through Sydney Harbour on a trip he should have been taking with his wife.

He closed his mind to thoughts of his beautiful Jane and pushed up from his chair. Maybe it wasn't too late to get off. He had only put his carry-on bag on the bed. Nothing had been unpacked. He gave a brief thought to his case. Were ships like planes? If you weren't on board would they hold up the departure? He picked up his backpack and opened the door. At the same time a voice began to speak through the PA system and the nice young steward who had helped him find his room appeared before him.

What had he said his name was? Jim glanced at the man's badge. Ricardo.

"Hello, Mr Fraser," he said in his stilted English. "You must leave your bag here for the muster drill, sir. Just bring your life jacket please." Ricardo smiled widely and went on to the next door. Jim stepped back into his cabin and closed the door. He'd missed his chance to get off this floating hotel.

Three

Day One – Sydney Harbour

"Can you believe we're actually here?" Maude shimmied in her chair to the beat of the music resounding around the deck but her words and the sounds of the band were lost in the long blare of the ship's horn.

Celia jumped and knocked over her glass of champagne. "Oh no!" She snatched it back up but the contents spread across the table in a trail of fizzing bubbles.

"You're so jumpy." Maude shifted her seat so the liquid dripped harmlessly to the wooden deck. "I didn't know that about you."

"Know what?" Celia drained the remains of the glass before she wasted any more.

"You're the nervous type."

"I'm not usually. The ship's horn was very loud." She glanced around as she had been ever since they'd come on deck. Ed was here somewhere with his new wife. Celia had only seen Facebook photos of Debbie. She wasn't sure she'd recognise her but she'd know her ex. They'd been married for twenty-seven years before she'd been traded for a new model. Celia was on this cruise to show Ed she'd moved on but she wasn't ready for him to see her yet.

The horn blared again as the ship steamed down the harbour and she was distracted by the sight of the Sydney Harbour Bridge looming nearer, like a giant gateway to her venture. She felt a stab of anxiety. There was no turning back, her plan was in motion. She just needed the courage to carry it out.

Maude stood and moved out to the open deck for a better view. "Oh look. There are people right near the top doing the bridge climb."

Celia joined her. They both waved then tipped their heads back as the ship slid beneath the bridge. From their vantage point it was as if they could reach out and touch the criss-cross of metal that supported the huge coathanger-like structure.

"It looks so close, as if the bloody funnels might hit." Maude grimaced. "No doubt they've done this before."

Celia lifted her sunglasses. "No doubt."

They returned to the table Maude had snared them, tucked in along the side of one of the upper decks. It was sheltered from the heat of the late afternoon sun by the walking deck above. Celia looked across the water to Circular Quay and the Opera House slipping by. She'd only been to Sydney twice before, both times with Ed on business. The last time had been three years ago. She remembered it like it was yesterday.

She'd spent an enjoyable afternoon wandering aimlessly among the quaint shops of The Rocks where she'd bought a brightly coloured painting of the harbour. Later she'd ambled on around the Quay, weaving her way through the constant tide of people to the steps of the Opera House. There she'd leaned against the rails close to the water and gazed up at the giant sails.

In the evening, after she'd indulged in a massage, she'd met Ed for dinner at a restaurant near their hotel. A cold shiver wriggled down her spine and gnawed its way around to the pit of her stomach where it remained to unsettle her. She remembered the events of that evening in detail. Not what she'd ordered and left uneaten, but Ed's declaration that he'd been unhappy for years and that he was leaving her; the disbelief, the shock, the idea that he was teasing and then the realisation that he wasn't. She'd felt sick and numb as waiters had come and gone with food and drinks. She swallowed too much wine, her face had felt stiff from trying to keep her emotions at bay as they sat at a table for two in the middle of the restaurant. Back at their room he'd come inside long enough to collect his things and for her to beg him not to leave her, then he'd let himself out. Their only conversations since had been via their lawyers.

"Whatever's the matter? You've gone quite pale."

Maude's question brought Celia back to the present. The Opera House was well behind them now. Like Ed, the bastard.

"Nothing." She looked back at the harbour, teeming with ferries, water taxis and sailing boats.

"Are you sure you're not feeling seasick?"

Celia was trying not to think about that possibility but it did lurk at the back of her mind. "Beryl was telling me about her last cruise the other day at bowls. It was really rough and lots of people got sick."

"You know how Beryl exaggerates."

Celia did but she hadn't been able to escape Beryl's regaling of her cruise experience, nor could she forget it.

"If you're worried you should have taken a pill like I did."

"I'd rather not take medication unless I have to."

"Suit yourself."

I will, Celia thought. She looked at her empty glass but couldn't face the crush of people around the bar. Everywhere you looked there were people pressed to spaces along the rails, or standing in groups chatting and laughing, taking photos, even dancing to the beat of the music. She didn't want to run into Ed unexpectedly. She wanted to pick that moment for herself.

"This is definitely a party cruise and by the look of it a real mix of ages." Maude drained her own glass. She turned her head and a soft breeze ruffled her dark wavy hair. "Isn't this wonderful?" she said. "Can you believe we're actually underway at last?"

Celia sucked in the fresh air swirling around her and lifted her chin. "Thanks for coming with me, Maude. I'm sure we'll enjoy it."

A waitress appeared. "Can I get you another drink, ladies?" she asked.

"Yes, please," Maude and Celia chorused in unison.

"My shout." Maude showed her card to the waitress then turned back to Celia with a triumphant smile. "I told you it would be easier to have the full drinks package."

"And I told you I'd be under the table instead of enjoying the cruise if I drank that much in one day." Celia settled back in the chair. Maude would be on her ear before they made the Heads where the harbour met the ocean if she kept drinking at this rate.

In no time at all the waitress was back with their drinks. Maude tapped her glass against Celia's. "Here's to good times ahead."

"To good times."

Maude was distracted by a man strolling past. She leaned in to Celia. "Plenty of possibilities this week, I think."

Celia sniffed. "There are plenty of possibilities at our bowls club."

"Like who?"

"Jack Higgins."

"Not my type."

"Jeff Sangster."

Maude screwed up her nose. "Bad breath."

"What about Clive Brown?"

Maude snorted into her drink. "Give me some credit please. Clive has tried to take out every available woman at the club. There's a reason they've all rejected him."

"Oh." Celia frowned.

"Full of talk and no action." Maude's eyebrows wiggled up and down.

"Oh!" Celia gave an involuntary shudder. How was she ever going to pretend she was looking for a fling? Ed had been the only man she'd ever slept with, and since menopause that had been rare. He had destroyed any idea of intimacy when he'd stabbed her through the heart and walked out, but she still yearned for companionship. People to chat to, go to the movies with, eat out. That's why she'd joined the bowls club when she'd made a sea change, two hours from Adelaide, after the divorce. She'd simply wanted to make new friends. To her surprise she'd also become quite good at bowls. Which had led to her pairing with Maude who was herself a talent at the game. They played in the same team but apart from her bowling skills, her drink preference and her outgoing personality, what did Celia really know about Maude?

Maude leaned back in her chair and watched two more men around their age pass by. "Plenty to feast on here." She giggled. "I might get lucky on this cruise."

"Not with those two." Celia nodded at the two women chatting intently only a few steps behind the men. "I suspect they're the wives."

"You and I both know that's of little consequence to some."

"Maude!"

"Don't look so horrified. No point in shying away from it. We've both been traded for new models but we're only just past fifty, not one hundred." Maude took another sip of bubbly and surveyed the crowd. "Use it or lose it, I say."

Celia emptied her glass. She needed some courage but she should also eat something if she was to have another. "What time did you say we were having dinner?"

Maude lifted the plastic credit-like card that dangled from a sparkling lanyard around her neck. "We've got the late sitting. The name of the dining room is on your card."

She leaned forward as Celia turned her own card to look.

"They're different names," Celia said.

"They can't be."

"Mine says Marlborough and yours says Gloucester." Celia was tugged forward as Maude took a closer look at her card.

"They are. That's odd. We booked together and asked to be seated together."

"We'll have to ask someone."

"Don't worry about it now." Maude finished her drink. "It's your shout and I think we should go for a bit of a look up front and watch the scenery from up there as we go out through the Heads." Maude stood up. "Let's go to the bar and move on from there."

Celia followed more slowly. She didn't imagine Ed would recognise her behind sunglasses and floppy hat but she had to keep a constant lookout.

Christine watched the two women move from the nearby table. "Let's sit down," she said to Frank and made a beeline for the empty table and chairs before anyone else had the same idea. All around them people grouped, moved, regrouped, some taking in the passing view, others intent on conversations; nearly everyone had a drink in their hand. Their enjoyment somehow eluded Christine and she felt a stab of envy.

Her legs and back were aching. She sank gratefully onto one of the chairs, pleased to have somewhere to rest her drink. It was some kind of cocktail, pinkish red in colour. A little umbrella jutted out one side and a slice of pineapple sporting a cherry on a toothpick was wedged to the lip. Thank goodness it had a straw. She'd never get it to her lips otherwise.

"I don't know how we'll ever find Dad in this crowd."

"I thought he answered your text." Frank lowered his tall frame to the empty chair beside her.

"He did, eventually, but the pool deck is huge." Her calls had rung out so she'd resorted to texting. It wasn't until the ship was pulling away from the wharf that her father had messaged back, saying he'd meet them on the pool deck.

"Relax, he'll find us."

Christine leaned forward, hunched her shoulders then pressed herself back against the chair. She closed her eyes. The air was warm and the breeze caressed her skin. Surely here she could let go of the stress. They'd left their home in Melbourne in the early hours of the morning to make the flight to Sydney in time for the ship's departure. The process of boarding had taken some time; there were queues and instructions and forms. Her head had started to throb by the time they'd made it aboard. It had been a long day after a busy week after a difficult couple of months.

She let out a long sigh. At least the pain in her head had eased. "It's so good to sit down at last."

"I'm glad we're doing this."

Her eyes flew open. "That's rich when I had to almost drag you kicking and screaming."

"Now that I've seen this ship I'm sure there will be benefits." Frank patted her leg. "I'll miss the kids but we could do with some time to ourselves."

"We have to include Dad."

"I bet Bernie doesn't want us hanging around every minute."

"What do you mean?"

"You know your dad. He'll be checking out the talent."

Christine stiffened. "This cruise is about us as a family."

Frank laughed. "Tell that to Bernie."

She had thought a cruise would confine her father. He'd be forced to spend time with her, but as she looked around she knew Frank was right. He'd be in full party mode, entertaining the ladies, as he liked to say. She shrugged her shoulders to rid herself of the image of her aging father lusting after women. "Anyway, I plan to do lots of relaxing."

"That's why you brought a laptop and an iPad."

"My iPad is an e-reader and we can facetime the kids, and the laptop has training packages for the new work software—"

"I checked out the wi-fi costs. Do you realise how expensive it is?"

"I don't need wi-fi for the training package but I do need to familiarise myself with it some more."

Frank pushed back in his chair. "You work too hard."

"I'd like to do less but it's impossible until we get new staff." The medical imaging company where she worked as office manager had opened another branch and changed the software program that ran all their bookings and referrals. Some staff had shifted to the new location. There was talk of hiring new personnel but that hadn't happened yet.

"You're only one person, Chrissie. You've got to learn to walk out the door."

"They don't pay me to walk out the door at set times."

"They don't pay you well enough to work such long hours either."

"It's private practice. It's easy for you working for the council. You just clock on and off."

The fine wrinkles along Frank's jaw deepened. He reached for his beer. Christine knew her words had irritated him but he didn't say anything more. They'd been down this path before. She hadn't meant to simplify his job. He had a senior position in their local council but he always seemed to be able to be home at a reasonable hour. Nor did he bring the worries of his day home with him like she did. And he did do things with the kids, but always the easy jobs like ferrying them around. He hardly ever cooked or cleaned, paid bills, made appointments or any of the myriad of details she attended to, and that was before she left for work.

Once more she was sorry that the words were out before she could stop them, but he had no understanding of how hard she worked and then when she got home it didn't stop. She felt as if all she did was snap at Frank these days. They hadn't made love in months. She'd been appalled when she'd worked out last night how long it had been. Frank had shown interest of course, but it always felt like the wrong moment. And she was always so tired. Now she studied his profile. He was turned away from her, staring in the direction of the pool where some younger ones were already swimming. She still found him such a good-looking man but she wondered what he thought of her these days. Her hair needed a cut, she'd put on a few kilos and had not had the time or the money to shop for a new outfit this summer.

She finally took a sip of the cocktail he'd bought her and wrinkled her nose; it was sickly sweet.

"Hello, Princess." Two strong arms came around her neck. She twisted to look up into the bright smiling face of her father.

"You found us."

"Of course." He leaned down and kissed her. The fruity smell of beer mingled with his spicy cologne and she got a close look at the curls of silver hair on his bronzed chest.

He trailed his big paw of a hand down her cheek. "You look like you could do with a holiday."

Her hand went to her hair. She'd meant to take out the ponytail and brush it before she came up on deck and now that she thought about it she'd forgotten to reapply her lipstick. She recalled the glimpse of herself she'd caught in the mirror just before her father had finally responded to her text and said he'd meet them on the pool deck. She'd looked years older than her forty. "It was a nightmare getting here."

"Good to see you, Bernie." Frank held out his hand. "You're looking well."

"Glad you could join us, Frank."

"You're very brown, Dad. It's not good for your skin, you know." Christine reached for a button on his open shirt but he evaded her and slid onto a seat opposite.

"Have you had a good look around yet?" He waved his beer at their surroundings. "It's a fancy ship."

"I have," Frank said. "Christine hasn't got much further than the cabin and here."

"The cases turned up. Someone had to unpack. Then we had that ridiculous life jacket drill."

"They have to be sure everyone knows what to do in an emergency." Frank drained his glass.

"There was no need to drag it out for so long. It's common sense, Frank."

He held her gaze a moment, a tinge of hurt crossing his face. Christine felt the knife of guilt again.

He rose from his seat. "I'll go and get a refill. Another beer for you, Bernie?"

Bernard nodded, waited for Frank to leave then leaned in. "So, what's up, Princess? We're meant to be on holiday and you two seem a bit tetchy."

"We're fine, Dad." Christine managed a smile. "We're both tired. We'll soon be in full unwind mode."

"That's good. You're always so busy, you lot." He reached out with the beer he'd been holding and tapped her glass. "Cheers, big ears."

"Cheers, Dad." Christine took another quick sip of her drink. Was it simply weariness that ailed them? Frank had been her dreamboat – they'd fallen in love at uni, travelled, found jobs and married. They'd both been eager to have kids, but when she thought about it, the arrival of the babies had been the start of the demise of their relationship. Life revolved around the children now. There had been so little time for each other and in the last few months hardly any. She couldn't stand the thought of her and Frank drifting any further apart than they already had. She'd planned this cruise to rebuild her relationship with her father but recently she'd added a second item to her agenda: mending her marriage. The thought of the work she had ahead sent a wave of panic through her. She took a gulp of the cocktail.

From his spot at the back of the ship, Jim watched the small boat that had taken the pilot back aboard swing around and power away to return through the Heads. Further along the coast, several large yachts cruised towards the opening in the cliffs that would take them to the safety of Sydney Harbour. How he wished he was on one of them instead of this cruise. Behind him music and the chatter and laughter of people getting into holiday mood carried on the wind. He stood slightly apart from the nearest group, watching the small trail of whitewater behind the ship flatten out to a dark blur on the deep green ocean. He should never have agreed to come. What was he to do with himself for the next ten days and nights?

A cruise holiday had been top of his dear Jane's bucket list, but they hadn't been given enough time to fulfil it. There was so much they hadn't done in the end. Her diagnosis and decline had been swift. He closed his eyes and imagined her here beside him. She would be loving it. She was always the social butterfly, taking in every new thing. He lowered his head to his arms and gasped in a breath. Dear, dear Jane.

The phone in his pocket vibrated, startling him. He had meant to turn it off. He tugged it free, amazed that he still had signal. Tammy's face smiled at him from the screen. He swiped at the button and pressed the phone to his ear.

"Dad?"

"Hello, love."

"Oh, Dad, I'm so cross with Anthony. I've just chewed his ear for ten minutes about how thoughtless he's being."

"You mustn't."

"He's saying it's work but I think that's an excuse."

Jim closed his eyes and tried to think what Anthony had said. Something wrong on a rig somewhere and he had to go.

"He can't ignore his job, Tam. They pay him big money to go when they call him."

"Money's not everything."

Jim could hear the exasperation in her voice. She sounded so like her mother when she was cross.

"He's known about this cruise for months." Her voice softened. "I can't bear the thought of you being all on your own, Dad."

Jim sucked in a deep breath. The sounds of the party going on around him drifted on the wind. "I'm not alone, love. There's a shipload of people here with me."

"You know what I mean, Dad. You don't like—"

"I'll be fine." He cut her off before she could sound any sadder and make him feel worse. "We're heading out to sea now and you're breaking up. I'll be in touch when I can. Don't worry about me, Tam, I'll be enjoying myself." He hoped he sounded convincing.

"Love you, Dad." Her closing words had been very clear as he moved his finger to disconnect.

Four

Night One – At Sea

First night at sea was Ketty's favourite, and the calm waters made the ship's movement barely detectable in the middle atrium level where she stood, one hand on the balustrade, as she took in her surroundings. It was the best place to be. There was a buzz in the air around her, not just the bubble of voices merging with the background sound of piano music, but an electric mix of expectation, excitement and even nervous tension. She watched the people strolling past, greeting friends, or exploring, looking in shop windows while others reclined in the luxurious seating of the lounges and bars that overlooked the central hub of the ship. She took in the looks of indecision on some faces, probably new cruisers still uncertain of their surroundings, and the more confident gestures of others hailing waiters, flashing cruise cards and sipping from elegant stemmed glasses. Such a mix of people. She felt the familiar thrill of expectation.

Ketty held her head high, gripped the polished wood of the handrail and slowly made her way down the curved marble staircase that led to the Marlborough dining room. There were lifts of course, like those found in the main lobby of any hotel, or the glass lifts that travelled between the four floors of the glittering atrium, but she preferred the atrium stairs. When she took what she thought of as the grand entrance to the dining room, it made her feel like she was a duchess instead of a dressmaker.

She hadn't wanted to miss the final voyage of the *Diamond Duchess*. She'd taken seven of her cruises on this grand old girl, now eight. It was on the *Duchess* she'd met Harry from the Hunter Valley; a romance that had barely lasted six months after the reality of their different home lives took hold but full of fond memories. And it was aboard the *Duchess* she'd helped a shy young man propose to the girl he'd loved since high school, and she'd used her creative talents to boost the confidence of a woman who went home and opened a shoe and accessory shop in her hometown which was still flourishing. There had been sad times too, of course; death was also part of cruise life although most passengers remained blissfully unaware. On her second cruise aboard the *Duchess*, Ketty had supported a woman from the cabin next door when her husband had died in his sleep. There were other deaths too but she preferred to focus on the happy times, like the first night of the cruise, which was always full of anticipation.

Ketty looked around at her fellow passengers and felt a bit like a grand old girl herself. Most were still wearing their casual boarding clothes but she'd changed for dinner. For this cruise, she'd packed her Jackie O–inspired collection and tonight she'd chosen a simple but elegant sheath dress, a deep purple silk with a boat neck and fitted waist. She'd felt instantly regal when she slipped it on.

A deep male voice sounded from nearby followed by a throaty chuckle. She stopped, and a prickle swept over her scalp and spread across her shoulders. She twisted to study the people seated in the lounge bar. She was searching for ghosts. What had brought this on? Perhaps she was being too nostalgic. She hadn't thought of Leo for years and here it was, the second time today she'd imagined his voice, the deep warm tones etched in her memory forever. She'd had her eyes checked recently, but maybe she should have had her hearing done while she was at it. Ketty straightened and took the final flight of steps down to the gleaming marble-floored waiting area outside her dining room.

The doors weren't open. She was early as planned. A couple still dressed in what Ketty thought of as 'day clothes' milled about reading the menus on display. She never read the menu in advance but preferred the revelation of each new meal once she was seated. She strolled to the etched glass door with its wooden surrounds and curved brass handle and waited. There was a hive of activity beyond the glass and she would be at the head of the line. It was another of her first-night rituals.

By the time the locks snapped and the doors were pulled open there was quite a queue behind her. Ketty's smile widened to see the maître d' who stood before her.

"Miss Clift, what a delight to have you aboard again. I was pleased to see your name on my table seating list."

His rich Spanish accent thrilled her as did the warm clasp of her hand in his.

"It's good to see you too, Carlos."

"I couldn't miss the final sailing of my beautiful *Diamond Duchess*."

"Nor I, once I heard. Thank you for letting me know. And I'm so happy my favourite maître d' is overseeing this dining room."

"Ahhh, Miss Clift, it is always my pleasure to look after you, and how delightful you look as always. You remind me of Jackie O in that dress."

Ketty smiled and nodded. Carlos had an eye for fashion and a smooth tongue but she knew from experience he was also genuine. She glanced back at the press of people behind her. "I'd better not hold up the works. I hope we'll get the chance to talk later. What table do you have for me this time?"

He beckoned to a young waiter who hurried closer. "Take Miss Clift to table fifteen."

"Thank you." Ketty smiled but Carlos was already greeting the next group of people. First night was always extra busy with everyone finding their tables. Ketty had cruised many times on different ships and the maître d's often changed but Carlos had made this job his life's work and he was her favourite. He was friendly, even familiar, once he got to know people, but Ketty had witnessed him putting a wayward waiter in his place, managing the most difficult of passengers and fulfilling unusual requests, such as the time a woman had booked a table for five and required a fresh lot of diners to fill the other four empty seats each night. Providentially that had been a short cruise, only five nights, but Carlos had managed it. There was no doubt he was in charge, overseeing the smooth running of all the ship's dining rooms and restaurants, their staff and diners.

Ketty followed the waiter past a row of smiling senior staff, resplendent in their white jackets and black pants. Her gaze swept the immaculate tables, with sparkling glassware and silver cutlery glistening on the crisp white tablecloths, and in the centre of each table a slim silver vase with a single orchid added some colour. At each setting a napkin sat neatly folded and shaped as a fan. The lighting from wall sconces and downlights was muted, enough to see by but creating a soft ambience. It was this glamour and attention to detail that Ketty adored, so different from dining alone in her flat.

"Please watch your step, ma'am." The waiter paused at the entrance to a group of tables set on a raised floor, a few steps higher than the rest of the dining room and enclosed by a balustrade.

She stepped up and frowned. Table fifteen was a large oval table. The waiter narrowly avoided her as she came to an abrupt halt and counted the chairs.

"This is a table for eight."

"Yes, ma'am."

Ketty glanced back towards the door where Carlos was dealing with the steady stream of diners for this second dinner sitting. He usually seated her at a table for four, sometimes six, but never eight. The waiter pulled out a chair.

"I think I'd prefer a different seat, thank you." She seated herself at the other end of the table with her back to one of the large pillars that rose from the floor to meet the ornate patterned ceiling. From here at least she would get a good look at everyone as they arrived.

The waiter draped the napkin across her lap, a brilliant white against the purple of her dress. "My name is Rupert, Madame Clift. I am your junior waiter. Phillip, your head waiter, will be along shortly." His smile was tentative. "May I get you a drink while you wait for the other guests?"

"Yes, thank you, Rupert. Bottled still water will be fine." Ketty glanced at his name badge but the little letters below his name stating his home country were too small to read. "Where is home for you, Rupert?"

"The Philippines, ma'am."

"And family?"

"My wife and son, ma'am."

She smiled warmly. "You must miss them."

"I will go home in two months, ma'am." He handed her a menu.

"Thank you, Rupert. And thank you for making me comfortable."

His smile was wide as he left to get her drink.

Ketty glanced around at the empty chairs. Seven new people to get to know. What on earth was Carlos thinking? She settled in her chair and looked at the menu. Tonight she could choose from sautéed seafood, spicy chicken and rack of lamb or even go vegetarian if she selected the pumpkin, walnut and mascarpone-filled crepe with thyme cream sauce, and that was only a few of the mains.

"Hello."

Ketty was startled by the booming voice from the other end of the table. She looked up at the tall man with a bald head and a shirt that looked bright white against his tanned skin.

"Good evening." She smiled as he moved to one side and a younger couple followed him to the other end of the table and began to seat themselves. Ketty sat perfectly still, studying each of the three in turn. The older man had to be the woman's father, there was a similarity about them – same dark eyes and tapered nose.

"Hope you don't mind us sitting way down here," the older man called across the table. "Chrissie thought we might want to make a quick getaway."

Ketty noted the glare the younger woman gave him but put on her most charming smile.

"Ketty Clift," she said. "The beauty of cruising is that there are no rules about how long you stay at the table."

"Bernard Langdon." He grinned and there was a twinkle in his eyes. Bernard was obviously a man who enjoyed flirting. "Good to meet you, Ketty. This is a first cruise for all of us." He waved a hand at the other two. "They call us virgins, I believe."

"Dad." The younger woman frowned.

"Loosen up, Chrissie, we're all adults here." Bernard winked at Ketty.

Yes, definitely a flirt, Ketty thought.

The woman had taken a seat next to her father. "I'm Christine Romano."

The man beside her stretched across and shook Ketty's hand. "And I'm Frank Romano."

"It's lovely to meet you all."

"Are you travelling alone, Ketty?" Bernard's dark brown eyes studied her.

"I am, yes."

"Looks like we're part of the singles set."

"What do you think of this menu, Dad?" Christine tapped the large printed page the waiter had put in front of her father and put a distracting hand on his arm.

Ketty observed them through lowered lashes; Christine discussing the food in detail with her father while her husband sat back in his chair, idly tapping the menu up and down on the table, his attention elsewhere.

"Hello."

A woman was being seated between Frank and Ketty. She wore a casual day dress that fitted her perfectly, although the beige linen did her no favours, nor did the pale lipstick. It was always so easy to dress customers with this woman's body shape. She had what Ketty thought of as a coathanger frame even if her look was a little on the plain side.

Before any of them could speak, the waiter ushered another person to the table. He looked rather distinguished with his short dark hair and neatly clipped beard. He gave them the briefest of smiles, as if the effort was too hard, then sat stiffly in his chair.

"Welcome," Ketty said. She glanced briefly at the two empty places then smiled deeply. "And how special that we have nearly a full table tonight. Often people don't come to dinner on the first night. I've sometimes eaten all alone."

"That would be a tragedy, Ketty." Bernard puffed out his chest. "Now let me do the introductions. Since my family make up half of our table it might be easiest."

Ketty settled back and watched as he rattled off the names for his end of the table and then added Ketty. He came to the recently seated woman and paused. She stared back at him a moment.

"Celia Braxton," she said.

A chorus of hellos came from around the table.

"I don't imagine you'll see me after tonight," she said.

"You're not leaving the ship at sea are you, Celia?" Bernard turned his charming smile on her.

"I'm travelling with a friend and they've put us in separate dining rooms. We'd prefer to be together."

"Don't worry." Ketty leaned towards Celia. "The maître d' will have it all sorted for you by tomorrow night. There are always a few hiccups on the first night."

"I'm not worried." Celia glanced at Ketty then looked away, twisting to take in the room.

"You sound like an experienced sailor, Ketty," Bernard said. "How many cruises have you been on?"

"This is my twenty-first." Ketty still counted her first overnight trip with her parents.

There was a collective gasp from around the table. Frank was the one to raise his water glass. "Happy twenty-first," he said.

"Thank you. I enjoy cruising." Ketty shifted her attention to the man on her left. "I'm sorry we haven't come to you yet." She held out her hand. "I'm Ketty, as you've heard."

He turned a pair of pale blue eyes on her. "Jim Fraser."

Once again there were welcomes from around the table. Ketty contemplated Jim, who had barely acknowledged his fellow diners and now sat, eyes downcast, staring at a point on the table in front of him. She wondered what his story would be.

Rupert and Phillip interrupted her thoughts as they introduced themselves, handed out menus and took drink orders. She requested her usual gin and tonic then glanced down at the menu again.

A loud laugh erupted from the other end of the table. "Enough of this Mr Langdon, Phillip. Call me Bernie."

"Certainly, Mr Bernie," Phillip said, a twinkle in his eye. "What would you like to drink?"

Bernard roared with laughter again then looked around the table. "Does everyone drink wine? How about I get a bottle of red and a bottle of white? My shout for our first night."

"Dad, really, you don't have to provide for everyone." Christine put a restraining hand on his arm once again.

"That's a good idea." Frank nodded at Bernard, ignoring his wife. "I'll buy tomorrow night."

"See, all under control, Princess."

Christine turned her glare from her father to her husband.

Ketty observed their interaction closely. "That's very generous of you, Bernard," she said. "I will be delighted to return the favour another night."

Celia spun back from her perusal of the room behind. "I probably won't be here to take my turn."

"Don't worry about it." Bernard spread his hands magnanimously. "It's my pleasure."

Christine gave an eyeroll that would outdo a teenager.

"I probably won't be here either, just for tomorrow night," Ketty said. "I like to dine in my room on my second night. It's a little ritual I allow myself, to get my sea legs as they say. But I'll be happy to buy wine the next night."

Phillip appeared at her right shoulder. "Are you ready to place your order, ma'am?"

"I am." Ketty had settled on the sautéed fish in saffron sauce. She so rarely cooked fish for herself at home and certainly never bothered to glaze carrots or crust her potatoes.

"Excellent choice," Phillip said with a broad smile.

Ketty watched the others while he took their requests, smoothly answering questions about styles of cooking, suggesting accompaniments, complimenting their choices as he had hers, giving each person individual attention as if they were the only diners, while all around the dining room this routine was repeated. Ever-smiling waiters in gold vests or white jackets moved on silent feet, learning the names, likes and dislikes of their diners and generally doing their best to please everyone. The murmur of voices from other tables were interspersed with the odd higher pitched laugh, the pop of a champagne bottle, the genial tinkle of glass against glass, the clunk of a door closing. And among it all Ketty was aware of the inscrutable presence of Carlos, watching over everything, his subtle commands ensuring the machinations of the huge dining room moved like clockwork.

Her attention returned to those seated around her own table. "Since we're to be dinner companions we should find out a bit about each other. I'm from Sydney. Where do you all come from?" She always found home was an easy conversation starter.

"Brisvegas," Bernard boomed.

"Oh, I love Brisbane," Celia gushed. "The climate is divine."

Ketty was surprised by Celia's sudden burst of enthusiasm and noted Christine's glare had shifted to the woman, who was leaning closer to Bernard as if suddenly fascinated by him.

"We're from Melbourne." Frank waved a hand that included his wife.

"I live in country South Australia now." Celia dragged her gaze from Bernard to take in the others. "A few hours north of Adelaide near the coast."

"Adelaide," Jim said as they all turned to him.

Ketty gave a small clap of her hands. "Between us all we've got quite a bit of Australia covered then."

"And what does everyone do to keep busy?" Bernard asked the next question as Ketty had hoped. "I'm semi-retired from the real estate trade but there never seems to be a dull moment. What about you, Jim? Are you still working or in the less frantic world of retirement?"

Jim looked up, startled. "Oh, still working...at least part-time... transitioning to retirement...insurance work..." He dwindled to a stop.

"I'm similar, I suppose." Celia took up the thread. "I work three days a week and volunteer the rest of my time."

Christine sniffed. "Frank and I both work full-time. With two teenagers, there's never enough money."

"We manage," Frank said.

"It's a struggle." Christine frowned at her husband.

"Lucky you could find the funds for a cruise then." Celia's tone held a hint of sarcasm.

Rupert returned with their drinks and took everyone's attention but not before Ketty noticed Christine give Celia a withering look. Ketty felt a warm shiver and the tantalising wiggle of her people antenna moving up a notch. At the other end of the table there were three from the one family and she had already noted undercurrents between them. Then there was the at first prickly and now almost flirty Celia, and the insular Jim. Ketty glanced at him just as he turned in her direction. She was concerned at the depth of sadness she saw on his face. The poor man was suffering.

She sat back as Phillip placed a prawn cocktail in front of her then continued on around the table, setting down the rest of the meals. Anticipation wormed deliciously in her stomach and Ketty allowed herself a small smile. Her table for eight could well prove to be an interesting mix.

By the time they'd finished sweets Ketty had some background knowledge of her fellow diners, all except Jim. He'd been harder to engage and was the first to excuse himself. He was swiftly followed by Bernard who'd invited Celia, and Ketty but she'd declined, for a drink on the pool deck and Christine had nearly dragged Frank from his chair to go with them.

Ketty remained at the deserted table and indulged herself in a post-dinner whisky while she pondered what she'd learned in the last hour and a half. Celia was a divorcee. Bitter, from what Ketty read between the lines. She'd spent half the meal looking over her shoulder, perhaps wanting to be somewhere else. Bernard was a widower turned playboy who was not missing a chance to enjoy life. Christine had done her best to gain her father's attention all night and if looks could kill poor Celia would be dead for trying to constantly engage Bernard in conversation. Frank had sat back, grinning agreeably but saying little and Jim, well, poor Jim was a grieving widower and it would take a bit of work to get him to smile.

"Was everything to your satisfaction, Miss Clift?" Carlos stood almost to attention at the end of her table. Even though she was alone, he maintained a formal staff-to-passenger manner.

"Perfect as always, Carlos. The food was divine."

"And the company?" He leaned in slightly, eyebrows raised.

She smiled at her old friend. "Interesting."

"And the two empty seats may be taken at tomorrow night's sitting."

"I think there's enough here to keep me busy." Ketty smiled. "I'm sure you will be working late tonight, Carlos, but perhaps we can have our usual catch up tomorrow night?"

"I would be delighted." His dark eyes twinkled. "Enjoy your evening, Miss Clift."

She raised her glass. "Thank you, Carlos." She watched him move on, weaving skilfully between the tables, pausing to adjust a chair, straighten a cloth, redirect a waiter and then come to a stop across the room where several other diners still lingered.

The warm murmur of his voice was followed by gentle laughter from the patrons. No doubt he was charming them with a compliment or a joke. It was an indulgence on Ketty's part to claim him as a friend but that was how she thought of him. Perhaps because their friendship had been struck in their younger years, they were comfortable in each other's company even though they met only once every few years. He had a cousin in Brisbane and liked to holiday in Australia. He'd even visited her once at her place in Paddington. It had been long before the renovations upstairs and the makeover out the back and she'd been living with a man who she'd thought might have been the one to replace Leo in her heart but he hadn't. Damn, she was back to Leo again. She rose from her chair and nodded at Phillip who had been waiting discreetly to strip the table and reset it ready for breakfast.

Why was Leo's memory haunting her so strongly now after all these years? They'd never cruised together so there was no connection there. Time and distance had been exceptional healers;

age and experience had created new memories, better ones, and yet as she walked through the almost-empty dining room she found herself wondering what if, what if things had been different and she and Leo had lived this life together? There were no guarantees that she wouldn't still be the single older woman travelling alone, worried about money and the future. She and Leo may have fallen out of love as had some of her friends whose marriages had ended in divorce or he could have become sick and died. She'd lost a few friends already, far too early.

Ketty retraced her steps across the sparkling tiles and up the atrium stairs. All around her people were still out and about enjoying their first night at sea while she walked alone, trapped in a memory of what might have been. It was a rare indulgence. Once more she blamed her approaching birthday. Seldom had the marking of another year bothered her before. She drew in a breath, straightened her shoulders and strode on past the overflowing bars, the happy voices and the bright tunes of a pianist playing an Irish jig. A good night's sleep would put it all to rights.

Five

Night One – Late Evening, At Sea

"Come on, Celia." Maude gave her friend a pleading look. "Just a little nightcap before we turn in. It's been such a terrific day I don't want to go to bed yet."

Celia groaned. Her new heels were rubbing and her legs ached. She'd run into Maude after dinner as Celia had followed Bernard, his sulky daughter and her bland husband in the direction of the lifts. Maude had wanted to go to the theatre for a welcome aboard show and Celia had been happy to make her excuses to the brooding family group and go with her, but now it was well after ten o'clock and she felt exhausted. The excitement of her first cruise, the tension of watching for Ed around every corner, the new shoes, a huge meal and more drinks already under her belt today than she usually drank in a week left her ready to collapse into bed.

"Can I have a cup of tea?"

Maude put her hands on her hips. "We're in a bar, not a tea room."

Celia glanced around the dimly lit space. At least there were some empty chairs drawn up at the small tables. "Just a mineral water then."

Maude pursed her lips but said no more and waved at a waiter who came immediately to take their order. They sat. Celia nestled into the comfort of the well-padded chair and discreetly slid out of her shoes under the table.

"What did you think of the show?" Maude asked.

"I enjoyed it. The singing and dancing were great."

"I thought it a little tame but I did enjoy the comedian."

"Yes, he was very clever."

"This must be the seniors bar. Not many young ones here." Maude had her back to the window. She was taking in the people around them rather than making eye contact with Celia.

"They're probably all out on deck. Wasn't there some kind of 'dance the night away' party happening?"

"I meant more our age. This lot all look to be over seventy." Maude fixed her determined look on Celia. "We need to find you some action. That chap you were with earlier, he looked like a possibility."

"Maybe." Celia was saved from elaborating by the arrival of their drinks.

She had decided by the end of dinner that Bernard would indeed be the man she needed to cultivate. Of the two available men at her table he was the obvious choice. Jim had been a dull and gloomy presence. If she was going to snub her nose at her ex-husband it had to be on the arm of someone much more flamboyant and Bernard fitted that bill. He was good-looking in a flashy kind of way, obviously had money and liked a good time, but it had not come naturally to her to flirt with him. That's what she needed Maude for.

That said, she did not want to hear more about finding a man tonight. Celia took a sip of her water and Maude her neat whisky. Celia was amazed at how much the woman could drink. She'd not seen that side of Maude before. She needed some sleep and time to work out how she could impress Bernard enough to want to be her escort when she was ready.

"Speaking of men." Maude suddenly sat forward. "That reminds me."

Celia braced herself for more of Maude's prattle.

"I wanted to talk to you about the evening meal. Would you mind terribly if we didn't sit together?"

"Why?"

"I'm at a table of six and there's only one couple, the other three are gents." Maude wriggled her eyebrows up and down and gave a silly giggle. "They're all single and out to have some fun."

"Oh." Celia tried to look disappointed but she was actually relieved. The thought of sitting beside Maude each night while she fluttered her eyelids and giggled was not appealing. At her table at least there was a mix of people and no real competition for Bernard. The Ketty woman, who had presided over the table as if it were her own, had responded to his attention but Celia was several years younger. Staying at her own table would mean she could cultivate Bernard without worrying about Maude watching.

"We'll still have plenty of time together," Maude went on. "There will be breakfast and lunch and all the activities and shows. We've got that destination presentation mid-morning tomorrow and plenty of other things we can do together."

"I've got an interesting group at my table as well."

"That's wonderful." Maude's hand shot out and grasped Celia's. "Is that man you were with after dinner from your table?"

"Bernard?" Celia extracted her hand from Maude's warm grasp. "Yes."

"Lucky you. Any other possibilities?"

Celia thought about the other man, Jim. He was working towards retirement, lived in Adelaide and was a widower like Bernard. "There's one other man but if the truth be known neither are my cup of tea."

Maude sat back and studied her. "And what kind of man is, Celia?"

"I don't know. And I don't care. I'm here to relax and enjoy myself." Celia hadn't told Maude her ex was aboard or anything about her plan.

"For goodness sake, Celia." Maude suddenly darted forward again and peered at her closely. "You're divorced but that doesn't mean you can't have a bit of fun in your life. I'm not suggesting you have to find a man to marry." She gave Celia's arm a gentle nudge. "You're on holiday, you can play you know."

Celia had every intention of appearing to do so but she was never going to do more than that. Maude waved at someone behind her.

"There's Pete," Maude hissed, then waved again. "Pete, over here."

A dark-haired man with a short pointy beard wearing a garish green shirt was heading their way.

Maude tugged on Celia's arm. "He's one of the chaps from my table. He said he might come this way later in the evening." Her face widened in a large smile. "Pull up a chair, Pete. This is my friend, Celia."

Pete swept an appraising glance over her and Celia pressed her hands to her lap to stop from putting one to her neckline as his gaze lingered there. "Hello, Celia." He turned back to Maude.

"I've come to see if you'd like to join us out on deck. There's music and dancing. We've got a bit of a group together."

Celia's heart sank as Maude rose from her seat.

"Sounds like fun."

Celia couldn't believe it but she'd actually seen Maude's eyelashes flutter up and down. She was quite sure she'd never be able to do that.

"Beauty."

Maude giggled.

Celia was amazed that at fifty-three her cheeks could still burn with embarrassment. Already she was doubting her ability to play this single and available game if Maude was anything to go by.

"What about you, Celia?"

Pete's question surprised her.

"Oh, I don't—"

"You're welcome to join us," he said.

"Yes, come on, Celia." Maude grabbed her by the hand. "Come on."

Celia reached down to slip on her shoes before she was dragged to her feet.

"Beauty," Pete said again.

Maude fell into step beside Pete who put a guiding arm around her waist and the two of them chatted like old friends while Celia trailed along behind. He pulled open the heavy glass door and immediately they were greeted by the thud of the music and the sounds of talking and laughter. The fresh outside air rushed to meet them as they stepped out onto the deck, which was lit with party lights and jammed with people making the most of the balmy night.

They wove single file through the crowd to a group gathered around some tables overlooking the pool below where Celia was amazed to see there were still people swimming. She did a quick scan of the area, hoping Ed wasn't among the partying passengers.

"Celia?" Maude tugged on her arm again. She was introduced to several people but their names were lost in the noise. She simply smiled and nodded.

One of the other men immediately whisked Maude away to dance. Celia took a vacant seat on the edge of the group next to a woman. She appeared to be about Celia's age, with a solid build and there was a walking stick hooked over the back of her chair.

The woman smiled and leaned closer. "Celia, was it? I'm Anne. My husband Pete and I are at the same dining table as your friend."

Celia nodded and glanced across to where Pete was in conversation with another woman whose name she'd missed. By his behaviour Celia had assumed he was one of the single men Maude had referred to. At that moment, he placed his drink on the table, gave Anne a wave, then took the arm of the woman and headed to the dance floor.

"Have you cruised before?" Anne asked.

Celia turned back. "No, what about you?"

"This is our second. I find the first day a bit overwhelming." She patted her leg. "And I've recently had a knee reconstruction so I won't be able to get around as well this time. Pete will have to dance with someone else this cruise."

Celia smiled and glanced across to where people were moving to the beat of the music, their clothes splashed with the bright colours of the flashing lights. Apparently, Pete had that under control already.

Anne began to talk with the woman on her other side and Celia sat and people-watched. She wished she could be as adventurous as Maude. Celia had always enjoyed dancing, and Ed had been good at it. But the last thing she felt like doing now was gyrating around the deck with a group of strangers. Maude was on the other side of the dance group and Celia could see she was now dancing with a different partner. Celia stared. The man wore a familiar green shirt. She stood and glanced around. The others were in pairs, heads close to be able to hear each other speak. No one noticed her slip away.

She went inside and down the stairs, jumping at every loud voice or closing door as she made her way towards her room. She was in no mood to run into Ed now. By the time she reached the little cabin she was wide awake again. A bulletin sheet outlining the next day had been deposited in the holder outside their door. She lifted it and let herself into the room where both their cases still lay open at the end of their beds and in front of each of their pillows sat a small wrapped chocolate. Maude's case had items overflowing everywhere.

Celia ate her chocolate and set about unpacking her case. She neatly folded and rearranged until she'd only taken up half the cupboard space available. Her empty case slid under the bed. Next, she read the bulletin then she used the pages as a fan. The air in the cabin felt close despite the air conditioner. She needed fresh air but she didn't want to be with the rowdy party she'd just left. Perhaps a walk around the promenade deck would help. She took her pashmina from the drawer, draped it over her head and shoulders, and let herself out into the long corridor again.

Outside, the sea breeze whipped her hair across her face and swept her pashmina from her head. She struggled with the silky fabric until it was firmly back in place and gripped tightly in one hand, then stepped up to the rail. Waves broke against the steel hull and whitewater foamed in a constant gentle hiss.

The heavy door swung open behind her. She froze. There was nowhere for her to hide here. There was a burst of laughter and a group of young men moved to the rail nearby with hardly a glance in her direction. This was getting rather ridiculous. She needed to work out where Ed was, make sure he got a good look at her enjoying herself, act all surprised to see him and then perhaps she could relax a little.

She moved further along the deck away from the noisy group, perched on the end of a deckchair and stared out into the inky night. Beyond the hiss and splash of the sea below, the giant motors hummed and a million stars glittered in the night sky but she barely noticed. All she could think about was Ed. Her ex-husband was somewhere on this ship and the bitterness that she thought she'd overcome bubbled to the surface.

She'd always wanted to cruise and Ed had earned plenty of money but they'd never done it. Resentment had broiled inside her when she'd heard from her sons that their father was taking his new wife on this cruise. More than that, she'd been so angry she'd thumped her favourite mug into the sink with such force she'd broken it. Then she'd cut her finger on the jagged edge and blamed it all on Ed. With her finger wrapped in a bandage and feeling sorry for herself, she'd hatched her plan. After some subtle probing of her sons, she'd found the name of the ship, the date of the cruise and the destination. She'd been surprised the cost hadn't been as much as she'd assumed but she needed someone to share it and that someone had been Maude.

Celia had suggested the trip over a few drinks at the end of a game of bowls. Of all the women at the bowling club who were free to accompany her, Maude had been the one who always flirted with the men. But Celia hadn't realised how small the cabin would be. Sharing it with Maude for the next ten nights might be the end of their friendship; a bit hard to play a game of bowls if you weren't speaking to your team member.

The voices of the young men grew louder again. Celia rose to her feet and began to walk in the other direction towards the front of the boat. The closer she got, the more dimly lit it became.

She was about to turn back when she noticed a shadowy figure against the rail further along. Someone was lurking there. Whoever it was leaned out over the rail. Celia wrinkled her nose; perhaps someone was being sick. Her heart rate quickened as the person put one foot on the lowest rung and the second foot on the next. Surely that wasn't safe.

Celia glanced back behind her. The young men had gone and she could see no one else on the deck. She took another step towards the figure perched on the railing. It was a man, and as she watched he bent further.

"Hello." Her voice was swept away by the breeze, lost in the sound of the waves and the engine. "Hello?" she tried again, moving another step closer.

The man turned, his foot slipped and he lurched forward, floundering over the rail.

Celia gasped, reached out with two hands and grabbed him around the waist. For a ghastly moment they teetered there and Celia thought he was going to fall, then he managed to right himself and they both collapsed backwards. She kept her feet but he slid to the deck, one shoulder against the rails.

She put her hand to her thudding chest. "Are you all right?" she asked then gasped as he turned his sad face to hers. It was Jim from dinner.

He stared through her, shuddered and turned back to stare at the water. "Yes." His reply was a whisper on the waves.

Jim sucked in a deep breath. His hand wrapped tighter around the rail as he stared at the foaming water below. He'd nearly gone right over. He'd thought about it ever so briefly, mesmerised by the water, but now, firmly back on the deck, he knew he never would have done it. The woman had startled him. He was aware of her now, hesitating beside him. He glanced up and she extended a hand.

He looked from the hand back to her face. Her lips twitched in a nervous smile and he realised she was one of his dinner companions.

"You're Celia, aren't you?"

She nodded. He ignored her hand and used the rail to stand, embarrassed that she'd been the one to see him almost fall in.

"I shouldn't have done that, the rail was slippery." He took a handkerchief from his pocket and wiped the tears that had welled in his eyes. "I like the ocean, the smell of salt and the spray. I used to sail and not so long ago I was a volunteer with the coast guard." He was babbling but he wanted to reassure her his slip had been nothing more than an accident.

"I've never been on anything more than a ferry before this." The wind got inside her pashmina and she shivered.

"The deck is quite breezy. I think we're going a bit faster than we were earlier." He glanced at the water again, wishing she'd go away.

"It is a bit cold." She took a couple of steps away from the rail. "It's better over here near the wall."

He hesitated, trying to clear the turmoil from his mind. He gave a small shake of his head as if that would help.

"Please come away from the rail, Jim."

Her look was imploring now. Mutely he did as she bid.

"Have you cruised before?" she asked.

Pain stabbed at him again. He shook his head. "My wife and I had planned to but...we didn't get the chance before she..."

"This is my first cruise too." She filled the silence. "I'm with a friend...well, more an acquaintance really. We play bowls together but what do you truly know about someone?"

"You're a bowler?" That was a less painful topic.

"Yes. Do you play?"

"I did. Only socially, night owls they called it."

"That's how I started."

They came to a stop in front of the heavy glass doors that led inside. He looked at them in surprise. Celia had been slowly walking back along the deck and he'd followed her.

She paused. Jim hoped she would go inside and leave him alone now but she hesitated.

"I was a bit concerned by the behaviour of a group of young men earlier," she blurted.

He looked around, his eyes taking in the empty deck as if he was seeing it for the first time. "Perhaps we should tell someone if you've been bothered."

"Oh, they didn't do any harm. Just a bit much to drink, I think."

"I see." He frowned, wondering why she'd bothered to tell him.

"It's just that..." Celia chewed her lip and blushed. "I hope you don't think I'm propositioning you or anything but I wondered if you'd walk with me back to my part of the ship?"

"I should turn in now myself." He pulled open the heavy door for her. His legs were still feeling wobbly after his near miss. "What deck are you on?"

"Nine."

"Me too, so we're going in the same direction anyway." He gave her the briefest of smiles as she stepped past him to the interior.

"The food was delicious tonight, wasn't it?" she said.

"Yes. I'm glad I went to dinner." Jim pushed the button for the lift. "I thought I'd stay in my room but I discovered I was rather hungry by seven o'clock."

"The other people at our table are friendly."

He paused, embarrassed to think he could recall little about any of them. "Yes."

The lift arrived and their small talk ceased as they stepped inside to find several others already aboard. They were the only two to step out at deck nine.

"I'm this way." Celia pointed left.

"And I'm this way." Jim pointed right.

"Well…thank you."

"Goodnight." He nodded and turned away, relieved to be out from under her scrutiny.

Ketty tucked her hair behind her ears, grateful for the natural waves and the cutting skills of her hairdresser. It required so little effort to keep it tidy. She replaced her brush on the shelf, flicked off the light and stepped back into her cabin. It was neat, everything in its place. She removed her robe and slid between the sheets. There was only one dim light illuminating the room but she hesitated before switching it off. She knew sleep would elude her for a while even though she'd spent time preparing herself with a warm shower and a cup of milky tea. The book she'd brought with her had helped pass the time but it was nearly midnight and she badly wanted to get some sleep even though the first night in a new bed was always bound to be restless.

She reached out, switched off the light and rolled over. The curtains were drawn across her balcony to keep out the light of the moon but there was a glow around the edges. She closed her eyes and took slow deep breaths. Two minutes later she was on her back. Perhaps counting sheep would do the trick although her favourite animal had to be cats. Trying to count them did not bring on the slightest desire for sleep.

She rolled to her other side and started reciting her times tables but she forgot to stop at twelve for the threes and started to muddle them up once she got past one hundred. There was no point in continuing, she was still not the slightest bit sleepy.

Her thoughts drifted to the days ahead. She'd been on this particular route five times before and she hadn't tired of the South Pacific islands they would visit. On her first trip to Vanuatu she'd been on this same ship and sharing an interior cabin with her girlfriend, Felicity. That had been nineteen eighty-two and, of all their friends, they had been the last two remaining singles. On their return Felicity's boyfriend had proposed, while Ketty's life had fallen apart.

On her back again, eyes wide open, Ketty felt the pain like it was yesterday. What was it about this cruise that was making her so melancholy, hearing voices that weren't there? She wondered where Leo was these days, what he had made of his life, what he looked like now.

They'd met in Adelaide during the Festival of Arts, in the foyer of the Festival Theatre at a late-night jazz event. He was sneaking out for a smoke, her to the loo and they'd literally bumped into each other. He'd laughed, made a joke, exuding confidence and she'd been in awe of him, already falling in love. They'd gone to several other Festival events together that year. They both worked long hours, he was several years older than her but doing a uni course outside his work as a financial planner. She was busy learning the dressmaking trade and doing extra tech courses but in the times they could be together they made the most of it. Leo had wooed her, they'd become lovers and had lived in their own delicious bubble of snatched opportunities for almost a year.

Only a year of her life but it had been one of the best. She could still recall the strength of his presence, the stare of his pale green eyes. Such vivid memories after all this time. There had been other men in her life since but no one like Leo, and yet it had all ended so badly. After her initial hurt and grief had come the anger. It had fuelled her for a long time. She'd wanted a husband and children then but it hadn't happened and once she'd come to terms with that, she had created a life that had been happy and rewarding but now...well, now she wondered what might have been had circumstances been different.

Ketty slipped lower down the pillows and her eyelids drooped. She took long slow breaths as she felt her limbs relax. At last sleep was edging closer and as she drifted off, a pair of twinkling green eyes hovered just beyond consciousness.

Six

Day Two – At Sea

Maude was still sleeping when Celia let herself quietly into the bathroom to have a shower. It had been a difficult night with Maude snoring, from both ends at times, and Celia didn't feel rested at all. She fiddled with the unfamiliar taps to get the water temperature right and stepped in. Once inside the miniscule cubicle she closed her eyes as the steam caressed her face then turned her back so the powerful flow could pummel her neck and shoulders. It felt luxurious to have some time truly alone.

She needed space to think. Somehow, she had to come up with a plan to show her ex-husband she had done brilliantly well without him. She was no longer the downtrodden wife he'd evicted for a younger model. She was Celebrity Celia. She'd thought of the title during the night and it had given her confidence so she'd kept saying it to herself.

"Celebrity Celia." She threw out her arms as she said it. "Damn!" Her right elbow hit the wall of the shower. She clutched it in her hand and thought about what she had to do. Bernard could be her escort and then she had to track down Ed at the right moment and look positively carefree and radiant on Bedazzling Bernard's arm. She'd thought of that name in the night as well but she'd been feeling really tired by then.

She turned off the taps and flung back the shower curtain. The tiny room was full of steam. She dragged her damp hair back from her forehead, her enthusiasm waning. How had she thought she would, firstly, find Ed among two thousand passengers spread across several floors and deck space and, secondly, convince Bernard to play along?

She rubbed a patch of steam from the mirror with her towel. She looked absolutely washed out. She pinched her cheeks, pouted her lips then pressed a finger to her cheek.

"Oh, Bernard you are so funny." She attempted to titter and broke into a cough. She leaned closer to the mirror. How had Maude done that fluttering eyelids thing?

"Oh, Bernard, what strong arms you have." Celia blinked several times then spent the next few minutes removing an eyelash from her eye.

She groaned, now her left eye was red.

She wrapped herself in a towel, gave one last attempt at a coy look and a giggle then opened the door and came face to face with Maude.

"I was just coming to see if you were all right in there." Maude peered over Celia's shoulder. "What was that noise?"

Celia stepped around her. "I was singing."

"Sounded more like a choking cat." Maude glanced back at her. "Have you finished in here?"

"Yes."

"I'll have a shower and we can go to breakfast."

Celia dressed quickly, spending a little more time on getting her hair and make-up right, then scribbled a note to Maude saying she'd meet her in the dining room for breakfast. What she hadn't said was she was going to find Bernard's cabin on the way. Last night she'd heard him talking to his daughter about their rooms. Christine had been annoyed about her room being such a distance from her father's. Turns out they were only several cabins apart. They'd mentioned level nine and the room numbers had been even and not much higher than hers which meant Bernard was along her patch of corridor somewhere. She hoped she'd find him still in his room.

The stewards were busy, their loaded trolleys dotted along the passage and their morning routine underway. Celia smiled at Maria who was looking after her room.

"Good morning, Mrs Braxton," she said in her singsong voice.

Celia moved away, trying not to look as if she was checking the names by each door. She found Bernard's name before she'd gone too far on the sea side of the corridor. Lucky Bernard had a balcony cabin. She knocked. Her heart raced. She hadn't thought through what she'd say.

She jumped as the door beside her opened and an older couple came out of the cabin next door, wished her good morning and set off along the corridor. Celia steeled herself and knocked again but there was no answer.

"Damn it," she muttered.

"Everything all right, ma'am?" Maria asked, her face full of concern.

"Oh, yes, thank you. Just hoping to catch a friend I met at dinner last night."

"Mr Langdon has already left his cabin, ma'am."

"Thank you, Maria."

Celia set off back along the corridor. Perhaps she'd find him at breakfast but he could be anywhere. She was headed to the dining room. The idea of being waited on silver-service style had appealed to her rather than the buffet that had been Maude's choice. They had agreed to alternate. The only problem for Celia was she imagined Ed would prefer the dining room too and there was only one open for breakfast. Her hair was longer now than when they'd been together and lighter in colour. She just had to wear her sunglasses and hope for the best.

"Seating for one, madam?"

"Oh, yes." Celia glanced behind her.

"Do you wish to sit with other people?"

Celia turned back to the maître d' who was smiling patiently.

"No…yes."

He raised an eyebrow ever so slightly.

"Yes, thank you." She gave a firm nod.

He waved at a waiter. "Table seven for this lady please."

Celia kept her dark glasses on and her head lowered, all the while watching in case she saw Ed or Bernard or both.

The only person she recognised was the woman from last night's dinner, sitting at a table with several different people. What had been her name? Betty? No, Ketty. A rather nosey woman with an intense stare, she'd asked lots of questions and when Celia thought back had revealed little about herself. Celia had thought the purple dress she'd been wearing last night rather over the top for a simple first night dinner and now here she was at breakfast looking like she'd stepped out of a vintage fashion magazine in a lovely linen top that sat at her waist and a pair of white pants.

Ketty looked up as she passed and smiled. Celia gave a brief nod in response and crossed to the table the waiter indicated where four others were already seated. She let out a sigh and slipped into her seat at the end of the table with her back to the room. None of them were Ed.

Everyone introduced themselves, another lot of names. Celia was beginning to wish they could all wear name badges like the staff.

An hour later she was replete after tropical fruit and yoghurt followed by a buttery croissant and then a delicate and unctuous sticky bun and was on her second cup of coffee listening to the suggestions for sightseeing in Noumea. One of the couples she was sharing the table with had been there before.

"Here you are."

Celia looked up in surprise at Maude's frowning face.

"I didn't know you were tucked away in this corner or I would have joined you." Maude waved a hand in the air. "They took me to the other side of the dining room."

The other four said their goodbyes and left the table as Maude lowered herself into an empty seat beside Celia. "Why are you wearing sunglasses?"

"I've got a sore eye." It wasn't really a lie, her left eye had stung after the eyelash incident. Celia changed the subject. "What did you have for breakfast?"

"Just coffee and some toast. I didn't feel like anything else." Maude looked pointedly at her watch. "Aren't we supposed to be at this destination presentation?"

Celia glanced at hers. "There's still plenty of time."

"Humph. My table were a toffy lot. Not on for a chat at all. And the waiters were rather aloof and brought me tea instead of coffee the first time." Maude rose unsteadily to her feet. "We'd better go."

Celia followed her friend out into the atrium where Maude paused, put a hand to her back and groaned. From that and her sour mood Celia assumed last night's good time was clearly giving her grief this morning.

"We should come back and look here after," Maude said as they passed by the glass-walled boutiques.

"I like these." Celia stopped by a rack full of floaty shirts set up outside the door of a clothing shop.

Maude rummaged through another rack of shirts. "What about this?" She held up an aqua blue linen-look shirt. "Just the thing for cruising."

Celia glanced up. Beyond Maude and the glass front she caught sight of a man who turned her blood to ice. It was Ed. He was in the boutique next door leaning over a display of handbags of all things.

Celia ducked her head and grabbed Maude's arm. "We'll come back later."

"Hang on." Maude shoved the shirt back on the rack as Celia tried to drag her away. "What's the rush all of a sudden?"

"We want to get a good seat in the theatre." Celia strode towards the stairs.

"Steady up." Maude was puffing behind her by the time they reached the theatre.

Celia slowed, her own breath coming in quick bursts. All the plotting and planning had kept her busy for so long that it had been a shock to actually see Ed in the flesh. And he'd looked good, damn him. She'd hoped marrying a younger woman might have left him looking haggard. No fool like an old fool was the thought that sustained her through the dark days when she'd raged between despair and jealousy. Now, from her brief glimpse of him, he'd looked fit and well, exceptionally so.

"I thought you were in a hurry," Maude said. "Shall we sit in the middle down the front?"

"No." Celia turned left. "Side aisle towards the back is always best." She moved on to the wall end of the row.

Maude gave her an odd look and sat down beside her. "We rushed so we could get a back seat?"

Celia ignored her, lowered the seat and slumped down. This business of trying to one-up Ed was fraught with more difficulty than she'd imagined.

"Come on, Chrissie, the pool awaits."

Christine looked up from her book and adjusted her position on the sun lounge. Frank towered over her looking relaxed and buff, wearing only his swimmers. How did he manage to look like he'd been on holiday for weeks? She was so pale. She'd plastered herself with sunscreen and had a towel draped over her legs, protection from the burning rays.

"I'm not going to swim this morning." She'd put her bathers on then taken them off again as soon as she'd seen herself in the mirror. Now she wore a black shirt and skirt that hid the bulges.

"Are you feeling okay?" He bent closer. "You took the travel sickness tablet, didn't you?"

She nodded. She'd taken the tablet first thing but she still hadn't felt like eating at breakfast.

"What's the plan for today?" Frank lowered himself to the empty lounge beside her and stretched out with his hands behind his head.

"I'm reading, Frank."

"You can't sit here all day."

"Why not?" Christine gripped her book tightly. The rolling of the ship was barely detectable but it was beginning to irritate her and so was Frank. "You go have your swim. I think I'll check out the shops later and I want to find Dad." She'd looked for her father at breakfast. He hadn't been in his room either. She'd been past three times and knocked. No sign of him at the coffee shop or here on the pool deck.

"I'm sure he's capable of enjoying himself without us."

Christine ignored Frank's sarcasm. "I thought we could have lunch up at the buffet. There's a movie on mid-afternoon then maybe we could go to the lounge where there's a few games and entertainment and then we'll have to get ready for dinner, perhaps go on after to see one of the shows."

Frank sat up. "So, you do have a plan."

Christine peered at him. His tone was accusatory.

"It's only ideas. We don't have to stick to anything." She flung out her hands. "We're on holidays."

"My point exactly."

"What's your suggestion?" She couldn't help the snappish way her question came out. The nagging nausea in the pit of her stomach wouldn't let up. She'd have to take another travel sickness tablet. One hadn't been enough.

He shrugged. "There's a family golf challenge. Your dad might enjoy that."

"Golf's not my thing."

"I don't imagine it will be proper golf, Christine." He stood now, the look in his eyes unreadable behind the sunglasses. "Then there's a lesson on how to play the casino games later. I wouldn't mind seeing how they do it here."

She gave a snort. "Going to win our fortune?"

He flung his towel onto the sun lounge and strode off to the pool without another word.

Christine dug her fingers into the flesh at the base of her neck where the muscles felt suddenly tight. What had happened? They were barking at each other like they did at home. Frank had no idea how exhausted she was. The only reason she wanted to shop was because she'd seen a nice dress she might be able to buy for one of the formal nights. She only had one decent dress with her. Something new would give her a lift. Frank's abrupt departure had been like a slap on the face.

A shadow fell across her legs. Christine looked up. The older woman from dinner was standing beside her, Ketty something.

The woman smiled, her eyes hidden behind big round sunglasses. "Hello, how are you enjoying the cruise so far?"

"What's not to like about being waited on? You obviously enjoy it enough to keep doing it."

"I do. During the sea days I have a few favourite spots around the ship I settle in to." She lifted the book she held in her hand. "Have a good day. I hope I'll see you at dinner tomorrow night."

"Yes." Christine nodded absently.

Ketty paused and Christine felt as if she was being summed up even though she couldn't see the woman's eyes. Instead of walking on Ketty leaned forward. "I'm sure you have tablets but the best thing for a queasy tummy is ginger ale. I swear by it." Then with a fluttery wave she was gone.

Christine frowned. How did Ketty know how she was feeling? She hadn't even admitted to Frank that she felt seasick. She'd said the tablets were only precautionary. She'd always thought seasickness was mind over matter. Her stomach churned. Anyway she was sure it was also Frank's curt behaviour that made her feel off and she didn't know what the cure for that was.

"Good morning, Princess." A set of warm hands gripped her shoulders as her father bent to kiss her cheek. "Did you sleep well? Where's Frank?"

"Swimming."

"The water's good but I came down early before there were too many about. I was just heading down for a coffee at that little shop near the dining room."

"I'd love a coffee." It was the last thing she felt like but she didn't want to miss an opportunity to talk with him alone. "I'll come with you."

The lights in the theatre went up before Jim had the chance to slip away. He'd wanted to beat the crowd but he was already hemmed in by others making for the door. The presenter had been enthusiastic and the big screen full of picturesque scenes of Champagne Bay and Port Vila but he'd not taken in much more than that. He hadn't planned to leave the ship at Champagne Bay anyway. The thought of sitting alone on such a beautiful beach brought back the cold dark feeling of loneliness.

His eyes narrowed against the brighter lights outside the theatre. Someone stopped in front of him.

"Good morning, Jim."

He realised she was from his table and they'd met up again on the deck last night. He hadn't recognised her behind the dark glasses.

"Hello…ahh…"

"Celia."

People squeezed past them, chatting and joking.

Jim felt like an outsider in their midst. He stepped to one side. "Yes, Celia, sorry, I'm a bit lost in this crowd."

"They can fit a lot of people in that theatre."

"Yes."

She glanced around.

"Don't let me hold you up," he said.

"Oh no, you're not." A frown creased her brow. "I was with a friend but I seem to have lost her."

"I'll let you keep looking." Jim wanted to escape. He was embarrassed that Celia had helped him back from the rail the previous evening. The crush of people thinned. He turned to leave.

She placed a hand on his arm. "I'll see you at dinner tonight?"

"I'll be there."

"I'm so glad. At least we'll all know each other tonight. I find it nerve-racking meeting new people sometimes."

"Hmm." Jim gave a noncommittal response; the woman was babbling.

Suddenly she leaned against him and slipped her arm through his. "Oh, goodness. I'm a bit wobbly. You notice the ship moving more in the theatre, don't you."

"It's because we're at the front of the ship." He looked down at her arm through his. It felt so strange to have another person's touch. "I must get going."

"Of course. I'm sorry." She leaned closer. Her cheek was twitching beneath the rim of her glasses.

He extricated himself from her grip. "I'll probably see you tonight then."

He hoped Celia wasn't going to be one of those people that clung to you at every turn. He moved away swiftly in case she tried to walk with him.

Celia watched Jim stride off. He couldn't get away fast enough. What had she been thinking, trying out her moves on him? It was just that Maude had left during the presentation needing the toilet urgently and when the theatre lights had come up, Celia had felt exposed. If Ed was in the theatre somewhere and happened to notice her she wanted it to be with a man, and Jim was rather good-looking even if he was a bit sombre. She looked in the direction he'd headed and hoped he wasn't going to spend all day shut in his cabin. Then she wondered what kind of cabin he had. Was there a balcony? Still, no point in her worrying about him. She didn't imagine a man planning to jump to his death would bother to attend a tourist information session first.

Celia strolled along past a bar and the entrance to the atrium that looked down over the next few levels. It was all glass and marble, very grand looking. She checked the floor below before she made her way downstairs. Ed hadn't ever been much of a shopper, so she hoped he wouldn't still be around. A quick recon revealed no sign of him and she spent an idle hour wandering from boutique to boutique until she ended up in the jewellery shop. It was full of pretty sparkling items from rings to necklaces and jewels of every colour. She recognised several designer names and knew there'd be nothing she could afford.

Ed had always bought her jewellery. She sucked in a breath. After he left she had sold the lot. Ed hadn't skimped on quality so she'd made a nice little amount from the sale. The only jewellery she wore now, besides her watch, was on her right hand and it had been her mother's engagement ring.

She bent to examine the pendants more closely. Maybe there would be something at the lower end of the price scale. A piece of jewellery would be a special memento of her holiday, a new beginning of sorts.

"Can I help you, madam?"

Startled, Celia looked up into the perfectly made-up face of the shop assistant.

"I was just looking at the pendants."

"Any in particular?" The young woman unlocked the drawer and slid the tray of pretty necklaces out.

"Oh." Celia hadn't seen anything she'd taken a real fancy to although one of the silver necklaces had a teardrop-shaped pendant with a sparkling white and blue starfish hanging from it. "That one." She pointed.

"Perfect choice. It's white gold with blue sapphires and diamonds."

Celia hesitated as the girl lifted the chain and laid the pendant across her hand. Just the mention of the gems made her think this would be out of her price range.

"It's very pretty."

"Would you like to try it on?"

"Oh, no. That's all right. I'm in a bit of a hurry. Perhaps later." Celia's words tumbled out but curiosity got the better of her. "How much is it?"

The girl twisted the tiny tag with the tips of her polished fingernails. "One thousand four hundred and fifty dollars." Her brightly painted lips turned up in a smile.

"Lovely." Celia tried not to swallow her tongue as she gulped. "I'll call back."

"Take one of these." The assistant offered a slip of paper. "There's a shopping spotlight show in fifteen minutes in the theatre. You'll hear all about the best of onboard shopping and everyone who attends will receive a pendant."

Celia let out a sigh of relief as the young woman turned away to serve another couple around the counter from her. A man stood slightly behind a woman who was tapping on the glass of the counter.

"I do like that one," she said and Celia realised they were her dinner companions, Christine and her father, Bernard. Celia felt her cheeks heat at the name she'd made up for him, Bedazzling Bernard, and the moves she'd practised in the mirror.

"How much?" Bernard asked the assistant.

Celia lingered, wanting to see their reaction. The two of them were so intent on the jewellery they didn't notice her anyway.

"That's a good choice," the assistant said as she drew the pendant out. "It's rose gold with diamonds set in the heart."

"How much?" Bernard asked again as the assistant placed the pendant around Christine's neck.

"It's almost half price. It was over twelve hundred dollars but it's on special this cruise for six hundred and ninety-five."

Christine leaned forward into the mirror. "It's beautiful, Dad."

Celia caught a glimpse of the pained expression on Bernard's face. She decided now would not be a good time to speak with him. She'd planned to spin him a yarn about wanting to be seen on the arm of a good-looking man. Surely she could play up to his ego. She wasn't going to tell him about Ed being aboard, she'd fluff over that bit. In a way she was glad he was with Christine. Celia needed more time to think and she would have to put her proposal to him when he was alone.

"Our shopping spotlight is about to begin." A young man addressed those present. His natty suit made him stand out from the casually dressed passengers. "Anyone who wants to be part of this fun-filled event should make their way to the theatre now." He glanced Celia's way, his smile charming and infectious.

Celia set off immediately, leaving Bernard and Christine to their deliberations. She may not end up with one of the beautiful pendants on display but at least she would have a memento of some description.

Seven

"My wardrobe is so much better these days thanks to you, Ketty." Josie lifted her champagne cocktail in a salute. "Now if only you could conjure me up a man like you did last cruise it would be perfect."

Ketty raised her glass of gin and tonic. "I didn't conjure him up. He was alone at breakfast and looking for company, all I did was introduce you." Ketty chuckled and looked beyond the rail of the ship to the sparkling green of the Coral Sea all around them, a brilliant contrast to the vivid blue of the sky. It was a glorious day for cruising. She felt so alive, free from concern and full of anticipation for the journey ahead. She'd run into Josie after lunch and they'd brought their afternoon drink to this secluded spot tucked away on one of the back decks where the sun lounges were often empty.

"I'm sure you sprinkled some Ketty magic on us." Josie popped the strawberry from the edge of her glass into her mouth.

"I'm sorry it didn't last much beyond the cruise."

"Oh well." Josie turned to Ketty as she swallowed. "And what about you? No man?"

"No, and I'm not looking."

"Why on earth not? You're a beautiful woman, only a little older than me. You've had a few men in your life." Josie leaned a little closer. "Don't you miss the companionship, the intimacy… the sex?"

Ketty concentrated on the view again. Sex hadn't been on her agenda for a few years now but sometimes, when she was alone at night in her apartment above the shop with only Patch for company, she did wish there was someone to share the events of the day with, a glass of wine, a meal. It had been several years since she'd had that kind of relationship. She shook her head. "You say the funniest things. Work keeps me busy and I enjoy the company I find when I'm cruising, male or female. That's enough for me." She had told herself that so many times over the years she actually said it with conviction.

"How is Ketty Clift Couture?"

Ketty gave a guilty thought to Judith and the others back in Sydney for the first time that day. "A little quiet."

"But you make the most beautiful clothing. I'm staying over in Sydney for a few days when we return and had planned to call in."

"I'm sure things will pick up again."

"You have regular customers."

"Yes, but not enough new ones."

"I do wish you were in Brisbane. I would be a regular for sure."

"I know you would." Trouble was, one more customer wasn't enough. Ketty needed a flood of customers, a miracle upturn if she was to save her business and the livelihoods of the women who depended on it. "And I'd want you to bring all your friends."

A small frown wrinkled Josie's brow. "Oh, I'm sorry Ketty. It's more than a slight slump, isn't it? You're worried about your business." She jerked forward and grabbed Ketty's wrist. "You should take your business online. Then I could buy from you whenever I wanted."

Ketty did an inward eyeroll. She already had a shop full of ready-mades. They were prototype garments or made to use up surplus fabric. A few sold from time to time but most of her customers came to her to have something made specially for them. "My clothes are individually designed and made to fit. I make sure my clients not only look exquisite but also feel special. That has to be done in person."

"But you have my measurements and they haven't changed." Josie sat back again. "I'm quite definite about that. I could email you a picture of the design."

"Email me?" Ketty shook her head. With emails there were none of the small nuances of face-to-face conversation. This was all getting too complicated. She wished she hadn't said anything.

Perhaps it was the second gin and tonic that had loosened her tongue. She put on a brave face. She wasn't going to make the mistake of telling Josie her troubles like she had Judith. And as for dealing with customers online – how could she maintain that personal touch that made her clothes unique? She shuddered.

"I have things to work out when I get home." She fixed Josie with a piercing look. "For now my job is to find a man."

Josie opened her mouth.

Ketty wagged a finger and cut her off. "Not for me, for you."

"Perhaps I'm glad you're not looking for yourself. You might steal the limelight."

"Never from you, my dear Josie." Ketty glanced at the strikingly beautiful woman who sat beside her. Today she was wearing a peach-coloured day dress that deepened the olive brown of her skin and caressed her figure without clinging to the rounded contours Ketty knew lay beneath the fabric. Her face was made up even though Ketty guessed she'd spent part of her day in the pool, and her hair was swept back in a casual roll that accentuated her high cheekbones.

Josie glanced at her watch. "I'd better go. I have to meet my brother." She stood and looked down on Ketty. "Now there's a thought."

Ketty sat up. "No pairing me up with your brother either."

"Good heavens, no. I wouldn't wish him on you at the moment. He's such a sad sack, not like himself at all." She pulled a pleading look. "I thought perhaps you should meet him. Maybe he would benefit from some Ketty magic."

"I'm sure your brother is a very nice man but—"

"Look at you getting all flustered. I'm teasing. I thought this cruise would be good for him but he's not been much fun so far." Josie swept up the panama hat she'd dropped beside her chair. "It was lovely to chat. Let's catch up again for a meal next time." And with a wave she was gone, leaving Ketty open-mouthed in her wake.

She put a hand to her cheek. Flustered? A raft of emotions surged through her but flustered wasn't one of them. Irritation that Josie thought she needed a man and then concern that perhaps she should look for company. Worry as she recalled her business problems even though she was trying her best to keep them at bay. Sadness that this could be her last cruise – what would life be like without the anticipation of another cruise? She lifted her shoulders. Where was the woman who had overcome loss, adversity, disappointment to build a business from nothing? The woman who had played the field, had enjoyed several relationships, travelled and was comfortable in her own skin. Is this what getting older was doing: draining her confidence, highlighting small issues, making them loom larger?

A gust ruffled the sarong she'd thrown over her legs to protect them from the sunshine that was creeping across the bottom of her lounge. She reached down to cover her toes again and pushed her troubling thoughts away. The breeze was stronger now than it had been earlier but it kept Ketty cool, tucked away in her cosy nook. She'd spent the morning getting some sun, swimming, reading her book before lunch and then she'd taken a stroll around the deck. There had been a few familiar faces from other cruises, prompting friendly waves and welcome hugs. She hoped to find someone she knew to join her for the trivia game later that afternoon. Then she'd run into Josie and forgotten all about trivia.

Ketty settled back against the sun lounge. This was one of her favourite places and at this time of day she had the shade thrown from the deck above. She always found it mesmerising to watch the sea bubble out behind the ship in a churning green and white trail and she wasn't alone. Several people lounged against the rail staring out to sea. Today the ocean was so calm that if you closed your eyes it was hard to imagine you were moving at all.

This morning she'd woken refreshed despite her late night. Now she drained the last of her gin and pushed away the final concerns that her talk with Josie had raised. Cruising was already working its magic. Troubles could so easily be left behind if you succumbed to the lure of this floating paradise. Unless of course you brought them with you and allowed them to fester.

She narrowed her eyes against the glare as she observed the couple who strode up to the rails. They barely glanced at the view before they began to talk, their faces grim. It was Christine and Frank, her dinner companions, and they didn't appear to be having fun. Ketty could only catch snatches of their conversation blown on the wind. Finally, Christine motioned wildly with her hands then strode off. Frank's shoulders slumped, he looked out to sea then slowly wandered on in the direction his wife had taken. Ketty tutted to herself. Poor Christine didn't even look like she was on a cruise holiday, wearing all that black. She was a little overweight but the shirt tucked into the short skirt only accentuated her extra kilos.

Sunshine reached Ketty's legs again. Once more she adjusted her sarong then pushed her sunglasses against the bridge of her nose and wriggled into a more comfortable position. Her book lay beside her unopened. This was always a perfect place for one of her favourite cruising hobbies – people watching.

"Hello, Miss Ketty."

She turned to the bronzed figure standing on her other side. And here was dinner companion number three. Bernard towered over her. He wore a pair of swim shorts and that was all, apart from a gold chain at his neck. A swirling pattern of greying hairs covered his toned chest. He was a fine looking man, albeit an aging one.

"You're enjoying the sunshine," she said.

"And you're not." He waved a hand towards her sarong-covered legs.

"My skin can only take small amounts of exposure each day but I love being out in the fresh air." She smiled. "How has your first day at sea been?"

He sat on the edge of the sun lounge Josie had recently vacated. "Expensive."

"Really?" He didn't strike Ketty as a shopper. Perhaps he was a gambler.

"I went to the jewellery shop with my daughter."

"Oh."

"She has expensive taste when it comes to spending my money."

"I see." Ketty thought about the scene she'd just witnessed with Christine and Frank. Perhaps he didn't approve of Bernard's spending.

"The rest of the time I've been by the pool reading and admiring the many pretty views." He winked. "Just as delightful here."

"I think you're a bit of a lad, Bernard."

"It's been a long time since I was a lad, Miss Ketty." He chuckled; a warm husky sound. He lifted his legs to the chair and lay against the backrest, hands behind his head.

"How do you know I'm a 'miss'?"

"No rings on your fingers."

"I could be a widow. Divorced."

He turned. "Perhaps but I think not."

It was hard to see his eyes beyond his dark glasses but Ketty could feel his scrutiny. What a funny afternoon it was. First Josie uncovering her worries about the business and now Bernard asking about her personal life. She wasn't used to having people analyse her. It was usually the other way around.

"What about you?" she deflected.

"I was married. My wife, Della, died nearly twenty years ago."

"Della's a pretty name."

"She was a pretty woman." He turned back to the view beyond the ship. "Unfortunately, the diagnosis took a long time to uncover and the illness dragged out."

"I'm sorry."

"I couldn't be. It was a release for her in the end. I was lonely after she went. We had a healthy relationship." He peered over the top of his glasses. "If you get my drift."

"I do."

"Hah!" He slapped his thigh and jabbed a finger in her direction. "I thought as much. There's more to you than meets the eye, Miss Ketty."

Ketty smiled. "So you didn't marry again?"

He leaned closer. "I'm still in the market."

"Your flirting is wasted on me, Bernard. I'm not in the market, as you say."

"A good-looking woman like you?"

She chuckled. "Your flattery is appreciated."

"You can't blame a man for trying. As long as my daughter's not around, at least."

"She doesn't approve?"

"After Della died I took up with another woman. Gloria was a lot of fun. She made me laugh again. Let's just say Christine didn't deal with it well."

"That's a shame."

"Gloria and I were very happy for quite a while but it didn't work out in the end. Nowadays I keep things simple. It's easier."

"I know what you mean." Ketty had been keeping things simple in the love department all her life since Leo. She cursed inwardly at her self-indulgent thoughts and sat up. "Do you enjoy trivia, Bernard?"

"I do."

"There are a couple of sessions each day in the main lounge. I like to go in the afternoons, keep the brain cells active. Would you like to join me?"

His brow creased. "What's the time?"

"I'm not sure but it's not until four o'clock, there's plenty of time."

"No." He sat bolt upright and swung his feet to the deck. "I'm meant to be meeting someone around three."

"I suspect you'd better get a move on then. It would be close to that now."

He stood, looking down at her. "I don't know if I'll make trivia today but perhaps tomorrow."

"If it suits. Never make plans too far ahead on a cruise."

"You're a gem, Ketty." He hurried off then stopped and waved. "See you at dinner."

She opened her mouth to say she wouldn't be there but he was gone. Oh well, it didn't matter. Ketty settled back into her lounge. She'd stay a few more minutes and then go in to change before she headed to the afternoon trivia session. The back of the boat was quite breezy now and there weren't many people sitting on the sun lounges let alone looking at the view.

A man walked slowly across the deck in front of her. His head twisted her way but he wasn't looking at her. Ketty recognised him though. It was Jim who'd sat next to her last night. That was companion number four. The only one she hadn't seen out here was Celia. Jim stopped at the corner of the deck and gripped the rail. His shoulders sagged and his head drooped. Ketty packed up her things and walked towards him.

"Hello, Jim."

He looked around, startled as she leaned on the rail beside him.

"Sorry, I didn't mean to surprise you. I'm Ketty. We met at dinner last night."

"Yes, I remember." His look belied his words.

He turned back towards the ocean. Ketty did the same.

"It's an amazing view from here isn't it?" she said. "All that water as far as the eye can see."

"Yes."

"Are you enjoying the cruise?"

It took a moment for him to respond. "My son was supposed to come with me but work called at the last minute."

"That's a shame. You must miss him?"

"He's in the oil and gas industry so he works away a lot. The cruise was my daughter's idea. She thought it would be good for me."

Jim's side profile was grim, his jaw locked.

"How long have you been a widower, Jim?"

"Two years."

She barely heard the whispered words.

"I understand your sorrow." She put a gentle hand on his shoulder.

Slowly he turned, searched her face with his ragged look. "You've lost someone?"

"Yes, much longer ago for me." But she wasn't a widow. She had never been married.

"How did you survive?" he asked.

"Not very well to begin with. I didn't have family; my friends were all happy newlyweds." Her parents were still alive then but she'd kept it from them, sure it would have broken their hearts to discover all she'd gone through. Her only sibling, her brother, Phil, had been overseas. It had been her dear friend Felicity who had taken her in and looked after her. When Ketty had left Adelaide, she'd renounced the shattered Kathy Clift, taken on the name Ketty and created a whole new life for herself in Sydney.

"You said you were young, you didn't remarry?"

"I've had some good friends, Jim. They haven't led to marriage." She let the softest of smiles lift her face and fixed her gaze steadily on his. "But my life has been very happy. I know everyone says it but time truly is a great healer."

Jim flinched as if she'd poked him. "I've got to go. I'll see you tonight."

"But I won't be...oh never mind." Her words were lost in the wind as Jim disappeared around the corner of the deck. "Dear, dear," she murmured. Jim Fraser was going to take a lot of work. Not only that but he was making her relive old pain that ran deeper than a lost love. Ketty gripped the rail, stared out to sea and reminded herself she was here to enjoy, not dig up the past.

Eight

Night Two – At Sea

Celia sifted through the shirts she'd brought with her. She was looking for something that would complement the marine blue pendant she'd received at the shopping spotlight show. From the bathroom behind her Maude's off-key voice belted out some kind of ABBA song compilation. Maude had brightened up considerably since breakfast. They'd caught up with each other at lunch where they'd shared a table at the buffet with Maude's dinner table companions, Pete and Anne.

After lunch the others went to play bridge leaving Maude and Celia to entertain themselves. It had been slow going with Celia keeping her eyes peeled for both Ed and Bernard. She'd stuck to the shadows where possible and scanned each new area they entered. They'd taken a few laps of the promenade deck, explored the upstairs decks and the various pools, checked out the different bars and eating areas on offer, and booked themselves in at the day spa; Maude for a massage and Celia for a manicure. Then they'd sat on the upper deck and enjoyed a strawberry daiquiri, in Maude's case two, before they'd headed inside to listen to a pair of Irish singers and then returned to their cabin to prepare for the evening. Celia had enjoyed the day immensely. Thankfully there had been no further sighting of Ed, but sadly none of Bernard either so she was no closer to inveigling him into her plan.

The sound of the shower stopped but Maude's singing continued. Now she was on to 'Dancing Queen'. Celia hadn't told Maude about the shopping seminar. It had mostly been about the jewellery, which was well beyond her budget, but she'd been happy to receive the pendant.

She slid a long-lined three-quarter sleeve white top over her crepe pants and ran her hands over her trim hips. During her forties Celia had put on some extra kilos. One of the positives from Ed's walk-out had been she'd lost weight – meals were simpler, she'd spent a lot of time walking – and she worked hard not to put it back on again.

The pendant was laid out on the desk. She lifted it, reached behind her neck to do it up then regarded herself in the mirror. The blue stone reflected the blue of her eyes and her trousers. The mirror also showed the crow's-feet at her eyes and she was still not used to the blonde colour in her hair which hid the silver. It had been slowly changing from the original blonde for years and hadn't bothered her until she'd planned this cruise. She turned her head from side to side. She still looked old. No wonder Ed had traded her for a younger model.

The singing stopped, the bathroom door burst open and Maude stepped out followed by a cloud of steam.

"That feels better," she said.

Celia turned to face her.

"Well, look at you." Maude paused towelling her hair. "You look a million dollars. Have you got a hot date?"

"Of course not." Celia scooped up her bag and stuffed her room card inside. She was glad Maude had said so though. Perhaps Bernard would see what Maude saw rather than the reflection Celia noted in the mirror. Tonight Celia hoped she would have the chance to work on Bernard. She'd even practised her flirty moves again when Maude first went in the shower and she thought she was improving. "I think it's lovely to have an excuse to dress for dinner."

"You're right there." Maude shrugged out of her dressing gown and wiggled her way into a multicoloured dress. "Although you might need to change those shoes later. Don't want you breaking an ankle while we're dancing."

"Dancing?" Celia looked down at her strappy sandals. The heels were a little higher than she usually wore but she had blisters from last night's closed-in pair. The Celebrity Celia look was proving hard on her feet.

"After dinner. There's an ABBA dance party up on deck."

"That starts at ten, doesn't it? I think I'll be ready for bed by then."

"Oh no." Maude gripped both her arms and gave them a jiggle. "You are not slipping away early tonight. How are we going to find you a man if you hide in your cabin?"

"I don't hide." Celia eased her arms from Maude's grasp.

"You keep peering around corners and looking over your shoulder and I've never known anyone to wear dark glasses and a sunhat as much as you do."

"I don't want to get sun damage."

"Inside?" Maude gave her a sceptical look then started applying her make-up. "It'll be fun tonight. Everyone from Pete and Anne's group will be there, including Nigel."

"Who's Nigel?" Celia knew as she'd asked the question she didn't want to hear the answer.

"Nice guy. Bit quiet but he seems to have money, he's single and he's not bad looking." Maude paused from applying her eyeliner to tick off three fingers. "There's the prerequisites marked."

"Why aren't you chasing him then?"

"First of all, I don't chase." She turned back to her make-up. "And second of all he's not my type. I like them with a bit more spunk." She wriggled her eyebrows up and down at Celia in the mirror.

"Time for dinner," Celia said and moved off towards the door. "Shall I meet you at the atrium bar after the meal?"

"I'll be there." Maude wagged a finger at her. "You make sure you are. No excuses."

Celia let herself out into the corridor and walked quickly towards the stairs. She had enough on her plate trying to cement her plans for Bernard without getting involved in Maude's matchmaking.

"Miss Clift." The maître d's eyes rolled in mock surprise. "We don't usually see you here after the first full day at sea. Have you changed your ways since we last travelled together?"

Ketty inclined her head. "Sometimes the element of surprise is needed, Carlos." She leaned closer, her next words for his ears only. "Four nine eight, level ten, for our nightcap?"

Carlos gave the briefest of nods. He turned to beckon a waiter. "Table fifteen for Miss Clift."

"It's all right, Carlos." She waved the waiter away. "I know my way. I'll leave you to get on."

He drew himself up importantly and turned to the next guests. They would have a good chat later.

She had met Carlos on her first cruise aboard the *Diamond Duchess*. Funny she'd thought her life was going in such a different direction back then. He had been a head waiter. She and her girlfriend hadn't used the dining room much but when they had Carlos had been their designated waiter, so full of charm and mischief. She had recognised him on her very next cruise when the two of them had conspired to matchmake for two passengers at Ketty's table.

Carlos wasn't supposed to mix with passengers but they'd managed many a secret catch-up over the years, usually in her cabin for a nightcap and a chat. There had been a cruise once a long time ago when she'd wondered if they were going to cross the threshold from friendship to lovers but the return of her travel partner had interrupted them and they'd never gone that way again. Ketty thought it for the best. She enjoyed Carlos's friendship but he lived so far away. She looked forward to seeing him whenever they ended up on the same ship.

She stopped beside the chair Rupert pulled out for her. Celia leaped up from the seat at the head of the table that Ketty had occupied last night. "I've taken your place."

"Not at all." Ketty motioned her to sit. "There are no set seats at the table."

"Only I thought you weren't going to be here." Celia still hovered over her chair.

"I changed my mind." Ketty draped her napkin across her lap. "It doesn't pay to make one's life too rigid in routine." She turned a brilliant smile on Celia. "I thought tonight I would break with tradition." The truth was, her chat with Jim earlier had unsettled her. She wanted to observe him some more, but she'd also decided she didn't want to eat alone.

"Good evening, ladies." Bernard's welcome oozed charm and Celia nearly fell off her chair, leaning over to pat the empty one beside her.

"Do sit here, Bernard. I want to hear all about your day."

He did as she bid. "How delightful you both look tonight, ladies."

Celia gave a stuttering giggle and Ketty raised an eyebrow. She sounded almost girlish.

"That's very kind, Bernard," Celia said. "You're looking rather dapper yourself."

Ketty tore her gaze from Celia's blinking eyelids to Bernard. Tonight's shirt was covered in swirls of vivid blue, pinks and oranges on a white background. Few could pull off wearing a shirt like that but it suited him. She could tell from the fit and the fabric it was expensive. Bernard obviously enjoyed quality.

"Are your family coming?" Celia asked.

"Christine and Frank will be along shortly, I expect." Bernard took a sip from the water Rupert had poured.

"That's lovely," Celia said, but her facial expression looked anything but pleased.

Another figure caught Ketty's eye.

"Good, Jim's coming."

"So, my company isn't enough for you?" Bernard put a hand to his heart. "I'm devastated."

"I'm sure you're not," Ketty said. "I'm just pleased to see he hasn't stayed in his room."

"Ahhh, so Jim is the real reason you've joined us," Bernard teased, not realising the truth in his words. "Welcome, Jim."

Bernard indicated the chair beside him as Jim drew level with the table. "Thanks for evening up the numbers."

Christine and Frank arrived next and she took the spare seat beside Ketty while Frank took the one beside Jim, leaving the two empty spaces at the end of the table between them.

Hmm, Ketty thought, still trouble in paradise.

"Are you feeling better, Princess?" Bernard asked.

"Yes." Christine settled herself in her chair and let out a long sigh.

"Seasickness?" Ketty asked.

"Exhaustion more like." Christine gave Ketty a haughty glance. "Seasickness is mind over matter."

"She's been drinking ginger ale," Frank said. "She's feeling much better."

Ketty pursed her lips to harness her smile.

"I wouldn't mind something stronger now." Christine leaned forward and fiddled with the pendant at her neck.

"Oh, is that new?" Celia's question and her wiggling finger pointing in Christine's direction drew everyone's attention to the pendant around the younger woman's neck. It was a rose gold chain, and a sparkling heart dangled from it.

"Dad bought it for me." Christine gave her father an adoring look.

Once more Ketty had to contain her smile. She laid it on thick, that one.

"It was a late Christmas present," Bernard said.

"That should cover a few Christmases," Frank muttered.

Christine glared at him but Frank sat stiffly studying the menu.

"It's very pretty," Celia continued. "I did see you as I was leaving the jewellery shop this morning."

"They have some beautiful things, and this will be my memento of this special holiday." Christine beamed at her father.

Ketty noticed Celia slip the blue glass pendant she wore inside her shirt.

"There are several jewellery shops in Port Vila worth a look," Ketty said. "It's duty-free and they have some lovely pearls."

"Perhaps you could buy me a pearl, Frank." Christine turned her wide smile on her husband but he ignored her.

"I promised to buy the wine," he said. "Shall I order a red and a white?"

Bernard raised his glass as soon as it had been placed in front of him. "Cheers, my dears." Everyone toasted with a drink of some kind. Bernard swallowed half of his before placing it back on the table. "Did you win at trivia today, Ketty?"

"No. I joined another couple who were on their own. None of us knew the sport questions."

"Dad's good at those," Christine said. "Not that you're a fan of trivia games, are you?"

"I don't mind testing the grey matter from time to time. What about you, Jim?"

"Pardon?"

"How are you with trivia?"

"Oh, not so bad, I suppose. I enjoy doing crosswords and the quizzes in the weekend papers."

The conversation faltered as Phillip and Rupert arrived with the first course. While the food was consumed and the wine drunk Ketty noticed Frank interacted little with his wife or his father-in-law but managed to have a few words with Jim. She wasn't sure about the relationship between Bernard and his son-in-law but there was still tension between Frank and Christine. Celia and

Ketty both chipped in from time to time but it was Bernard and Christine who did most of the talking.

Bernard was the first to sit back from his empty plate. "I am going to put on weight if I keep eating at this rate. How do you cruise often and stay so trim, Ketty?"

"I don't eat between meals, I rarely eat sweets and I take the stairs."

"The stairs!" Christine patted at her chin with her napkin. "Don't talk to me about them. I don't know how many times I've been up and down today. I thought I was fit but I'm quite puffed and my legs are aching. And the maid seemed to be in our room a lot. Does anyone else find her a bit strange?"

"Do you have Maria?" Celia asked. When Christine nodded, Celia went on to say how helpful she'd been. Bernard agreed.

"They're called stewards aboard ship," Ketty said. "And my chap is very helpful."

"Well, I think Maria is rather lazy if you ask me. It took her forever to finish our room today. Twice she was still there when I went back. I had to send her out so I could use the bathroom."

The waiters came to clear the table and Ketty thought it best to steer the conversation away from a discussion of the staff. In her experience they all worked very hard for their passengers and didn't earn much to support their families at home. "What did you do today, Jim?" she asked.

Jim twisted his water glass slowly then glanced up. "Not a lot. Took it easy mainly."

"That's what cruising's for." Ketty gave him an encouraging smile.

"I couldn't find you this afternoon, Dad," Christine said. "What did you get up to?"

"Moved from one sunny spot to the next, had a spa, sat at the bar." Bernard shrugged his shoulders. "Relaxed."

Ketty thought his reply evasive. He'd been in a hurry to go somewhere this afternoon. She wondered what he'd really been up to. "It's so easy to do that," she said.

"Frank and I are going to the show." Christine rose from her chair. "Would you like to join us, Dad?"

"Oh, Bernard." Celia leaned over so that she was almost in his lap. "I was hoping we could have that drink we missed last night."

For once Bernard looked a little startled. "I'd love to but all this relaxing has worn me out. I'm having an early night. Perhaps tomorrow?"

"See you at breakfast then," Christine said. "Eight o'clock at the buffet?"

Bernard nodded.

"Goodnight, all."

Murmurs came from around the table as Christine strode ahead of Frank across the dining room.

Bernard stood as soon as his daughter was out of sight. "I'm off too."

"I plan to be at the afternoon trivia session tomorrow." Ketty made eye contact with Jim who was still sipping the last of his red wine. "I could do with some help if anyone else is keen."

"Perhaps."

"Maybe."

Celia and Bernard spoke at once.

They all looked at Jim.

"I'm not sure what my plans will be tomorrow," he said.

"Well, you know where I'll be if you're at a loose end in the afternoon. The information is in the cruise newsletter." Ketty rose. "Goodnight."

She crossed the dining room with barely a nod at Carlos, keen to see which direction Bernard had gone. She had a rather strong feeling he wasn't heading to his cabin.

Jim swallowed the last of his wine. Now that the others had left he felt Celia's scrutiny keenly. He looked up to make his excuses to leave but she had such an anxious look on her face.

"Is everything all right?" he asked.

"Yes." She folded her napkin into a neat square, placed it purposefully on the table and glanced at her watch.

"Are you going to the after-dinner show?"

"No, I'm supposed to be meeting my friend."

Jim nodded. She was being polite, waiting with him.

"Only I don't want to," she blurted. "I don't mean I don't want to meet my friend. I just don't want to go dancing and she's insisting." She twisted the corner of the napkin then flattened it again with a firm pat. "I'm being silly."

"Surely your friend will understand."

"Maude can be quite…emphatic." Once more the napkin got a work-out. "She's trying to set me up with someone."

Jim could relate to that situation. "I've had friends who've tried that with me."

"What did you do?" Her look was desperate.

"Mostly I simply didn't turn up. Sounds a bit rude but I'm not looking for anyone and after the first time it was all so awkward I couldn't face another evening like it."

"Maude's so determined I should meet this Nigel fellow." Celia picked up her bag. "I'd better go."

"Would you like to do something else instead?" Jim surprised himself, and Celia too by the look on her face.

"Have my toenails extracted by hot pincers?"

Her expression was so comical Jim laughed. It felt good. "I slept quite a lot today," he admitted. "Now after that big meal I'm not at all tired. Would you like to get some fresh air?"

"As long as it's nowhere near the ABBA dance floor."

They set off across the dining room. Jim walked a few steps behind.

"Goodnight, Mrs Braxton, Mr Fraser." The maître d' inclined his head as they passed. "Enjoy your evening."

Celia nodded then leaned a little closer to Jim as they walked away. "He's quite clever remembering our names, isn't he? Truth be told I'm a little scared of him though."

"I suppose he has to run a tight ship, if you'll excuse the pun."

They made their way up the sparkling staircase and the golden sounds of a piano reached his ears. He hesitated, one foot mid-air then lowered it to the step and stopped. The tune was 'Moon River', one of Jane's favourites. What was he doing here without her? It had been her dream to cruise, not his. Celia had reached the top of the stairs ahead of him and he was about to make an excuse to leave her when she turned abruptly, hurried back down the stairs and stood behind him. The horror on her face as she passed shook him from his own despair.

"What's the matter?" he asked.

"Oh." She dipped her face and put a protective hand to her forehead. "There's someone I've realised is on this cruise that I'd rather not see. An old acquaintance, we had a falling out..."

Jim took a deep breath and turned his back on the melancholy sounds of the piano. "Right," he said. "This calls for evasive action. We'll take the back stairs."

"That's good of you but you don't have to stay with me." She peered over his shoulder, the worry still on her face.

"Let's go." He took her arm, careful not to get too close, and drew her down the stairs.

"Thanks, Jim. This is very kind."

He nodded, surprising himself with his action.

Ketty ambled along at a discreet distance behind Bernard. As she'd suspected he hadn't headed for his cabin. She stopped and smiled as he turned into a doorway ahead of her. Unless the sports bar was his new bedroom he was definitely not having the early night he'd said he was. Ketty strolled up to the door. The vibrant sounds of band music filtered out into the walkway. She continued on, sure there was a solos and singles get-together in there tonight. She'd made her fair share of visits to that group over the years. It started out for all ages in the first days of the cruise, then seemed to break up as different age groups collected for their own fun or, even better, you found someone to pair up with. She'd had several shipboard romances and yet here she was alone.

She sat in one of the soft lounges of an intimate bar and closed her eyes. Why was she looking back so much? And sad for lost love, if she admitted it. She had her brother and his family, and along with her dressmaking team they were her nearest and dearests, and her scallywag Patch, of course. Add in a few holiday flings and she'd always told herself that had been enough for her. She'd be sixty-five in a few days and yet never since Leo had she found someone who ignited the same passion and who she thought she might want to spend her life with. Josie had been encouraging but surely it was too late for Ketty now. While she still had her business and the women who worked there she was happy but what did the future hold? Even if her business was booming she couldn't work forever.

"Blast it!"

"Are you all right, Ketty?"

Her eyes flew open. She must have spoken out loud. Celia and Jim were watching her with concerned expressions.

She drew in a breath and rose to her feet. "I'm perfectly fine. I just remembered something I forgot to do before I left home," she lied. "What have you two been doing?"

Both of them looked flustered by her question.

"A walk on the promenade deck," Celia said. "It was kind of you to go with me, Jim, but I think I'll call it a night now."

"The same," he said.

They said goodnight to Ketty, walked towards each other, stopped then walked in opposite directions.

"Well, well." Ketty smiled then glanced at her watch. Time for her to collect a couple of drinks and take them back to her cabin. She was rather looking forward to sitting out on her balcony with company tonight. A comfortable chat with Carlos catching up on all that had happened since they last met would do her the world of good.

Twenty minutes later, back in her room, Ketty replaced the phone headset and looked out the open balcony door to the two drinks she'd placed on the table. It seemed she would have to drink them both. There had been a message on her stateroom phone, the voice was Carlos's, his tone polite; he'd obviously been still working. The message said her friend was unable to come tonight but hoped to catch up with her again the next night instead.

Ketty moved the deckchairs so that they were opposite, sat in one, kicked off her shoes and put her feet on the other. She reached for the first glass of Tinto de Verano and took a sip. Carlos had introduced her to it and she only ever drank it when she was with him. Ketty savoured the taste on her tongue. Poor man's sangria, they called it, but she preferred the mix of chilled red wine, lemon juice and soda to the real thing.

"To you, Carlos, my friend." She raised the glass to the part moon and took another sip.

Nine

Day Three – At Sea

"You should read this newsletter." Christine waved the ship's daily paper at Frank, who was still propped up in bed, a sheet draped over his naked body. "There's so much on you'd never know about otherwise."

He dragged his gaze from the television. "I can think of plenty to do without adding all of that."

Christine felt a wave of irritation. "Lazing around all day."

"We're on holiday. That's what holidays are for."

"That and spending time as a family, with Dad."

Frank flicked the channels with the remote control. Christine moved between him and the television.

"Let's sit out on the deck." She glanced towards the glass doors. The curtains were open and the sun sparkled off a dusky blue sea. "Get a few minutes private fresh air."

He dropped the remote and reached for her, a silly lopsided look on his face. "I can think of something else that's private, Chrissie."

Even though her heart thudded in response she side-stepped and blew out a sharp breath. Why did he have to be in the mood now? "I've just showered and dressed. It's nearly eight o'clock. We said we'd meet Dad."

"Why did you make it so early?"

"We're usually up well before this at home."

He flopped back against the pillows and took up the remote. "My point exactly."

Christine stared at her husband who remained doggedly focused on the television and tried to remain calm. They were snapping at each other again. She knew she had to try harder with Frank but she also needed to spend this time with her father if she was to make any headway on her plan to renovate their house. It was more than a house, it was the place she'd put her heart into making a home. And she had. It was so full of memories of the fun she and Frank had had as newlyweds: they'd made love in every room, they'd spent hours on weekends finding furniture in op shops and markets. Then they had babies. Lucca and Anna knew no other home. Bernard had sold her childhood home too soon after her mother had died and Christine was determined her children would never be forced to leave the home that she'd created for them.

"You go and meet your dad." Frank cut into her thoughts. "You don't need me to be there."

"What about your breakfast?"

"I'll have a swim first. I'll meet you by the pool later."

"You should eat."

"For goodness sake, Christine, I'm not a kid." He flung back the sheet and stood, his naked body a silhouette against the blue of sea and sky outside. "There's nonstop food here. I can eat whenever I like." He turned away and dragged on a pair of shorts.

Christine was surprised by his anger. Frank was usually so placid. Yesterday he'd become cranky when they'd gone for a walk around the ship. He'd noticed the pendant her father had bought her straight away and thought it a ridiculous amount of money for what he called a trinket. She'd been hurt by that. Then he'd wanted to sit on one of the sun lounges on the back deck, have a drink and watch the view but, still feeling miffed, she'd said she'd prefer the pool bar out of the wind. They'd argued again. She looked at him now as he dragged his fingers through his hair. Perhaps he was tired like she was.

"All right," she said. "I'll see you in about an hour."

He didn't answer.

"Frank?"

"Yes." His tone was sharp and he didn't look around.

Christine let herself out and made her way along the all-but-deserted corridor. The maid, Maria, spoke to her as she passed but Christine was on a mission. She paused to knock on her father's door but there was no answer. Not that she'd expected there to be. He'd gone to bed early last night so he should have been awake first thing. At least he hadn't gone with Celia. She made Christine sick the way she fawned all over Bernard. And that Ketty woman was little better with her smart quips and sparkling smiles. Christine hoped her father wasn't going to indulge in any holiday flings. He'd openly flirted with Ketty and Celia but thankfully they weren't Bernard's type at all. That's if his girlfriend, gushy Gloria, as Christine had called her, and the women that had followed her were anything to go by. He was attracted to loud flashy women, so different to her mother.

Christine pressed the button for the lift. There were five of them but she could see from the illuminated numbers none were near her floor. She took a deep breath and set off up the stairs. By the time she reached the top she was puffing loudly. She paused to catch her breath as the glass doors to the pool deck opened and her father stepped inside. He was dressed in a polo shirt and shorts, his gold necklace shone against his tan and he had a pool towel draped over one shoulder.

"Good morning, Princess." He kissed her cheek and she could smell the chlorine on his skin.

"Have you been swimming already?" she asked.

"You know I like to swim first thing." He glanced around. "Where's Frank?"

"Back in the room. He's not ready for breakfast yet."

"I thought eight would be a bit early for you. You're meant to be on holiday, you know."

She threaded her arm through his. "I've hardly seen you yet. I didn't want to miss meeting you for breakfast."

"Let's eat then, shall we? That swim has worked up an appetite." Bernard drew her along with him into the buffet.

They were finished and almost ready to leave before Christine broached the subject she'd been planning to discuss with her father.

"Frank and I want to do renovations."

"Wasn't it expensive last time you got a quote?"

"Yes, but we've come up with a few changes." She reached across the table for his hand and gave him one of her wide-eyed looks. "If you helped us out we wouldn't have to borrow the money."

"You're talking big bucks, Princess."

"You've got plenty, Dad. Your house is paid for and you enjoy a good lifestyle."

"Because I don't waste money on things that won't bring me a return."

"I'm your only child." Christine sniffed and sucked in her bottom lip.

"I know you are, Chrissie, and because of that it's important I give you sound advice." He squeezed her hand and let it go. "It would not be wise to throw good money after bad and renovate your current house."

Christine could feel a knot of anger twisting in her stomach but she swallowed hard. She had to keep calm. "You often said a good renovation added much more value."

"Not in the case of your place. It needs knocking down and starting again. I told you a few years ago you should quit it and move further out and closer to the beach. You could get a newer bigger house with a decent yard for the same mortgage and it would be a better lifestyle."

"It's not a house, it's our home. Besides, being near the beach isn't all it's cracked up to be." Her dad didn't understand a house was more than a saleable commodity to be swapped for another.

"Have you run that past Frank and the kids? They love the water."

"How would you know what they love, Dad, you hardly see them."

"Anna and Lucca holiday with me once a year. You could send them more often."

"Melbourne to Brisbane flights are expensive."

Bernard's jaw clenched. "I shout them one a year. Perhaps you could pay to send them up."

"Or you could come and visit us more often."

"You're never home. I think last time I visited I only saw you at evening meals."

The knot in Christine's stomach twisted tighter. "I work long hours and the children are busy with school and sport and music, but it's still good to have you stay."

"Melbourne weather doesn't suit me any longer, nor does sleeping on the fold-out couch in the lounge."

"That's one of the reasons for the reno, you see." She managed a smile. He wouldn't deny his only child. He owed her this. "You could have a guest room and en suite all to yourself."

He flopped against the back of his chair. "You always were persistent, Chrissie, I'll give you that."

The knot slipped away. She'd won him over. It hadn't been as difficult as she'd thought. "You're the best father."

He stood up, came to her side of the table, bent and kissed the top of her head. "Don't lay it on too thick, Princess. The answer's still no. I'll catch you later."

Christine's jaw dropped as she watched him stride away. She stood as a waiter came to ask if she was finished. Ignoring him completely, she swept out. She was not done with her plan yet, not by a long shot.

Bernard paused once he reached the pool deck and took a deep breath of fresh air. He'd thought Christine would ask him for money sometime on this cruise. He'd often given her handouts over the years and he'd been happy enough to buy her the necklace, but he hadn't been expecting to be asked to pay for renovations to their house. He had more than enough to give her but that wasn't the point. It didn't matter how much he gave her, she always wanted more and renovating that little inner Melbourne house in the manner she wanted was over-capitalising. At least they'd dealt with it now and he'd done his duty for the day, breakfasting with his daughter. He hoped not to see her again until dinner. Give her time to cool off. She'd had a face like thunder when he'd left.

He glanced at the Rolex on his wrist then made his way past the fully occupied sun lounges towards the back of the ship. Almost there, he paused. Ignoring the few other people strolling past, he focused on the ocean. The fresh sea air swept over him and the sun was warm on his back. He stretched, feeling like a lizard absorbing its energy. He could get used to this easy existence. Especially if his next rendezvous worked out the way he hoped.

Yesterday he'd attended a get-together for singles and there had been several women he'd chatted to. Two had joined him for drinks at last night's singles get-together and taken his interest. One had been a bit on the shy side but the other was a rather attractive sixty-something woman with a ready laugh and a sparkle in her eye. They'd arranged to meet at the pool and spa area this morning. It was an adults-only zone so he was hopeful it would be less crowded and it was also well out of sight from passing foot traffic. After his awkward breakfast with Christine he was looking forward to chatting with someone with no strings attached.

He rounded the corner to the entrance and his smile returned. She was already seated at the bar, a panama-style hat perched on her head, a see-through shirt hinting at dark bathers underneath, and she was alone. Last night her brother had been with her. Bit of a pretentious bloke. Bernard hadn't taken to him so he was pleased she had come on her own. On the bar in front of her there was a lime green drink with an umbrella poking jauntily from the top. She looked up and he grinned. Josie was his kind of woman he could tell. His day was improving one hundred per cent.

"Good morning."

Ketty looked up from her magazine to see Celia taking a seat beside her in the day spa waiting room. "Hello." She smiled. "Isn't it a beautiful day?"

They both glanced towards the huge plate-glass windows looking out over the expanse of ocean beyond. The water was a divine peacock blue today. Ketty imagined it as fabric rippling softly through her fingers, knowing no fabric she'd ever seen held quite the same colour or lustre.

"Gorgeous." Celia turned to the woman who had taken a seat beside her, her hand clutching the familiar clipboard. "Maude, this is one of my dinner companions, Ketty."

"Hello." Maude waved her pen at Ketty. "So, you're part of the group that kept Celia from dancing last night."

Celia threw Ketty a desperate look. "We all kept talking till quite late, didn't we?"

Ketty nodded. "Yes, we lost track of the time completely. Easy to do on a cruise ship."

"Mrs Harris?" A young woman in a white coat stood in front of them.

"That's me." Maude grimaced. "But I haven't finished the form yet."

"That's all right." The woman smiled, revealing a perfect set of pearly white teeth. "Bring it with you and we'll get started."

"I hope you've got strong hands, dearie," Maude said as she followed the masseuse.

Ketty looked back at Celia whose cheeks had coloured deep pink.

"I'm sorry to draw you into my fib, Ketty. Thank you."

"I'm sure you had good reason."

"Not that good, I'm afraid. It's easier than telling the truth."

Ketty wanted to ask but people often said more if you remained silent.

Celia went on. "I didn't want to dance and Jim, well, when he offered to go for a walk on the deck I took him up on it."

Ketty waited.

Celia's eyes widened. "I'm not interested in Jim…not as a…" She flapped her hands. "I'm not looking for a man."

"I think it was very kind of you."

"You do?"

"I think Jim's in need of a friend. Male or female, it doesn't matter."

Ketty stared at Celia. The other woman looked down at her hands then back at Ketty. "Yes, I think you're right. I was a bit concerned about him so I was pleased he was happy for company, you see."

Ketty nodded and remained silent.

"The first night I went out onto the promenade deck after dinner. I saw someone perched…well, not perched exactly, more like leaning over with a foot on one of the rails. It gave me a start and then I realised it was Jim."

A lump formed in Ketty's throat. "Did you speak to him?"

"Yes. Although he didn't answer at first. It was as if he was far away. It took him a while to acknowledge my presence." Celia gripped her hands tightly in her lap. "And then…well, he slipped. I grabbed him so he didn't fall in."

"Slipped?"

"Overbalanced or something. I'm not sure. He looked shocked and then he said he'd been watching the sea, that he used to sail and he loved the ocean. I felt a bit silly then. He'd probably been simply watching the water but there was something about him, that made me not want to leave him. I told another little fib to get him to walk me back to my deck." Celia chewed her lip.

Ketty smiled. "Seems you've told a few little white lies."

Suddenly Celia doubled over, moaned and clutched her head in her hands.

Ketty put a hand to her back. "Whatever is the matter?"

"It's all getting too hard."

"What is?"

"Miss Clift?"

Ketty looked up. Blast. Another white-coated woman was waiting expectantly. "That's me. I'll be right with you." She looked back at Celia who had lurched upright, her face twisted with worry. "Is it Jim?"

"No…yes. Yes, that's it." She had a wild look in her eyes. "It's just Jim. That's all."

Ketty studied her closely.

"We had a bit of a chat last night about bowls and where we live, football teams, music." Celia's face brightened. "We have a mutual dislike of ABBA music. There is an underlying sadness about him, though."

"He's only been widowed a couple of years. Grief is different for everyone and can't be rushed. I do hope this holiday will give him some new happy memories." Ketty stood up, aware the masseuse was checking her watch.

"Yes." Celia had resumed the aloof look she'd had on the first night at dinner. "Enjoy your massage."

"See you at dinner. Don't forget it's formal night tonight. Dress-up time."

Ketty felt a little thrill as she followed the masseuse into the small room with its soft lighting and her thoughts turned to formal night. She made many beautiful gowns for other people but there was rarely a reason for glamorous dressing in her own life. Formal nights gave her the opportunity to wear gowns she would never have the opportunity to at home and she loved it.

After the usual questions, the young woman turned on the background music and left her to prepare. Ketty slipped out of her loose dress and into the spa robe. She made herself comfortable on the table, inhaled the sweet scent of lavender and geranium and focused on the soothing sounds of the flute. The masseuse returned and Ketty settled back as the warm fingers began their magical work. She wanted to slip into total tranquillity but she couldn't shake the thought of Jim standing on the rail. She would need to keep a closer eye on him, and encourage Celia to do the same.

Ten

Night Three – At Sea

Ketty studied her appearance in the mirror. Her black satin top had a boat neck and buttoned down the back, sitting just below the band of the straight silver skirt, which finished above her ankles. She had altered the top herself after discovering it in a vintage flea market and it fitted her like a glove. The skirt had been made from a piece of leftover fabric. Her black pumps were one of the few pairs with heels she owned these days. How she used to love heels. Nowadays she worried about wobbling over and breaking an ankle.

She gave a little snort. "How sensible you've become, Ketty." She shook her head at her reflection and turned way.

Her pearl necklace was laid out on the desk. She picked it up and opened the clasp. It had been her mother's. Her dear dad had given it to her when they'd been sorting her mother's things after her death. Now he was gone as well. They said pearls should be worn often but hers rarely came out of their velvet box. Thank goodness for formal nights on cruise ships. The catch was a fiddle but she got it in the end, once she'd put her glasses on.

Once more Ketty looked at herself in the mirror. Happy with what she saw, she picked up her clutch, then looked back at her reflection.

"If only there was someone else to appreciate it," she muttered. Then, berating herself, she flung open the door and nearly walked straight into a passing couple. They looked like they'd stepped from a movie set. She was blonde, dressed in a long floaty black dress, fitted at the top to flatter the bust. Ketty knew the dress well.

Her door slammed shut behind her.

"Ketty!" Josie's voice was pitched high with excitement.

Bernard's face mirrored Ketty's surprise. He looked from her to Josie. "You two know each other?"

"We're old shipboard friends," Ketty said.

"I didn't realise we had rooms on the same deck. How convenient." Josie's laughter was warm. She looked positively dazzling in the dress Ketty had made for her after her last cruise, and Bernard looked so different in a black jacket, bow tie and cummerbund at his waist. Very dashing.

"I was walking Josie to the captain's welcome." He offered his other arm. "Are you heading down? I'd love to escort two beautiful ladies."

The diamonds at Josie's neck sparkled as she leaned closer. "Do join us, Ketty. You look so glamorous."

Ketty could barely drag her eyes from the pair. They made a handsome couple. "I'd be delighted." They moved on together to the seductive sound of rustling fabric. Ketty glanced across at Josie's wide smile and saw the adoring look she gave Bernard.

Ketty smiled too although she couldn't help but wonder what Christine's reaction would be.

Downstairs the crowd was strengthening as people gathered along all levels of the atrium, making the most of the chance to wear their finest clothes and their brightest jewels, and partake freely of the captain's hospitality. Bernard led the two women into the throng where dozens of waiters in tails, wearing white gloves, carried trays filled with glasses of sparkling champagne.

"Here's to the two most beautiful women aboard." He raised his glass. Josie and Ketty both tapped theirs against his and their eyes met. Josie's vivacity was contagious.

"To us," Ketty said, her mood much improved.

"We have to have our photo taken with the champagne tower." Maude grabbed Celia's hand and began to weave her way through the crowd.

Music played, cameras flashed, voices and laughter filled the air. Celia's head swivelled in every direction. Surely every passenger was gathered in the one area. Ed was bound to be here somewhere.

She stopped, jarring Maude to a halt. Both their glasses of champagne rocked precariously.

"I don't want to, Maude."

"Why on earth not?"

"I don't want to stand up there, that's all." There was a queue of people waiting to have their photo taken in front of a tower of effervescing champagne glasses, which had been set up on one of the landings between stair flights. Everyone standing up there was in clear view of the rest of the passengers. Celia didn't want to risk Ed seeing her. "Besides the queue's long. It will take ages."

"Don't be a wet blanket." Maude took a sip of her drink. The gold-sequined dress she'd told Celia she'd found at an op shop clung to her every curve and sparkled in the bright lights. Celia felt like the proverbial wallflower beside her in a simple sheath dress.

Maude tugged at the hem of her own outfit. "I'm glad I brought this. Would you look at what people are wearing? It's as if we're at the Oscars."

"There are certainly some magnificent outfits."

Celia took another sip of her drink and looked around, feeling at ease with her back to a poorly lit corner. She was pleased to see that among the tuxedos, long lacy frocks, diamonds and even some tiaras there were simpler outfits like hers. Some men were in shirts without ties and there were women in casual dresses. She hadn't been sure what to expect and had felt quite drab beside Maude's dazzling outfit but she was also glad not to feel conspicuous. Far better to blend in.

"We haven't scrubbed up too badly." Maude struck a pose and Celia chuckled.

"For old ducks."

"Who are you calling an old duck?" Maude gave Celia a mock pout then reached for her hand. "Please come with me for a photo. It's not very often we look like this, girlfriend...hot to trot." Maude wiggled her hips and nearly knocked over a man leaning on a walking stick as he passed.

Celia looked at each of the photographers with their backdrops depicting different scenes and each subject brightly illuminated for the camera. There were several set up around the atrium. She needed to be on Bernard's arm – he was looking like a film star and a perfect companion for her, except he already had a woman on his arm, two if you counted Ketty. She'd seen them arrive. "Maybe another night. You go on."

"All right." Maude sniffed and weaved away through the crowd.

Celia felt a little bad she couldn't go with her. They'd had fun getting dressed. It had reminded her of her boarding school days and preparing for a social. There had always been swapping of jewellery and make-up, giggling and posing in front of mirrors; a similar scenario to what had happened in their cabin earlier but with a slightly different spin as Maude had produced what she called a sucker-inner and had needed Celia's help to get into it. Other than that Celia hadn't contributed anything to Maude's outfit but Maude had loaned her glittering beads to brighten up her plain black dress. She looked up to where a couple posed for a photograph with the champagne tower and sucked in a breath.

It was Ed and the child bride. He was looking handsome in a tux and she like a young film star in a shimmering emerald green strapless dress. Celia pressed back against the wall as a new wave of jealousy raged through her like a thousand burning fires. She fanned frantically at her face with her free hand. Damn Ed. She hated he could still make her feel this way.

"Hello, what are you doing hiding back here?"

"Ketty." Celia gasped and the rage hissed out, leaving her with a prickling dose of irritation. "I wanted some space out of the crowd."

"It can be a bit overwhelming with so many people filling the atrium."

Celia frowned. The woman didn't get the hint. She looked out over the press of people. "Maude's having a photo."

"And you're not?"

"Not tonight."

"Me either. I've had my fair share of them over the years."

Celia glanced towards the champagne tower. Ed had gone. She looked around frantically trying to see where he was now. She jumped at the touch of Ketty's hand on her arm.

"Would you like to sit down? I know where I can find us a seat."

"No, thank you." The last thing she wanted was to be alone with Ketty making small talk. She'd been on the verge of spilling her story at the day spa. How tempting to share her burden with this amiable woman. Or was she simply being nosey? Celia pulled her arm away and glanced around. No sign of Ed.

"It's a quiet nook."

Celia tensed. "I'm fine here, thanks."

Ketty leaned closer, studying her intently. "Are you all right?"

"Of course," Celia snapped then felt churlish. "I am a bit annoyed at Maude trying to set me up with a man, that's all. I'll see you at dinner."

She spun away. Ed was strolling in her direction with his wife on his arm. She twisted, wobbled on one heel and dashed into the ladies loo.

"Let's have a photo while we're all dressed up." Christine looked to Frank.

He shrugged his shoulders. "If you want."

She bit back her sigh. She did want and she also wanted him to show some enthusiasm. Today had gone from bad to worse. After her flop of a breakfast with her dad, she and Frank had hardly agreed on anything. It had not been the relaxing day she'd planned. By the time he'd stomped off to the casino she'd been too angry to read her book or sit down with her laptop and she'd ended up pounding the promenade deck. At least they'd made polite conversation over a few drinks prior to this event starting. She looked around at the photographers. "What about the ocean sunset? Or maybe the tropical scene. That has the shortest queue."

"Fine."

He started off, leaving her to follow along behind. No sooner had they reached the end of the line than he took off his jacket.

"Frank." Christine frowned and brushed at his shirt. It had creased in the case and there hadn't been time to find an iron.

"I'm hot. I'll put it back on for the photo."

"You look so good in a jacket." She meant it. There was something about Frank in a suit and tie that turned her on, like a fireman's uniform did for other women. Heat flooded through her. Bugger! This was their third night aboard and they hadn't yet consummated the holiday.

"I ought to look fantastic for the cost of it." His face hardened with a frown. "It was a ridiculous price."

"You'll wear it again." Christine used the jacket to fan her face then ran her hand over the fabric. It was wool, lightweight with a sheen to it like silk. "We've got your cousin's wedding later in the year."

Frank draped the jacket over his arm and waved at a passing waiter with a tray of drinks.

"Here we are." He passed her a glass of bubbly and the smile returned to his face as he tapped his against it. "Cheers, big ears."

"You sound just like Dad." She scanned the crowd. "I haven't seen him yet, have you? I was hoping he'd be in the photo with us."

Frank shrugged, the sullen look back on his face.

"I hope he turns up soon." She wanted to add *without a woman on his arm*, but she kept that to herself. She hadn't told Frank about her attempt to get money from her father for the renovations. He'd made enough of a stink over the cost of the pendant Bernard had bought her. There was still plenty of cruise time left for her to work on Bernard. He'd said no but she hadn't given up and she still had her trump card if necessary.

"Look," Frank exclaimed. "That woman has something dead around her neck."

"Shh, Frank."

He shook his head with a glare of irritation. The lady wearing the fur around her neck swept by, oblivious. They shuffled along the queue. Christine studied her husband's profile. He really was doing his best to annoy her at the moment. How had it come to this? Sometimes she felt as if she no longer knew him at all, as if they were two strangers cohabitating.

She thought back over the last few months. November and December had been busy and Christmas with his family was always a huge affair that went on over days, leaving them exhausted. New Year they'd spent with friends. They'd only had time to talk in snatches and that had been mostly about organising their schedules so that one of them was always available to pick up, drop off and supervise children. Their couple time had become almost non-existent along with their sex life. Tonight she had to get that back on track. It was part of the reason for this cruise, but maybe she was too late. There was plenty of much younger eye candy where he worked. Was it possible Frank fancied someone else? She took a gulp of her drink this time. They said the wife was always the last to know.

"There's Bernie." Frank nodded over Christine's shoulder.

She looked around and frowned at the sight of her father chatting animatedly to a woman.

"He's scrubbed up all right for an old bloke." Frank's voice held a hint of awe as if he admired her father when Christine knew the opposite was true.

"The woman's a good-looker."

"She's old enough to be your mother."

"Surely I can still say someone looks good." The annoyance was plain on his face. "It's nothing to do with their age."

Christine drained her glass. He hadn't said anything nice about her black dress. Admittedly she'd squeezed herself into it and there were rolls around her middle but he'd liked it when she'd bought it a year ago for her work Christmas party and she'd spent ages blow-drying her hair, a luxury she rarely had time for these days.

"There's a man with them." Christine took in the cut of his tuxedo and the neatly brushed silver hair. "He reminds me of someone. The man who played James Bond, Sean, what's his name?"

"Connery."

She clicked her fingers. "That's it. That chap's not as old as Connery but he has that look about him. A very handsome man." Two could play the admiration game.

"He's old enough to be your father." Frank's voice dripped with sarcasm.

Once more Christine took a deep breath. "Oh look, it's our turn." She smiled at the photographer who beckoned them forward. "Put your jacket on, Frank."

The captain was speaking from the balcony of the next level up in the atrium when Jim joined the back of the crowd gathered at the lowest level. A waiter offered him a drink but he declined. He had nearly waited until it was time for dinner before coming down, but once he'd dressed in his suit he'd become restless.

He glanced around. Everything sparkled, from the jewellery-clad women to the marble steps. People lined every balustrade on all levels. He was amazed to see so many men in tuxedos and women in evening gowns, and was glad he had a dinner suit to wear. The only other dress suit he'd owned was the one he'd worn to Jane's funeral and he'd relegated that to the local op shop never wanting to see it again.

All faces were turned to the captain who looked resplendent in his white uniform with gold epaulets on his shoulders, a commanding presence. Jim had to strain to catch his words, which were laced with a distinctive Italian accent. No doubt he had done this many times before but when he held his arms wide and welcomed them aboard it was as if to his private home.

The end of the speech was followed by loud applause and then the murmur and chatter of the huge crowd as they began to disperse. He waited in the corner, in the shadows, until there was room to navigate his way to the dining room.

"Hello, Jim."

Ketty was coming around a now-empty arrangement of chairs.

"Don't you look smart," she said.

Jim shuffled his feet. He was so out of practice at complimenting a lady on her looks. Jane would have poked him in the ribs. "You're looking rather flash yourself."

"I do so love to dress up. I lead a rather simple existence at home. What about you?"

"I wore a suit nearly every day of my working life. I'm a casual clothes man at home."

"Well, I'm glad you donned a dinner suit tonight."

"And at home my existence is very plain and solitary."

Ketty smiled kindly. "I do understand but I've been on my own a long time. It does get easier."

Jim couldn't imagine that and yet here he was on a cruise ship.

"Sometimes we have to step outside of our simple existence and try something else, don't you think?" Ketty cast her hand towards the space of the atrium. "Another reason I love cruising. I'll go back to my quiet life soon enough. Might as well live it up while I can."

He squared his shoulders a little and returned Ketty's smile.

"Are you going in to dinner?" he asked.

"I am." She looked around. "I came down with Bernard but I lost sight of him not long after we got here."

He offered his arm. "Would you do me the honour of walking in with me?"

Ketty's smile widened and she slipped her arm through his. "Why, Mr Fraser, I would be delighted to accompany you."

Once again he flinched at the surprise of the soft warmth of another human touch, then he settled into the comfort of it and strolled along beside Ketty with more confidence than he'd felt in a long time.

Bernard had enjoyed Josie's company for most of the day. After a swim and a spa this morning they'd had a late and lingering lunch together in the little Italian cafe where they'd had a quiet table to themselves. Josie had expressed interest in a salsa dancing class and he'd gone along, prepared to do nearly anything to keep her by his side, and then surprised himself by actually having fun. What wasn't to like, having an excuse to hold her warm body in his arms?

Later they'd taken a drink on the pool deck where he'd been pleased not to run into his daughter, but then Josie had to leave to find her brother who was her travelling partner. Bernard hadn't been able to settle after that, watching his clock until it had been time to collect her from her cabin as planned. When she'd opened her door he'd been momentarily blindsided by a surge of heat that had left him speechless. He'd almost drooled as his gaze had swept the dress that outlined her shapely body with just enough cleavage on view to leave him wanting more. Her brother had greeted him gruffly and left. Bernard had been glad to have her to himself but it only turned out to be for a few minutes before they'd run into Ketty who also knew Josie. Another surprise.

They'd lost Ketty among the throng in the atrium but had found the painful brother. Josie had wanted a photo with him, and now the three of them were sitting in the club bar where they'd had a good view over the atrium during the captain's speech.

"I'd ask you to join us for dinner," Josie said as she rose gracefully from her chair. "But our table is full."

"Why don't you join my table?" The words were out before Bernard had time to wonder if it was allowable to swap tables. Surely he could slip the maître d' something to accommodate their needs. "We are a table for eight but we've had two empty seats so far. Perhaps they will be again tonight."

"That would be enjoyable." Josie smiled and looked to her brother. "What do you think? We could meet another group of people."

He gave a shrug. "Fine by me."

"There are a couple of single ladies at my table," Bernard said. He knew the other man was on the lookout for a companion. If Bernard could line him up with someone it would mean Josie would have more time to be with him. "They're nice women but not my type." He winked at Josie.

She slipped her arm through his. "Let's check with the maître d' and see if it can be arranged." She put her other arm through her brother's and the three of them trouped down the stairs towards the welcoming aromas of the Marlborough dining room.

Ketty glanced at her fellow diners, Jim and Celia on her left and Frank and Christine on her right. Bernard hadn't arrived yet, no doubt waylaid by Josie. It had been a surprise to see them together but she could tell they were smitten with each other and she was delighted for them.

Ketty suspected the Romanos had both enjoyed a few of the free drinks by the look of their laid-back behaviour. Jim also appeared a little more comfortable tonight.

Only Celia looked around as if expecting something rather nasty to pop out in front of her.

The waiters hovered nearby.

"Doesn't everyone look splendid tonight." Ketty raised her hands in a little flourish. "Are you all ready to order?"

"A very worthy-looking bunch," Frank said.

"Shall we wait till Dad gets here?" Christine looked around. "I saw him before the captain's speech and then I lost track of him but he shouldn't be far away."

"I'm ready for a drink," Frank said. "Surely we don't have to wait for your father to have that."

"It's my turn to get the wine," Ketty said as Christine glared at her husband. "Let's get the drinks ordered and we can wait till Bernard gets here for the food."

The wine was poured and Ketty was deep in conversation with Celia and Jim about the wide variety of South Australian wines when Bernard arrived at their table.

"Hello, everyone. I've brought guests." Josie was still on his arm.

"Dad, I don't think you're allowed to rearrange the seating." Christine was smiling but Ketty could see it was through gritted teeth.

"All taken care of." Bernard beamed his big wide smile, held up his hand and waved two crossed fingers at them. "The maître d' and I are like that. It's all arranged. This is Josie and her brother..."

Bernard looked around as a tall man stepped up behind him.

"Ah, there you are," Bernard said. "And her brother. I told him what delightful ladies we had on our table and he couldn't wait to meet you."

"You are a tease, Bernie." Josie patted his arm and stepped aside. "This is my brother, Leo."

The sip of wine Ketty had just taken caught in her throat. His hair was silver now and not as much of it, and there were more lines on his face, but he was still exceptionally good-looking.

"Leo," she gasped then spluttered as the wine caught the back of her throat and spattered down her black top.

"Kathy?"

The noise of the dining room receded, replaced by a loud whooshing as the air went from her lungs, and she sagged back against her chair. A gentle hand rested on her shoulder and gradually the sounds of the dining room returned.

Jim's face appeared in front of her. "Are you all right, Ketty?"

She nodded and took the glass of water he offered.

"Talk about sweeping the lady off her feet, Leo," Bernard said.

"Not only are we on the same cabin deck but you know my brother." Josie chortled. "How funny life can be."

"So you two know each other already?" Bernard said.

Ketty braced herself as she regained her breath and sat stiffly upright again. "We do…or at least did." She stared steadily down the table into the surprised look of the man she had once loved with all her heart. "It was a long time ago." She tilted her chin upwards ever so slightly. "I haven't been called Kathy by anyone outside my family for over thirty-five years."

Eleven

Ketty wasn't sure how she made it through dinner but she did. Somehow, she'd been civil when required, which thankfully hadn't been often tonight. She'd felt isolated at the end of the table, as if there had been a great flashing sign above her head pointing her out as the woman who had been duped by the man who sat at the opposite end. The curiosity of her fellow diners had been short-lived after her explanation that she'd known Leo for a short time back when she'd lived in Adelaide. No one seemed to have noticed that she'd played with her food rather than eaten it, that she'd had an extra glass of wine or three, that she had barely said a word, except perhaps Leo whose gaze was on her whenever she risked a glance in his direction.

Bernard had been louder and flashier than ever and flirting outrageously with Josie. Christine had nearly drunk herself under the table and Frank had taken her to their room as soon as the main course was finished. Celia had almost disappeared into her chair and Jim had been the only one who tried to make conversation with Ketty. She had made it as far as dessert but her stomach had clenched tightly when her favourite citrus tart had arrived. Not even the scoop of creamy vanilla ice cream Phillip had added could tempt her. She had broken off a spoonful but not lifted it to her mouth, finished the last of the wine and then excused herself. Josie had thrown her a questioning look but had been quickly distracted again by Bernard.

Now as Ketty reached her cabin door her hands shook and she fumbled her card. She tried again, the catch released and she was inside. She slumped against the door, her knees threatening to buckle beneath her, her heart pounding in her chest and not just because she'd walked as quickly as she could up several flights of stairs.

Leo, the man she had loved, had imagined herself marrying, the man who had broken her heart, was here on the *Diamond Duchess*. She hadn't conjured him up like some ghost from the past – he was aboard ship, very much alive and looking wonderful.

She jumped as someone tapped gently on the door behind her.

"Kathy?"

Her pounding heart thumped harder at the sound of Leo's voice.

"Please, Kathy. Let me in. We need to talk."

She pressed herself against the door not daring to move and closed her eyes. She was twenty-nine again and he was outside her flat in Adelaide. Then he'd hammered on the door, begging her to let him in. This time she was startled by a much gentler knock close to her ear.

"I'll call you Ketty if you prefer but please...let us talk."

Oh, God, what was she to do? Damn, she was no shrinking violet. Her life had been testament to that. She couldn't spend the rest of the voyage worrying she would run into him. He was right. They needed to speak.

She spun and tugged the door open. Leo stood there, his hand raised to knock again, his beautiful mouth rounded in a surprised O. All she could do was look at him. No words would come.

"Please can I come in?"

He looked down at her with a softness that melted her heart and a voice so gentle it was as if she had a choice, when she knew she didn't. She stepped back and pulled the door open to allow him in then closed it. The solid clunk it made filled the room and then there was silence. She took a deep breath and turned. Leo was standing so close that if she put out her hand she could touch him without stretching. He filled her room with his presence. Josie had said he'd been sad. Each time Ketty had risked a glance at him over dinner she'd seen other things, a frown, a laugh at a joke from Bernard, concern at something Christine had said and yearning when he'd glanced at her across the table, but not sorrow. Now he was studying her expectantly.

"What do you want to talk about?" At last, the words came.

"Us. We could avoid each other but now that I know you're here I couldn't stand it. Fate's brought us together for a reason, Ka…Ketty."

She was edgy, like she had been when she'd first met Leo all those years ago but then she'd been a naive young woman in awe of his maturity, his sophistication, his magnificence. She was no longer naive or in awe but she felt diminished somehow by his commanding presence taking up most of the space in her room.

"Let's sit outside." She held out her arm to point the way. If she tried to lead she would have to squeeze between him and the end of the bed.

He moved along the wall ahead of her, into the small lounge space, and rolled the door open. Immediately the room was filled with the soft swish and splosh noise of the waves against the hull.

It was a reassuring sound. Ketty took her wrap from the chair, draped it around her shoulders and stepped past him out into the night. A gentle breeze ruffled her wrap, brushed over her hair. She dragged her chair a little further away from the table that separated the two balcony seats and sat, waiting for him to do the same.

She stared out into the night, lit by a partial moon and a million twinkling stars, aware he was regarding her steadily.

It was Leo who broke the silence between them.

"Where did you go, Kathy?"

She took a careful deep breath, to steel herself against the longing look she'd seen across the table in those pale green eyes. She was glad she hadn't switched on the balcony light. When she turned her head to look at him, his face was part of the shadows.

"To Sydney."

"But we were so happy. I never understood why you left suddenly with no explanation."

She shook her head and a small wave of anger built. He was making it easy for her. "Why, Leo?" She took another breath, not caring if he noticed her agitation now. "Because you were a married man." Her voice sounded loud in her own head but she knew she had barely murmured the words.

Even though his face was in shadow she saw the shock register. "No," he groaned.

"Adelaide is a small place. Did you think I would never find out?"

"I loved you, Kathy."

"But you were not free to love me, Leo." Tears stung her eyes and she blinked hard. "And I discovered I was pregnant."

"You had a baby?"

"We." Ketty struggled to keep a hold on the lid to the box that kept those sad memories locked away. "We didn't have a baby. I miscarried."

"You should have told me."

"I was not the kind of woman to break another's heart."

"Yet you broke mine."

He reached forward but she put up a hand. She had to be strong, keep him at bay or she would be completely undone.

"How is your wife?"

He didn't answer straight away. "I expect she's well." He settled against the back of the high deckchair. "We've been divorced a long time. I don't see her."

Ketty's head spun at that news. These days, on the rare occasions she thought about him it was as still married with children, perhaps even grandchildren.

"I loved you, Kathy," he said again. "My marriage was over when I met you. After you left I stayed with Marjorie but it was all a sham. We only lasted a few more years."

"I see." It sounded so prim but Ketty had no other words, she was too busy asking herself what if she'd stayed. What if she'd told him she'd found out? She wasn't naive enough to believe she would have been the exception to the rule, but her heart leaped nevertheless. "Why didn't you love your wife?" Ketty had never known her name and even now that she did she couldn't bring herself to say it out loud, as if it had the power to summon the other woman in Leo's life.

His shoulders hunched and his hands drew apart. "We married when we were both students but in the end, we wanted different things. When I met you, my life made sense again but I knew I had to tread carefully."

"So you wouldn't be found out?" Ketty's anger still simmered. She was surprised at how easily it came to the surface.

"Of course, but it wasn't about me. I didn't want to hurt Marjorie and I didn't want to hurt you. I was torn. I'm not that callous." He leaned forward, his forearms resting along the top of his legs and his hands gripped tightly in the space between his knees. He was close enough so that she could see the pain in his eyes even if she couldn't see the colour. "I tried to find you. I kept going to your flat until one day a stranger answered the door. She didn't know you. Said she'd moved in the week before and there was no forwarding address for the previous tenant. I went to the places where we'd met. I even spent time at the tech campus looking for you. It was as if you'd disappeared."

"I did in a way." Ketty thought about her move to Sydney, her first year when she'd dragged herself to work because she had to, to pay the rent and eat. She'd eventually been dismissed because of her lack of enthusiasm, her careless work, her poor health. Her grief had consumed her. Her overseer had been sympathetic but Ketty had mucked up one too many times. In a way, losing that job had saved her. It had jolted her out of her misery and she'd vowed she'd move on and not look back. She'd done that most successfully.

"Did you find someone else? Marry? Have more babies?" he asked.

The stab at her heart was as sharp as any knife but she swallowed the pain. "No, I'm not married but I haven't been lonely. In a way, my business is my marriage and my family."

"What is your business?" He leaned a little closer and a chink of light from inside fell across his face. Now she could see the green of his eyes. "There's so much I want to know."

"I'm a dressmaker. I've had moderate success in Sydney, own my own establishment." Ketty's sense of pride in what she had achieved suddenly ebbed. She shivered and pulled the wrap tighter. She didn't mention that it was all crumbling beneath her. She owned the building that housed her shopfront, her work space and her, but she'd borrowed against it to make renovations. The accountant had warned her it was more than the business she could lose if things didn't improve. She had a moderate super fund, some dwindling savings and little else. How did a woman her age build herself back up if she lost everything? She swallowed. "What about you?"

"There hasn't been anyone else since you."

Ketty thought back to what Josie had said about her brother a few days before, something about him needing cheering up because of work and a relationship ending.

"I'm not saying I've been celibate," he added quickly as if he'd read her thoughts. "But there truly has never been anyone I've felt the same about since you."

The last of Ketty's anger ebbed away. She understood what he meant. When she had eventually started showing some interest in men again none of them had ever measured up to the feelings she'd had for Leo, and it wasn't his fault she lost the baby.

This time when he reached for her hand she let him take it in his, watched as he pressed it to his lips, felt the soft brush of his beard and the ripple of anticipation that touch invoked.

There was a tap at her door. Ketty snatched back her hand. They both looked around startled. She rose, dazed, caught herself on the back of the chair as she stepped inside. She glanced at her watch. It was almost eleven. The gentle knock came again.

She put her eye to the peephole and saw the top of a cap. The head below it lifted to reveal Carlos's big smile. She'd forgotten all about him coming to visit. She glanced over her shoulder to the balcony then opened the door a crack.

"Hello." She smiled. No one would recognise this man in his baggy pants, oversized sweat shirt and baseball cap as the man who commanded the ship's dining rooms.

"It's late but I called on the off-chance you were still up, seeing I couldn't come last night."

Further down the corridor a door clunked shut. Carlos pulled his cap lower as a woman strode past.

"I'm sorry, Carlos, I'm very tired tonight." Ketty kept her voice low and clutched her wrap to her shoulders. She felt awful lying to him but how did she explain Leo being in her cabin, or Carlos coming to visit her for that matter. "Do you mind if we put off our catch-up again?"

"I should have phoned first," he said.

She reached out one hand and squeezed his arm. "Another night? I'll make sure of it."

"Sleep well."

Ketty shut the door to find Leo had come to stand behind her.

"Who was that?"

"A friend."

"At this hour?"

She stiffened. "I hardly need to ask anyone's permission to have visitors at any hour."

He sighed and shook his head. "I'm sorry, Kathy. I have no right to make any claims on you or your time. I'll go."

Ketty's gaze swept the silver of his hair brushed away from his forehead, revealing the deep creases produced by seven decades of life, and on to the crinkles at the corners of his eyes. She wanted to know what had happened over the years to form those creases, the things those eyes had seen. She wanted to reach out and touch the soft, neatly clipped beard the same colour as his hair. Instead she reached again for the door handle. "It is getting late."

"Before I go I have to ask." His voice had a brightness about it now. "We've found each other and we're both free. Why not spend some time getting to know each other again?"

Ketty gripped the handle tighter. Was it even possible? She still couldn't believe it was really Leo who was standing here beside her after all these years.

"There's no rush," he said. "And we don't have to be together every minute but…I would so like to get to know you all over again, Kathy."

Is that what she wanted? Her head was full of so many doubts and questions. Perhaps if they spent a little time together, in a more neutral environment than her cabin, it would be easier. "I'd like that too." She said it before she had a chance to change her mind.

"What about tomorrow? Are you going to the beach?"

"Of course."

"A walk on the beach would be perfect, don't you think? No strings attached." He gave a quirky smile.

She remembered it from when she first met him. He'd always looked like that when he thought he was being funny.

"We could meet at the beach," she said. "There's a path along from the jetty past some stalls. There are some shady trees there. Shall we say eleven?"

His smile widened and he leaned forward. Ketty pulled open the door to put a barrier between them. Surely he wasn't planning on kissing her.

"Goodnight," she said.

"Goodnight."

He started to turn back but Ketty shut the door on him, took the two steps to her bed and lowered herself to the soft cover before her quivering knees gave way. A million thoughts and emotions whirled inside her. How was she to deal with them? Slowly she began to undress, the ritual of preparing for bed helping her to calm a little, but she could not get the catch to undo on the pearls.

She humphed in frustration. It was the image of herself in the mirror wearing a pink nightie sprinkled with white hearts and the pearls still around her neck that was her undoing. She began to laugh and before she knew it the laughter had turned to big shuddering sobs. The ferocity of her grief overwhelmed her. She cried for everything she'd lost, until ultimately the tears ran dry.

Twelve

Day Four – At Anchor, Champagne Bay, Vanuatu

Ketty had dressed early, the clasp on the strand of pearls coming undone at her first attempt, and she'd been down for breakfast and was ready to set off to catch the tender to the beach when there was a tap on her door. She'd slept poorly and felt exhausted but she knew a swim at Champagne Beach would revive her. She'd done enough thinking while she'd tossed and turned and now she was ready to meet Leo. They'd have a chance to talk and then, if she wasn't happy with continuing their – what would she call it? Reacquainting? – she'd never have to see him again, apart from some simple shipboard connections.

The tap came again as she reached the door and Josie called from the other side.

Ketty took a breath, put on her brightest smile and opened the door. "Good morning." She was fairly sure she knew why Josie was visiting so early.

Josie looked her up and down. "You look like you're ready to go."

"Yes. I've got my tender ticket but I'd forgotten my hat."

"Doesn't the beach look divine?"

"It truly is."

Josie glanced over her shoulder. "Can we have a quick chat before we go downstairs?"

"Of course." Ketty stepped back to allow Josie in. She had expected Leo would have told Josie about the affair. What did it matter anyway? It was so long ago, water under the bridge of life.

"So, you and Leo?" Josie began as soon as Ketty had shut the door.

Ketty felt a small stab of remorse. Would her friend think less of her because of the long-ago affair? "I'm sure he's filled you in."

"No. He was asleep when I got in last night and gone before I was awake this morning. Left me a note to say he'd meet me over on the beach later. I can't believe you and I met on a cruise and all those years ago you knew my brother. Isn't it funny how life pans out?"

"It was a long time ago." Ketty felt she'd had a reprieve. Perhaps Leo didn't want his sister to know about his affair any more than Ketty did.

"But you knew each other well? I hardly saw Leo in his early Adelaide days. Our family were from Melbourne and I was just out of high school when he married and moved to South Australia. I was doing my training, living it up and giving our parents grief. Were you a friend of Marjorie's?"

"No." Ketty had decided to tell it as close to the truth as she could without revealing the finer details of her relationship with Leo. Unless he chose to tell his sister, she wouldn't hear it from Ketty. "Leo was part of a group I met at a jazz concert. We ran into each other from time to time – Adelaide was a small place for people who liked the same things – but I never met his wife."

"Poor Marjorie. They had such a beautiful wedding, I always thought Leo adored her. We were all shocked when they divorced. Still I've learned for myself that those watching usually have no idea of what really goes on in a marriage." Josie gave a snort. "All I know is, after two divorces of my own, I'm not going down that path again."

"We'd better get going." Ketty turned to collect her bag, desperate to change the subject. She felt sure her guilty conscience was displayed on her face.

"I know I joked about setting you up with my brother, Ketty, but if you were friends once...well I just thought you might be again and maybe you could cheer him up. Our parents are gone, he's my only sibling and he's on his own. I feel I must do what I can for him." Josie's look was hopeful. "Maybe you could work some of your Ketty magic."

"It was all a long time ago when I knew your brother. We're quite different people now but we have agreed to meet ashore later for a chat."

"Oh, Ketty, that's fantastic." Josie's eyes sparkled.

"It's only a chat."

"I know, but it might be all he needs to brighten him up. Goodness knows I've tried. Things can't be any worse."

Ketty pulled open the door, not wanting to see the expectation on her friend's face. They stepped out into the corridor and walked together.

"Bernie's getting our tickets," Josie said. "He wants to get ashore early too. I can't believe someone as confident as Bernie wants to hide from his daughter."

"She doesn't appear to deal well with her father's...friendship with women."

Josie threw her head back and laughed. "Ketty, you are always so discreet. He's a bit of a hunk, don't you think?"

"He's certainly aged well." Ketty took in Josie's radiant smile. "Just watch out for Christine."

They paused at the bottom of the stairs.

"Don't worry about me, Ketty." Josie's look was steely now. "I've dealt with my share of Christines."

"Here you are."

They looked around at the sound of Bernard's booming voice. He walked towards them, arms outstretched. He was hard to miss in his colourful Hawaiian shirt.

"You're up bright and early too, Ketty."

"I love Champagne Beach."

He drew Josie against him, his large arm draped casually across her shoulders. The three of them made their way to the lower atrium level where groups of people were waiting to go ashore. Ketty found herself searching the faces, wondering if Leo might be among them, but she saw no sign of him.

"There are a lot of people waiting already," Josie said. "How long will this take?"

A voice over the loudspeaker interrupted them, asking for their patience – there had been a delay but the tenders would be ready to depart soon and people with tickets numbered from one to one hundred and fifty should prepare to be called.

"Oh, here's Christine." Bernard's smile didn't match the annoyance in his voice.

"I think I'll get a coffee," Josie said. "Would anyone else like one?"

Bernard and Ketty shook their heads and watched Josie weave her way to the cafe.

"Dad." Christine had spotted her father and was headed his way.

"If they haven't got their tickets yet they'll not be on the same tender as you," Ketty murmured.

Bernard gave her a grateful smile. "You're a trouper, Miss Ketty."

"Dad, there you are." Christine arrived with a bag hanging from each arm and her dark glasses firmly in place. "Hello, Ketty. You're an early riser too, it seems."

"Yes, I like to get to the beach first thing."

"What do we have to do?" Christine asked.

"You need tickets for the boat." Bernard nodded over her shoulder. "Frank's got the idea. He's in the line."

Christine slid her bags to the ground. Ketty saw her wince as she lifted her head. The younger woman was looking particularly pale this morning. Perhaps she was still recovering from the large number of drinks she'd consumed last night.

"I thought you might have got tickets for us, Dad."

"No, I haven't, I'm sorry." Bernard shook his head. "You can only get them if the people are present."

"That's ridiculous."

"I think they just try to make it fair for everyone," Ketty said.

Christine sucked in a breath, clearly annoyed.

"I would have been gone by now if there hadn't been a hold up," Bernard said.

"I've got the tickets." Frank joined them and nodded a greeting. "Hello Bernie, Ketty." He turned back to his wife. "We may as well go and get some breakfast after all. The purser said it will be an hour before we get called."

"But we want to go when Dad goes."

"You can't, Princess."

Christine glared from her father to her husband. "Give them to me." She snatched the tickets from his hand. "I'll sort this out."

She stalked away to the line of people waiting and moved straight to the front. No sooner had the next person finished than Christine pushed up to the desk. The man behind her complained but she simply lifted her shoulder and kept her back to him.

Frank and Bernard turned away. Both wore pained expressions, Ketty noted.

"I've got my tickets already." Christine's demanding tone carried easily. "But I need to change them. My father has earlier tickets and we want to travel together."

"I'm sorry, madam." The young officer spoke in a clear English accent, polite but firm. "We can give you all a later ticket but I can't change any that have already been issued."

"Of course you can—"

Christine's voice was lost in the call of the overhead speaker for tickets one to one hundred and fifty to board.

"That's us," Bernard said. "I'm sure you'll find me when you get there, Frank. Let Christine know I've gone."

He put a guiding hand in Ketty's back, propelling her forward. Josie met them as they left the atrium.

Bernard smiled. "Just in time."

"What about your daughter?" Josie looked back.

"She's coming later." Bernard paused as they reached the narrow stairs leading down to the tenders, his grin wide. "After you, ladies."

"Isn't this great." Pete smiled across at Celia. "We're all on the same tender so we can hang out together when we get to the beach."

Celia hoped she managed a smile. 'Hanging out' was something she hadn't done since she was a teenager. She gripped the seat beneath her hands as the boat accelerated away from the ship. She was seated between Nigel and another of Pete's friends, Bob, and trying hard not to make body contact with either. Pete and Maude were seated opposite with Bob's wife, Freda.

"It's such a shame Anne can't join us," Freda called above the noise of the boat.

They were crammed inside the cabin of the tender with a large number of other passengers. Celia felt claustrophobic.

"Her knee's like a balloon and quite painful," Pete said. "I've had her to the medical centre. The doctor said the stairs on and off the tender and the long walk from the jetty to the beach would be too much for her." He patted the camera hanging around his neck. "I've promised to take lots of photos." His hand dropped to his side and Celia saw it rest on Maude's hand a moment.

Maude was busy staring out the window and took no notice. He gave her hand a pat. She turned back and smiled. Celia looked away and came face to face with Nigel.

"Do you like to swim, love?" he asked.

She shuddered at his use of the word *love*. It was a pet hate of hers when people used that word for someone they barely knew. Like one of the checkout operators at her local supermarket. Celia was old enough to be her mother and didn't know the younger woman personally but she always asked Celia if she had any bags and added the 'love'. She swallowed her distaste. "Sometimes," she said. "I'm more of a pool person but I have been known to swim in the sea when the temperature's high enough."

"Me too. They say the water's quite warm here. And I've got my snorkel and goggles." He patted the bag he clutched to his chest. "I've never used them before but it shouldn't be too hard to learn."

"I've got a pair of swim goggles so I can look at the coral from the surface. I've never used a snorkel before. I didn't want to drown myself."

Nigel laughed. "Pete's going to teach me."

"Nothing to it." Pete grinned and nudged Maude. "I'm looking forward to teaching you too."

Maude laughed, a little bit too loudly, Celia thought, in spite of the engine noise. The boat slowed.

"We're here," Maude called. "Isn't it divine?"

Celia could only nod in agreement as they tied up at a small jetty. She took the hand of the crew member helping her to step ashore, but her attention was taken by the aquamarine ocean sliding onto the dazzling white sand. Beyond the beach were palms and broad-spreading trees sheltering umbrellas and little huts with brightly coloured fabric fluttering in the breeze. Behind it all was the lush green backdrop of a foliage-covered mountain reaching up to the brilliant blue sky. The tension slipped from her shoulders. She felt as if she'd stepped into paradise. "It's like a postcard," she murmured.

"Let's go." Pete led the way along the jetty, a guiding hand at Maude's back.

The rest of the group followed. Celia sighed. She looked down at a gentle pressure on her arm. Nigel had cupped her elbow with his hand.

She strode ahead and out of his clammy grasp. Her plans to relax on the idyllic beach evaporated with every step. How was she going to get through the day? It was hard enough keeping an eye out for Ed, she'd not seen Bernard, and now she'd have to spend her day trying to avoid Nigel. On top of that Pete was making eyes at Maude. He was a married man and Celia didn't take kindly to cheaters.

⚓

Ketty sat with her back against one of the palm trees and looked out over the beach and bay in front of her. Her fellow passengers were spread in every direction and beyond them the tenders were still busy traversing the sparkling blue water between the jetty and the ship.

Bernard and Josie had stayed with her for a time. They'd swum, and Bernard had snorkelled while Ketty and Josie had floated in the temperate water, but then the other two had wanted to hire one of the taxis and see more of the island. They'd offered to take Ketty with them but she'd declined. Apart from not wanting to be the third wheel, she had said she'd meet Leo and she was determined to do so. Josie had given her arm a squeeze along with a smile before she left.

Normally Ketty enjoyed nothing more than soaking in the warmth, content to swim, wander among the stalls or sit in the shade, but today nothing about her favourite beach was helping her relax.

She'd thought she was ready but now she was nervous about meeting Leo. What would they talk about? How to begin? They'd known each other intimately, but for such a short time. He'd always come to her little flat if they were staying in. He'd told her he lived in a shared house with no privacy. Ketty shook her head recalling how gullible she'd been. Shared house all right. What he'd neglected to say was it was his wife he was sharing with. She sighed and looked out over the bay but she hardly took in the view. The swim had been refreshing. It had washed away the final cobwebs of her broken sleep but now she fought her seesawing emotions as the time to meet Leo drew nearer.

Raucous laughter attracted her attention further along the beach to where a group of people were settled on the sand. A man had donned a set of the coconut bras and a colourful grass skirt that were on sale from the huts behind. He was doing a very bad imitation of a hula dancer. He reached down and pulled up one of the women in the group to join him. Ketty recognised Celia's friend, Maude. She stared harder and saw Celia was sitting beside another man. It appeared as though he was talking in her ear while Celia gazed out to sea. Perhaps he was the chap she had said Maude was trying to set her up with.

Ketty glanced at her watch, stood and shook out her towel. She didn't have time to ponder Celia. All she could think about was meeting Leo and what they might say to each other.

She took a deep breath of the sweet-smelling air and set off. The sand was hot beneath her feet and the sun warm through the turquoise blue shirt dress she had thrown over her bathers. When she drew level with Celia, the others in the group were hooting with laughter except for Celia who looked up at that moment, a pained expression on her face.

Ketty nodded a hello as she passed and was surprised to see Celia leap to her feet and pick up her bag. The others were still distracted by the joke except for the man she'd been sitting beside. He began to get up but Celia waved him back.

Maude also noticed her friend's movement. "Where are you off to?"

"Catching up with Ketty." She slipped her arm through Ketty's. "Back later."

Their feet sank into the sand as Celia dragged Ketty along the beach.

"You're a lifesaver." Celia glanced over her shoulder but kept walking. "They're nice people. I especially like Bob and Freda but Nigel won't give me a minute's peace."

Ketty glanced back. "Was he the man sitting beside you?"

"Yes, and if he calls me 'love' one more time...ohhh! I'll scream!" Celia squeezed Ketty's arm tighter. "But what really bothers me is the way Pete's playing up to Maude. He's married and he's acting like a single man."

Ketty hadn't been able to get a word in. How was she going to get rid of Celia in time to meet Leo?

"Thank goodness you came along," Celia said and looked at her with such relief Ketty felt as if she could have just saved her life. Then Celia's mouth dropped open. She was staring at something over Ketty's shoulder but before Ketty could turn she was being dragged up the beach to where throngs of people wandered between the colourful stalls.

"Have you bought any souvenirs?" Celia babbled as they merged with other passengers. "You've done this before. What do you recommend?"

They were heading along the path between the huts at such a pace they could barely look at any of the souvenirs on offer let alone purchase any. Finally, Ketty stopped, Celia did the same, and with a glance over Ketty's shoulder she turned to one of the stalls and picked up a shell necklace. "What about this?"

"You have to be careful of Customs when you get home." Ketty wasn't sure what to do now. Celia had commandeered her and it would be such bad manners to desert her but—

"Oh, look who's coming. Isn't that the man who joined us at the table last night? You know him don't you? Leo?"

Ketty turned and once more the sounds around her receded for a few seconds and then came flooding back. It was Leo, just mere metres away moving towards them. He wore a plain white polo shirt and loose blue shorts, looking at ease and staring straight at her.

His smile widened, self-assured. He was obviously not feeling the turmoil inside that she felt. He stopped beside them. "I saw you coming this way so I thought I'd meet you."

"How lovely," Celia gushed, obviously assuming he was including her. "Ketty and I were just going for a walk. Why don't we go together?" She reached for Leo's arm. "You can escort us."

Ketty's stomach lurched as Leo's other arm slid through hers. He looked at her, a quizzical smile on his face, then he turned back to Celia.

"I'd be delighted," he said.

They moved off together, Celia talking to Leo as if she'd known him for longer than one night and Ketty lost in the whirl of thoughts being so close to him brought on. Not able to say anything personal and yet still unsure how she would have begun, she was relieved that she had some respite.

Thirteen

Josie leaned back against the cracked vinyl seat of the four-wheel drive and smiled. "This has been a lovely day, thank you Bernie."

"I've enjoyed it too." He knew he was acting like a besotted schoolboy but it was how he felt.

Today they'd spent their time swimming and touring the island with only the taxi driver as their guide. They'd bought fruit at a roadside stall and ate it on a small secluded beach, marvelling at the sweetness of the small bananas and the beauty of the scenery. They had talked about where they lived, both in Brisbane as it turned out, and what they liked to do: swimming, tennis, movies, wine. They had a lot in common.

He studied her now as she looked out the open window. Her blonde hair flicked in the wind and her white shirt ruffled around her shoulders. She'd reapplied her lipstick but much of her make-up had washed off during their swims, first at Champagne Beach then at a lagoon further inland and finally at their picnic stop. She was an attractive woman with or without the paint.

She turned suddenly and caught him studying her. Her lips turned up slowly in a smile. "I think I'll be ready for another swim at the beach when we get back."

"Yes."

"Is something wrong?"

He looked into Josie's eyes shaded by her sunglasses. He knew they were pearly blue and they sparkled when she laughed, which she did easily. And not a nervous half-laugh, Josie's laugh was vibrant, full.

"No, it's nothing."

"Tell me."

That was another thing he liked about Josie, she looked like a fluffy blonde but she cut to the point. He'd been physically attracted to her, still was, but he was discovering there was more to her than just a pretty package.

"I should meet up with Christine and Frank," he said.

"Of course. Why shouldn't you?"

"It's complicated. My daughter can be…"

"Protective?"

He pushed his sunglasses to the top of his head and took her hand. "Chrissie thinks I'm a bit of a flirt."

"A bit." She raised her eyebrows at that.

"I enjoy the company of women, I'm the first to admit it. I know we've only known each other a few days but I really like you and I'd—"

"Steady up there, Bernie." She slipped her hand from his and placed it against his chest. "You're not about to propose are you?" She laughed.

He laughed too. "Of course not."

"That's a relief."

Bernard looked the other way through the window where the coconut palms had given way to thicker bush. What had he been trying to say? Josie was the first woman since Della that he'd felt more than a flash of attraction for. There had been Gloria and then Kath but neither of them had worked out and since then, well, it had all been about having fun, no strings. Even though they'd only just met he felt a strong connection to Josie.

She slid her hand up and patted his cheek. "No need to complicate things."

"No." Bernard turned back. Her hand was soft and warm on his skin. "I've been a widower a long time."

"And I've divorced two husbands."

"Do you have children?"

"Three sons."

"How are they, when you, if you…" Bernard knew he was spluttering but he couldn't get it out.

"When I meet other men?"

"Yes."

"My first husband was violent and my second a womaniser." This time it was Josie who lifted her glasses to study him closely. "I've worked hard to raise three young men who I hope are neither of those things. They are happy for me to have my own healthy relationships."

Bernard flopped his head against the seat. "I have one daughter and I'm afraid I haven't managed to instil such liberal ideas in her mind."

"Oh, I see." Josie slid her glasses back onto her face. "You think she won't approve of me."

"Nothing personal but yes, I know she won't."

"And here I thought her cool manner with me last night was because she didn't like my dress."

He gaped and she laughed, placing her fingers softly against his lips.

"You're an adult, Bernie."

"I know that, so is Christine. Maybe it's different with daughters."

"Perhaps."

They travelled on in silence a moment then Josie spoke.

"Look Bernie, I've been having fun with you but if this is going to be a problem for you we can cool it. You spend some time with your daughter. We can catch up again for a drink at some stage, see how things go. There's still plenty of cruise time left."

"Would you like to stop for photo?" The taxi driver glanced in the rear-view mirror.

"Oh, look at that view." Josie took out her phone. "Yes please."

Bernard tugged his own phone from his pocket. They had been wending their way downwards catching only glimpses of the sea between the trees but now the panorama before them was extensive. The varying greens of the lush vegetation met the iridescent blue sea on which their ship sat at anchor, the only craft visible from their vantage point. Further away, smaller islands appeared as if they were green broad-brimmed hats floating on the ocean.

Josie threw out her arms. "Our own tropical island and there's our personal yacht waiting for us."

He stepped up beside her and took a selfie with the ship behind them.

She threw an arm around his neck. "I feel like I've escaped reality."

He understood what she meant. It was easy to forget the world and enjoy the moment. This was a beautiful island but he suspected he felt this way more because of Josie's company than the setting.

She planted a kiss on his cheek and he snapped another picture.

Josie laughed. "Aren't you worried your daughter might see that?"

He kissed her lips. She tasted sweet like berries. "No."

"Quick, get in quick." The driver tooted his horn. "Another car coming."

They jumped into the back seat and slammed the doors as a jeep hurtled past them, heading down the road.

Josie laughed and clutched his hand as their driver sped off at a similar breakneck speed. Bernard grinned and reached across to cover her hand with his other. There was no way he was going to miss spending time with Josie. He was more than keen to see where this might lead.

"I feel terrible." Christine groaned and put her head in her hands. They'd come back to their room to freshen up after the beach. She was still in the chair she'd slumped into as soon as they'd entered the cabin, her bag by her feet on the floor. Frank had been through the shower and put on the palm tree-patterned shirt he'd bought on the island. It hurt her eyes to look at the bright colours.

She'd felt miserable all day with a queasy stomach and a headache. Frank had hinted that perhaps it had been the number of drinks she'd consumed but she wasn't admitting that, not even to herself. She'd said it was something from dinner the night before. You often hear about fish causing upsets, and she'd had the fish.

"Have some water." Frank offered her a bottle now from the fridge.

She took it from him then eased back into her chair. "Could you get me some headache tablets as well?" She managed a wan smile. "Please."

He retrieved them from the bag in the bathroom and watched while she swallowed them.

"Thanks." She leaned back in the chair, her eyes closed.

He sat on the edge of the bed and she could feel his stare. She peered at him through one partly open eye.

"Why don't you read a book or go for a walk? Give these tablets time to work then I'll have a shower and I'll be fine."

He took a deep breath and leaned forward. "I need to tell you something."

Christine's breath caught in her throat. "Not now, Frank."

"Yes now."

She opened both eyes. What was he going to say? She wasn't strong enough to deal with whatever had him looking so serious. "I don't feel well. Later we can—"

"Later doesn't come with you, Christine. Last night I'm sure you drank too much so you could avoid me."

"I didn't drink too much and anyway I could hardly avoid you. We share a room and a bed."

"You were snoring before I'd finished cleaning my teeth."

"We're on holiday, Frank." She put her hand over her eyes and settled back against the chair again. If she could get rid of this headache and the queasiness, then she could focus. "Whatever it is that's so serious can wait."

"I'm thinking of applying for a new job."

Her hand dropped as a wave of relief swept through her. "That's your important news?" She'd imagined another woman or an illness.

"Yes."

"That's great, Frank. What is it? Head of garbage now instead of second in command?"

Frank lurched back as if she'd punched him, his face crumpled in a scowl. "Why is it that what I do is never good enough for you?"

She sat forward slowly and reached for his hand. She hadn't meant to hurt him, only she was feeling so miserable. Headache or not, she had to try harder. "I was only joking, Frank."

He glowered at her.

"Tell me, what's this new job?"

"Waste management will be part of it but it's a much broader department with—"

"That's great, Frank. I'm pleased for you. I guess it will mean a pay rise as well. The extra money will come in handy." Perhaps they could put something towards the extensions and her father might be willing to put up the rest.

Frank gripped her hands tighter. "There's more."

Once more her stomach dipped. He looked worried. Perhaps he was planning to leave her after all.

"It's a different council."

"What?" Her head thumped. She really was having trouble keeping up.

"We could sell and move south. You've always wanted more room. Our place is small and we could buy something bigger and still be paying the same mortgage."

"Wait, stop." She put up a hand. "You want to sell our house?"

"It would save renovating."

"But I love that house."

"You want to do a total makeover."

"But it's still our home. The only one we've ever had together." Her stomach roiled. Surely he didn't want to leave the haven they'd created and its sixteen years of memories.

He reclaimed the hand she'd held in the air. "We'll still be together."

"But it's in such a good area and easy for me to get to my work in the city."

"Your firm has that new office in the south. It's close to where I'll be based. You said yourself they wanted staff for it."

"But I'm in charge of everything where I am, and what about the kids' school?"

"They travel now. It's about halfway between where we are and where we'd move to. They'd simply be travelling in the other direction."

"You can't do this to us, Frank." Her fear slid away replaced by anger. She yanked her hands from his and stood up. "You've planned all this and not a word. How could you keep such a secret?"

"I've taken my time to look at what a change would mean for us and I think it would be good but I haven't applied yet. I might not get the job."

Her legs felt wobbly. She sat down again. He was only thinking about it. "That's all right then."

He crouched down, wrapped her in his arms and kissed the top of her head.

"I want this job, Christine. It's a fantastic opportunity and a big step up."

She stiffened as the resolve tightened around her heart. "I don't want to move, Frank. Everything works where we are."

"What?" He pulled away.

"No harm done if you're only thinking about it. Something will come up where you are. You won't be second in command forever." She had to smooth this over. She reached up a hand to pat his cheek but he intercepted it, gripping her hand tightly in his.

"You're not listening to me. If we move we can get a better house with the features you want. It won't affect the kids' school and—"

The thumping in her head grew stronger. "And you're not listening to me. We're not moving."

"We can make it work." He dropped her hand.

She could see the hurt in his eyes but she wasn't giving in on this. Everything she cherished was tied up in their home. They'd bought the house together when they'd become engaged. They hadn't had a honeymoon but spent their first week of married life there without letting on where they were or leaving the house for anything. That week was one of her treasured memories. The roses her friends had given her after her mum died bloomed there. Their children had been conceived there and started their lives in rooms prepared with care and love. When they'd repainted a couple of years back she hadn't let the painter go over the patch of wall in the little store room where they'd marked the kids' heights each year on their birthdays. The house was everything to her even if he no longer felt the same. "No Frank, we can't."

"Then I'll have to commute and you'll have to be the one to get home on time for the kids and run them around."

"What do you mean? I do that most nights. You haven't thought this through."

"I've done nothing else but think about it for months. I'm tired of your digs that I'm only in charge of garbage." He stood and folded his arms across his chest. "You know what would happen if no one was in charge of removing the rubbish, Christine. You'd be up to your neck in it. This job has a larger portfolio and I'm going to apply. I think I've got a good chance of winning it."

He glared at her with such a determined look she was speechless. She'd not seen him this resolute before and it bothered her to think perhaps she wouldn't be able to get him to change his mind. She'd not realised her teasing about rubbish collection had been such a sensitive issue. It was hard to think straight with her head pounding and their argument had made her stomach churn harder. They needed some space. "Good luck then," she said sadly and got up from the chair. "I'm having a shower."

She shut the bathroom door then slumped against it as she heard the door to their cabin bang shut. She put her head in her hands. So much for lighting the fire in their marriage. There was heat all right but not the kind she'd hoped for.

Jim leaned on the rail at the front starboard side of the ship and studied the beach. He hadn't planned to go ashore today but his steward, Ricardo, had chastised him when he came to drop off the bottled water and found Jim still in his cabin.

"Mr Jim, why aren't you on the island? It's so beautiful there," he'd said.

Jim had no good reason. He'd made his way downstairs, eaten a late lunch, wandered the ship then had decided he should go ashore and had taken one of the mid-afternoon tenders with half-a-dozen other passengers. Once there he walked among the stalls then back along the beach, paddled in the shallows and caught the next tender back to the ship. At least he could say he'd been to Champagne Beach if anyone asked, but instead of the delight he saw on other faces he felt hollow, as if he was viewing it all through grey-coloured glasses.

Now he leaned forward to watch the tenders returning the last few passengers to the ship. He took out his phone and snapped some photos. He hadn't thought to do it during his brief journey ashore. Tam would want to see some pictures when he returned home. He'd better have something to show her.

Music began to play from the pool deck behind him and his thoughts wandered to Celia and Ketty. He'd seen no sign of anyone he knew among the people spread around the beach and in the water. No doubt they'd made the most of the day like he should have but being on that tropical beach made him long for Jane again and he'd come back to the ship as quick as he could. He didn't want to slip into the terrible state he'd been in on the first night aboard.

After that first dinner he'd taken himself outside. It had been stupid to climb on the rail. He'd been mesmerised by the ocean swirling past, feeling so desperately lonely for Jane, then Celia had come along. He shuddered at the recollection of slipping. He'd given himself quite a fright realising how close he'd come to falling overboard. Sad as he'd been at that moment he knew he didn't want to die.

He squared his shoulders and focused on the present. A few people began to spread out along the rail watching the preparations for departure. Jim noticed a man in a bright shirt walking towards him. It was Frank and he was waving one of the bottles he was carrying.

"Would you like a beer?"

Jim took the offered drink. "How did you know I was here?"

"I didn't." They clinked the necks of their bottles together and took a swig.

The beer was icy cold and refreshing. Jim licked his lips. "Thanks."

"I'd planned to drink them both," Frank said. "But there're plenty more at the bar."

"I'll get the next one."

Jim and Frank both leaned on the rails, sipping their beers, gazing towards the land.

"Did you go to the beach?" Jim asked.

"For a couple of hours." Frank shook his head. "Christine didn't feel well. She sat up under the trees most of the time. I swam. The coral and the fish were worth a look. I bought myself this shirt thinking we might make it to the Pacific night deck party later."

Jim glanced at Frank. The orange shirt with the green-and-brown palm trees was certainly bright. Frank's expression was gloomy in comparison.

"Not in the mood for dancing now?" Jim asked.

Frank shrugged. "Tell me, Jim. You were married a long time. How did you manage?"

Jim took another swig of his beer. "My motto was always 'happy wife, happy life'." He was selling his dear Jane short but he was trying to make light of Frank's dark mood. Jim was in no position to be counselling anyone on relationships.

Frank's gaze remained towards the coast. He laughed but the sound was mirthless. "What if there is no way to keep her happy."

They drained their beers.

A blast came from the ship's horn and the music behind them cranked up. Jim took Frank's empty bottle from his hand. "I'll get the next one."

Fourteen

Night Four – At Sea

Ketty sat with her back to the porthole-styled window, giving her a view of the entrance, and settled into the plush leather couch to wait for Leo. The low mahogany table at her knee shone in spite of the soft lighting and the scent of wood polish lingered. She loved the atmosphere of this more intimate bar, tucked away off a small corridor near the front of the ship. In the past she'd witnessed others meet here, their clandestine nature revealed by the positioning of furniture away from the door, the surreptitious glances, the furtive caresses. This time she was having her own meeting rather than being a bystander. She smiled. All those years ago her meetings with Leo had been in secret but she had been too caught up in her own happiness or too naive to realise it. When they'd gone out together it had always been to late-night jazz concerts in poorly lit clubs or back corners of eateries. Then she'd simply relished having him to herself.

This meeting was similar in a way. They'd planned it without letting Celia hear. They hadn't had any time to talk alone on the beach and by the time they'd returned to the ship Ketty's lack of sleep and time in the sea and sun had caught up with her. It had been the strangest of days. She had been anxious about meeting with Leo but she needn't have worried, Celia hadn't given them a moment to themselves. The other woman's behaviour had been furtive at times and openly flirtatious at others. Ketty couldn't work her out at all. She suspected Leo was becoming a little fed up too by the time they'd returned to the ship. Celia had wanted to have drinks on the pool deck but both Leo and Ketty had declined and had managed to make a time when they would meet for pre-dinner drinks alone.

Ketty glanced at her watch. He was late. He often had been when they'd been together but Ketty had put it down to juggling study and work. She'd been so busy herself back then it hadn't mattered. When he did arrive he never seemed rushed, he'd join their little mismatched group of jazz enthusiasts, filling whatever space they were in with his presence. Always making sure they had drinks, the best seats, whisking her to the dance floor, or if they were alone at home – it was always her flat – he'd be full of talk about work, music, something that had happened, and when they made love it was passionate, demanding, wonderful. She shivered. And then the devastating end. Perhaps she was being too eager, sitting here waiting for him to arrive, but punctuality was important to her. It had to be, in her business. All part of the attention to detail and personal touches that were vital. How on earth that transposed to the online world was beyond her.

She was just thinking she'd get herself a drink to steady her nerves when he appeared in the doorway. She held her breath and watched him look around, a small frown on his brow. The frown changed to a smile when he saw her and he headed in her direction. He wore clothes well, looking casual but smart in his black shirt, cuffs rolled back, and dark denim jeans. He was tall, and passed through the room with an air of self-assurance. Heads turned to look at him but his eyes were fixed on her. Only when he stopped in front of her did he appear to hesitate, perhaps, like her, unsure where to begin.

"I was about to get a drink." It was Ketty who broke the tension between them. "Oh, but here's a waiter."

They ordered and Leo lowered himself to the soft padded chair opposite her, his back to the room. They stared at each other a moment.

"These cruise people seem to have everything worked out don't they." He tucked his card back inside his shirt. "A very smooth operation I must say."

"Have you cruised before?" At least this was a topic Ketty felt comfortable with.

"Never was on my radar. Josie wanted company. I wasn't keen but she begged me to join her. She can be very persuasive, my sister."

"I find her good company."

"Oh yes, she's always good company."

She wondered if he was mocking his sister but the waiter arrived with their drinks and Leo was quick to reach across to tap his glass against hers, regarding her intensely.

"To you, my sweet Kathy. You look just the same except your hair, like mine, is a different colour. You're as beautiful as ever."

Ketty chuckled to hide her pleasure that he should still think her attractive after all this time. "I do like the muted lighting in here." She took a sip of her drink. His eyes didn't leave her. She put her glass carefully back on the table. He hadn't lost his movie-star looks and instead of grey hair like hers, his was what she thought of as a more distinguished silver. "You're looking well, Leo."

"I've had some setbacks lately but..." He lurched forward, his hands resting on his knees. "Seeing you again, Kathy, it's been like a panacea. And I love this dress." He lifted his hands now holding them open. "You look so regal. You always did dress well."

Once more she felt satisfaction at his words. She'd spent some time after her shower deliberating on what to wear. In fact, she'd tried on several outfits. She liked to dress for dinner but didn't want Leo to think she was making a special effort just for him, although part of her knew she was. The dress was soft grey brocade with a subtle red pattern, short sleeves, high neck, fitted waist, a day dress really but she had decided it was right for tonight.

"Clothes are my business," she said. "I enjoy getting the chance to dress up."

"You said you are a dressmaker."

"Yes."

"All that hard work and study you did back in Adelaide must have paid off."

"It did, and I learned so much more when I moved to Sydney."

"You must be doing well to survive there and in the current retail climate."

Ketty smiled. If only he knew how tenuous her hold on her business was. "It's not easy but we're managing."

"We?"

"I employ five staff."

He leaned closer, his green eyes not so vivid these days but still as mesmerising. Ketty found herself telling him about building her business. Not the earliest days, but from when she found her current premises and employed first Ning and then Tien and then

Judith, the renovations, more staff and even some of the foibles of her well-heeled clients, without revealing names of course. They'd laughed together and he'd mentioned he was retired now and suddenly it was time for dinner.

"Josie is keen for us to sit at your table again." His look was questioning. "Are you happy for me to be there?"

"If you are."

Leo stood. "Shall we go together?"

She glanced from his outstretched hand to his questioning look, reserved but with the hint of a smile.

"Of course." She accepted his hand to stand then fell into step beside him and their conversation continued to flow easily all the way to the dining room.

Celia was pleased to see she was the first to arrive for dinner. She felt more relaxed tonight. Something to do with the bottle of wine she and Maude had shared before dinner and also Celia was fairly sure Ed was booked in the other dining room meaning she didn't have to keep a watch for him here. She ordered another bottle of wine and hoped Leo might arrive soon so that she could get him to sit next to her.

She took a mouthful of wine and pondered her day. Celia had done her best to charm Leo and she thought her attempts had been working. Pity he hadn't wanted a drink once they got back to the ship. Celia had hoped Ketty would retire for a rest and Celia would have him to herself. She was desperate to cultivate the attention of a good-looking man and Bernard only had eyes for Josie last night. If he was no longer available Leo could be her plus one. Like Bernard he was several years older than her but a very good-looking man all the same, more distinguished than Bernard.

Her heart sank when she saw Ketty and Leo arrive together. Perhaps it was a coincidence and they'd met at the door. She took another gulp of wine and put on what she hoped was a captivating smile.

Christine arrived late to the dining room. She'd been sitting alone in the cabin for the last couple of hours assuming Frank would at least return so that they could go together to dinner but he hadn't. Now she was annoyed he wasn't at the table already, and the sight of her father with his arm draped across the back of Josie's chair, leaning in close to her, didn't help her mood. Christine stalked across the room.

She took a deep breath relieved that at least the headache and nausea were gone. "Hello everyone. Dad." She slipped into the seat beside him and kissed his cheek, totally ignoring Josie's smiled greeting.

"Where's Frank?" Bernard looked at his watch. "We should order."

"I have no idea." She picked up her menu. "If he doesn't have the manners to arrive on time we should go ahead."

"Jim's not here either." Ketty glanced around. "Perhaps we should wait a few more minutes."

"Yes, let's," Celia gushed. "Now, Leo, you must tell me more about the trip to New York you mentioned. It's somewhere I've always wanted to go."

Celia drained her glass and literally grabbed Leo's attention by placing her hand on his arm. Her eyes were bright and her cheeks flushed. Christine's stomach turned. What was with these oldies all falling over each other like lovesick teenagers while she and Frank, the only couple both young and married, were getting no action at all.

Rupert refilled Celia's glass and then the bottle was empty. Christine decided to stick to non-alcoholic drinks tonight and ordered a nojito. When it arrived her spirits lifted and she wished she had a flower in her hair and bare feet. The tall glass sported three different coloured citrus wedges and a sprig of mint. She took a sip and closed her eyes as the refreshing tang of the lime tingled over her tongue. A burst of laughter from Josie, Ketty and Phillip made her begrudgingly open her eyes. Her father was telling his soppy jokes again and he was even including the wait staff.

"Did everyone enjoy the island today?" she asked.

"Yes." Celia and Bernard both answered as one with great enthusiasm and Celia gave a strangled giggle and bumped against Leo who looked rather put out.

"I appreciated having a look at the country beyond the beach," Bernard said. "So interesting to see the people and the different landscape. But hell, driving flat out down the middle of the road was crazy!"

Christine swallowed her chagrin and took a sip of her drink. "I wondered where you'd got to, Dad. I looked up and down the beach for you when we finally got there."

"Here comes Frank," Celia said. "And Jim's with him."

Christine watched her husband approach then felt a wave of heat spread through her as he chose the seat beside Celia rather than the one next to her. He wobbled a bit as he tried to pull out his chair and Jim corrected him with a helping hand.

"Have you blokes been on the booze?" Bernard laughed.

"Sorry we're late," Jim said. "We did have a few drinks and then tried our luck at blackjack. Time got away."

Christine gave a soft snort. "Let's order."

"My fault entirely," Jim said.

"Did you win?" Ketty asked.

Frank had a silly grin on his face and pressed a finger to his lips. Jim shook his head.

"I'll have to come with you next time," Bernard said. "Show you how it's done. You'd join us, wouldn't you, Josie? Be my lady luck."

"Of course."

Bernard squeezed her hand.

Christine waited for Frank to suggest that perhaps she could be his good-luck charm but he leaned in to talk to Jim.

The waiters took the dinner orders. Conversation flowed but it didn't include Christine. Her father was more interested in Josie than he was in her. He'd been like it ever since her mother died, always chasing after women, putting his floozies before his own daughter. And Frank. She looked across the table to where her inebriated husband was now giving Celia some detailed explanation about the coral he'd seen today while he was diving. Christine felt a stab of envy. He hadn't bothered to tell her so animatedly about what he'd seen. Even Ketty was leaning a little closer to Leo who was speaking in such a low voice Christine couldn't hear him. To hell with them all. She downed her nojito, poured a wine, took a big swallow and sat back in a silent pool of misery.

Ketty was startled by a sudden chorus of happy birthday from behind Celia. Everyone stopped talking and turned to watch the waiters, who included Phillip and Rupert, gathered around the next table. A small sparkler crackled in a slice of cake placed in front of one of the other diners.

"Oh, it must be someone's birthday," Celia gushed.

"You don't say." Leo's mutter was directed at Ketty, his look tetchy. He'd been on the receiving end of Celia's ceaseless chatter all through dinner. Ketty understood his irritation but her heart went out to Celia, who'd worked her way through several glasses of wine. There was something amiss with her. Ketty was sure this wasn't her normal behaviour. The song finished to cheers and laughter from the people at the next table and the staff returned to their work.

"Beautiful singing." Celia clapped her hands as Rupert and Phillip cleared the last of the plates.

"Would anyone like the drink of the day?" Rupert asked. "It's a Raspberry Collins."

"Oh, that sounds interesting," Celia exclaimed.

"I'll join you," Frank said.

Christine glared at her husband. "I think you've had enough, Frank."

He flung himself back against his chair. "Is that so?"

Ketty could see the others shifting uncomfortably in their seats just as she was. It was never wise to argue with someone who'd had a few too many but she could see from the scowl on Christine's face she would not be deterred.

"You won't be in any shape to go out tomorrow," Christine continued.

"Ha!" Frank huffed. "You should know."

Christine rose to her feet and placed two hands on the table. "You'll thank me in the morning."

"If I do as I'm told, you mean."

Ketty was mortified that the Romanos were being so openly hostile in front of everyone. She could see an equally uncomfortable look on Jim's face at the other end of the table and she didn't dare look sideways at the others.

"What are you trying to say, Frank?" Christine's face had turned red.

"Keep your voice down, Christine," Bernard growled.

"I suppose you're on his side."

"There is no side."

There was silence around the table. Ketty noticed the waiters and a few other diners glancing in their direction.

"Perhaps we should all call it a night." She rose steadily to her feet.

"Now you've broken up the party." Frank scowled at his wife.

Christine turned a sad look on her father. "Perhaps I'll see you tomorrow, Dad. Goodnight everyone."

Among subdued farewells the others stood, everyone except Frank and Celia. He was sitting arms folded with a face like thunder and she was red cheeked, eyes darting from one person to the next.

"Josie and I thought we might go to the show," Bernard said. "Ketty, Leo, would you—"

"I'll come with you." Frank stood and swayed against his chair.

Bernard stepped behind Jim and patted his son-in-law on the shoulders. "Might be a good idea to call it a night, Frank."

"Probably good advice," Jim said. "I think I'll get an early night myself."

Frank glanced from Bernard to Jim then down at the floor. His shoulders sagged. "Yes...well...okay." He looked up again. "Thanks for your company, everyone. I'm sorry about earlier."

"Please don't worry, Frank," Ketty said. "We're all friends here."

He leaned on his chair and shook his head, his colourful shirt mocking his woeful expression.

"Things always look brighter after a good night's sleep," Ketty said.

He turned and made his way slowly across the dining room. Ketty hoped she was right.

"Now, what about the show?" Bernard drew Josie to his side and glanced around.

"Not for me," Jim said.

Ketty was startled by Leo's arm slipping around her waist.

"Count us in," he said.

She twisted to look at him. There was a possessiveness in the way he returned her gaze. Then Ketty caught the startled look on Celia's face. She was watching Leo intently, then abruptly leaped to her feet.

"Me either," she mumbled. "Suddenly I'm very tired. Good-night." She spun around, wobbled against the rail, regained her balance, took the step down carefully and walked away.

Ketty extracted herself from Leo's arm by moving to pick up her purse. She'd been looking forward to tonight's show, but now Leo had made her feel uncomfortable. She moved ahead of the others towards the door where Celia had already made her exit. Poor woman. She must have been as surprised as Ketty when Leo had pulled her in close.

Carlos appeared as she reached the maître d's station.

"Did you enjoy your meal, Miss Clift?"

"It was delicious, Carlos."

"And everything is in order?" He raised one eyebrow and glanced over her shoulder.

No doubt he'd seen the kerfuffle at the table even if he hadn't heard it.

"I think so." She leaned in closer. "Let me know when you're free next and we'll have a chat."

He nodded, then said goodnight to the others who had come up behind her.

Celia walked quickly up the marble staircase. She wanted to put as much distance between her and Leo as possible. What a fool she'd been. He and Ketty were obviously good friends and he was simply being polite, putting up with her attempts to enthral him with her scintillating conversation and her Celebrity Celia impersonation—

Damnation! She hadn't been watching where she was going and now Ed and Debbie were only a few steps above her, heading down. She turned swiftly and scurried back down the stairs, glancing over her shoulder as she went. A shudder of panic went through her, now she couldn't see them. Which way had they gone? She paused, searching the crowd, and caught her heel on the last step. Then she was flying, arms and legs flailing across the floor. It was as if time had slowed; she could see shoes, men's black leather, women's vibrant pink toenails peeping from glittering sandals, and she could hear gasps, and then a piercing shriek. It was her own, coming from deep inside her as her cheek collided sharply with the tiles.

Fifteen

For a few seconds Celia lay there. She was dazed, then amazed that nothing hurt, not yet at least. As the sound of her scream faded she heard the murmurs and worried voices around her. She twisted her head slightly to see Ed coming towards her, a look of distaste on his face. Debbie peered down, fingers to her lips suppressing a smile. Celia turned away hoping the floor would open and swallow her up.

"Stay there a moment." It was Ketty kneeling beside her. "Catch your breath then tell me if anything hurts." A gentle hand rested on her back.

"Move on everyone, thank you." The authority of the maître d's voice sounded somewhere behind Celia. She rolled to her side, her back to the crowd of feet and legs. She put a hand to her head and groaned.

"What's hurting?" Ketty asked.

"I'll call for the doctor." The maître d' again.

"No." Celia managed to sound firm. She tested her arms and then her legs. "I'm all right. Just a shock that's all, nothing broken."

With Ketty's help Celia shifted to a sitting position, and pulled her dress down from where it had scrunched around her hips. She glanced up, the heat of humiliation seeping over her as the crowd dispersed, some still muttering, others throwing backward glances; and there was Ed, his back ramrod straight, one arm around Debbie guiding her away. Celia dropped her head and groaned again.

"You probably should let the doc check you." This time it was Bernard.

Celia risked glancing up again. Now it was only the maître d', Ketty and her remaining table companions who stood around her, their faces full of concern.

"I just need to sit somewhere a moment."

"Of course, if you're sure." Carlos's strong arm and Ketty's gentle hand helped her to her feet.

"You go on," Ketty said to the others. "I'll stay with Celia."

"I'll be fine, Ketty, don't stay on my account." Her cheeks were burning, partly from embarrassment and the right one from its collision with the hard floor. Of all people to witness her spectacular idiocy it would be Ed and Debbie.

"I'm not leaving until I know you're truly all right," Ketty said.

"We'll head off to the show but let us know if you need anything." Bernard shepherded Josie and Leo away but Jim remained.

"You should put some ice on your cheek," he said gently.

Ketty leaned in closer. "Oh yes. You're going to have a shiner there."

"I hope you're okay." Jim's calm look was encouraging.

"I'll look after her." Ketty put her arm around Celia's waist.

Carlos despatched a waiter for an icepack then guided them back to a quiet corner of the dining room where he sat Celia down and produced a glass of water. "Are you sure you're not hurt, Mrs Braxton?"

"Only my pride." Celia looked up. His face, usually set in a firm smile, was softer and his look full of concern. Tears brimmed in her eyes. "Damn." She looked around, blinking frantically. "My bag."

"I have it." Ketty took the chair next to her and offered a tissue.

"Damn," Celia said again. "I can't bear to sit here and make a bigger fool of myself by crying."

"If you're up to it I can walk you back to your room." Ketty put a gentle hand on her shoulder. "You probably should have someone with you, just in case."

"Maude won't be there." Celia dabbed at her eyes and winced as her cheek throbbed.

"Would you like to come to my room then? We can sit for a while, take it easy, let you regain your composure."

A waiter arrived with a neatly wrapped icepack.

"Thank you." Ketty took it from him. "Let's settle you upstairs and get this on your cheek." She put a guiding arm around Celia and helped her to her feet.

"Let me know if you need anything more." Carlos saw them to the door.

Celia let herself be led away. It was strangely comforting to give herself over to Ketty's care. Her cheek still throbbed and she'd probably be a bit sore in the morning but she knew she was lucky she'd done no real damage. It was the spectacle she'd made in front of Ed that truly hurt.

⚓

Ketty ushered Celia into her room and was met by the disarray she'd left behind in her endeavour to find the right thing to wear. There were dresses and scarves on the bed, several necklaces on the desk and shoes around the floor. Peter had left her chocolate on the only clear space near one of the pillows.

"Sorry about the mess." She scooped a wrap and a jacket up from the padded armchair, settled Celia into it and handed her the icepack.

"This room is so much more spacious than mine." Celia looked around while Ketty returned the dresses to their hangers, flicked on the kettle for tea then began to fold the wraps.

"Oh, that looks gorgeous." Celia was admiring the black lace wrap Ketty had picked up.

"I always bring it with me and never end up wearing it but someone else usually does."

Celia spread it across her lap with her free hand. "What exquisite lace."

Ketty took it and wrapped it around Celia's shoulders, leaning in close as she did, holding the other woman's gaze. "It looks lovely on you."

"Even with my battered face?" Celia grimaced.

Ketty lay a hand over Celia's clutching the icepack. "Even with that." She smiled then turned away to set out cups in their saucers. "Tea or coffee?"

"Tea, please, weak black."

Celia lowered the icepack and brushed her cheek over the wrap. "It's so soft," she murmured. "This is kind of you, Ketty. I was a bit shaken up but I'm feeling much better already."

"It would have been a nasty shock." Ketty placed the cups of tea on the stool-come-coffee table and sat on the edge of the bed beside Celia's chair.

"I've kept you from the show…and…and Leo." Tears brimmed in Celia's eyes again.

Ketty reached for the tissue box and placed it beside the cups of tea. "Please don't worry, Celia. I'm not. I've seen plenty of shipboard shows and Leo will still be here tomorrow." He had given her a forlorn look before he'd left with Bernard and Josie but Ketty had been too concerned for Celia to worry about Leo's feelings.

Celia groaned and gripped her head in her hands. Ketty watched in silence.

When she finally looked up Ketty passed her the cup of tea. "Do you want to talk about it?"

Celia shook her head. Ketty didn't press her. The air conditioner hummed overhead, a background noise to the soft rattle of china and the gentle sipping of tea. After several minutes, Celia placed her cup and saucer back on the table and picked up the icepack, pressing it back to her cheek.

"Is it hurting?" Ketty asked.

"Throbbing a bit, that's all."

"You may get quite a bruise out of it."

"Nothing compared to what I feel inside."

Ketty studied Celia, who was staring at the curtains drawn across the glass door.

"I hope Leo didn't offend you, Celia."

Celia remained silent. She fiddled with the icepack, shifting it to another position, gripped the arm of the chair with her other hand then let it go again. Next, she stood and paced the tiny space between the chair and the balcony door, the lace wrap slipping from one shoulder.

"I've made such a fool of myself."

"It was an accident."

"Not just my tripping on the stairs." She stopped pacing and stared down at Ketty, eyes brimming with tears again. "Ohhh!" She slumped into the chair and put the icepack on the table. The cheek where it had been pressed glowed red. "I've got to tell someone or I think I'll go mad." She turned to Ketty, desperation on her face. "Please don't tell anyone."

"Have you committed a crime?" Ketty was sure Celia hadn't but just in case.

"Only the one of stupidity."

"Surely it's not that bad."

Celia took a tissue from the box. Dabbed gently at her eyes then crushed it between her fingers. She took a breath. "My ex-husband is aboard ship with his new wife."

That wasn't quite what Ketty had been expecting her to say. "That must have been a bit of a surprise."

"No." Celia ripped the corner off the tissue. "I knew they were going to be here." She ripped a bit more. "I'd always wanted to cruise and Ed wouldn't go, said it wasn't his kind of holiday. Next thing he's married for five minutes to the new woman and he takes her on a cruise. When I found out I was so angry I decided to book myself on the cruise as well."

Ketty watched as the poor tissue was shredded into tiny pieces.

"I devised a plan to make Ed jealous, to show him I could make a new life just as well as he could." Celia snorted and reached around to drop the bits of tissue into the bin. "You should see his child bride. She's gorgeous, almost young enough to be his daughter. I don't know how I thought I was ever going to make Ed even half care if I was alive let alone be jealous. Anyway, back home it seemed like a good plan. I asked Maude to come with me. I play bowls with her and she's so at ease with men and such a flirt, I thought I could find a good-looking man, learn how to be a flirt and then…" She flung her hands in the air and the wrap slithered down her back. "There I would be looking glamorous on the arm of a handsome man enjoying myself beyond measure, rubbing Ed's nose in what he'd given up."

Ketty kept a serene look on her face but Celia's tale certainly explained a lot about her behaviour. First, she'd tried to attract Bernard and then Leo. The poor woman must have been having a terrible holiday.

"So when you tripped down the stairs…"

"I nearly ran into Ed and Debbie." Celia plucked another tissue from the box and went to work on it with her fingers. "The only impression I gave Ed was of his tipsy ex-wife spreadeagled across the floor."

"Perhaps he didn't notice."

Celia's mouth fell open. She pressed her fingers to her lips but couldn't stop the laughter erupting. Ketty laughed too.

Celia paused to catch her breath. "There's no avoiding it. Ed could be vague but even he couldn't have missed my slide across the floor with my dress around my waist and my underwear on show for all to see."

"He might have seen someone fall but did he know it was you? We all surrounded you very quickly and Carlos moved people on."

"Oh thank you, Ketty." Celia gripped her forehead with one hand. "You're so kind to try to make me feel better but he saw me. I've been such a fool."

"You're not the first and you won't be the last."

"I can't imagine you doing something so stupid."

"I've been a fool over a man."

"I don't believe it. You seem so self-assured, as if nothing would faze you."

Ketty smiled inwardly at that. A month ago she would have described herself as such but with the worry of her business, and now meeting Leo again after all these years, her confidence was in a perpetual state of flux. "I'll admit it was a long time ago but when I look back I still can't accept how stupid I was."

Celia shook her head as if she still didn't believe Ketty.

"He was a married man."

Celia gasped, a frown crossed her face.

"Trust me, I had no idea he was married. I put our erratic meetings down to our busy lifestyle. We were both working and studying nights. How naive do you think I was? I was so in love and then...well, then I found out and I ended it immediately." Ketty shook her head. She'd only meant to empathise with Celia. "Anyway, I'm glad you've told me what you were doing."

"You are?"

"Yes, you see I thought your behaviour a little odd. You acted like a person who wasn't being themselves."

"I did?"

"Shall I make us another cup of tea?"

"Please."

Ketty truly was relieved. Beneath the pretence there was a different Celia and Ketty suspected it was that Celia she'd like to get to know. She made them a fresh cup each and settled back on the bed.

"I hope you don't mind me asking this, Celia, but do you still love your husband?"

"Good heavens, no. My love for him was destroyed when he left me for Debbie."

Ketty understood the response. "But you still feel anger, resentment?"

Celia frowned. "I did once I got over the shock of his leaving me but it's been three years and I thought I'd left the worst of it behind."

"Grief affects everyone differently."

"It was when I heard from our sons that he was going on a cruise I…well, the bitterness returned and I couldn't let it go."

"You mentioned you'd made a fresh start in the country."

Celia sighed. "Yes. I really do like it there and I've made new friends, not all of them like Maude but she's a good stick, and I've got plenty to do. After the divorce I realised there was little to keep me in Adelaide. Our friends were mostly Ed's friends and my old girlfriends are flung around the state. My eldest son had just won his first job in Western Australia and the other had headed overseas. Now at least when they come to stay I feel I have more time for them and them for me. Ed always dominated the conversation, the house, our lives in general. Now I'm rediscovering my boys and the men they've become. I like that. In fact, life is more interesting than it was. Being married to Ed I spent time alone but I had little time for myself, if that makes sense."

Celia's face had lit up when she spoke of her sons. Ketty's stomach twisted but this wasn't about her. She reached out and gripped Celia's hand. "I think you must ask yourself why you care what your ex-husband thinks?"

"I suppose I wanted to show him that I'd moved on."

"Do you need a man on your arm to prove that?"

Celia gave a shrug that turned into a shiver.

Ketty leaned forward and tucked the lace wrap back around her shoulders. She kept her gaze firmly locked on Celia and went on, her voice slow and even. "It sounds to me as if you've settled in to your new life, you've made friends, you're busy, content. You've always wanted to cruise and now here you are doing it.

Forget about Ed." Ketty squeezed the warm hand clasped in hers. "Make the most of it, Celia."

Celia's eyes widened and she shook her head slowly. "I truly have been a fool."

"Put it behind you. Don't waste what's left of this cruise. Enjoy yourself."

Celia sagged in the chair. "I feel exhausted."

"No wonder. You probably haven't relaxed since you came aboard. Why don't you lie on my bed for a while? You shouldn't be alone, just in case, and I've got a bit more tidying up to do."

"I don't want to impose."

"Nonsense. I don't mind."

Ketty helped Celia to get comfortable and put the icepack in the freezer for later.

"I'm going to change out of this dress." Ketty loved it, but after the large dinner she'd eaten it was feeling very tight around her middle.

Celia looked at her watch. "Maude will probably be back to our room soon. I'll head off in a while."

"No rush." Ketty took her baggy pants and loose top and went to the bathroom. By the time she'd changed, washed her face and let herself back out again, Celia was asleep. She crossed the room and stared at the sleeping woman a moment. Her cheek was red and her eye make-up smudged but she looked peaceful, the wrap clutched in her fingers. Ketty took out one of her large pashminas and draped it over Celia. It was a lovely aqua blue and the colour looked so much better against the younger woman's skin than the drab dress she was wearing.

Ketty turned out all but one of the lamps. Then she moved quietly around the room finishing the tidying she'd started when they'd arrived. Once she was satisfied all was where it should be she took her book and sat in the chair to read. After a few minutes she tossed the book aside. She wasn't ready for sleep herself but she found it hard to concentrate.

Everything she'd talked about with Celia had dredged up her own feelings for Leo. She'd been comfortable chatting over drinks but at dinner she'd been reminded there was another side to him. She suspected he'd been annoyed at Celia's attempts to claim his attention but was too polite to ignore her. It was at the end of the meal when she'd sensed both his arm and his manner were claiming her that had made her bristle. It had been a while since she'd been in a man's arms. Perhaps she was too set in her ways.

There was a tap at the door. Ketty hoped it wasn't going to be Leo. She wasn't sure what to make of her feelings for him tonight. She put her eye to the peephole and opened the door with relief. Carlos, wearing casual clothes now and his old cap, stepped inside. She put a finger to her lips and he glanced over towards the bed.

"Is she all right?" He kept his voice low.

"She'll have a bruise on that cheek but otherwise she seems okay. I think she's very tired and I don't have the heart to wake her."

"Shall I find you an empty room?"

"Oh no. That bed's huge. We'll be fine but her friend, Maude, might worry if she doesn't come back. Could you possibly have a message delivered to her cabin? I don't know the number."

"Of course." Carlos nodded. "I'll take care of it." He remained just inside the door studying her. "This group of people is keeping you busy."

"I've so much to tell you but I don't think I could face another drink tonight. I could make you tea or coffee though, and we could sit out on the balcony."

"No, no. You look tired yourself. I'll go and organise a message to Celia's cabin. We'll catch up another night."

Ketty smiled. She could always rely on him for help. She wanted to hug him but that would not be appropriate. "Thank you, Carlos."

"Goodnight." He let himself out, softly closing the door.

Ketty made sure Celia was covered by the pashmina, turned out the lamp and slid under the sheet on the other side of the bed. Celia's confession replayed in her mind for only a short time before she too fell asleep.

Sixteen

Day Five – Alongside, Port Vila, Vanuatu

Christine was awake early. Frank's back was to her. She lay still listening to the gentle sound of his regular breathing. Last night when he'd eventually returned to the cabin she'd lain rigid in the bed. She'd hoped he would want to talk, to make up, beg her forgiveness, and they'd make love and everything would be right again. Instead he'd removed his clothes, fallen into bed and begun snoring almost immediately. Another lost opportunity. She'd simmered with anger for a while and then had given him a shove. He'd rolled over and she'd managed to go to sleep.

This morning she would have the upper hand. He had made a fool of himself last night and he'd realise that in the light of day. She would forgive him, of course, perhaps they'd finally have sex. But first she needed the bathroom. She eased herself from the bed and let herself into the en suite. The fluoro above the handbasin threw a harsh light over her face. She cringed at her own reflection. Her hair was lank, her eyes puffy and her skin sallow. No wonder her husband wasn't interested in her. She leaned against the bench and took a deep breath. Somehow she had to make things right between them. She turned on the shower and stripped off, twisted away from her reflection in the mirror and stepped under the steaming jet of water.

By the time she opened the bathroom door again Christine was feeling much more positive. The shower had been restorative. She'd used some of the face scrub she'd been given a few Christmases ago and the new lavender body wash she'd brought with her. When she'd stepped out of the water she'd spent time blow-drying her hair and applying some light make-up. She felt ready to fall into Frank's arms; they'd make love and then they'd be ready for breakfast and plan their day.

She stared around the cabin in dismay. Frank was gone. The clothes he'd dropped on the floor last night were still where he'd left them. She crossed to the balcony but the curtains were drawn. She tugged them open; the space was empty barring the furniture. Frank hadn't bothered to wait for her.

A strange prickly sensation deepened in her chest. It was hard to put a finger on how she felt. Sad, on edge, as if things were spinning out of control. It was such an unusual sensation for her. She'd always felt in charge of everything in her life, from her marriage and children, to her work. She took a deep breath then swallowed to disperse the uncertainty. If things weren't going the way she wanted she needed a new plan, that was all, and making up with her husband was a start. If Frank had already gone to breakfast she would join him.

She strode across the room to the bench where she'd left her jewellery. Frank's watch had been dropped on top of her things, scattering them. She retrieved one gold hoop earring from the floor and put both in her ears then looked for the new pendant her father had bought her. She hadn't wanted to wear it to the beach yesterday and hadn't thought to put it on last night. It was nowhere among the other jewellery scattered on the bench. She rummaged in the bag she kept chains and earrings in but it wasn't there either.

Swearing under her breath, she began to search the room, trying to remember where she'd put it when she'd taken it off two nights ago but her memory of that night was foggy. Frank's shoes and clothes were scattered across the floor. She picked up his shirt and pressed it to her nose, drawing in the scent of him. She had a small pang of guilt at her anger over his excessive alcohol intake when she'd done the same herself only the night before. She plonked down on the unmade bed. At least she hadn't made a scene like he had.

Ketty stepped out of the bathroom to find the bed empty. Through the open curtain she could see Celia on the balcony, leaning on the rail, taking in the view, her crumpled beige dress partly covered by Ketty's blue pashmina, the black lace neatly folded on the chair. The ship had been approaching the wharf at Port Vila when Ketty had peeped around the curtain before taking her shower.

Now she straightened the bed covers. It had been strange to wake up and find someone else in her bed. She smiled. Celia wouldn't be her choice of partner. Immediately Ketty thought of Leo and for a moment she wondered what she would do if meeting him again lead to something intimate. She felt anxious at the thought and yet there was an unbidden surge of anticipation. Her mind and her body were pulling in opposite directions.

Celia turned and saw her through the glass, waved and moved to the door.

"Stay out there if you like," Ketty said.

"I should go. Maude will wonder where I am."

"Carlos was going to get a message to her. He called in last night to see how you were."

"The maître d'? That was kind of him." Celia shook her head. "He must think I'm a klutz."

"I've known Carlos for years and, believe me, in his work he's seen many things. He takes it all in his stride."

"The others from our table saw it all." Celia closed her eyes and groaned.

"No more of that. It was an accident." Ketty switched on the kettle. "I'll make us some tea. Did you sleep well?"

"Like a baby as they say, although mine never slept that deeply."

Ketty set out the cups she'd rinsed the night before. "How's your face?"

"A bit tender. I looked in the mirror while you were in the shower. There's a shadow of a bruise."

"You should ice it again, now. I think they say to keep icing for twenty-four hours." Ketty took out the pack and handed it to Celia. "Sit down a moment. Enjoy the view."

Celia turned back and beyond her Ketty could see the lush green of a small island nestled in the sheltered turquoise blue water of the harbour. A ripple of expectation wiggled over her. She had previously enjoyed the relaxed lifestyle of Vanuatu and the welcome smiles of the people, especially the women she visited at the craft centres, but now her anticipation had a sharper edge to it. There had been no chance to organise anything with Leo and she wondered what today would bring.

There was a sharp knock on the door. The peephole revealed Josie on the other side.

"Ketty, I'm calling to see if you know how Celia is." Josie was in as soon as Ketty opened the door. "Oh, you're here. No adverse effects from last night?" She made her way to Celia who was standing in the balcony doorway. "That bruise will be a beauty."

Celia's hand went to her cheek.

"What a gorgeous wrap. The colour suits you so well."

"I love what you're wearing." Celia said. "I never feel brave enough to wear such vibrant colours."

"You should. That blue brings out the colour of your eyes."

Ketty followed her visitor across the cabin. "You're both wearing colours that favour your natural complexions." Ketty studied the bright watermelon pink of Josie's sleeveless blouse, tucked into a skirt that flowed in soft folds to her knees. The skirt fabric was deep green and patterned with bright pink and orange hibiscus flowers. "I like your skirt, Josie."

"I found it in a little boutique near home. Thought it would be good for cruising. You could so easily make this kind of thing, Ketty, and sell it online. Standard sizing, no fittings needed." Josie tugged at the fabric then turned to Celia. "Has Ketty given you a makeover yet? She's the queen of style. I would never wear a shirt tucked in at the waist until she convinced me it looked all right."

Ketty was still pondering Josie's mention of selling online when she realised Celia was studying her with a questioning look.

"Josie had a great body under the big shirts and shapeless dresses she wore." Ketty waved her hands through the air to give the impression of a curvaceous figure. "I encouraged her to make more of her assets."

"Ketty's polite way of saying I'm 'well rounded'." Josie laughed.

"I simply made a few suggestions when we cruised together last, that's all." She gave a small shake of her head. "I was making tea. Would you like a cup?"

Josie glanced at her watch. "I'm meeting Bernie and Leo for breakfast. We're going to plan our Port Vila excursions. That's the other reason for my visit, to see if you'd like to join us. You too, Celia. Ketty, we're keen to hear from you the best places to visit." She stepped out onto the balcony beside Celia. "I've certainly got time for tea though. Isn't it a glorious day?"

Celia and Josie chatted about Port Vila while Ketty made the tea, reflecting on Josie's remarks about making skirts like hers. Earlier, while she'd showered, Ketty's thoughts had inevitably turned to home and business and the women who depended on her. She'd decided that instead of trying to keep the worry of it at bay she should embrace it. Without actually being in the thick of the day to day, she could give her mind free rein to ask the 'what if' questions. Change was needed. The kind her accountant was suggesting was unpalatable but Josie's idea might have some merit. At least the ready-made skirts part. Could it be possible to sell them online? She'd resisted it for so long, clinging to her mantra of making sure each client got the personal treatment. Perhaps there was room for both in her business and yet selling online still felt so foreign to her.

She handed out the cups and dragged the stool outside, eager now to go ashore. Port Vila was the perfect place to find fabric that might suit the ideas turning over in her head. And once she'd finished her jobs this morning she looked forward to meeting the others for lunch and seeing what panned out from there.

Celia let herself back into her little cabin, which seemed even smaller after Ketty's room. Maude's usual morning tune sounded beyond the bathroom door. Celia sat on the end of her bed to take off her shoes. She'd been surprised to find herself still in Ketty's room when she woke this morning and then after Josie's arrival they'd settled on the balcony, enjoyed a cup of tea and talked about their sons. Josie had three, two of whom were a similar age to Celia's two, and Ketty had talked about her nephew who she said she claimed as her surrogate son. It had been such a peaceful start to the day, chatting as they contemplated the aquamarine water. The company and the surrounding tropical paradise had been so relaxing.

Celia looked around the little cabin she shared with Maude. You had no idea of the passing scenery from in here.

The bathroom door opened and Maude stepped out, a towel barely covering her naked body.

"You're back." Her eyebrows wiggled up and down and then she leaned closer. "What happened to your face? I hope your lover boy isn't responsible for that."

Celia put a hand to her cheek. "There's no man, Maude. I had a bit of a fall last night and banged my face."

Maude gave her a sceptical look. "I didn't know what to think when I found a note in the door on ship's letterhead saying you were in good hands but wouldn't be back to your stateroom for the night."

"Ketty took me back to her room after I fell." Celia waved the icepack she'd brought back with her. "I needed to ice my cheek. We had a cuppa and a chat and then I was suddenly very tired. I slept in her room." Celia put the pack in the freezer of the little fridge and picked up her brush from the bench.

Maude sat on the edge of her bed watching Celia brush her hair. "You missed a great dance party again last night. Are you sure you haven't got a man hidden away somewhere?"

"Definitely no man hiding. I tripped on the bottom step straight after dinner and Ketty kindly looked after me." Celia put down the brush and leaned in to take another look at her bruised cheek.

"What about your disappearing act yesterday from the beach? You went off with Ketty then. You're not turning, are you?"

Celia glanced at Maude in the mirror. "Turning?"

"You know, batting for the other side like Beryl and Dot at bowls. Not that I care one way or the other but Nigel will be disappointed."

Celia shook her head and opened the cupboard to find her robe. "I am not batting for anyone, male or female. Ketty has been very kind to me, as a friend. Now I'm going to have a shower before I go down for breakfast."

"You'd best be quick. We don't have long before we go."

Celia paused at the bathroom door. "Go where?"

"Celia, I do wonder if you take in anything I say. We discussed it over our pre-dinner wine last night, remember? The six of us are sharing a water taxi into town."

"Us?"

"Perhaps you hit your head last night as well. Pete and the rest of his group, remember? Except Anne, of course."

Celia swallowed her sigh. "Yes, I remember." She turned to look at Maude, face to face. "Don't you think it's a bit odd that Pete comes with us instead of staying with his wife?"

"Not at all." Maude stood and began rummaging for her clothes. "Pete and Anne have got one of the cruise ship tours of the island booked for a few days' time. She hopes to be a bit more mobile by then and the travel will all be by bus so she can stay put if she needs." Maude sniffed and lifted her chin. "Anne wants Pete to enjoy himself. The way you keep disappearing poor Nigel is glad Pete's part of the group. And Bob and Freda, of course."

"About Nigel—"

"The poor guy is desperate to get to know you a bit better. And he's quite a catch."

"Why don't you get to know him better?"

"I told you he's a bit quiet for my taste and anyway, it's you he's smitten with."

Celia grimaced. "I wish he wasn't."

"Don't you like him?"

"No…well, yes but—"

"Oh, for goodness sake, Celia. Just chill. Now hurry and have your shower and make sure you bring everything you need when you come down for breakfast. We're leaving straight after."

Celia shut herself in the bathroom and began to undress. She'd left Ketty's room this morning feeling as if a huge weight had lifted from her shoulders. She hoped she wouldn't run into Ed now. She wasn't so sure he hadn't recognised her last night as Ketty had suggested. Celia had convinced herself she didn't care anymore but she was feeling fragile and not in the right frame of mind to come across Ed face to face.

Now she felt uneasy. In her relief at sharing her troubles with Ketty she'd forgotten all about today's proposed outing. It was arranged so she would go, but she was feeling quite determined she wouldn't let Maude rope her into any future plans she wasn't comfortable with. Celia peered at herself in the mirror. Perhaps Ketty was right, she could be her own person and stand on her own two feet. She'd done it when she'd left Adelaide after the divorce without realising it.

"What are you doing?"

Christine sat back on her heels in surprise at Frank's voice behind her. She hadn't heard the cabin door open. "I'm looking for the pendant Dad gave me. It's missing." She took in his tousled hair and crumpled t-shirt. He looked like he'd just got out of bed. "Surely you didn't go down to breakfast like that?"

"I didn't go to breakfast. I needed the toilet urgently and you were in the bathroom." Frank picked up his watch and began to rummage in the tumble of jewellery on the bench. "It must be here somewhere."

"What?" Christine staggered up from the floor where she'd been searching under the bed.

"The pendant."

"It's not there, not anywhere. I think it's been stolen."

Frank frowned at her. "Who would steal it?"

"That maid is often hanging out in the corridor when I pop back to the room. She can come and go from here whenever she likes."

"Maria?" He shook his head. "She's lovely. Very helpful."

"There's a shifty look about her."

Once more Frank shook his head.

"Don't look at me like that, Frank. The necklace is missing and she's the one with opportunity."

"It could be caught up in something. Maria was out in the corridor when I came back. We should ask her to keep an eye out when she's cleaning. She might find it." He pulled the sheet back from the bed.

"I've looked there." Christine threw up her hands. "I've looked everywhere."

"Don't worry about it. I'm sure it will turn up."

"It's a special gift and worth a lot of money. How can I not worry about it?"

"Steady up, Chrissie. It's got to be here somewhere. I'll ask Maria if she's seen it and to keep an eye out."

"All right but if she knows nothing I'm going to report it."

He reached for her hand. "I'm sorry about last night."

His look was contrite. She met him halfway with a small smile.

"I'd had too much to drink and behaved badly." He hugged her against him. "I think we both need to go easy on the drinks, hey?"

Christine drew in a deep breath and recoiled at his stale man smell. He had overdone it far more than her but she wasn't going to spoil his apology with a contradiction. "Have your shower, Frank, and we'll get some breakfast. I'm looking forward to checking out Port Vila." She eased out of his arms and took in his bleary eyes and stubble-covered chin. "I'll go down now and have a look for Dad while I wait for you. Meet you in twenty minutes?"

He nodded.

She gave the bench one last inspection, slipped on her lanyard and let herself out into the corridor. There was a trolley loaded with sheets and towels a bit further down but no sign of Maria. Christine's eyes narrowed. She didn't trust the smiling maid one bit.

"Are you expecting someone?" Josie's bright eyes locked on Bernard. They were in the ship's coffee lounge enjoying a cup before they set off for their day in Port Vila.

He shook his head.

"You keep looking over your shoulder as if you're about to be arrested." She took a sip of her coffee and looked at him over her cup. "I assume you're not."

"Going to be arrested?"

She gave a wry smile.

"My slate is clean." He sighed. "Except where Christine is concerned."

"Really, Bernie. I don't mind if she and Frank join us. Leo's coming, why not them?"

"I want to enjoy myself. It's hard to relax when Christine's around. You don't know her very well."

"But I know you." She put her hand over his, resting on the table. "You're a real man, not someone easily cowed by your daughter of all people."

He lifted her hand and pressed it to his lips. "Are you calling me a wimp?"

She laughed and slid her hand from his, resting her back against the chair. "I haven't decided yet."

Bernard let out a soft growl. "My room or yours?"

She threw her head back this time and her laugh was throaty. "Slow down, cowboy."

"Are you ready to go?" he asked.

"Shouldn't you check what Christine's doing?"

"Better she and Frank have the day together. They've got a few issues to sort out that don't involve me."

"I'm happy if you are. And here comes Leo."

Bernard felt a niggle of irritation as he took in Leo's sour face. "It's a shame Ketty's not coming with us."

"She has some jobs to do in town first."

Leo came to a stop beside them. "I still don't understand why someone who runs a couture dress shop in Sydney would bother with fabric from here."

"Don't be such a snob, Leo," Josie chided. "Ketty said there are all kinds of gems to be found if you know where to look."

"Are you sure her business is as good as she says?"

"I'm sure she wouldn't have given herself any praise but I've been there and she has an outstanding business in the midst of similar establishments. There's nothing fancy about her place but her work is exceptional."

Bernard watched Leo's expression change from cynical to calculating and gave an imperceptible shrug of his shoulders. Bernard could think of no reason to be interested in a women's dress shop but each to their own.

"Ketty will catch us later." Josie stood. "Let's go ashore."

She walked beside her brother and Bernard followed behind. If only Ketty would have agreed to come with them. Leo on his own would put a dampener on the day.

Seventeen

Jim stepped through the barrier that had been constructed at the land end of the wharf and straight into a chaotic barrage of men offering taxi deals. He'd been musing over the photo he'd just had taken, squeezed between a welcoming chief and his wife in traditional costume, and now he stood surrounded by men calling and waving at him. The humid air was full of the smell of lush vegetation mingled with the sweat of the closely pressed bodies. From behind him the ship's sirens blared.

He stepped sideways then twisted round as a firm hand pressed against his back.

"Keep walking, Jim."

It was Ketty. She slipped her arm through his and propelled him forward.

"Don't make eye contact," she murmured. "Keep walking."

A man stepped in front of them, waving a laminated sheet of colourful scenes.

"No, thank you," Ketty said brightly and side-stepped him, dragging Jim with her.

They were soon past the haggle of taxi drivers and among the stalls loaded with souvenirs set up either side of the road. Ketty let go of his arm.

She chuckled. "He who hesitates often ends up in a taxi he doesn't want." She lifted the brim of her big hat and peered closer. "Oh, unless you did want a taxi. How silly of me."

"No, it's all right, thank you, Ketty." Jim squared his shoulders, embarrassed that he'd been rescued. "I'd been planning on a walk up the hill to look around. I was surprised by the crush, that's all."

"It's quite different to catching a taxi at home." She watched him closely. "It can be overwhelming when you're not used to it. Anyway, I'll leave you to get on." Ketty smiled. "I'm taking a water taxi across to the town."

Jim glanced around. He couldn't see the water from where they stood. They were hemmed in by street stalls where brightly coloured sarongs and t-shirts depicting scenes of Vanuatu swung in the breeze. "Well…enjoy your day."

Ketty had partly turned away but she stopped and looked back at him. "You're welcome to share it with me if you like. I have some jobs to do in town then I plan to have a swim, and then meet some of the others from our table for lunch at a little bar on the beach." Her lips only lifted in a brief smile but there was a warmth about the gesture that somehow reminded him of Jane.

They stepped to the side as a horn tooted and a car loaded with tourists edged along the narrow road.

"Maybe I will, if you don't mind."

"Not at all." She waved her hand in the air like a magician. "Follow me."

Ketty stepped into a stall and wove around the tables and racks to the back. Jim followed her out through the canvas flap and found himself standing on a stone ledge above the bay.

"Taxi?" she called to the man who had several boats lined up along the rock wall below them.

He beckoned them down, then reached up and took Ketty's hand as she went ahead of Jim down the rocks that had been fashioned as crude steps to the water's edge. Ketty negotiated the price, gave the driver the destination then let him help her into the boat. Jim followed, feeling totally useless, and sat in the middle seat facing Ketty who was perched at the front. They motored slowly forward. She took off her hat and draped her scarf skilfully around her head and shoulders. She reminded him of an actress but he couldn't think who. Jane was always better at the film trivia than he was.

Once they were away from the wharf the little boat picked up speed and his own hat threatened to blow from his head. He pushed it down firmly and held it with one hand. The fresh salt air was refreshing and the breeze cool on his skin.

"What kind of jobs are you doing, if I'm not being too nosey?" He had to raise his voice over the burble of the motor.

"Not at all. I like to check out the fabrics while I'm here. There's often something a bit different. I don't collect souvenirs but I like to spend some money in the town and the colours and prints are quite diverse."

"Jane liked to sew and passed the talent on to our daughter."

"You might see something you could take back for her." Ketty pointed to some battered yachts on a bush-covered stretch of island. "They had a devastating cyclone here a few years back. The islands still haven't fully recovered from the damage. I like to think if everyone on the cruise ship spends some money here it helps the local economy."

Jim nodded. Ketty's kindness extended beyond her fellow passengers. He sat back and sucked in the salty air as the boat sped across the harbour. Scooting along so close to the water was as near to pleasure as he'd felt in a long time. He stared across to the island they were passing where the bush had been cleared. A thatch-covered jetty extending into the water had a sign on it naming a resort. The vegetation was thick and deep green with the odd small grey roof hinting at bungalows below. Along the water's edge were thatched huts built out across the white beach sitting over the ocean just like a travel brochure. If you wanted to lose yourself and forget, this would be the place to do it. He drew in another deep breath. If only he could.

Nigel's sweaty body pressed against Celia's in the back of the mini cab. She tried to ease away but she was jammed against the side of the vehicle on the other side. The only air conditioning was the wind coming through the wide-open windows and she welcomed the rush of air on her face and through her hair.

The driver had promised to show them sea turtles and that's where they were headed but it felt as if they'd been travelling for ages. They'd left Port Vila behind and had driven through lush green countryside that gave way from time to time to more open vegetation where cattle roamed in knee-high grass, then the bush would crowd in on them again. Celia caught glimpses of life beyond Port Vila; shanty-style houses dwarfed by coconut palms with more cattle grazing among them, groups of laughing barefooted children, and women washing clothes on the edge of a river. Everywhere the colours were vibrant, so different to the dry yellow summer she'd left behind in South Australia. If it wasn't for Nigel pressing closer trying to see past her, making foolish comments about some of the things he saw, she would actually be enjoying the ride. She cringed when he pointed to the huts they passed and repeated several times he didn't know why people lived like that. The driver's English was basic and she hoped he couldn't understand Nigel's ignorant responses to what he was seeing.

The vehicle slowed and turned off the bitumen road where it bounced along over a dirt track.

"Oh look," Maude exclaimed from the middle seat of the van where she was equally as close to Pete as Celia was to Nigel.

They all craned forward to catch glimpses of brilliant blue and stark white through the bush. Their driver pulled up beside a gate and a sign with a welcoming message and sketches of sea turtles.

The driver explained they needed to pay to enter and Celia was embarrassed as Nigel first complained that they were being ripped off and then insisted on paying for her. He put a guiding arm around her as they followed a sandy path towards the water's edge. She walked steadily ahead to escape him and arrived at the water first. There were already people swimming in a protected enclosure and beyond them, the waves of the Pacific Ocean broke and pounded the shore in a constant roar. There was the odd call or squeal of delight and Celia realised the swimmers were sharing the enclosure with turtles.

"Would you look at that," Maude exclaimed. "There really are turtles here."

"Let's get swimming," Pete said.

They found a place in the shade of a thatched shelter to leave their bags. The others were in a rush to reach the water but Celia hung back. Unfortunately, so did Nigel.

"Are you going in, love?" he asked.

She gritted her teeth. When he used that word it grated on her very soul. "I'll see."

They walked back to the water's edge. Maude and Pete were more intent on splashing each other. Freda and Bob were already under with goggles and snorkel. Celia put her toes in the water and nearby a small child and her dad fed seagrass to a turtle. She didn't have to go in to see the turtles – she had a good view of them from where she stood.

"I'll stay right beside you if you're nervous." Nigel tried to put his arm around her again but she bent down pretending to take a closer look at a passing turtle.

"I'm fine here, thanks." She continued to study the turtle as it slowly drifted away. She knew Nigel would be looking at her with his imploring gaze. Guilt stabbed inside her but she really couldn't rustle up the slightest bit of reciprocating fondness. "You go in." She turned his way. "Tell me what it's like."

"Are you sure?"

He placed a hand on her arm. She edged away.

"Quite," she said firmly. He shot her a hangdog look then donned his goggles and snorkel and stepped carefully into the water.

"It's lovely in," he called back to her.

She smiled and waved, watching as he adjusted his snorkel and ducked his head under, then she wandered on a bit further. The sun was very hot and she was glad of her hat and the sarong she'd draped over her shoulders. A large turtle surfaced between Bob and Freda, who was busy snapping pictures with her underwater camera. Celia knew she should go in but she had the awful feeling Nigel would use it as an excuse to get close. The thought of it made her squirm. He wouldn't leave her alone for a minute.

She walked the edge of the enclosure, cooling her feet in the water then went back up to the shade and sat down. Last night she'd made a fool of herself but talking with Ketty had made her feel so much better. She would like to have gone to breakfast with Ketty and Josie but she no more wanted to be the odd one out there than here with the constant tension of avoiding Nigel and watching Maude play up to a married man.

Celia stood up, walked out into the heat of the brilliant sun again and made her way further along the sandy beach. What was she doing? Ketty had helped her to see that she didn't need to pretend she was with a man to make Ed jealous and here she was dodging the attentions of another man. It was not how she wanted to spend the rest of this holiday. It was ridiculous behaviour. She wasn't a silly schoolgirl who didn't know her own mind. She had to tell Nigel – politely – that he wasn't for her and she also had to tell Maude that she didn't want to be paired up with him anymore.

Celia turned and retraced her steps. Nigel waved at her from the water. She gave a small finger flutter in return. She'd do it once they got back to the ship. It was such a relief to have made the decision and now that she was no longer bothered about proving something to Ed she felt so much better, stronger even, as if she truly was moving on. Ketty, who she'd thought to be rather a busybody at first, had proved to be such a help. Celia was surprised to think she was thankful to the older woman for her nosiness.

Ketty strolled beside Jim along the stretch of beach bordered by clear blue water. The sun was hot and there were few people on the brilliant white sand but several children played on a giant blow-up ball anchored just offshore. Conversation had been punctuated by their squeals and laughter as Ketty and Jim had walked the length of the beach and back towards the little beach bar, where they would meet Leo, Bernard and Josie.

Ketty was pleased Jim had stayed with her all morning. She'd taken him to the duty-free shops where he'd bought some jewellery and some alcohol, then he'd come with her a bit further out of the town to the strip of shops that sold bolts of colourful material. She'd enjoyed chatting with the women, some of whom had enough English for them all to understand each other. Ketty had bought several pieces of fabric that she planned to take home.

Judith would raise her eyebrows at them but Ketty had an idea, triggered by Josie's vibrant skirt, that the bright designs would suit a couple of sketches Lacey had shown her recently. The young woman had tentatively suggested a different style of ready-to-wear range. Ketty had put the thought aside – it just wasn't Ketty Clift Couture. But desperate times called for desperate measures and she realised now her young assistant had been cleverly urging her to experiment with the best of intentions. And perhaps she was right. Ketty owed it to her team to try something different and she was sure Lacey's sketches would be brought to life by the talents of Tien, Ning and Birgit.

Many of Ketty's clients travelled, quite a few on cruise ships like her. She had a shop full of ready-made, some of which had been there for years. Perhaps it was time for a clean out and she could try the addition of a unique line of holiday wear. It was that uniqueness that would retain the *special* for her clients. She would provide fabrics and styles only available at Ketty Clift Couture. It gave her a little glimmer of hope. At least it was a positive thought.

They'd drawn level with the umbrellas and chairs in front of the bar. Jim stopped and turned to her.

"Thanks for including me in your morning, Ketty. Being spontaneous – doing things like this – is not one of my strong points but neither would I have described myself as reticent or even fearful…until Jane died."

Ketty studied him a moment. When she spoke, her voice was low and calm. "Losing someone dear certainly knocks your confidence. Especially if you've been together for a long time like you and your wife."

"I wish we'd had longer." He sucked in a breath and shook his head. "But you said you'd lost someone too."

"Our circumstances are quite different. I was much younger. But there have been close friends since then, and my parents of course." She put a gentle hand on his arm. "We all deal with grief differently, Jim."

"This holiday has pushed the edges of my boundaries. I've been hiding myself away from family and friends at home. I hardly leave the house except to work, shop and attend the odd social function, though mind you the invitations have dwindled away. My daughter is the only person I see regularly, and she lives on the other side of Adelaide. I wake up every day expecting to feel better but I don't. Today I've enjoyed myself and…" He closed his eyes and put a hand to his chest.

"Jim, are you all right?" Ketty shifted her hand to his shoulder. The colour had drained from his face. "Come and sit down." She led him to a chair in the shade of an umbrella, eased his canvas carry bag from his shoulder and took out the bottle of water she knew he kept inside. "Have a drink."

He took several gulps and the colour slowly returned to his face.

Ketty watched him closely. "What is it?"

He shifted in his seat. "Nothing."

"Only you looked as if you were in pain."

"I…it's not my heart or anything. I've had all that checked out…I'm…I'll be all right in a minute."

Ketty leaned closer and lowered her voice. "Jim, we hardly know each other but I do hope you'd consider me a friend."

He inhaled deeply through his nose and let it out slowly through his mouth. The light returned to his eyes. "You're a generous woman, Ketty. You remind me of the counsellor I was seeing." He looked away then as if embarrassed. "It was my daughter's idea."

"Did it help?"

"A little. Sometimes the pain is so severe it takes my breath away. It's brought on by…well, anyway, the counsellor taught me some strategies to cope."

Jim gazed out over the water. "Jane's illness wasn't nice." He swallowed his voice, and it was little more than a whisper. "We knew it would be bad at the end. We had a palliative care nurse, the kids were there. I stayed by her side day and night but I felt useless."

He turned to Ketty with a look of raw despair.

"Seeing my beautiful Jane fade away was the cruellest thing but I have accepted she's gone. It's the guilt I can't shake. Every so often it overwhelms me. There were things I could have done better to help ease her pain. I let her down when she needed me most." He put a hand to his chest again. "It gnaws at me."

She reached out and put a gentle hand on his. "Part of grief is to blame ourselves, to ask the what-ifs, and it's important to feel the pain of grief. You have to, and I know it hurts but it also heals. With the passing of time the pain doesn't ache as much and getting on with life isn't so hard."

Jim nodded and turned his face seaward again. "I'll be all right."

"Yes Jim, you will be." Her voice was firm and she gave his hand a quick squeeze before she let it go. Across the carpark she caught sight of a group clambering out of a taxi. "There's Celia and her friends. I told them about this place. Would you rather some time to yourself?"

"No, I'll be fine, Ketty, thank you. One thing I've discovered since I came on this holiday is that I'm looking for company again."

"Good."

Celia stood looking around, a little apart from the others. Ketty waved over Jim's shoulder catching her attention. Celia waved back and wended her way through the tables to join them.

"Have you had an interesting morning?" Ketty asked.

Celia nodded at Jim and sat in the empty chair beside Ketty. "You might describe it as that. The rest of the group are having a quick bite to eat here then heading to the main street." She looked expectantly from Ketty to Jim. "What are you two doing?"

"We've had a stroll on the beach." Ketty smiled at Jim who seemed calm again. "I was thinking I'd have a swim. Leo, Josie and Bernard are coming here but not till later. I said I'd have a late lunch with them. You're both welcome, of course."

"A swim sounds lovely." Celia looked towards the ocean. "It looks divine here."

"That boat keeps coming and going from the end of the jetty," Jim said. "Do you know what that's about, Ketty?"

"For a few dollars you can go over to that little island just offshore. There's a resort there and you can swim. It's rather pretty, lovely lush gardens and a beach even nicer than this one."

They all looked around as loud voices and laughter carried from the other side of the tables.

"Celia!" Maude beckoned her. "We're having a quick swim here before we eat."

Celia turned back to Ketty, a look of dread on her face.

"I wouldn't mind going for a look at the island," Jim said. "Would either of you like to join me?"

"Yes."

"Lovely idea."

Ketty and Celia spoke at once.

"There's a boat coming now," Jim said.

They all stood up.

"I'll tell Maude not to wait for me." Celia set off to where her party were dropping their towels and bags on the sand.

"Perfect. We'll meet you on the jetty," Ketty said.

Eighteen

Christine was feeling more relaxed as she sat in the shade, watching Frank splash around in the water at the base of the waterfall. It had been a bit of a hike to get there but worth it; the tension between them as they had toured the island in a taxi had been dispersed by the refreshing swim. The constant sound of the water, the fine misting spray and the earthy smell of the tranquil setting stirred something primal in her. Pity they didn't have it to themselves or perhaps she and Frank could have enjoyed exploring that feeling further.

"How good is that water?" Frank came towards her grinning, his bathers and hair spraying drops on her as he reached for his towel.

Christine flinched away, the water cold on her warm skin, her racy thoughts dampened. Frank sprawled on his back in the sun, eyes closed. Even though he had a desk job he was fit and lightly tanned from his regular walks and gym workouts. He looked so handsome, and she felt so dowdy in the loose top she'd put on to cover the bulges her bathers didn't hide. When they got home she would get back into exercising and be more careful about what she ate. She stared at his tanned chest as it rose with each breath. She badly wanted to reach out and trail her fingers over his skin. Warmth flooded through her at the thought of sliding her hand further.

Squeals and laughter came from the family group splashing each other in the water nearby.

Christine sighed. "We should get going, Frank." She packed her book and phone back into her bag. "I'd like to stop off in Port Vila on the way back. Have a look at the shops and markets we passed."

"If you like." He didn't say it with any enthusiasm.

"Everyone says they have the best duty-free shops here. I thought I'd look for a pearl."

"We're on a budget, Chrissie." He rose to his feet and shook out his towel.

She studied her husband as he gathered his things. They hadn't mentioned the job or moving again. If her planned chat with her father went the way she hoped, they'd have plenty of money for renovations. Frank could have his job if his heart was set on it but they wouldn't need to move from the family home. "I've been thinking I might see if Dad will have dinner with me one night, just the two of us."

"Why?"

"Now that he's spending most of his time with Josie I hardly see him, and dinner is busy with such a large group."

"And I'm not included in this little get-together of yours?"

"He's my dad and I rarely spend any time with him. You don't mind, do you?"

He stared at her then slowly shook his head. "No."

"Good. I'll organise it soon. It won't be a late night."

Frank hefted his backpack over his shoulder. "Let's go." He set off ahead of her down the track.

She bent to pick up her towel and at the same time lifted her big beach bag. An intense pain stabbed in her lower back. "Oww!" She couldn't help the expletive that followed. She was rooted to the spot, breathing quick shallow breaths like she had in childbirth. The pain radiated across her lower back then gradually eased to a dull ache. She straightened cautiously and slipped her feet into her sandals.

Frank was now out of sight. She set off down the rugged path, carefully placing her feet but her back jarred with every step. She hadn't gone far when he appeared further down the track. He paused, then, noticing her slow hobble, he strode back.

"What happened to you?"

"I've hurt my back," she grumbled. "You shot off and left me."

He took her bag carefully from her shoulder. "I thought you were right behind me. How did you hurt your back?"

"I don't know." She let out a long sigh. "All I did was bend over to pick up my things."

He offered his arm, she leaned into him and they set off again.

"Perhaps we'd better go straight back to the ship," he said.

"I'll be all right," she said quickly and in a voice that held just the right amount of stoicism. "It will be better once we're on flat ground I'm sure."

She'd heard about the pearls in the duty-free shops and she was keen to have a look. The ache in her back wasn't so bad now and a bit of pain was worth it if it made Frank more solicitous.

Jim sat on the beach on the little island in the sun, drying his shorts. He was glad of his hat. He hadn't come prepared to swim and had simply slipped off his t-shirt and swum in his shorts.

Celia and Ketty were still in the sea. They were several metres away standing in water nearly up to their shoulders. He couldn't hear their exact words but the rise and fall of their voices reached him as they chatted together. He allowed himself a smile. If someone had told him a week ago he'd be swimming in a tropical paradise with two women he'd have told them they were mad, and yet here he was and it wasn't that terrible. Except for the odd upset like he'd had earlier, each day he felt a little more relaxed with them. The other people from his table were easy enough to get along with now that he knew them better.

Jim wondered what Jane would have made of them. The two of them would have joined in the conversation, been a part of it, especially Jane, and then when they got back to their cabin they would have discussed everyone. Ketty's presiding over the table and the surprise arrival of Leo who she'd known before. No one else had seemed to notice her shock and discomfort. Bernard's flirting with the women, which Jane would have enjoyed and laughed at. Christine's jealousy and poor Frank with his hangdog look. Jane would have had them all summed up in an instant: she was far better at understanding people than he ever was.

How she would have loved all of it, the whole experience from the cruise itself, to their fellow passengers, to the destinations like this beautiful beach.

"Jim!"

He looked up. There had been fear in Ketty's call. She was beckoning him but her movements were slow. Celia was wide-eyed, her elbows in the air. He was on his feet immediately and striding into the water.

"What's the matter?" he called.

"There's a snake."

Ketty's response hissed over the water. Jim frowned, trying to remember all he'd heard about sea snakes. All he could think of was their venom was deadly. He arrived beside the two women. Ketty was holding one of Celia's hands above the water line and Celia's face had lost all colour.

"It's at Celia's back." Ketty's voice was a whisper now. "I didn't know what to do. I thought if we stayed still it would swim away."

Jim looked behind Celia who was wearing a brightly coloured sheer shirt over her bathers. There was indeed a small snake nudging up against her back. Jim took Celia's other hand. Her fingers gripped his.

"It's being inquisitive." He kept his voice calm. "I'm sure it will swim away."

"I can feel it." Celia's eyes were shut now and her voice came out in a sob. "Tapping against my back."

"You're fine." Jim recalled what had been said about inquisitive sea snakes; small mouths, not likely to bite. It all came back to him from the shipboard presentation about Vanuatu. "Listen, Celia, Ketty and I will hold your hands and we are going to walk slowly with you towards the beach." He glanced across at Ketty and gave her a nod. "The snake will lose interest and swim away."

Celia's eyes were scrunched shut now, her brow deeply furrowed and her jaw rigidly clamped. "I can feel it."

"Look at me, Celia."

Her eyes opened. Poor woman was terrified and who could blame her?

"We're going to start walking."

Celia tried to look back.

"Celia." Jim gripped her hand tighter. "Keep looking at me. Ketty and I are with you, you're going to be fine. Walk with us."

"I can't. If I move it might bite me."

"It can't bite you on the back, Celia." Jim kept his voice low and steady. "It only has a very small mouth." He had no idea what the snake was capable of but somehow he had to get Celia to move slowly out of the water. He took a small step forward so that he was in front of her. "Keep looking at me. You're going to start walking now."

She took a step, gasped and stopped.

"Celia."

She looked at him.

"Keep your eyes on me and keep moving forward. Ketty's going to tell us when the snake loses interest and swims away. All you have to do is look at me and keep moving."

Celia took another step and he kept his gaze locked with hers. He could see the fear in her eyes. He kept talking to her softly, willing her to be brave.

From the corner ofhis eye he saw Ketty look behind. She grimaced and gave a slight shake of her head. The snake was obviously still following. He felt the slope steepen beneath his feet.

"Nearly there," Ketty said.

"You're doing well, Celia." Jim gave her a reassuring smile. "Keep walking steadily."

Finally, they were out of the water. Celia collapsed against Jim's chest and he held her tightly, watching the snake swim away. It had followed them almost to the shore. Behind him, he could hear worried voices. There had been people sunning themselves on chairs further up the beach and they had come to see what was going on.

"Thank you, Jim." Ketty said. "I couldn't get her to move."

"What's happened?" A man in a white shirt and khaki shorts strode along the beach towards them from the direction of the resort, a manager's badge on his chest.

"Everyone's all right," Jim said. "There was a sea snake."

"No one's been bitten?" The man glanced at each of them with a worried expression.

"It was nudging Celia's back," Ketty said and several people gasped. "I'm sure that's all it did though. I saw it immediately and kept an eye on it."

Jim was acutely aware that Celia was still clamped to him. He eased her away and held her at arm's length. "You've not been bitten, have you, Celia?"

She shook her head, her eyes bright and her skin pale. "I…I don't think so."

The manager urged the onlookers away then turned back to take a closer look at Celia. "But what happened? How did you hurt your face?"

Celia, still wide-eyed, put a hand to her cheek.

"She fell yesterday," Ketty said. "That's fine, nothing to do with the snake. I think she's a bit shocked, that's all."

"Is there somewhere we could sit in the shade for a moment?" Jim asked the manager. "And perhaps we could have a cup of tea."

"Of course. Follow me and I will see to it straight away."

He seated them in comfortable chairs in the shade of a huge umbrella. Ketty helped Celia to remove her wet shirt and replace it with a dry one and Jim dragged a footstool closer so she could put her feet up. A pot of tea was delivered, with some sweet pastries and a large jug of iced water.

Ketty passed Celia a glass of water and they both watched her drink with shaking hands.

When the glass was empty, Celia settled against the back of her chair and let out a long sigh. "Thank you both," she said. "It's silly but I have a morbid fear of snakes."

"Not silly," Ketty said. "I don't like them myself."

Ketty handed out cups of tea and sat back in her chair. Jim was pleased to see the colour returning to Celia's cheeks.

She rested her cup and saucer in her lap and stared at him. He found it hard to look away. "Jim, I was a mess." She leaned a little closer. "I don't know what I would have done out there if you hadn't been so courageous."

He shifted in his chair. "Glad to be of help."

There was a brief silence then Celia shivered. She put the cup back on the table. "I don't think I'll be going swimming again."

"Not today anyway." Ketty's voice was warm and reassuring. "I think we should catch the boat back, see if Josie and the men are at the bar. We could probably all do with food and I think maybe a glass of something stronger to fortify our nerves."

"Thanks for organising this visit to the waterfall, Ketty." Josie stepped carefully over the rough path as she followed Ketty down the rugged incline later that afternoon. Leo and Bernard followed a few steps behind. "So refreshing in the water, and part of a small group rather than aboard ship with two thousand people."

"This one's a bit more out of the way. It doesn't usually get so many tourists." Ketty stopped and glanced down at the ground in front of her. She was relieved Celia and Jim had decided to go back to the ship after lunch.

"Are you okay?" Josie asked.

"The ground's a bit slippery here."

"How about taking my arm?" Leo moved down beside Ketty, stuck out his elbow and gave her one of his charming smiles. "If one goes we both go."

Ketty slipped her hand around his arm. "Thanks."

"You seem very strong to me but it's wise to be cautious."

"Oh, blast." Ketty shook her head. "Am I showing my age? I've become cautious."

"We're still thirty inside." He grinned. "It's only the bodies that are a little older."

They moved on together. He was right. Ketty didn't normally dwell on thoughts of old age but there was no denying she would be sixty-five in a few days and the face she saw in the mirror reminded her more and more of her mother. And yet today she felt like the young woman she'd been. It had been a pleasant afternoon with just the four of them. She was pleased to be able to spend time with Leo, not on their own, because Josie and Bernard were with them, but under less scrutiny. No deep conversations, simply easy banter between the four of them, not discussing anything too personal. She was losing the reticence she'd felt in Leo's presence. He was being courteous and attentive. She even felt comfortable with his arm in hers as it was now.

They stepped from the bush and the shaded path into the bright sunshine. A group of taxis and an ecotour bus waited in the carpark.

"I'm a little disappointed with my choice of taxi driver," Ketty said. "I don't think this chap has been doing it very long."

"He said he was experienced."

Josie and Bernard stepped out of the bush and came to a stop beside them. They all looked across to where their driver, Delmar, lounged against a car. He was talking to a group of drivers.

"They all say that,' Ketty said.

"It's getting late," Leo said. "We'd best be on our way."

Delmar hurried to his vehicle as he saw them crossing the carpark.

"You enjoy?" he asked in his broken English.

"It was beautiful," Josie said and moved to the other side of the battered four-wheel drive.

Bernard and Leo stowed their bags in the back and Ketty had barely had a chance to climb into the backseat when Delmar shut the door. She yelled and then swore as a pain shot through her arm.

"What's the matter?" Josie cried.

Ketty leaned away from the door as Delmar whipped it open again.

"Sorry, sorry," he stammered. "Are you okay?"

"Ketty?" Leo bundled the driver out of the way. "What's happened?"

She drew her arm to her chest and cradled it with her other. "It's my arm. It got caught in the door." Her words came out in rasps. The pain made her nauseous.

Josie leaned in from the other side. "You do look pale."

Bernard squeezed into the open-door space beside Leo. All three of them studied her. She leaned back, and took a long slow breath to keep the nausea at bay.

Josie lifted Ketty's good arm gently to her side and peered at the injured arm. "It's got black around the elbow."

Leo inspected it too. "Probably grease from the car."

"There's some broken skin and some blood but it doesn't look misshapen," Josie said.

"I think it caught me on the funny bone," Ketty gasped. "That always hurts like hell when you bump it."

"Does it hurt to move?" Leo asked.

Ketty tried to lift her arm but the pain shot up to her shoulder like a jolt of electricity and she gasped again.

"I think that's a yes," Josie said. "Can you get my bag please, Bernie?"

"I'll be all right." Ketty put her head back against the seat. "Took my breath away that's all. Give me a minute."

Bernard came round behind Josie and handed in the bag. He gave Ketty a reassuring smile.

"What are you going to do?" Leo asked.

"I want to wash that broken skin with my bottled water. Then I'm going to bind it," she said. "Just in case."

"In case what?" Ketty frowned. All this fussing wasn't necessary.

"It could be broken."

"It's not," Ketty snapped. The pain was making her irritable.

"Better to be safe and I'm sure it will be more comfortable regardless." Josie rummaged in her bag and pulled out her water bottle. Then she climbed out of the car and came round to the open door. "You fellows can leave us a minute." She shooed Leo and Bernard away. "Now Ketty, can you lean out a little for me?"

Ketty did as she asked and Josie poured the water and wiped gently with a clean tissue, glancing at Ketty's face as she did. Ketty's lips tingled and she could feel perspiration forming on her brow. Her stomach still swirled with nausea and she concentrated on keeping it at bay rather than the pain of her arm.

Josie worked quickly. "There are a few cuts but I don't think they're deep. Doesn't look so bad now the grease is gone." She looked around. All three men stood together only a few metres away. "Is there any ice here?"

"Ice?" Delmar said.

"Cold." Bernard waved his hands. "Frozen water."

"Yes, ice." Delmar nodded eagerly then frowned. "No. No ice here. Maybe one of the others." He dashed off towards the group of drivers.

Josie reached across Ketty for her tote bag and pulled out a sarong. "How are you feeling?"

"I'll live."

Josie passed her the water bottle. "It's clean. Take a sip."

Ketty did as she suggested and they both looked around as Delmar called excitedly.

"My friend has ice." He held up a small esky triumphantly.

Leo looked inside and his face creased with distaste. "It's only muddy water with a few chunks of ice."

"Thank you." Josie beckoned the driver towards her.

"You can't use that," Leo said. "Ketty could catch anything from that water."

"She's not going to drink it, Leo," Josie said. "Just drain off the water and keep the ice for me." Once more she rummaged in her tote. This time she pulled out a small plastic cosmetic bag. She tipped the contents back into her tote and then held the smaller bag out to Leo. "Put the ice in here."

Leo did as he was bid and handed it back. Josie gave Ketty a reassuring smile. "Nearly done." She placed the makeshift icepack carefully on Ketty's arm at just below the elbow, which appeared to have been the part gripped in the car door. "Can you hold that in place for me, Ketty?"

"Of course."

Josie proceeded to fold the sarong then worked carefully, binding the arm to Ketty's chest. When she was finished she helped Ketty to ease back more comfortably in the seat, well away from the door.

"Right." She turned to Delmar. "You must get us back to the ship quickly." She put a restraining hand on Delmar's arm. "But carefully."

"Yes, missus. I will take good care."

Leo climbed in and settled cautiously beside Ketty with Josie on his other side and Bernard took the front seat.

"Thank you." Ketty looked past Leo to Josie. "It feels much better already."

"That's good." Josie shot a glare at the back of Delmar's head as they bounced over a pothole on the way out of the carpark.

"Were you a nurse?"

"No." Josie laughed. "But I keep my first aid up to date, just in case." She gave Ketty a quick smile. "You're my first ever real patient."

Leo shook his head.

"Look out, Ketty," Bernard teased.

"How's the pain now?" Leo asked.

"Bearable," Ketty said but couldn't help wincing as they swept around a corner.

"As soon as we get back to the ship we'll have the doctor take a look at you," Josie said.

"That's not necessary."

"Yes it is."

"Even if it's only to check she hasn't done any further damage with her first aid attempts," Leo said.

The three of them kept up their banter. Ketty clenched her jaw against the pain and the rocking of the vehicle and wished she was back aboard ship with a glass of whisky in her hand.

Nineteen

Celia tagged along at the rear of the group as they all trooped up to the pool deck. She'd run into Maude and her friends as they'd crossed the atrium. They'd only just come back on board whereas Celia had been back for a couple of hours. She'd showered and had a nap in the cabin and, now refreshed, had decided to wander the atrium in the hope of finding Ketty or even Jim. He'd been good company today. The sad shadow that hovered over him had been almost non-existent and when he'd helped her escape the snake she'd seen a different side to him altogether. They'd shared a water taxi back to the ship then gone their separate ways. Unfortunately, in her search for company it had been Maude she'd found. The only relief for Celia was that Nigel wasn't with them.

Anne waved to them from a table with vacant chairs. Pete rushed over, hugged and kissed her, and was asking all about her day when the rest of them arrived. It made Celia want to puke. What a sleaze he was. And Maude was no better. She joined in the attendance as if she was Anne's best friend.

"Hello, gorgeous."

Celia clenched her teeth at the sound of Nigel's voice. In her efforts to keep away from Pete and Maude she'd sat in a chair at the end of the table with an empty seat beside her and now he was sliding onto it. Damn, she should have known he'd turn up. He'd stuck so tight to her during the morning that at one point he'd even gone with her to the primitive ablutions to stand guard outside her door.

"This is for you." He pressed a plastic bag with something firm inside it into her hands. "Sorry about the wrapping paper."

She glanced at the others but they were all still busy chatting. She turned to Nigel. "What is it?"

"Take a look." His face twisted into a sloppy grin. "Something special for a special lady."

Celia's heart sank. She felt as if she were in some terrible nightmare that she couldn't wake up from. She opened the bag and looked in. One of the pretty turtle souvenirs she'd admired at the stalls, but had thought too expensive, was inside. "Oh."

"I knew you'd love it." He leaned in closer as if he was going to kiss her.

Celia twisted sideways in her seat. She'd avoided the brush of his lips but it meant she was facing Nigel full on now and she had her back partly to the others.

"Take it out." He took the bag from her hands and reached inside.

She had to put a stop to this. Now that she'd given up on her 'make Ed jealous' quest she felt stronger.

"Nigel." She hoped her voice wasn't too loud but carried some authority. "I can't accept this."

"Why not?" He looked at her with such adoration she was reminded of a puppy. Her resolve wavered.

"You're a nice man, Nigel."

"I think you're more than nice." Once more he leaned in.

Celia turned away quickly to see if the others were paying them any attention. Pete was telling a story, holding the limelight as usual.

"I didn't come on this cruise to find a partner." Celia let out a sigh. There, she'd said it.

"Neither did I." His smile widened and he took one of her hands in his and squeezed it. "Then I met you."

Celia groaned inwardly. He hadn't understood what she was trying to tell him.

"Please, Nigel, you must listen." She extracted her hand from his sweaty hold.

"At your command, my lady. Speak on."

Celia thought she was going to gag.

Nigel filled the space she left. "I've something to tell you when you've fin—"

"I've met other people on this cruise who I'd like to spend time with." The words blurted out. "I'm not looking for a man and even if I was..." She took a breath. "Nice as you are Nigel..." She blew out the breath. "You are not my type."

The smile stayed on his face a moment then changed to puzzlement as he digested what she had said. He opened his mouth, closed it again then shook his head.

"You've been very kind." Celia felt terrible now. "Looking out for me and the gift was lovely."

His face brightened. "You do like it then."

"Yes, but—"

"Please keep it." He pressed the bag into her hands.

Celia didn't have the heart to reject it again.

"You're probably tired." Nigel stood. "I'll see you tonight after dinner." Without a word to the others he walked away.

Celia collapsed back against her seat. Nigel was right about one thing, she did feel exhausted but not because of her day, because of him.

She turned to the group. They were all still chatting animatedly, filling Anne in on their travels. She caught Maude's eye and indicated she was going down to the cabin. Pete saw her and looked around.

"Where's Nige?" he asked.

Celia froze as all eyes looked her way. "Ah. I'm not sure. He might have gone to his cabin."

"Trevor's on a diving tour." Pete dug his elbow into Maude and winked. "Won't be back till just before we sail."

Trevor was another of their friends and he shared Nigel's cabin. They all laughed. Even sensible Freda sniggered.

Celia felt heat warm her cheeks. "I'm off to see if I can catch up with Ketty. See you later." She almost tripped on the chair leg in her hurry to get away. She prayed she'd run into someone else she knew. She certainly didn't want to give the slightest impression she might be following Nigel to his cabin. All the same she was relieved. She'd spoken up to Nigel and made her feelings clear. Now there was only Maude to put straight and then Celia could truly relax.

Christine spied her father as soon as she stepped out onto the pool deck. He was sitting with his back to the bar, alone she was pleased to see, watching the passing parade of people.

She came up beside him. "Hello, Dad. I wondered if I might find you up here."

"Hi, Princess." He patted the seat next to him. "Just waiting for Josie." He indicated a glass filled with swirls of lime and yellow liquid, topped up with ice and a slice of lemon perched on the rim. "She loves her cocktails. This one's called Illusion."

Christine swallowed her annoyance, winced and eased onto the stool.

"What's the matter?"

"I hurt my back today while Frank and I were visiting a waterfall. Just a twinge. I'm fine." Her back was hardly hurting at all now. She'd had a shower as soon as they'd returned to the ship and that, along with some painkillers, seemed to have done the trick but Frank had remained attentive. It wouldn't hurt to lay it on a bit thick for her dad.

"Have you seen a doctor?"

"No need for that," she said. "I'm sure it will get better of its own accord." She shifted on her stool and winced again for good effect.

Bernard lifted his beer. "Can I get you a drink?"

"That'd be great, thanks, Dad. I'd better stick to a nojito though. I'm taking tablets for the pain."

Bernard ordered her drink then turned back to peruse the pool area again. "Maybe waterfalls are bad luck. We went to one today too and Ketty got her arm jammed in the car door."

"Oh?" Christine wasn't interested in Ketty's problems.

"She's still with the doctor as far as I know."

"I guess when you get older things get hurt more easily." She put a gentle hand on her father's arm. "I hope you're not overdoing it."

"I'm having the time of my life. Apart from Ketty's accident we had a great time together with Josie and Leo," he said brightly. "I hope Josie turns up soon, her drink will be warm."

Christine swirled her straw in her fingers. "She's very attractive, isn't she?"

Bernard paused about to take a mouthful of beer. "Nothing wrong with a good-looking woman."

Christine leaned closer. "You're always a sucker for a pretty-faced damsel in distress, Dad." She saw the start in his eyes and knew she'd hit her mark. After her mother had died he had taken up with a woman called Gloria who had been deserted by her husband with barely any money in her account. She'd latched on to Bernard and his money.

"Josie can stand on her own two feet," he said.

Christine took another sip of her drink. Bloody Gloria was the reason he'd moved to Brisbane leaving his family behind in Melbourne. He had even thought he might marry her but it hadn't worked out in the end. Only trouble was he'd taken to Brisbane life and decided to stay.

"I hope she's at least single," Christine said, studying her father closely. After Gloria he'd taken up with Kath until Christine had done some digging and discovered she wasn't divorced as she'd said but had a husband who worked away a lot. She'd had a lot of disposable income though, one of the reasons Christine suspected her father had been attracted in the first place.

"Josie is divorced." Bernard glanced around as if he was watching for someone.

"And you believe her?"

"Of course I do. Leave it alone, Christine."

She pursed her lips. She was sure Josie was a gold-digger like the others had been but decided to change tack for now. "Why don't we have dinner together one night, Dad. Just the two of us. We so rarely get time alone."

"We're alone now."

"You're expecting Josie at any moment. If we had dinner together in one of the restaurants we could have some uninterrupted time… to ourselves." Christine shuffled on the stool and sucked in a breath. She could barely feel a twinge but she could see she needed to play the sympathy card to get her father's full attention.

"Okay, Princess," he said. "But not tonight."

"Oh no, I'll need an early night with my back." She grimaced. "Perhaps tomorrow night?"

"Why don't you have a decent drink?" Bernard said. "It might help."

"I suppose one won't hurt. Thanks." She gave a feeble smile and nodded towards Josie's glass. "I'll have one of those Illusions, and would you book us at that nice restaurant at the front of the ship for tomorrow night?"

He barely hid his sigh. "Of course."

When her drink arrived, he slid from his stool. "Can you stay and keep an eye for Josie? I need to go to the mens."

"Sure." This time she gave him a proper smile and he strode away.

She felt much better now that she'd arranged to spend some time alone with her father. She was sure this time she'd be able to convince him to help with the renovation costs. By one means or another he would have to hand over some money.

And things were getting back on track with Frank, or at least had been except for the blip with the phone call to the kids. When they'd first arrived back in their cabin he had left her for a while then he'd come back with a smug smile on his face and presented her with an appointment for a massage. She'd already seen the expensive price list for treatments. That, along with the pearl-drop necklace he'd bought her at the duty-free shop in Port Vila, would blow out their expense sheet but she didn't want to think about budgets when he was being so very attentive. It reminded her of their early married days before children, and she liked being the centre of his world again.

Frank had wanted to go to the gym and they'd decided to put in a call to the kids before he did. It had been so good to hear their voices. They were full of what they'd done on their beach holiday with their cousins. For a while it had been hard to get a word in. They'd told the kids a few of the things they'd seen and done and when Frank had told them about all the swims he was having Lucca had mentioned wanting to join a surf club.

"A surf club." Christine shook her head at that. "We're nowhere near any surf and I'm not driving you to another thing."

"Dad said we might be shifting and we'd be closer to the beach." Lucca's reply was full of teenage outrage.

"Did he?" She glared at Frank over the phone they'd put on loudspeaker. He stared back giving nothing away.

"I don't want to join a surf club," Anna whined.

"No one's joining anything at the moment." Frank reached for the phone. "We'd better go. Calls are expensive."

Lucca had said a quick goodbye but Anna's voice sounded teary and Christine spent a few minutes jollying her daughter along. Mentioning the surprises they'd bought today for them had helped, then Frank had joked with her and she was laughing by the time they ended the call.

"You told them we were moving?" Christine hissed as soon as she disconnected.

"I told them we might."

"You had no right going behind my back."

"I didn't go behind your back. I talked to the kids about it just before we left to sound them out, knowing I'd talk to you while we were away."

"But what's the point if we're not moving anyway."

"We might."

"It's not an option."

She'd put her hands to her hips and he'd slammed out of the cabin to go to the gym. It was then that she'd known she couldn't fail in her next attempt to get her father to hand over some money. She'd pinned her father down to dinner alone and that's when she'd put her plan into action. Frank might still want to go for the job but if they renovated he wouldn't go on about moving.

The deck area was getting busier now and the bar was crowded as it got closer to sailing time. Music played from the speakers and voices began to rise. She took a slug of the cocktail, tapping her feet in time to the music. Among the crowd she saw a familiar figure. Josie was headed towards the bar but she hadn't seen Christine, who took the opportunity to study her. She was tall and wore long white pants with a bright floral top. It had an off-the-shoulder neckline and the hem hung at hip level but it was gathered at the waist on a drawstring. Begrudgingly Christine had to admit she was attractive in a flashy kind of way. She had expensive tastes, judging by her clothes and jewellery. There was a small fortune hanging off her arms and neck and she was heavy-handed with the make-up. Christine gave a wave to catch her attention. Perhaps they'd actually get a few minutes alone so that she could find out a bit more about this woman who was making a play for her father.

"Hello." Josie came to a stop in front of her. "Have you seen Bernie?"

Christine gritted her teeth. She hated it when people shortened his name even though her own husband often did it. "He asked me to keep an eye out for you. He'll be back in a moment. He bought a drink for you."

"He's a good man." Josie perched on the empty stool and reached for the colourful drink. She took a sip then replaced the glass on the bar. "Did you have a good day?"

"Yes, until I hurt my back."

"Oh, that's no good. Ketty injured her arm." Josie glanced around. "I hoped Leo might be here by now and let us know how she is. He had to take her to the medical centre when we got back. Poor thing got her elbow slammed in the car door."

Christine took a breath. Even when she wasn't here Ketty demanded attention.

"You do look like your dad when you make that face. The family likeness is strong." Josie locked her gaze on Christine.

"Do I?" Christine smiled sweetly back. "People who know us always say I look like my mother."

"People say that about my sons but I think they're clones of their father. I can never find any likeness to me."

Christine continued to smile through gritted teeth. "So, Dad said you are a divorcee?"

"Yes. Not once but twice." Josie waggled two fingers in the air and laughed.

"That must have been a difficult time."

"Not once they'd settled me with their money."

Christine's eyes widened.

Josie laughed louder. "I'm joking."

Maybe, Christine thought, but interesting that she would raise the topic of money.

"Actually your dad and I have been talking about investment property."

"Have you?"

"He's very knowledgeable about the market in Brisbane."

Very, Christine thought. She wondered who had brought it up, Josie or Bernard? She decided to change the subject. "Do you have grandchildren?"

"No, and I'm not sure I ever will. Two of my sons are still single and the other and his partner are too busy for children."

"That's a shame." Christine caught sight of her dad approaching from over Josie's shoulder. "Dad adores his."

Bernard came up behind Josie and slipped his arms around her waist. "What do I adore?"

"Your grandchildren." Josie leaned against him as he kissed her cheek. "As you should."

Christine did her best to keep her smile in place, when all she wanted to do was groan. Really, how old were they and behaving like young lovers? Once more she was reminded of her own lack of success in that department.

"What is your surname?" she asked Josie.

"For heaven's sake, Christine." Bernard frowned at her. "I hope you haven't been quizzing Josie the whole time I've been gone."

"That's all right, Bernie. It's Keller." Josie chuckled. "I've married a plain Brown and then a fancy Duponte but decided to make a clean break with the past and return to my maiden name. My three sons however have stuck with Brown. What else would you like to know?"

"Where do you live?"

"Really, Christine." Bernard glared at her from his stool on the other side of Josie.

"Brisbane." Josie patted his knee. "Not all that far from your dad as it turns out."

"I see." Christine didn't like the sound of that at all.

"And you're in Melbourne?" Josie said. "Such a long way from Brisbane. Bernie said you don't get up to see him all that often."

Christine glowered at the woman. Was she having a dig? "I work long hours and the children are busy with school and sport and music." She pulled a tight smile and turned to her father. "He's always welcome to come our way."

"You're never home," Bernard said.

"Well, at least we'll have some private catch-up time soon." Christine smiled sassily at Josie. "Dad's taking me to that nice restaurant at the front of the ship. Just the two of us. You understand, don't you? We don't see each other all that often and we haven't had a proper catch-up since we came aboard."

"That's lovely," Josie said.

"Tomorrow night." Bernard squeezed Josie's shoulder. "I haven't told you because we only just organised it."

"That's all right, Bernie. We'll have other nights. And we have plenty more days to spend together. You should devote a few hours to your daughter." Josie nestled closer to Bernard and gazed back at Christine with a smug smile.

Christine stiffened. The bitch had all but made a declaration of war.

"Leo's coming." Josie leaped to her feet and lifted her arm in a wave. "I hope he's got good news. How's Ketty?" she asked as soon as he reached them.

"They don't think the arm is broken but they're going to X-ray it just in case. They took her into a cubicle and there was nothing more I could do."

"I hope she'll be all right," Josie said.

"They gave her some painkillers. She's in good hands." Leo gave his sister a nudge. "And the doctor said your first aid was well done. I'll go down again before I get changed for dinner and see how she is."

"It's so nice to see you two getting to know each other again," Josie said.

Christine straightened on her stool, remembering at the last second to wince. "Again?"

Leo turned the full force of his charming gaze on her. "Ketty and I, or Kathy as I knew her, were friends in our younger days. We lost touch and then, here we are, meeting up again on this cruise."

Christine did recall something being said the first night Leo and Josie had turned up for dinner. "Were you close?"

He cleared his throat. "We were both interested in the jazz scene at the time."

"You were getting along well at the waterfall this afternoon," Josie said. "I think it's so romantic."

"Leave the man alone, you women." Bernard clapped a hand on Leo's shoulder. "You look like you could do with a drink. A beer?"

"I'll have a martini, thanks Bernard."

Christine's eyes narrowed. Leo's response had been more a command than a request and her father obliged. There was quite a difference in price between a beer and a martini. She eased herself from her chair and put a hand to her back.

"How are you feeling, Princess?" her father asked.

"I'm starting to fade. I think I'll go back to my room and stretch out before dinner. Too much sitting seems to make it worse. Frank and I were thinking we'd grab a quick bite in the buffet tonight and turn in early." They hadn't actually discussed it but Christine was fed up with vying for attention from her father. She'd pinned him down to dinner tomorrow night so tonight she was determined to seduce her husband.

"Take care." Josie slipped her arm casually through Bernard's.

"Yes, take it easy, Princess. See you tomorrow then."

Before she'd had a chance to turn away, the three of them had dismissed her and were discussing Ketty. That busybody of a woman stole the limelight even when she wasn't there. Christine walked carefully towards the lifts in case one of them did bother to watch her. She was actually going to go to the dress boutique as soon as the ship left port but she hadn't mentioned that. At least she'd found out some information about Josie. With a bit more digging she'd find her weak spot like she had with Bernard's previous women.

Twenty

Night Five – At Sea

Jim leaned over the rail of the smaller front deck intent on watching the men on shore cast off the ship's ropes. He was bemused by the whole process. The three men hefting the thick ropes that held the ship to the shore were casually dressed in t-shirts, shorts and thongs. Not a fluoro vest in sight or boots of any description. Beyond them families gathered outside the fence to watch and wave as the ropes were cast aside and farewells were called, echoing from the vegetation-covered cliff behind, and the ship swung away from the wharf.

The door behind him opened and Celia stepped out. He hadn't been sure if she'd come.

She'd changed into a long red shirt over white pants and the gentle scent of a sweet perfume wafted with her arrival. She smiled and Jim brightened in response. He offered the glass of wine he'd been holding in his left hand. "I got you a drink but it might be a bit warm now. You don't have to have it. I wasn't sure what you'd feel like."

"That's very kind of you. Wine's perfect, thank you."

Celia took the glass and he held his beer towards her.

"Cheers," he said. "Happy cruising."

She tapped the glass against the neck of his bottle and took a sip. She sighed. "That's good. Just what I felt like."

"I'm glad." Jim took a sip of his beer and realised he meant it.

"Look at that view." Celia was watching the port as the ship slowly swung out to turn its nose to the sea. "It's a beautiful place. I'd love to come back again."

"And swim?"

"Don't remind me."

They both grinned and leaned on the rail, silently enjoying the changing vista until they were past the islands and moving towards the golden rays of the setting sun and the open sea.

Jim took his phone from his pocket and snapped a picture. He hadn't taken many but the sunset over the water was certainly noteworthy. He needed a few more snaps to show Tammy when he got home.

"Oh, I forgot to tell you," Celia said. "I ran into Christine on the way here. It seems she's done something to her back and is in a lot of pain but she also mentioned Ketty had been taken to the medical centre. Something about hurting her arm but Christine didn't think it was bad."

"I wonder what happened?"

"I thought I'd pop down to her room in a while to see if she's there." Celia looked out over the ocean. "She was so good to me the other night. I feel a little guilty."

"Why?"

"I thought her a bit of a busybody to begin with. I was so caught up in...well, in my own problems, I thought her conversation too personal."

"We had a long chat this morning before you joined us. She's not a widow but lives alone."

"I think she had an affair a long time ago and it's burned her for life."

"From what she told me she's moved on. I wish I had some of her self-determination."

"I for one think you've got it in spades." Her look turned fearful. "I thought I was going to die today. I'd heard so much about how poisonous sea snakes were and not to go near one." Her lips trembled and tears pooled in her eyes. "I was so scared."

Jim put out one arm and she fell against him. He felt the familiar prickle of panic begin in his chest. Jane had been scared too and he hadn't been able to help her.

Celia snuffled quietly against his shoulder. He held her stiffly, reminded of the days and weeks after Jane's death; so many of her friends had sobbed in his arms. All he had felt was numb. Now he still had no idea what to do with a tearful woman.

Celia straightened and stepped back. She brushed the tears from her cheeks with her fingers.

"I'm sorry, Jim. I don't know where that came from. I've had a bit happening lately, it must have all piled up." She took a tissue from her pocket, blew her nose and glanced around. "Here I am making a fool of myself in public."

Jim glanced around too. There had been several others on the deck when he'd first come out but only one other couple had stayed on once they left port, and they were locked in each other's arms on the opposite side. "It's only me really," he murmured. "I don't think those two know we're here."

Celia dabbed at her eyes and looked past him. "Probably not." He was relieved to see her smile return.

"It's just that I keep mucking up. This cruise is not turning out at all how I imagined."

Jim felt the same. On the first day, once he knew he couldn't escape, he thought he'd spend most of his time in his cabin. Now he discovered he was beginning to look for company. "Is that good or bad?"

"Good in some ways, not so in others." She huffed out a sigh and looked out to sea. "I'm avoiding Maude."

"You don't enjoy her company?"

"Oh yes…no…well, it's not that I don't enjoy her company, just not so much of it. I hadn't realised how different we are. We're partners at bowls and we have the odd meal out or coffee together back home. We get on all right there, but here she wants me to do what she's arranged and that often includes Nigel and his other friends. I'm embarrassed by her open flirting with Pete. He's a married man and his wife is on the cruise. It all leaves me feeling most uncomfortable. I don't…at least I…oh, damn." Her face contorted into a stricken look. "I'm sorry. I've said too much."

"I don't mind. It might help you to speak with her later if you get it off your chest now."

Her face softened. "Thanks, Jim. You're very kind but you don't need to rescue me twice in one day." She lifted her empty glass. "Would you like another drink? I feel I could do with one."

"Yes, I would." Jim opened his mouth to say more, closed it again as she turned to the door. He pulled it open for her. "I was thinking I'd go to the early session of tonight's theatre show," he blurted. "Would you like to come?"

"I would, yes." She glanced at her watch. "That's soon, isn't it? I'd like to see how Ketty is first. Shall I meet you at the bar outside the theatre?"

He nodded. "Let me take your glass."

"See you shortly."

Jim let the door close and went back to the rail. Beneath him the deck rose and fell gently as the ship met the swell of the ocean and the wind ruffled his hair. He watched as the last glow from the sun slipped into the water and was filled with a sense of anticipation. A feeling he hadn't experienced in a long time. It was as if he was sailing towards something rather than away from it.

Celia checked the names beside the doors as she walked along the corridor of the deck one level above hers. She knew approximately where Ketty's room was but not the number. Up ahead a steward pushing a trolley draped with a cloth stopped at a door. He tapped and called out.

"Room service, Miss Clift."

Celia smiled and strode ahead, arriving as Ketty opened the door. The older woman was wearing a deep purple silk robe and a garish blue sling kept her arm to her chest. She looked elegant even with her injury.

"I've arrived with the food," Celia said.

The waiter gave them both a big smile and Celia followed him into the cabin. He wheeled the trolley skilfully past the bed and into the space beside the desk.

"Don't worry about setting it out," Ketty said as the man began to lay out cutlery. "I'll manage."

"Just call us if you need anything at all, Miss Clift," the steward said as he made for the door.

"I will, thank you." Ketty smiled at him. "You've all been very kind."

Celia waited for him to let himself out then she turned to Ketty. "How are you?"

"I'm fine." Ketty sat on the bed and waved Celia to the chair.

"What happened?"

"My arm got caught in the car door as we were about to head back to the ship."

"Did it do much damage?"

"Not broken, thank goodness. Just a bit sore and sorry for myself. Bit like you the other night."

"Don't remind me." Celia put her hand to her cheek. "It's enough I have to see the bruise every time I look in the mirror."

"It's certainly spread and got darker. You should ask Josie to help cover it up if it bothers you. She's a whiz with make-up."

"I might if it gets any worse. How does your arm feel?"

"They gave me some pain relief so I'm quite comfortable. I'm sure I'll be a hundred per cent again by morning."

"You're so strong, Ketty."

The older woman studied her intently. "So are you."

"I went to pieces today."

"I would have too if it had been me with a snake at my back."

A shiver wriggled down Celia's spine at the memory. They lapsed into silence.

"I should go," she said. "I don't want your dinner to go cold."

"It's only a salad."

Celia glanced at the tray loaded with several lidded plates. "There are a lot of dishes for a salad."

"They sent me some extras in case I got hungry later." Ketty straightened out the lids. "And some cake. I thought I'd give myself a treat."

"Good idea." Celia stood up. "I'm meeting Jim for the show."

"I'm glad." She paused, looking steadily up at Celia. "Say hello from me and tell him I'm fine."

"I will." Celia turned away, relieved to be released from Ketty's scrutiny.

The older woman stood and moved to the door ahead of her blocking her way.

"How's it going with Maude and Nigel?"

"I've spoken with Nigel. He took it rather well I think, so that's a relief." She wrinkled her nose. "But I haven't had a chance to have a private word with Maude yet."

"You'll feel so much better once you've done it." Ketty placed her hand on Celia's arm and gave it a little squeeze. "Be firm and make it clear what you'd like to do. This is your holiday as well as hers. Just imagine I'm on your shoulder as you talk."

"Hmmm," Celia said. "There's an interesting thought. Between you and Jim I've had lots of moral support."

Ketty looked her steadily in the eye again. "I'm glad you and Jim are getting along."

"Oh...yes...well," Celia mumbled. Jim had been very kind to her but there was nothing more to it than that. "We're both lame ducks in one way or another."

"You're not a lame duck, Celia, and neither is Jim." Ketty opened the door. "Enjoy your night."

Celia stepped into the corridor and turned back. Ketty was framed in the doorway. She looked small, vulnerable perhaps.

"I don't like to leave you."

"I'm fine. The staff have been very helpful and Leo, Josie and Bernard are calling in later to check on me. All this fuss over a bump on the arm."

Celia noticed Ketty's jaw tighten as she lifted the arm in the sling. "Shall I call on you in the morning? See if you need a hand with anything?"

"I'm sure I can manage."

"For my peace of mind then." Celia smiled.

So did Ketty. "See you in the morning," she said and closed the door.

Celia's footsteps, muffled by the carpet, receded. Ketty let out her breath and looked back at the trolley loaded with dishes. She'd ordered for two but she didn't want to tell Celia that Leo was dining in with her. Silly really, as she'd probably find out at dinner from Josie or Bernard.

She moved around to the mirror, leaned in and flicked her hair into place then reapplied her lipstick. She had been more than happy to dine alone after she'd been cleared by the doctor. They had wanted to take her to her room in a wheelchair but she was having none of that. Then Leo had reappeared as she was leaving the medical centre and he'd walked with her to her cabin. She'd mentioned room service was being organised for her and he'd suggested he join her.

She looked up at a tap on her door. And that would be him.

She opened the door. He waved a box of chocolates and a bottle of wine at her.

"Hello."

She stepped back to let him in.

"I know you're not supposed to drink when you're on medication," he said. "But I thought one little glass wouldn't hurt and the chocolates are mandatory."

"Thank you, Leo. That's very thoughtful."

They sat on the balcony, or at least Ketty did while Leo rearranged furniture, bringing the trolley outside and setting it between the two deckchairs. When he was satisfied everything was organised he sat, passed her a glass of wine and raised his.

"Here's to the marvel of us meeting again after all this time."

"Indeed," Ketty said as she touched her glass to his. *Marvel* wasn't quite how she'd put it, perhaps more disbelief, but it was all semantics. Here they were, almost thirty-five years on from when they'd last seen each other. She took a small sip of wine and set the glass back down.

"Purple is your colour," Leo said. "You looked so pale when I brought you back to your cabin but you look...well, you look beautiful."

"It's amazing what a bit of make-up can hide." Compliments were rare these days and she wasn't sure what else to say. She began lifting lids from the dishes Leo had set out in front of them. "I must say it's quite a while since I've had dinner alone with such a handsome man." She glanced up. He was watching her closely and the intensity of his gaze sent a warm shiver through her. It had been risky to agree to dinner with him, on their own with no others to keep their conversation on neutral ground. She thought it best to change the topic to something practical. "Would you like some of these prawns? They look good."

He studied her a moment longer then dished some for her and then for himself. He peeled her prawns, cut the slices of salami and ham into small bites and served her some salad. She could have managed but she let him do it and kept the conversation on cruising, where she'd been, which ships she'd liked the best. He talked about a trip he'd taken to New York and one to Japan. They didn't discuss family or work – Ketty felt it easier not to. She had decided that being with Leo was like meeting someone for the first time. She wanted to start as if from new and not spoil it with conversation that might lead to the past and things she'd prefer not to recall.

Leo had several glasses of wine to her one and finally they could eat no more. Ketty sat back and Leo stacked their dishes before resting against his own seat. They both stared out into the night, cocooned in the warm tropical air and lulled by the soft sounds of the waves against the hull.

It was Leo who broke the silence. "Your business must be doing well."

She hadn't expected that.

"I looked you up today when I was in Port Vila. Made the most of the free wi-fi. Your online shopfront is very professional."

She frowned. "You must have looked at someone else's. Mine's terrible. Has hardly been touched since a young chap set it up for me, years ago. I get feedback saying how awful it is."

He gave her a puzzled look. "Surely there can't be two Ketty Clift Coutures?"

"I don't believe so."

"I can't understand how you don't know you've got such an expert site."

Ketty bristled. "Online has never been a priority. I've built my business by making sure each of my customers have been made to feel special. The personal touch has always come first and I can't see how that can be achieved via a computer..." Her voice trailed away as she recalled Lacey's parting words and giving the go-ahead for the website makeover. "I have a very capable young assistant. I gave her free range to make some changes."

"Is that wise?"

"Obviously if the website is as good as you say it is." Ketty was full of curiosity to look at it herself now. Had Lacey somehow managed to transfer the 'special' from the shop to its online presence? "I have full confidence in my staff."

"What about a financial manager? Or do you do that yourself?"

"I do, with the help of an accountant."

"Finance is my thing, you know." He leaned closer, his look intense. "I could help you."

She tried to imagine what that might be like, to share the responsibility of managing the finances. She opened her mouth and closed it again. Looked away.

"I am sorry for the pain I caused you, Kathy."

His voice was soft, contrite. She reached for her glass but it was empty. He poured the last of the bottle into it. She took a sip. "It's all so long ago and best left there, don't you think?"

"If that's what you want." He reached for the hand she rested on the table. "I'm glad I did end up meeting you again. At least I could be of some help today. Take care of you. I could continue to do so."

Ketty slid her hand from his. "I don't need a carer. I've managed much worse than a bung arm on my own."

He looked surprised and she immediately felt sorry for being so sharp, reminding herself how grateful she'd been for a shoulder to lean on getting back to the ship.

"I'm used to fending for myself," she said more gently this time. She'd learned the hard way not to burden anyone. Perhaps that's why her other relationships hadn't worked out. She'd been in love since Leo. There had been other men who she'd thought could be his replacement but it never worked out. She'd always thought it was because they hadn't measured up but maybe it had been more about her needing to show she could manage alone. Had she pushed them away? The realisation startled her.

"I'm sorry, Kathy." His voice was full of remorse. "I don't know what else to say. I know I can't go back and set it right."

She looked up to find him studying her, a slight frown creasing his brow.

He leaned in again. "I've a lot to make up for, I know, but I had this small hope that we could at least be friends, get to know each other again…see what happens."

Ketty's shoulders sagged. For years she had managed on her own, made every major decision alone, now she wondered what a difference it would make to be able to share the load.

"Is it possible, Kathy?"

Ketty thought about that. She'd overcome great sadness, grief and disappointment to build the life she had now. A life where she hadn't shied away from challenges, new ideas. She drew herself up again, gathering her inner strength to form the protective layer she always kept close and smiled. "Anything's possible, Leo."

Twenty-one

A loud laugh came from the table beside Celia. She looked around at the group who were intent on the man speaking. They all looked so animated and she was acutely aware of the silence at her table. The nightly dining was in full swing all around them and she was used to the routine now, but tonight was different with only herself and Jim. Rupert had cleared Ketty's place as soon as Celia had told him the older woman wasn't coming and then the other places when Jim finally announced they probably weren't coming either.

"Oh, you are all alone tonight," Phillip said. He moved the silver vase with tonight's flower, a red rose, closer.

Celia took in his cheeky grin, then focused on the water he was pouring into their glasses.

"I will be back with your entrées very soon," he said with enthusiasm.

She took a sip from her water glass and glanced along the all-but-empty table. "I wonder where the others have got to? It feels strange to be only the two of us."

"It won't be so busy." Jim's smile was tentative. "It gets noisy when everyone's here. Hard to get a word in sometimes."

They both took sips of wine and lapsed into silence. Celia felt as if they were playing charades. Guess the movie. She immediately thought of *When Harry Met Sally* then imagined the look on Jim's face and other diners if she suddenly started writhing and moaning, imitating Meg Ryan's famous fake orgasm scene. She'd truly be Celebrity Celia then.

She pressed her fingers to her mouth to stop the giggle that burbled up just as Phillip arrived with their entrées. They'd both chosen the smoked duck carpaccio with orange cranberry relish, which he set before them with a flourish. Jim gave an enthusiastic moan. Celia strangled her laugh with her napkin. Not daring to look Jim's way, she snatched up her cutlery. The first mouthful was a mixture of tart and smoky and melted in her mouth, a welcome distraction from her crazy thoughts.

"I hope Ketty's all right," Jim said.

Celia took a calming sip of water and composed herself. "She's recovering but a bit fragile. Something like this could spoil her holiday."

"Somehow I don't think Ketty will let a wounded arm slow her down too much." Jim sat back from his empty entrée plate. "That duck was delicious. Another good reason to come to the dining room."

"The trip's half over already." She pulled a sad face. "I'm not looking forward to going home and cooking for one."

Rupert whipped in to remove their plates.

"I don't know how I'll go back to stir-fries or meat and three veg." Jim grimaced too.

"Were you always a cook, or out of necessity?" Celia asked.

"Jane always got the meals in our younger days but once the kids left home I developed my rather crude skills to perhaps a bit more than basic. And then when she got sick…well…"

"I'm sure your wife appreciated it. Ed never cooked. Except the barbecue but that was only the meat and only ever sausages and chops. If we had steak or shasliks I did it and I made the salads."

"My insurance work kept us in the country, we moved around a lot so barbecues were a good way to meet people."

"More often I would prepare three or four-course dinner parties for staff or clients. He selected the wine. Always made sure there were plenty of drinks. Didn't matter what the event, he stood there and took single-handed praise for the result every time."

"What's his line of work?"

"He runs a firm that looks for people to fit jobs. Headhunts for clients. Mainly engineers in mining."

"I have to admit it was more my forte to cook the meat but the meal was a joint effort. When we moved back to the city Jane made some friends who held regular dinner parties. It was a good way to meet new people and I added to my skills. We always cooked for guests together."

"That sounds like fun." Celia drew in a breath. "I sometimes wonder if that's where Ed and I went wrong. I managed the home and he led a totally separate life at work that I knew little about."

Jim studied her and Celia found herself fiddling with her glass to avoid his scrutiny.

"I must sound bitter," she said. "I don't mean to be. We had a lovely home, two great boys, and I enjoyed entertaining."

"Why did it end?"

She lifted her gaze from the glass and this time he looked away.

"I'm sorry," he said. "That was very nosey of me."

Celia hardly heard his apology. She was back at that restaurant in Sydney again and Ed was telling her it was over. "I was traded for a younger model."

"I'm sorry, Celia. I didn't mean to—"

"In my case it was true the wife was the last to know." She gripped the stem of the glass. "When I look back there were signs, personal things of course, and Ed was away more often and the dinner parties that I was so good at were moved to restaurants and I was invited less often. Then one weekend Ed had to go to Sydney for business and I remember being so excited. The boys had left home and I saw it as a new beginning. Ed travelled all the time for business but I didn't go often and here he was taking me to Sydney.

"We stayed in a beautiful hotel overlooking the harbour. The first night he took me out for dinner and in the middle of the restaurant surrounded by strangers he told me clearly and succinctly he was leaving me."

She looked up, steeling herself to the horror on Jim's face.

"Our two sons had both set off, one overseas, the other to a job in WA. My parents are dead, and my brothers and their wives thought I must have done something to make him stray. I believed it myself for a long time. Most of our nearby friends were his friends. I felt so terribly alone."

"What a cad."

It brought a smile to her face to hear Jim use the old-fashioned word.

"Yes," she said. "That describes Ed to a tee."

Phillip set a plate in front of her. She'd ordered the beef wellington with truffle madeira sauce for mains, and the aromatic scent of it made her mouth water. She glanced over at Jim who was looking equally enraptured over his lobster tail and king prawns in lemon and caper butter. She'd been tempted by the lobster but the beef had won. Rupert topped up their glasses and Jim picked up his knife and fork.

Celia felt a sudden wave of remorse. "Listen to me prattling on. Your wife died. That must have been so terrible."

He paused, a forkful of lobster part way to his mouth. "No point in saying which is the more awful thing. We've both lost our partners and been through the wringer."

They ate in silence for a moment. Celia's delight in her food soured a little as she thought about her failed marriage and the way Ed had treated her. It hurt still but not as much. She hadn't poured it out to anyone like she'd just done with Jim for a long time.

She looked up as he did. "It probably seems odd to say it but there were times in those first months after he left me when I wished Ed had died."

"Understandable after the way he treated you."

"No, not because of that." She drew in a deep breath. "It was because...in spite of everything I still loved him. If he had died I could have at least believed he loved me and mourned that loss. It's so hard to move on when you know the person you love is living a different life without you."

Jim studied her a moment. "Celia, I feel as if I might be speaking out of place." Now it was his turn to fidget with his wine glass. "We haven't known each other long but you seem to be a happy person, content."

She thought about that a moment. "I don't love Ed anymore." She said it with conviction knowing it was true. Then she recalled her reason for booking the cruise and her spectacular tumble on the stairs. She pressed her fingers to her lips but couldn't stop the laugh that erupted.

Jim looked at her in surprise.

She took a sip of water and composed herself. "My ex is on this cruise."

"Really?" Jim glanced around as if he was about to meet Ed.

"The thing is I knew he was going to be here with his new wife."

Jim remained silent, his eyebrows rising a little.

"Do you fancy another wine while I explain?" Celia said.

The bottle was empty. Jim ordered them a glass each and Celia talked as they ate, amazed at first that she wanted to share her sorry tale and then strengthened by it. By the time she got to her embarrassing slide across the floor they were both laughing.

"So you see what a mad woman I truly am," she said.

"Celia Braxton." Jim had laughed so hard he was dabbing tears from his eyes with his handkerchief. "That is the best story I've heard in a long time." Then he looked contrite. "I hope you realise I'm laughing with you, not at you."

"Please don't worry, Jim. I'm past caring either way. And you know the strangest thing, since I no longer care about running into Ed, I haven't seen him once."

"And it was Ketty who helped you to face facts?"

"Yes. I've come to truly like her, you know."

"She's a good woman." He smiled at her. "As are you."

"I don't know about good but I'm certainly feeling a lot more settled." Celia sat back, sated from the delicious meal and at ease from sharing her story.

"You've come through it stronger."

She snorted. "Unless it's Maude I'm talking to."

"Perhaps it's not in your nature to enjoy confrontation."

"No, but tonight I must talk to Maude. I promised Ketty."

"She's a determined personality too."

"But in a good way." Celia lifted her chin. "And she's been right so far. I've had much more fun since I gave up on my project to make Ed jealous." Another giggle erupted as she thought of the stupidity of her plan. "Now it's only Maude I have to set straight. I'm determined to sit her down and have a talk soon." Fortified by alcohol, she actually believed it.

They each had a mouthful of wine left in their glasses. He raised his.

"Here's to you, Celia Braxton. A kind, generous and courageous person. Good luck."

Celia's cheeks felt warm. Other than Ketty she couldn't remember the last time someone had spoken so supportively to her.

Bernard put a guiding arm around Josie as they made their way out of the intimate Italian restaurant.

"I enjoyed that so much," she said. "The food was delicious and," she smiled at him, "it was just the two of us."

"I enjoyed it too." Bernard slipped his arm around her waist. He loved the way she fitted snugly against his body. It was getting late but he didn't want to say goodnight.

"Fancy a nightcap?" he asked.

"I'd actually like one of those non-alcoholic mojitos."

"It's called a nojito. I fancy something sweet myself. Let's go to the bar up on deck."

Josie nestled against him while they waited for the lift. He thought about tomorrow and dinner with Christine. It almost felt like a wasted opportunity. He'd much rather spend his time with Josie. Perhaps he could wriggle out of it.

Up on the pool deck they were greeted by party music and the enveloping warmth of the tropical night.

They found a table for two and Bernard shifted his chair beside Josie so they had a view of the dance floor. He caught the eye of a waiter, ordered their drinks then draped his arm around Josie's shoulders and looked out over the pool where a young couple were still swimming. Bernard didn't want to call it a night. He was keen to see more of her. Very keen, and he got the feeling she felt the same way but he wasn't a hundred per cent sure.

Their drinks came and they both took big mouthfuls.

"That's good," he said.

"I've enjoyed tonight." Josie's eyes sparkled, reflecting the flashing disco lights. "Just you and me."

"I like being with you."

She traced a finger down his cheek and the electric sensation it caused surged through him.

He captured her hand in his. "I'd like to spend some alone time with you."

She glanced around, a smirk on her face. "There aren't many people here."

"I mean somewhere with only the two of us." He leaned across the table and murmured in her ear. "Completely alone."

Josie's eyes shone. "I'm sharing a cabin with my brother."

"I'm not." He kissed her.

"Shall we take our drinks?"

Bernard smiled. He took his glass in one hand and her hand in his other. "This way."

The corridor to his room was totally empty but he couldn't help the sigh of relief as he closed his cabin door behind them. No sign of Christine.

"A queen bed." Josie turned back to look at him. "Not two singles?"

"I asked for it. I hate single beds."

"And two chocolates?"

"The steward is doing her bit for me." Bernard winked. "Don't feel too special. She's given me two every night so far."

Josie stepped out of her shoes and into his arms.

"What about Leo?" he asked. "Won't he wonder where you are?"

She smiled up at him. "I already told him not to expect me home tonight."

Bernard's chest swelled. "Is that so?" He bent his head to meet her lips and this time their kiss was long and slow.

Christine smiled at Frank as he passed her a cocktail in a long tall glass. It was the colour of ginger ale with enough fruit protruding from the top to start a shop. He slid into the spa beside her. After their dinner at the buffet they'd gone back to their room but, just when she thought the night was theirs, the pain in her back had come back in earnest and she couldn't relax. Frank had been the one to suggest they sit in the spa to help her loosen up.

She adjusted the large chunk of pineapple to reach the straw poking out from among the fruit. "Yum, this is good. Refreshing with a bit of a bite." She took another sip. "What is it?"

"Drink of the day. Some kind of punch. It's got dark rum and pineapple juice and a mix of other things."

Christine slid her tongue around her lips. "Pretty sure there's grenadine in there too and it's even got kiwi fruit."

Frank tried it. "Mmm. Perfect cruise drink. We'll be nice and relaxed." He grinned at her, leaned in and as he kissed her his hands slid over her breasts. "We've got to do some making up for lost time."

"Not in a public spa," she hissed and pushed him away.

He grinned. "Not many here to see us."

He was right about that. They were the only two in this spa. A group of four younger people occupied another and a few more sat at the bar but other than that they had the place almost to themselves. She leaned back and closed her eyes. Her back wasn't too bad but she wasn't taking any chances.

"We could have a spa like this."

Christine's eyes shot open. She smiled. She had hoped for a chance to bring up her new ideas for improving their home. If Frank was keen on a spa it might be enough to swing him to her way of thinking. "It could fit with our renovations."

He sat up straight. "No way. I meant if we bought somewhere else."

"I love our home. We've made it special together, it's where every important family event has taken place."

"We'd still have those memories and we'd make new ones at the next place."

"We're not moving, Frank."

"We could even get a pool," he persisted.

"I told you, Frank, no."

"That's just it, you told me." He glared at her. "This is important to me, Christine. Why can't we at least discuss it?"

"We could but I won't be changing my mind." She looked away and took another sip of her drink, fighting back the tears. She couldn't make him understand how lost she'd felt after her mother had died. She'd loved her mum even though they'd had their differences. The family home had been her solace and then her dad had sold it. If it hadn't been for Frank she'd have lost her way completely. When they bought their own place they both put all their energy into it and she vowed her children would never be uprooted from their only home.

"Damn it, Christine, we're a partnership, not a dictatorship."

"Something you only remember when it suits you, Frank. Most of the time you sit back and I have to make the decisions or we would get nowhere." She stabbed at the ice in her glass with the straw. This was not how she'd imagined the conversation going at all. She had to calm things down. She took a moment to drain her drink and place the empty glass on the edge of the spa then she drew in a breath and gave him a smile. "I think dictatorship is a harsh term, don't you? You said yourself we're a team. It's swings and roundabouts and I don't want to argue."

He set down his glass beside hers, then leaned back, arms folded against his chest.

She would leave any reference to renovations until she'd spoken with her dad again. All she could do now was try to distract him. "Let's not spoil this lovely night with an argument. Please, Frank."

He turned to look at her. His brown eyes were troubled but still sparkling in the light from the lanterns swinging overhead.

"We should head back to our room," she said. "I'm ready for a shower."

She leaned in and kissed him. His lips were firm beneath hers then they softened as he responded. His hands swept her body. She pulled back. His gaze was full of desire leaving her in no doubt what he was planning once they were back in their room. She sometimes forgot how easy it was to sway Frank. But her back was giving her curry now in spite of the spa. Bugger, another missed opportunity.

"My back, Frank." She lifted her hand. "Can you help me out?"

He stepped out of the spa ahead of her and offered his hand, the scowl back on his face. "I think I'll have another drink."

"Please yourself." She turned away desperately hoping he'd follow.

"Which clearly means I can't," he muttered.

At the entrance she paused and looked back.

Several people were gathered around the bar. The murmur of their voices drifted on the warm breeze. Frank was headed to join them.

Celia walked through the bar outside the theatre. She had looked in all the bars and lounges and this was her last stop before giving up and going to bed. There were several groups of people either at the bar or seated in the plush sofas at low wooden tables but no sign of Maude and the group she spent most her time with. Celia felt a mix of relief and disappointment. She had worked herself up to talking directly with Maude and now she'd have to wait until tomorrow. Unless perhaps Maude had returned to their room in the time Celia had been looking.

Movement in the far corner caught her eye. She hadn't noticed the couple in the little nook before because the seats had been turned with their high backs to the room. She moved closer. A burst of sharp snorting laughter confirmed Maude's presence.

Celia sucked in a breath and stepped around the chairs. Maude and Pete looked up in surprise, their heads were close together and Pete had his hand on Maude's leg. He snatched it away and they drew apart.

"Hello, Celia." Pete grinned and looked past her. "On your own again?"

Maude tugged at her dress, which had ridden up well past her knees. "There you are," she said as if she'd been the one searching for Celia. "Some of the others are going to the rock star show."

"We're going to join them soon." Pete's grin widened. "Are you coming?"

"No." Her response was sharper than she'd intended. "Thank you." Celia looked directly at Maude. "I need to have a quick word with you...alone."

Pete gave Maude a nudge and a wink.

Maude looked up at her. "We'll catch up later."

"Now please, Maude. I won't keep you long."

"I've been evicted." Pete pulled a mock pout and stood. "Have my seat, Celia. I have to slip off to the gents anyway. I'll get us another drink on my way back, Maude."

"Thanks." Maude gave him a coquettish smile, fluttering eyelids and all.

Celia gritted her teeth as Pete winked back.

"Sit." Maude patted the empty chair next to her.

The wine swirled in Celia's stomach. She'd hoped the wine over dinner, and then one more after her deck walk with Jim, would give her courage but instead she felt nauseous as she took Pete's seat.

"What's so urgent?" Maude said.

Celia perched on the edge of the soft chair and turned her knees towards Maude. Everything she wanted to say sounded mean. She wasn't sure how to start.

"If this is about Nigel, don't worry. He didn't ask after you and tonight after dinner he found another woman to talk to. You're off the hook."

"It's not about Nigel, although I'm glad he's found some other company." Celia also thought he hadn't waited too long before finding someone else but she really didn't care.

"What then?"

"It's about you and me."

Maude gave her a puzzled look.

Celia pressed on before her courage left her altogether. "We're friends but we have quite different tastes, wouldn't you say?"

"Are we talking men here?"

Celia looked down and smoothed the wrinkles in her trousers. "In general. You're obviously having a good time with Pete and Anne—" Celia emphasised her name "—and the others and it's kind of you to include me but I sometimes have my own plans."

"Reading a book or walking the deck is not a plan, Celia. It's a cop out. You need to—"

"You don't know what I need, Maude." Celia lifted her shoulders and looked Maude in the eye. "That's for me to decide, not you, and I'd prefer it if you didn't expect me to do everything you do. It's fun to do some things together but don't suppose that I'm going to join you every minute of the day."

"Well, you haven't, have you?" Maude sat back and folded her arms.

"And that's okay, isn't it? We don't have to do everything together. I've made a few friends of my own."

"So you don't want me to include you in my plans?"

"It's not that." Celia fought desperately for the right words. She didn't want to upset her friend but she had to make herself clear. She imagined Ketty sitting on her shoulder. "We should discuss our plans. You might want to do something I suggest sometimes."

"Trivia and shopping." Maude rolled her eyes.

"Each to their own." Celia stood her ground. "I want to be able to do my own thing without upsetting you."

"I don't get upset."

"Good." Celia nodded her head, relieved now. "I've made friends at my table too. We've done a few things together. So from now on you and I *suggest* things to do and if we want to go our different ways then that's okay."

"I don't know what you're going on about, Celia. It's always been okay."

Celia smiled and nodded. Maude didn't get it but from now on Celia would have to stand her ground. She was about to say goodnight when Maude shot forward in her chair.

"You've found a man, haven't you? That's what this is about." Maude nodded, her face wide with a knowing grin. "Who is he? Someone from your table?"

Celia gaped at her.

"Can't be the buff bald guy. I've seen him drinking with a flashy blonde." Maude's eyes widened and she jabbed one short finger in the air. "It's the other one. The guy with the brooding sad face."

Celia frowned. "Jim?"

Maude gave her a playful tap. "You're a sly one."

"What's going on?" Pete came round the chair carrying two drinks. "I'm sorry, Celia, I should have got you something. I can go back."

"No." Celia shot to her feet, nearly colliding with him. "I'm leaving now." Her cheeks were warm again. She glanced at Maude. "I'll see you later."

"Maybe." Maude winked.

"Goodnight."

Celia spun on her heel and hurried away, her conversation with her friend going around and around in her head. She was quite sure now Maude hadn't got the gist of anything she'd been trying to say and instead had put two and two together and come up with six. The thought of Jim as anything more than a friendly table companion was simply ludicrous.

Twenty-two

Day Six – At Anchor, Lifou, New Caledonia

The sound of knocking on his door woke Bernard from a deep sleep. He peered through slitted eyes at the light filtering into the room from around the curtains and tried to remember where he was. The knock came again.

"Dad?"

He sat bolt upright as his memory flooded back. He glanced at the bed beside him. It was empty. Then he realised he could hear the shower. Josie must be in the bathroom. He swung his legs to the edge of the bed and sat waiting to regain his equilibrium. If Christine could hear the sounds of the shower through the door she would hopefully think it was him.

The knock didn't come again. He picked up his watch. It was not quite eight o'clock. No doubt she was wanting him to go to breakfast with her but dinner tonight would be enough.

He stood up, stretched, drew back the curtains and couldn't help but smile as he recalled last night with Josie. He dragged on his shorts and opened the balcony door. The warmth of the tropical day greeted him. He felt like a new man.

"Good morning."

He turned. Josie stood outside the bathroom door wearing his robe. He smiled, crossed the space between them, took her in his arms and planted a kiss on her lips. He pressed his face to her neck. "Mmmm. Don't you smell good?"

"Much better for a shower." She eased away from him and crossed to her neat pile of clothes where she slipped on her underwear, completely unperturbed by his eyes devouring her. "I need to head back to my room for some fresh things." She gave him a wicked smile. "Shall we have breakfast later?"

"I'd like to spend the day with you." He lowered himself to the bed. "I've promised to have dinner with Christine tonight... just the two of us."

"That's okay, Bernie." She slipped her dress over her head. "She's your only daughter and you don't see each other often. I get she wants to have you to herself at some stage."

He reached for her hand and pulled her gently down beside him. "I told you Christine has not been very accepting of my past relationships."

"And I told you." She patted his nose with her finger. "I can take care of myself."

Bernard couldn't raise a smile.

She escaped his wandering hands and stood to look in the mirror. He watched her drag her fingers through her hair and apply some lipstick from her purse knowing he would do whatever it took to keep seeing her.

Her gaze shifted to meet his in the mirror. "I'd better check in on Leo."

"Shall we meet in half an hour?"

She glanced at her watch. "I might need longer than that. Can we make it nine?" She bent down and kissed his cheek.

He stood up, pulled her close and kissed her. "Sounds like a plan."

"I'll meet you downstairs where they gather for the tender." She brushed her fingers down his cheek and let herself out, leaving Bernard with a warm tingling feeling coursing through his body. Josie was one hell of a woman. Now he was wishing neither of them had family on this cruise with them.

A knock sounded on Ketty's door. She berated herself for the lift in her spirits as she imagined Leo at the door even though they'd agreed to meet later, on the island.

"Coming."

She got up from her seat on the balcony where she had been watching the scenery as the ship had anchored off Lifou. This island was high on her list of favourites in this region. There was a lot of cloud cover but she'd enjoyed small bursts of early morning sunshine as she ate the breakfast that had been delivered to her room.

When she opened the door it was Celia who waited on the other side.

"Oh, you're dressed already," Celia said.

"Took me a while but I managed. I had to pick things with no buttons."

"How are you feeling?"

"Much better, thank you." Ketty hoisted her arm. "Except for this sling. It's driving me mad. Are you in a hurry? Would you like to come in?"

"Yes. At least, no…"

Ketty waited.

Celia looked her squarely in the eye. "I'm not in a hurry and I'd like to come in."

"Good. Go out on the balcony. It's glorious out there this morning."

"Oh gosh, what a view. Lifou looks beautiful. And we've stopped."

Ketty followed Celia out. "We've been at anchor for a while."

"This is the first I've been outside. I was awake early and went down for breakfast. Thought I'd call in here on my way back to my room."

They both sat. Celia kept staring towards shore, while the fingers of one hand fiddled with the edge of her shirt. Last night she'd looked vibrant in the red blouse she wore over white pants but today she was insipid again in a wishy-washy top of pale yellows and muted browns.

"Is everything all right?" Ketty leaned forward a little. "You look distracted. Did you talk to Maude?"

"Yes, I did, and no it's not."

"Oh, I'm sorry. Didn't she take it well?"

"Maude?" Celia blew a little puff of breath over her lips. "She took it in her stride as Maude does with everything. I couldn't have made it any plainer." She grinned. "I even imagined you sitting on my shoulder, but I don't think she got my point at all."

"Perhaps after she's slept on it."

"She certainly slept all right. She tends to snore after a few drinks. I on the other hand tossed and turned all night. Thus this sallow complexion and I might see if Josie has something to help hide this." Celia put her fingers to her cheek.

Ketty could see the bruise was turning the colours of the rainbow.

"This morning when I left for breakfast Maude was still sleeping. I couldn't face her."

"Sounds like you had a good try at a talk. If she didn't..."

Ketty's voice dried in her throat at Celia's stricken look.

"She thinks I'm having an affair with Jim."

Celia looked very distressed. Ketty opened her mouth and closed it again. She suppressed the chortle that wanted to escape.

"An affair?"

Celia flapped her hands. "Well, a relationship. I can't remember her exact words."

"And are you?"

"Ketty! I'm friends with him, same as you, and that's it. And you of all people know how fragile Jim is. He's still up to his neck in grief for his wife."

Ketty nodded but didn't speak.

"I like his company and we're definitely friends...but...damn." Celia flapped her hands again. "We're not in a relationship."

Ketty thought about her dinner with Leo the previous evening. If someone had put her feelings under the microscope she'd be flustered like Celia. They'd kept things casual in the end. After they'd made plans to meet on Lifou this morning he'd given her a chaste goodnight kiss on the cheek and left. Ketty hadn't slept straight away with so many thoughts whirring in her head and her arm aching on and off.

"Try not to think about it," she said. "Putting a label on feelings often makes them into something they're not." She shifted her arm slightly into a more comfortable position.

"Ketty, I'm so sorry. Here you are helping me with my problems and you have your own."

Ketty studied Celia. No doubt Josie and Bernard had filled her in about Leo's dining with her and their past link.

"Your arm," Celia said. "You've got enough to deal with."

Ketty let out a breath. "Truly, it's much better this morning. The odd twinge that's all. How was dinner last night?"

"Strange but nice." Celia grinned. "It was only Jim and I." The smile slipped from her face. "Not because we planned it. None of the others turned up."

"Really, that's odd. Bernard and Josie may have taken the opportunity to dine alone. Leo was here—"

"Was he?" Celia glanced around as if she was expecting him to appear. "I thought you had a lot of dishes for one person."

Ketty regretted her slip. "I didn't say anything because I didn't want you jumping to conclusions like Maude."

"You're right. I'm sorry." Celia's look was contrite. "You said you knew each other a long time ago. It must be strange to catch up after all these years."

"Strange is the perfect word for it." Ketty felt a sudden urge to share. Instead she changed the subject. "Why don't I give Josie a call? She's only down the hall and if she's still in her room she could pop by with her make-up bag of tricks."

Celia nodded and Ketty put in the call.

"She's on her way," she said as she replaced the handset.

Celia had followed her back into the cabin. With the sun shining across her face the bruise was prominent.

"Celia, I hope you won't be offended but I've been looking at your top and it does nothing for your complexion."

"Oh." Celia looked down. "I got this at the op shop at home. I didn't think about the colour. Thought the fabric the right weight for the tropics."

"So it's not dear to your heart?"

"Good heavens no. I'll probably donate it back when I go home."

"I have a suggestion."

Ketty crossed the cabin, opened the wardrobe doors and began to rummage with her free hand.

"Oh my goodness," Celia said looking over her shoulder. "How on earth did you get all these clothes aboard?"

Ketty laughed. "Years of practice. And I didn't have to fly so weight's not an issue."

There was a knock on the door and Celia opened it. Josie came in carrying a small case and flapping an envelope that she passed to Ketty.

"You had mail in your door holder."

Ketty glanced at the envelope embossed with the ship's letterhead. No doubt another invitation to something in the Diamond Lounge, one of the perks of her frequent traveller status.

"That looks like one considerable make-up bag," Celia waggled a finger at Josie's bag.

"I take my make-up very seriously." Josie looked at the open wardrobe. "Ooh. Are we doing a makeover? I love the chance to delve into Ketty's collection."

Celia looked from Josie to Ketty.

"Not a makeover," Ketty said. "I was searching for a top to give Celia a bit of a lift. With her poor bruised face she's in need of some colour."

"Won't that make it worse?" Celia said. "Last night my red top made the bruise look like it was glowing."

"Your make-up would have been wrong." Josie's tone was matter-of-fact. She reached in and swiped a towel from Ketty's bathroom. "Have a seat and I'll get started."

While Josie went to work on Celia's face, Ketty pulled out several tops and laid them on the bed. Her arm forgotten, she went back for scarves and necklaces. This was where she felt at home. She and Josie had had a lot of fun last cruise. Not that much of Ketty's clothing had been any good to Josie, she was a good size bigger, but they'd played with styles, colours, accessories. Celia on the other hand was more Ketty's size. Her bust was a little smaller but other than that they were similar.

"There we are." Josie stepped away from the front of Celia's chair so she could see herself in the mirror.

Celia's mouth dropped open and she leaned forward. "You can barely see the bruise but that lipstick…you don't think it's a bit bright?"

"What do you think, Ketty?" Josie asked.

Ketty took in the earthy orange tone. "Perfect." She lifted a shirt from the bed. "And this should brighten up your face and those black pants."

Celia studied the garment in Ketty's hand. "But that's yellow. I thought you said yellow washed me out."

"There's yellow and there's yellow." Josie took the shirt from Ketty and draped it across Celia's chest. "This is a soft colour, not too pale, not too bright, and the little black palm tree pattern ties it in with your pants."

They both looked from the mirror to Ketty. "Exactly right."

"Why don't you try it on?" Josie urged.

Celia still hesitated.

"We're used to clothing changes but if you'd prefer, use my bathroom," Ketty said.

Celia had her old shirt over her head before any more could be said and Josie helped her into Ketty's offering. The top was semi-fitted with a side zip, and finished just below the waistband of her capri pants.

"There you are," Josie said. "A few years younger already. Not that you didn't look good before but..."

"It's all right," Celia turned her head from side to side. "I do see what you mean."

"Try these with it." Ketty held up a set of black wooden beads. When Celia put them on they sat above the square neckline of the shirt.

"So, is this to impress Jim?" Josie's question fell like a blanket over the room but she didn't seem to notice. "He's a good-looker." She glanced from Ketty to Celia's stunned face reflected in the mirror. "Don't look so horrified. He's very debonair, relatively trim still. He must look after himself." She fluffed at Celia's hair with her fingers. "I'm very happy with Bernie but I can still admire a good man when I see one. Surely you've both noticed Jim's rather attractive."

Ketty took in Celia's jaw which had dropped nearly to her chest and had to stifle her laugh.

"There is never a dull moment with you two," Celia said.

"Pot, kettle, black, Celia," Ketty said.

"I'd better get going." Josie packed up her bag. "I'm meeting Bernie in a while to catch the tender ashore. Leo said he was meeting you mid-morning, Ketty."

"Yes." She began to put away the clothing and accessories she'd spread over her bed, aware that Celia was watching her closely.

"I think it's wonderful you two have found each other again after all this time. He told me you knew each other before Marjorie came on the scene but you lost touch. Pity he married her instead of you. We could have been sisters-in-law."

Ketty remained rigid on the spot, clutching a bundle of necklaces tightly in her hand. What on earth had Leo been saying?

Josie had a mischievous gleam in her eye as she reached Ketty's side. "Still could be." She gripped Ketty's hand as she passed. "Since he caught up with you Leo's been a different man to the one I came aboard with. I do hope things work out." She began to hum a tune.

This time it was Ketty's turn to gape as Josie departed, the door clunked shut and the sound of humming faded away down the corridor. Behind Ketty there was the soft rustle of clothing and the squeak of a chair.

"He's the one, isn't he?" Celia's voice was little more than a whisper.

Ketty turned slowly, clutching the necklaces to her chest.

Celia was standing now. "Leo is the man you said you were a fool over...the married man."

Ketty nodded then sank to the bed, her back to Celia again. Now she wished she'd never shared her story. What had possessed her? She was usually the master of keeping things close to her chest.

"Josie doesn't know the full story, I gather?"

This time Ketty shook her head.

Celia came to stand beside her. "How do you feel about him now?"

"I..." Ketty looked up at Celia's concerned face. "I don't know."

"But you did love him once?"

"A long time ago."

"He's not married now."

"No."

Celia sat beside her on the bed. "This cruise has thrown us both some curve balls, hasn't it?"

"You might put it that way." Ketty rubbed the beads between her fingers. Meeting Leo again had been a shock and stirred up so many memories and emotions but above all it had renewed hope. Not that Ketty had given up being hopeful about life in general. In the face of obstacles and in her darkest moments she'd always had hope. People talked about resilience, perhaps it was that way of thinking that had kept her afloat. But now she found her hope focusing on Leo all over again and she worried that could be a mistake.

Celia shifted slightly, turning to look at Ketty. "You know you said to me you were pleased when I told you about me trying to make myself into something I wasn't for Ed."

Ketty frowned. Had she said that? Then she remembered. "I was only relieved you weren't that person you were trying to be."

"Well, now I'm relieved. It's petty in a way but apart from your confession to an affair so long ago, you seem to have life all stitched up. You're so self-assured, knowledgeable, as if nothing would ever go amiss for you."

Ketty wanted to laugh at that. If only Celia knew all the things that had gone wrong and not just little things, life-changing things.

"And here you are uncertain like the rest of us mere mortals."

Ketty shook her head. "I'm human. Cut me and I bleed."

"Oh, I think we've had enough injuries between us."

Ketty smiled at Celia. She badly wanted to direct the limelight away from herself. "And now I'm going to dispense more of my wondrous wisdom." She patted Celia's leg. "Jim has become your friend and I think he's in need of one. Don't let something Maude said spoil that friendship. Not only that, I think Josie's right. He's darn good-looking and if I were a younger woman I'd give you a run for your money." She laughed.

"Ketty!" At first Celia looked shocked then she began laughing too. "Oh, Ketty." She shook her head.

It felt good to laugh. Beside her Celia tipped her head to one side.

"What was that tune Josie was humming as she left? I feel as if I know it."

"'Love is in the Air'."

"Oh, yes."

They looked at each other and chuckled again.

"When are you going ashore?" Ketty asked.

"I had planned to meet Jim…that was before I spoke to Maude."

"Forget about Maude. What time?"

"Nine, downstairs."

Ketty thought about the lesson she'd booked at the internet cafe. She was keen to see what Leo had been referring to regarding her website but she could do that later. "Do you mind if I come too?"

"I'd love you to, as long as you're feeling up to it. I'd rather it was more than Jim and I."

"I'm not letting this arm stop me from going ashore." Ketty dropped the beads and sat up straight. "Anyway, I'm meeting Leo there later."

"That's right." Celia stood. "I have a few things to do first. I'll see you at nine."

Ketty remained on the bed after Celia had let herself out. In the past she'd not allowed herself to rely on others emotionally and now she was contemplating allowing Leo to get to know her again, to perhaps draw back the screen she put up around her feelings. Was it foolish? Ketty stood up, inhaled deeply and prepared to go ashore. There was one thing for certain, she wasn't going to find out sitting in her cabin.

Twenty-three

"Come in together, folks." The photographer waved a hand.

Jim slid his arms around Ketty then Celia. Mindful of Ketty's sling he drew both women closer. Behind them the rail of the small landing jetty pressed against his back. A soft breeze ruffled their clothes and Ketty laughed. He smiled for the camera and surprised himself with the thought that he might actually like to keep this photo.

The photographer leaned in, snapped and looked at his screen. "Great, thanks," he said. "Enjoy your day on Lifou."

Celia busied herself picking up her bag. The next group were already lining up for their photo. Jim took up Ketty's bag in spite of her protests and began to move off down the jetty towards the beach.

"Shall we find ourselves a spot under the trees?" Ketty suggested. "I'm going to sit and enjoy the view while I wait for Leo but you two should explore."

"Oh, yes...well...if you're sure." Celia's head was bent over her bag again.

Jim nodded and led the way to the grassy area above the beach. He wondered if he'd said something to upset Celia. She'd hardly said a word to him since they met to board the tender and she was rather jumpy.

He stopped at a flat clearing where the grass was short and the area shaded by palms. "What about here?"

"Perfect. Would you be a gem and spread my towel under that tree, please Jim?" Ketty pointed at the thick base of a palm.

He did as she asked and helped her to sit.

"Isn't this beautiful?" Ketty waved at the vista in front of them.

Jim turned to take it in. It was very much like Champagne Beach but this time he noticed the white of the beach, the turquoise of the sea and the earthy smells of the lush vegetation. He felt a different man from the one who'd boarded the ship six days ago.

Two little pigs darted between their feet. Celia squealed and he chuckled, delighting in the surprise on her face.

"Certainly is," he said. Celia ducked her head away from his look and set her towel down on the other side of Ketty.

"You two should walk up to the little church at the top of the hill," Ketty said. "The church is interesting and the view amazing."

"Are you sure you're feeling okay?" Celia asked.

"Quite sure. I've hardly any pain this morning." Ketty lifted her arm inside the sling.

She was being very stoic but Jim had noticed her wince once or twice when she thought no one was looking.

"I'm going to ditch this sling soon," she said.

"Keep it on a little longer," he said. "It probably helps to keep it immobilised."

Ketty studied him closely. "Words of wisdom and caring," she said softly. She turned to Celia. "You've both been so kind. Thank you for checking in on me."

Jim smiled at Celia who once again looked away quickly, a pink tinge deepened the colour of her cheeks.

"Oh look," she said. "There's Christine from our table."

Jim shifted his gaze to a woman standing below them on the beach. "So it is."

"She's on her own," Ketty said. "Perhaps we should—"

"No, she's not." Celia nodded in the direction Christine was facing along the beach. "That's Frank coming, isn't it? I recognise his shirt."

They watched as Frank arrived in front of Christine whose hands were now on her hips.

"I wonder what Frank has done wrong now?" Ketty mused.

"It looks like he's getting a tongue lashing," Jim said.

"She can be very brusque," Celia said.

"I think she's simply got a case of no-filter mouth."

"Do you?" Ketty turned her piercing look on Jim. "You see, I think she's quite calculated with what she says. And when someone is deliberately hurtful or antagonistic I find there's usually an underlying reason." She looked back to where Frank and Christine were now moving off along the beach. "Something's bothering that young woman and I can't put my finger on it."

"You're very kind, Ketty." Jim didn't find Christine a particularly nice person.

"At the moment all I feel is weary." She put a second rolled-up towel behind her back. "I was awake very early this morning and I've come prepared to snooze. What are you two going to do?"

Jim glanced across at Celia. "Do you fancy a walk up to this church? Then we could come back for a swim."

"I'm not going near the water," Celia said. "Not after yesterday."

"A walk on the beach then," Jim said.

"As long as you'll be all right here on your own, Ketty."

"Me and half the ship, you mean." Ketty waved her hand with a flourish. "I'm perfectly fine." She glanced at her watch. "Anyway, I'm meeting Leo in half an hour."

Jim rose to his feet and held out his hand to help Celia up. She looked at it a moment as if it might bite her then accepted his offer.

"We shouldn't be long," she said.

Ketty had already lowered her hat over her eyes. "Take all the time you like. Just make sure you're back before the last tender leaves."

"We'll be back long before that," Celia said.

Jim smiled as they walked away. "Ketty is amusing. I wish I had half of her spark."

"But you do, Jim," Celia said. "I know you're finding it difficult at the moment but I think there's a cheerful man within. You'll find him again eventually."

They'd stopped and Celia was looking at him earnestly.

"I've been in the doldrums so long I'd forgotten how to smile. You and Ketty have helped me to find it."

"Oh…well…let's do this walk, shall we?"

Jim had to suppress a laugh as she almost tripped in her hurry to move ahead.

Christine watched from her position on the beach as Frank ducked under the water again. He was some distance from shore, and several other people were snorkelling nearby, but even so she was edgy with him being out there by himself. She was cross with him as well, which didn't help her mood.

She'd been asleep when he'd eventually returned to their room last night but she'd been woken by his fumbling about and then kept awake by his snoring. This morning he'd been a bit seedy but behaving as if nothing had happened. When they'd come over to the island they'd lost each other and she'd spent fifteen minutes looking for him, eventually tracking him down on the beach. He'd wanted to go off exploring but she'd said her back hurt and told him how terrible he looked and his drinking better not ruin their day, to which he'd had a dig about her drinking.

He was swimming towards her now, shortening the distance between them with his easy strokes, then he stopped, saw her watching and waved. She waved back. Frank was never one to stay angry for long. She tried hard to swallow her own resentment. He stood in the shallow water and walked slowly out towards her. Her eyes drank him in and a different fire started to build, warming the pit of her stomach and moving lower. Frank's usually short hair had been left to grow over the summer. It dripped with water as he swept it back from his face, his jaw still covered in the shadow of his overnight stubble. It was hard to stay cross with him when he looked so desirable. And annoying to think it was already day six. They were halfway through the cruise and had barely more than kissed each other.

"Feel better?" she asked as he reached for his towel.

"Much." He rubbed himself all over, spread the towel on the sand beside her then he stretched out on his stomach, rolled to his side and propped himself up on one elbow. "It was beautiful in the water. You should go in."

"I can't be bothered."

"You would cool off." He trailed a finger down her arm.

His touch made her shiver. "I don't want to swim on my own."

"I'll come with you." He leaned in and kissed her shoulder. His lips were cool on her sun-warmed skin.

"You've just been in."

"I'll go again." He nuzzled her neck.

It felt so good. She groaned. Why couldn't they be like this in the privacy of their cabin instead of on a beach they were sharing with a thousand other people? A dull ache radiated between her hips as she leaned against him. And why of all times did she have to have hurt her back?

He stopped suddenly and got to his feet, reaching for her hand. "Come on."

"My back."

"A swim will be good for you."

She let him help her to her feet then she slipped off the floaty short caftan she'd worn over her bathers. Frank's eyes devoured her as if she were naked.

"We're not alone you know, Frank."

He let out a low growl. "Do we care?"

Then he winked and her legs went to jelly. How she loved it when Frank acted like she was hot. She glanced down and all she could see were black rolls trapped inside her sculpted control bathers.

He took her hand and started pulling her towards the water.

"Wait," she cried but he towed her with him. She shambled forward over the rocky bottom, the water deepening quickly. She toppled and went under with a splash then came up gasping for breath. She was about to complain even though her back hadn't so much as twinged but his lips pressed to hers and this time they were warm. He took her hand and led her out deeper then wrapped his body around hers.

"Frank." Her protest was lost as his mouth closed over hers again. She groaned.

He slid around behind her and drew her body against his.

"Hello." A couple swam past them. "Beautiful in, isn't it."

She nodded. Frank's hands were massaging her breasts under the water, while a few metres away a family snorkelled past. She gripped his hands.

"Frank, stop," she hissed.

He laughed, let her go and ducked under the water, swimming away. When he came up he was grinning.

Christine couldn't remember the last time he'd been this playful. "You're obviously feeling a lot better."

He swam back to her, his eyes glazed with desire. "No matter what happens, we are having an early night tonight, babe."

"We could have had one last night if you hadn't stayed out drinking."

His smile slipped away. She was immediately sorry she'd snapped.

"You have a bad back, remember?" He looked at her pointedly.

Her mouth fell open. "Are you suggesting I'm making it up? It comes and goes you know but the pain is a lot less now."

He shrugged. "Tonight's the night then." He smiled but there was no mirth in it.

"I'm having dinner with Dad," she said. "I'll try not to be late."

Frank made no comment. He stared at her a moment, looked away then back at her again and this time his look was rigid with determination. The warm day receded and she felt a chill wriggle down her spine.

"I'm going to apply for that job as soon as we get back."

That wasn't what she'd expected. "What job?"

"The one I told you about the other day."

"Oh." She'd pushed it to the back of her mind hoping he'd given up on the idea.

He glared at her. "Head of garbage, remember?"

She remembered the argument. Opened her mouth to protest. She'd apologised already for that.

"I need another dip," he said, gave her a mock salute and sank under the water, kicking with his feet so that water splashed in her face.

"Frank!" She brushed at her eyes.

He came up a few metres on and swam away with long steady strokes. Where was the Romeo he'd been only a few minutes before?

She watched him a moment then turned for the beach but a small niggle of fear wormed inside her. Nothing was going to plan with Frank. She took a deep calming breath as she reached the shore. The cruise might be half over but there was still time. Once she had this dinner with her father and got their money sorted she was sure Frank would come round. They'd turn their current home into something from the home magazines and perhaps he wouldn't want to change jobs. Not that she minded if he did, as long as they could stay in their home. She thought of it now. The roses would be in full bloom and if she opened her bedroom window, their delicious scent would waft through. She and Frank had painstakingly rubbed back and painted each section of the five-panelled bay window with its leadlight glass. It wasn't a huge room but if they built a walk-in robe and en suite off the side, it would be perfect. She picked up her towel. After dinner with her father she'd bring drinks to the cabin and she and Frank would celebrate and make up for lost time.

"Excuse me."

Celia looked around. An older woman was beckoning her from the lookout.

"Would you mind taking a photo of Harold and I with the ship behind, please dear?"

"Of course." Celia took the camera the woman held out. She lifted it up and peered at the screen. It was a great picture. There was a vivid green tree behind the man and the sea behind the woman with their ship just over her shoulder. Celia snapped a couple of shots.

"I hope one of them will be all right." She handed the camera back.

"Thank you. Would you like one of you with your husband?"

Celia stiffened. "Oh…no…" She shook her head. "We're not—"

"I've got my phone." Jim cut her off. "We can use that." He drew his phone from his pocket and prepared it for the woman, who was smiling kindly. Then he stepped up to the rail and looked expectantly at Celia. He was taller than her, thin but not reedy. His arms and chest filled out the t-shirt he was wearing very nicely. "Celia?"

Both Jim and the woman were looking at her expectantly. Celia moved to stand next to him trying hard not to touch him, but his arm reached around her shoulders and drew her close.

"What a lovely couple," the woman gushed. "Smile, dear."

Celia tried but all she could think of was the warm arm resting across her shoulders. She held herself rigid but her stomach felt like a herd of butterflies had erupted inside her. It had been a long time ago she'd last felt like that.

"There you are." The woman handed back Jim's phone. "I hope I've got you in the picture. I'm not so good with phones, I'm afraid."

"Thank you," he said as the woman took Harold's arm and moved on.

Celia turned back to the view but her eyes didn't take in the ship at anchor in the bay. She was conscious of the quick drop away of his arm and his shuffle away from her.

"Sorry to go along with that woman assuming we were a couple," Jim said. "It seemed easier."

"Yes." She risked a sideways glance. He was leaning stiffly on the rail, staring forward.

He turned to look at her. His face was full of anguish. "I hope it didn't bother you when I put my arm around you. No point in explaining we hardly know each other."

"No." Celia looked out to sea again; her mind in turmoil. He was obviously regretting the moment of intimacy that had hit her like a bolt. She had long forgotten that warm rush of adrenalin. She'd realised in that moment when Jim's arm had slipped around her that she liked him very much. Maude and Ketty had both been right. He was a lovely man, decent and kind and what she felt for him was more than friendship. Ed's rejection had all but destroyed her self-esteem and left her terribly hurt. After her confession to Ketty the other night, Celia had realised she didn't care about him anymore and she truly could move on. But it was different for Jim. He was still deep in grief and she could tell by his look he was embarrassed.

He walked further away. "I'm glad Ketty suggested we come up here."

"You are?" Celia gripped the rough wooden rail that edged the viewing platform.

"Don't you think the view was worth it?"

"Oh...yes." She focused on the panorama before her. Stupidly she'd hoped he was going to say because of her company.

The warmth that his touch had brought ebbed away, dampened by regret. She knew she had to swallow any feelings for him other than friendship. Even if he, by some wild chance, felt something for her, he wasn't in the right space to reciprocate. How ironic that she had rejected Nigel only to find a man who would no doubt reject her. She shook her head. Unrequited love at her age.

"What do you think about Ketty and this Leo bloke?"

"Leo?" Celia was still struggling with thoughts of Jim.

"He's making a play for her."

"A play?" Celia tried to concentrate on what he was saying.

"Perhaps that's the wrong term but he's laying on the charm with her."

"They knew each other a long time ago."

"I gathered that. When he appeared at our table that first night Ketty was shocked."

"Was she? I don't remember. I suppose it would have been a big surprise. They had been lovers—" She clamped her hand to her mouth. "Oh damn! Please don't say anything. Ketty confided in me."

"Of course I wouldn't. It's just that Ketty's been very kind to me and I wouldn't like to see her hurt."

"She seems quite happy to get to know him again." Celia thought about Ketty's self-assurance. "You think Leo would upset her?"

"I don't know. It's a feeling I have about him, something I can't quite put my finger on."

"I'm sure Ketty will manage him." She gave Jim a worried look. "Please don't say anything."

"Of course not." Jim inclined his head towards her. "Don't worry, your secret's safe with me."

There was nothing more than reassurance in his look but Celia's heart thudded in her chest regardless. She turned away and fanned herself with her hand. "It's quite humid, isn't it?"

"Shall we head down then? We could paddle in the water if you don't want to swim." His serious look was replaced with a grin. "I'll be on snake watch."

"Good idea." Celia turned, stepping quickly forward. In her hurry she missed her footing on the edge of the viewing platform. Just as she thought she was going to repeat her awful tumble aboard ship, a strong arm steadied her. She looked down at Jim's hand grasping her elbow.

"Careful."

She glanced up, the heat in her cheeks so strong now she could act as a lighthouse for this look-out point.

"You didn't hurt yourself, did you?"

"No."

"I'm glad. I was wondering how I was going to carry you down that mountain if you'd turned your ankle." He grimaced. "I'm sorry. I wasn't meaning that you're too heavy, more that I'm not as fit as...I used to...be." His words dwindled to a stop.

Celia turned away. "We should go." She moved ahead and took the lead back down the steep path. The journey would give her time to compose herself. The last thing she needed was to make more of a fool of herself than she already had.

Ketty was grateful for the seat Leo had found for them in the shade of one of the thatched shelters. The day was humid and she was feeling it. In front of them a group of islanders in bright red sarongs and headdresses were preparing to act out a welcome ceremony. They were all ages, shapes and sizes, and being directed by one older woman, her grass headpiece wobbling wildly from side to side as she moved her ample arms.

Leo arrived back with ice creams.

"I didn't expect to be able to buy ice cream on the beach at Lifou," he said as he removed the wrapper from hers and then his.

Ketty could have unwrapped her own but she let him do it. She took a bite. "Mmm, thank you. This is exactly what I felt like."

"Can't remember the last time I bought an ice cream."

"Really? I love ice cream. It's a staple in my freezer." Ice cream had always been a favourite. They'd eaten it together. He'd obviously forgotten.

"My freezer's a bit depleted these days. I'm not very good at managing for one." His look was glum.

Ketty felt a flick of annoyance at that. She was used to living alone. He'd said there'd been no one serious since Marjorie but she wondered about that now. He was sounding like one of those men who was accustomed to being looked after. She took another bite of her ice cream and decided to change the subject. "You mentioned earlier you were going to set up a new financial planning practice when you get home."

He sucked in a breath, groaning as he let it out. "Yes."

"You don't want to?"

"Yes and no. At my age and in my line of business I imagined I'd be financially well off, not starting again from scratch."

"Oh." Ketty understood the sentiment and felt the re-emergence of anxiety for her own business.

"Marjorie took me to the cleaners after we split and the kids needed money."

"Kids?" She'd known he'd had at least one child.

"Well, they're adults now. Three of them."

Three! Ketty swallowed the hard lump that had formed in her throat. There was a time when she'd have given anything to have one child. The other two must have come after she'd left

Adelaide. He must have stayed with Marjorie for longer than he'd intimated, unless someone else was the mother. She wanted to ask but couldn't bring herself to.

"All doing their own thing but still with their hands out," he went on. "Anyway, after Marjorie...well, let's say she got the house and nearly everything else, I started from scratch, was finally doing okay again, then last year my partner did the dirty. It's all been messy, court proceedings, lies and smoke screens but in this case the truth didn't out and...the bottom line is I've been left with little." His voice was bitter and he stared off into the distance as ice cream dripped down his hand. He took out a clean handkerchief and wiped at the white dribbles as if they were poison. The stick and the remaining ice cream were shoved into the wrapper and stuck under his chair. "You're lucky to have remained sole owner and manager," he said giving her a smile now. "You're a smart woman, Ketty."

"It hasn't been easy."

"Running your own business never is but you're one of the lucky ones, successful."

Ketty thought about that. It was on the tip of her tongue to tell him how close to losing everything she was. He'd offered to help. Perhaps he would be able to suggest something the accountant hadn't thought of. And how good would it be to share the burden of her worry? Not with an employee like Judith but with a friend, that's how she thought of Leo now, and a friend who understood business.

"Josie and Bernard have turned up." He gave a nod.

She followed the direction he was looking. A crowd was forming closer to where the dancers were setting up and Josie and Bernard were standing among them.

"How well do you know this Bernard fellow she's taken up with?"

Ketty wiped ice cream from the corners of her lips. "Little more than you do, why?"

Leo turned to her and leaned closer. "Don't say anything to Josie but I've had to bail her out in the past. She's…she's got a poor history when it comes to finding men. She's got some money behind her now. I hope this Bernard isn't after that."

Ketty felt offended for Josie and for Bernard. "They're both independent adults."

Leo looked back across the clearing. "I just hope I don't have to pick up the pieces again if it doesn't work out."

Ketty too stared across at the couple who were chatting to someone beside them. Josie's head tipped back and Ketty caught the sound of her deep laugh. It had only been a few days but there'd obviously been an instant attraction between them. Ketty's people radar was usually quite accurate but she made mistakes sometimes. She hoped not in this case, she liked Josie very much and Bernard was fast turning into a friend as well.

"Looks like the show's about to start." Leo stood as people came from other directions and filled the space between them and the dancers. "Shall we move closer?"

Ketty took the arm he offered and they stepped forward together. It was difficult making herself accept his gestures of kindness. Her injured arm was not giving her much bother but he was solicitous nonetheless. She tried hard to appear grateful but she was so used to doing everything alone.

Twenty-four

Bernard shepherded Josie in front of him as they stepped back aboard ship. He had hoped for a bit of time alone with her before his dinner with Christine but they'd been on the same return tender as Christine and Frank who were walking ahead of them up the stairs. Now he felt obliged to include his daughter and her husband in his plans.

"Anyone in a rush?" Bernard asked once they'd all arrived in the space between lift and stairs. "We could have a drink together on the pool deck." He was hoping they'd say no but Frank jumped in straight away.

"I could go a beer."

"I'd love a cocktail." Josie looked at Christine. "How about you?"

Christine glanced at her watch. "We've still got plenty of time before dinner. Why not? But I'd like to get out of my bathers first."

They all boarded the lift. "Shall I take your things?" she asked Frank.

"Thanks." He handed over his bag.

Bernard glanced from Christine to Frank. They were being very polite to each other, more like acquaintances than husband and wife. The lift door opened and she left without a backward glance.

Josie jabbed at button ten. "I might do the same." She kissed Bernard's cheek as the door opened for her. "I'll see you up there."

"Looks like it's down to you and me, Frank," Bernard said.

He led the way out to the bar where he ordered two of the drink of the day for the ladies and a beer each for himself and his son-in-law.

"So how are the kids?" Bernard asked. "Have you spoken to them since we've been away?"

"Yes, we've phoned twice and I think Christine plans to face-time them from Noumea. They've been away at the beach and reception hasn't been good but they'll be back at my sister's in Melbourne tomorrow."

"I wish I could see them more often. They're nearly grown up already."

Frank took a sip of beer, watching Bernard over the rim of his glass. "You know you're always welcome to visit, Bernie."

"Ditto, Frank."

They looked at each other, both knowing that the status quo of a visit once a year was unlikely to change. They'd never spent a lot of time together over the years, especially not alone, but he did like Frank. He just wished he would stand up to Christine a little more and not let her walk all over him.

"I'm applying for a new job."

Bernard was surprised at the way Frank blurted it out. As if he was making a declaration.

"Something different?" Bernard gave an encouraging smile. Christine often played down Frank's work but Bernard was a firm believer in everyone having their niche. Frank was honest and hardworking, that was all that mattered.

"Director of Engineering and Horticulture. It'd be a step up from what I'm doing now."

"Good luck." Bernard raised his glass.

"Thanks. Nothing's certain but I think I've got a good chance of getting it." Frank swallowed half of what was left in his glass. "Thing is it's with a different council, a bit further south. I'm thinking we should move house as well. Buy something closer to the beach." Frank turned away, looking out over the pool deck where the usual late afternoon crowd were gathering. "We wouldn't have to move but I think it would be better. A bit more commuting for Chrissie perhaps, but it would be close to their new suburban office so she might be able to transfer."

"What about the kids' school? They're pretty settled there by the sounds."

Frank turned back, his face more animated now. "No more distance for them, purely a different direction."

Bernie nodded.

"I think we'd be better off." Frank pressed on. "We could buy a bigger house, maybe even with a pool, for the money we could sell our current place for."

"Christine said something about money for renovations."

Frank frowned at that. "We wouldn't need to renovate if we moved."

"Are you moving?" Josie slid onto a spare bar stool the other side of Bernard and slipped her hand through his arm.

"Maybe," Frank said. "Christine's not keen."

"Oh." Josie pulled a face.

"We looked at doing renovations a few years ago," Frank said. "Got some plans drawn up and a quote but it was a lot of money and we shelved it."

He looked at Bernard and once again there was a kind of desperation in his eyes. Perhaps this was why the two of them were being so cool with each other. Christine hadn't given up on the renovations idea if their breakfast a few days ago was anything to go by. The idea of moving was apparently a bone of contention and one Bernard didn't want to get involved in.

He passed Josie one of the chartreuse-coloured cocktails with little rounds of fruit bobbing on the top. "Try this. It's called a Melon Ball."

She put the straw to her lips. "Mmm. Fruity. Love it, thanks."

"Here I am." Christine joined them.

Bernard passed her drink then raised his glass. "Cheers, my dears."

They all paused to sip their drinks.

Christine licked her lips. "Thanks, Dad. That's delicious."

Josie smiled. "I don't think I've had one drink that hasn't been amazing yet and I'm determined to work my way through their cocktail list."

Bernard grinned. Everything about this woman he liked.

"You said you live near Dad, Josie. Which suburb?" Christine asked.

"Teneriffe, overlooking the river."

"Mmm." Christine's eyebrows raised. "Expensive suburb."

"Not necessarily. I bought my apartment at a good time."

"Like us with our place. We bought at a good time didn't we, Frank?"

Bernard shifted on his stool. He sensed trouble brewing.

"But the house isn't very big. The kids are teenagers now and we need room for visitors." Christine looked pointedly at Bernard. "We need to extend."

"Sometimes you're better off to move," Josie said.

"I think you're right." Bernard scratched at his chin. "Renovating is a messy business."

Christine opened her mouth but Josie cut her off, waggling a finger towards Lifou. "Oh look, we're underway again. I thought the view was changing."

They all turned.

"The sea is so smooth," Christine said. "You hardly know you're moving."

Bernard rested a hand on Josie's shoulder and twirled a loose piece of her hair. He loved the silky feel of it between his fingers. "It's such a beautiful evening. We should go and watch from the front of the ship," he said. "You two don't mind, do you?" He slid from his stool, wrapped his arm around Josie's waist and pulled her close.

"I owe you a drink," Frank said.

"Next time."

Christine opened her mouth but Bernard cut her off. "See you at dinner." He gave a wave and propelled Josie forward.

The cabin door had barely shut behind them before Christine started.

"Did you see the way Dad and Josie were carrying on?" She took off her lanyard and tossed it on the desk. "Old people acting like teenagers. It's disgusting and worse when it's my father."

"Josie seems nice enough."

Christine glared at him. "She's a gold-digger. After his money, that's all. Why else would she be chasing him?"

"That's a bit tough, Chrissie. Your dad's a pretty good-looking bloke, fit and healthy."

"He's nearly seventy."

"The new fifty, they say. Anyway, she's at least sixty and it sounds like she's got her own money. As you said, apartments in Teneriffe don't come cheap."

"No doubt a pay-out from one of her divorces. She's probably looking for a new income source."

Frank sighed. "Do you want a shower first or shall I?"

"You go." She waved towards the bathroom.

She had to get her thoughts in order and her plan sorted before she met her father for dinner. Christine was the only one going to get her hands on his money, not anyone else and certainly not that floozy of a woman, Josie.

Ketty sat on one of the deckchairs on the promenade deck and watched as Lifou Island slowly disappeared from view. She'd had such an enjoyable day. Up until now anyway. She tried to focus on the good rather than what unsettled her. She was expert at that. Pushing the bad stuff away. Trouble was, it involved Leo and she was unsure what to do about it. How to move forward.

The island had been as beautiful as ever. After the welcome dance they'd run into Celia and Jim and taken a stroll along the beach. They'd caught the tender back together, enjoyed a late buffet lunch then gone on to trivia. Ketty relished trivia. It was so interesting to watch how people participated. Some were too shy to put forward a suggestion and others would calmly lean in with an answer, while there were always some who almost burst with the telling, eager to show off their knowledge.

Celia had slipped away as soon as the quiz was finished. She'd been acting like a startled rabbit again, at one moment nearly knocking all their drinks flying when she'd reached for her glass, and then tapping one fingernail on the edge of the table. They hadn't had a chance to speak alone. Jim had started talking stock markets with Leo, the discussion had led to investments and then Jim had asked about Leo's previous business but Leo had changed the subject then and the conversation had fizzled. Jim had headed off and then it had been just her and Leo finishing their drinks together before they went off to prepare for dinner.

They had been chatting about family. Ketty knew his sister Josie now of course, but he hadn't ever met her brother Phil and then there was Phil's wife and their son Greg. Perhaps Ketty had glowed a little too much when she spoke of Greg but she did feel a special bond with him. Leo started talking about his own children. They were all the product of his marriage to Marjorie. Ketty found it difficult to accept he'd stayed on in the marriage and they'd had two more children when he'd been adamant he no longer loved his wife.

Next, he'd talked about his grandchildren. For some reason that had hit her hard, almost a physical reaction as if she'd been punched in the stomach. It was then that he'd pulled out his phone and she'd sat stiffly beside him looking at photo after photo as he scrolled through pictures of several children, she'd lost count of how many, of various ages from babies to young teens. He didn't look like stopping so she'd said it was time for her to go but she hadn't returned to her cabin, instead she'd come to the promenade deck where she sat and watched the view.

Now she probed the grandchildren thing and it hurt, like poking at a sore tooth. Perhaps because children had been denied her, but she'd got over that a long time ago. It wasn't until her friends and clients began having grandchildren and she saw the love and fulfilment it gave them in their later years that she felt a sadness.

Ketty Clift, who controlled most things in her life, had no control over that, and Leo's obvious pride and joy over his own grandchildren had opened old wounds. It wasn't his fault she didn't have grandchildren of her own and yet a part of her couldn't help but feel it was.

"Quite ridiculous, Ketty," she muttered, then smiled sweetly at a young couple who gave her an odd look as they passed.

She'd been so deep in her own thoughts she hadn't noticed another couple had come to sit on the deckchairs further along from her. They were intent on their own conversation and not looking her way but the woman gave a snorting laugh which set the hairs on the back of Ketty's neck on end. She caught glimpses of the man with Maude, lavishing attention on her. It was Pete. Ketty glanced up and back along the deck. No sign of anyone else. She wasn't one to judge others but she understood Celia's concerns for her friend and the implications of this dalliance. She pondered a moment then she recalled the invitation to the Diamond Lounge for late night cocktails and canapes, and a plan formed. She'd been going to suggest to Leo that they go there after the show but she could always take him another night.

Ah, Leo. She stood and walked along the deck away from the chummy couple till she was alone again. The sun was getting low and the light was golden. She breathed in the salty air. She had rebuilt her life by not looking back, not regretting what wasn't to be. Here she was on a cruise where she'd rediscovered the man who she'd loved so desperately and she needed to focus on that. If something came of this meeting and their friendship continued, it was possible Leo's grandchildren could be kind of adoptive grandchildren for her. She pulled herself up at that. She was getting far too ahead of herself.

Twenty-five

Night Six – At Sea

Christine settled into her chair and glanced around the restaurant, taking in the potted palms and floral decor. It didn't look as luxurious as their dining room. She swallowed her disappointment and turned back to her father who was studying the wine list. He was dressed smartly in a jacket and tie and she felt rather glamorous even if the surroundings weren't. She wore a sparkling silver and black dress, the one she'd had her eye on in one of the ship boutiques. It was the perfect fit – at least it was once she pulled on her spandex and squeezed her boobs in. She had justified the expense thinking she'd wear it tonight and on the next formal night.

At her neck was the pearl Frank had bought her. Her father's gift was still missing and she hoped he wouldn't make mention of its absence. Christine was sure Maria had taken it but Frank had made a fuss when she'd said again she wanted to report it. He was determined it would turn up, said they hadn't had a proper look and how silly would they feel if they reported it and it was among their things. But Christine had had a good look and she didn't trust Maria. She quizzed the maid each day to see if the pendant had been discovered during cleaning. Maria's responses were always emphatically 'no' and there would be vigorous head shaking before she would ease away and disappear into wherever she went when she wasn't skulking in the corridor. And her cleaning left a lot to be desired. There'd been a black hair in the shower one day and a mark on the mirror another, and she usually hurried off in the other direction when Christine approached. Definitely shifty but Frank stood up for her.

He wasn't usually one to dig his heels in but these last few days he had on several occasions, defending Maria, this new job he wanted, moving house. Still, she would work on that and if all went to plan they'd be able to celebrate as soon as she got back to their room. She was determined that tonight she would seduce her husband one way or another.

She pushed thoughts of missing necklaces and changing jobs aside and smiled at her father who had just ordered an expensive bottle of wine. She felt confident tonight was going to be a good one in all respects.

"Isn't this lovely, Dad?"

"Yes." He glanced around. "But the downstairs dining room is very nice too."

"I know. I was thinking more about it being only the two of us."

"Of course."

His gaze shifted to the big front-facing window beside their table. The night was black beyond it and their reflections were mirrored back at them in the glass. The restaurant was on a high level at the front of the ship and Christine was more aware of the rolling motion here. She'd not felt unwell since the first few days at sea and now she found the movement comforting.

"How's your back?" Bernard's question drew her attention.

"It's not too bad." She felt hardly a twinge now but it wouldn't hurt her case to rustle up some sympathy.

"What about you and Frank, Princess?"

"We're both well. I was only queasy at the start of the cruise."

"I don't mean your physical health."

Christine frowned.

"You don't seem very happy together."

"We're fine." She fiddled with her cutlery. "Work's crazy at the moment. The kids are involved in lots of things. Life gets so busy."

"You have to make time for each other."

"We do, Dad. We're fine, don't worry."

Christine was relieved the waiter arrived at that moment with their wine. She didn't want to defend her current relationship hiatus.

The waiter poured then watched as Bernard tasted. They had ordered steak for main and were sharing a bottle of red. Once their glasses were filled he raised his and she did the same.

"Cheers, big ears," he said.

"Ciao, Dad." She took a sip and the peppery taste rolled around her tongue. "Mmm, that's good."

"So it should be. It's one of their better ones."

"You spoil me."

"I like to."

Christine's chest swelled with warmth. At least her dad made her feel special and valued. She'd have to work carefully tonight to make sure it stayed that way.

⚓

"Miss Clift, I'd heard you were injured." Carlos drew her aside from the line of people entering the dining room for dinner.

"Not badly, Carlos. I'll live. The doctor insisted on a sling for a day or so, he's being cautious. It's a nuisance that's all." Ketty was aware of the scrutiny of the other passengers passing behind Carlos. "I mustn't keep you."

He made a dismissive gesture. "Tonight has been uneventful. Everyone knows their seating and I haven't had any requests for table changes for a couple of days."

"That's good then." She leaned in closer. "Calm waters."

"Indeed. We must have that chat."

Ketty felt torn. She wasn't sure what the night would bring. They would probably go on to the after-dinner show and then maybe drinks. Every moment with Leo was intriguing; she felt alive in his presence and yet a little on edge, uncertain of where it might lead. It was unsettling and yet on the other hand exciting. Something that had been lacking in her life for a while. "Perhaps tomorrow?"

His look was sage, as if he understood her prevarication. He offered his arm. "Let me walk you to your table."

"That's not necessary, Carlos."

"I know but it would be my pleasure."

Ketty accepted. When Carlos did things for her it made her feel special rather than bossed about. Leo was charming but a part of her railed when he held out a hand, or ordered a drink, or made way for her on a seat. She frowned at that, feeling a little disloyal. After all Leo was simply being thoughtful.

He leaped to his feet as they approached. "Kathy, I could have come to collect you."

"I didn't need collecting." She smiled as Carlos pulled out her chair and draped the napkin across her lap. "Carlos thought I might trip over my sling." She waggled her bandaged arm and glanced around the table. Only five of them tonight. "Is this us?" she asked.

"Bernard's dining out with his princess tonight." A muscle in Josie's jaw twitched.

Leo leaned closer to Ketty. "Josie says she doesn't mind but she's in a mood."

"I can hear you, Leo," Josie said. "You're lucky Ketty has no one else aboard to demand her attention."

Leo smiled indulgently and patted Ketty's hand. "I got you a G and T," he said.

She slid the sling from her neck and picked up the glass. "That was kind of you."

"And we don't know where Frank is." Celia shifted in her seat.

"Well, I'm sorry I was late." Ketty lifted her arm. "This bothersome elbow slowed me down."

"I could have helped you," Celia said.

"Or me," Josie said. "I'm only down the corridor."

"Thank you both but I've been managing."

"I don't think Frank's coming." Leo tapped the menu that had been placed in front of Ketty. "Let's order." He sat back, arms folded across his chest. He'd obviously already decided what he would eat.

Ketty picked up the menu and began to peruse it slowly, determined to take her time.

Christine had thought of little else but this dinner with her father and how she was going to bring up the discussion of money but now that she was here she wasn't sure how to begin. "So you enjoyed Lifou?" she asked.

"I did, yes."

"It's a pity we didn't keep in touch today. We could have spent the afternoon together."

"We're together now."

"I meant the four of us."

Bernard put his head to one side. "I thought you wanted it to be just you and me."

"Now, yes, but earlier...well..." Her words dried up. In actual fact she wanted it to be the three of them, her father, her and Frank but she couldn't say that. She decided to take a different approach.

"Did you love Mum?"

Bernard almost spluttered into the glass of wine he'd lifted to his lips. "Why would you ask that now?"

"I sometimes wonder if she loved us."

"Of course she did. Della was the love of my life and I know that love was reciprocated."

Christine hung her head. "Until I came along and spoiled it."

"Don't be ridiculous, Chrissie. How could you say you're not loved?"

"I think Mum would have preferred it had stayed the two of you."

"We were deliriously happy when you came along."

"But I cramped your style."

"Never."

"Well, Mum's anyway."

Bernard's face softened. "Your mother was a good wife and mother. She was devoted to you and a talented homemaker."

"But she didn't like to share that talent." Christine let the familiar ache of her mother's remoteness work its way to her core. Della had loved her but Christine had never felt the closeness she saw with her friends and their mothers. "I never learned to take up a hem or sew on a button, and when she cooked I had to keep out of her way. She didn't let me help like my girlfriends' mums did."

"We entertained a lot. Your mother was a fabulous cook."

"A skill she didn't want to share with her only child."

Bernard rubbed at his head and took another sip of wine.

"I thought perhaps you weren't so special to her either," Christine said. "You've had so many women since she died."

His gaze narrowed. He shook his head and then he leaned towards her, his voice low. "First of all, I did love your mother and she loved me but she's been dead for over twenty years. And second, I have not had *so many* women. You make me sound like a gigolo."

"Goodness, there's no need to be so defensive."

"I'm a man, Christine, and I enjoy the company of women."

"But you don't have to marry them."

"Who said anything about marrying them?"

"You were headed that way a couple of times."

They were staring at each other in a stalemate across the table when the waiter arrived with their entrées. He offered cracked pepper for their scallop mousseline with prawn sauce, and topped up their wine glasses.

Christine enjoyed the creamy scallops before she tried again. "Frank has his eye on a new a job. He wants to move."

"He said."

"Did he?" Christine wondered when they'd had that conversation. It seemed Frank was telling everyone. "I know you have concerns but I'd rather stay in our current place, extend it, build up. It's in a good area."

Bernard didn't reply to that but carefully replaced his napkin in his lap.

Christine had to press home her point. Get him onside. If he gave them the money for renovations she knew Frank wouldn't try to move them. "Anna's very musical and she wants to take up piano. They're expensive and we've nowhere to fit one. Lucca has his drums in the shed so we can't park the cars in but if we did the renovations on our current house we could stay where we are."

"I've already said you'd be crazy to renovate—"

"It's my family home, the only one I have."

"You're not still pining for our old place, surely?"

She felt a stab of anger. She'd never forgiven him for selling her childhood home and auctioning off most of the contents. "Perhaps if you'd kept one of Mum's wall hangings for me."

"We've gone over this, Chrissie. You were travelling when I had to move out. I wanted a fresh start. I was never one for those wall hangings your mother made."

"She wove the one in my bedroom specially for me."

"I'm sorry that I can't go back in time and fix this."

"Keeping the home Frank and I have made together is important to me, Dad."

He sighed. "If it's what you really want."

She smiled, sure he was coming round. "It is, Dad."

"I thought money was an issue."

"It is of course, but—"

"Have you ever heard of saving?" Bernard cut her off. "That's what your mother and I had to do. We worked hard and we saved. It wouldn't hurt for your kids to learn that too."

Christine's jaw fell open. She sat back suddenly as the waiter placed her filet mignon with its side of garlic and herb French fries in front of her then she leaned forward again as Bernard received his spice-rubbed rib-eye. "There's always something to pay for with two kids, the council rates have shot up and my car needs new tyres."

"The car I put money up for?"

"That was a big help, Dad. My old one kept breaking down."

"And you're enjoying the balcony cabin?"

He looked at her steadily across the table. He didn't say it but she understood he was reminding her he'd paid for the room upgrade.

"Of course."

"And the necklace you had to have so badly." He wiggled his knife towards her throat. "I haven't noticed you've worn it since the first night I bought it."

Christine put her fingers to the pearl Frank had bought her. "It's been stolen."

"What?" His cutlery went to his plate with a clatter. "From where?"

"From our cabin."

"Have you reported it?"

"Frank won't let me. He thinks it'll turn up but I think the maid took it."

Bernard frowned. "You mean the steward, Maria? It surely wouldn't be worth her job to steal it. She seems like such a nice woman."

Christine sniffed at that. Maria had all the men wrapped around her little finger. With Frank she was always smiling, and it was "yes, Mr Frank, no, Mr Frank". As soon as she saw Christine coming she would duck away.

"You've searched everywhere?" Bernard asked.

"Turned the room upside down."

"Perhaps you should report it." He picked up his cutlery again.

"I'll get it back one way or another." Christine softened her voice. "I do appreciate all the things you've done for me...for Frank and the kids and me."

"Mmm." Bernard murmured through a mouthful of steak. "This is good."

She glanced at her plate and gave a brief thought to the grilled asparagus side she should have chosen instead of the fries. She no longer felt hungry anyway. This wasn't working out as she'd hoped. Even though her father had said no the last time she asked she wasn't giving up.

"You could loan us the money for the renovations."

Bernard cut another piece of his steak and put it into his mouth. He chewed thoughtfully then once he'd swallowed it he looked at Christine. "Interest free, I suppose? Or maybe a gift you don't have to repay?"

She sat forward eagerly. "That would be fabulous, Dad."

To her dismay he shook his head.

"You don't need my money, Christine. You and Frank both have good jobs. I've told you I think Frank's idea of a move would be for the better rather than to plough more money into your old place. You should give it some thought, but whatever you decide, make the best of it."

Christine put down her cutlery, her food untouched. "That's easy for you to say. You don't have the responsibilities we do." She willed the tears to form in her eyes and then she blinked them back.

"But that's it, Princess. At your age I did. Your mother didn't bring in an income. I had both of you to support. It hasn't been till my later years that I've become more comfortable financially and I can enjoy the rewards of my hard work."

Instead of leaning forward to comfort her he took another bite of his rib-eye. Christine reached for her purse as a tear dribbled down one cheek and then the other. She took out a tissue and dabbed at her face while her father continued to eat.

"It's good steak," he said. "Don't let it go cold."

She took up her cutlery again and cut a piece, all the while thinking about a different way to tackle her father. Usually he saw things her way but she was making no progress tonight. He had plenty of money. He could easily give her some for renovations and not miss it. She looked up just as he glanced at his watch.

"Somewhere else to be?"

"Not yet." He smiled. "Josie and I are meeting up outside the theatre later for the show."

Christine sat back, the steak a lump in her throat. Josie again. The witch had her hooks in him already. She was the reason Bernard wasn't as amenable as usual. Christine hadn't wanted to play tough but she was going to have to.

"Josie appears to be well off."

"I think she's comfortable. We haven't discussed it."

"Haven't you?" Christine stared at him but he was intent on his plate. "I thought how much money she had would have been one of the first things you found out."

He looked up now and frowned. "You're not going to rake up the past again, are you? Why can't you let things be, Chrissie?"

"You only started making your fortune after Mum died. Her life insurance was what set you up."

He patted at his lips with his napkin and sat back, his expression unreadable.

"Poor Gloria didn't last because she was a drain on your finances, wasn't she? Then came Kath who had plenty of cash." She watched the hurt flick across his face and then the bland expression returned, set like rock. Christine had come this far, there was no turning back now. She took a deep breath. "I know you fleeced Kath, Dad."

His eyes widened, his mouth opened a little.

"The kids and I were staying with you not long after you broke up with Kath."

"That was after you did some dirt-digging."

She flinched. "She wasn't divorced like she said."

He gave a soft snort. "I wasn't going to marry her, Christine."

She was momentarily baffled then she got his meaning. She steeled herself and pressed on. "I saw the forms for that house you sold for a small fortune. Kath's name was on the paperwork as well as yours but she didn't see any of the profits, did she? And after Kath came a string of other women and your fortune kept growing. How many of them did you fascinate and then fleece, Dad?"

His eyes darkened and the muscles twitched along his jaw.

"What do you do? Convince them something's going to be a great investment then tell them it didn't make as much as you'd thought? Have you asked Josie to invest in something yet?"

This time she saw him flinch.

The waiter came to take their plates. "Would you like to see the dessert menu?"

"No, thank you." Bernard answered without so much as a glance at Christine.

The waiter poured the last of the wine into their glasses and moved away.

Bernard took a sip. Sat the glass down again carefully and folded his large hands on the table in front of him. "I have to take my hat off to you, Christine. You never give up on something. I assume in return for your silence, I am to fund your renovations?"

"You have plenty to spare."

He shook his head. "You have no idea of my financial situation. It isn't what you've imagined." He held her gaze a moment, his eyes narrowed. "Unless you've been going through my paperwork when you come to stay. Is that what brings you to visit me?"

"Dad." That stung. "Of course not." She looked down at her lap. She had come across bank statements though and she knew he was a very wealthy man.

He raised his glass to her. "One day, what's mine will all come to you."

She felt a twinge of remorse. "Don't be morbid, Dad."

"It's true. I'll drop off the perch one day but I'm making bloody sure I'll enjoy myself until I do. There might not be much left for you."

She looked up, shocked to see the scathing look he gave her. "Dad…I…" Her words dried in her throat under his scrutiny.

"I like Josie a lot. I'd go as far as to say I feel a love for her I haven't felt since your mother." He leaned across the table, pinning her with his glare, his voice low. "Don't you dare spoil it. Not this time."

"What do you mean *this time*?"

"I knew you didn't like Gloria but I thought you'd get used to her. Then I thought moving to Brisbane would be the answer, putting some space between us, but you wouldn't let me have my happiness. I didn't need her to have money. I had enough for the both of us, but my fun-time Gloria became irritable and snitchy. You drove a wedge between us. I didn't know it at the time, of course. She never let on but I ran into her a few years later. She was happy with someone else and she told me why it hadn't worked out with me. You wore her down with your snooping and bothering phone calls."

"She wanted your money, Dad."

"What did that matter?" He tossed his napkin on the table. "Happiness isn't about money, Christine."

"Then why did you diddle Kath?"

The colour that had been building in his cheeks drained away. He slumped back as if the fight had gone out of him. She felt bad about raising the Kath thing but her father had forced her into this corner. She was not giving up on her home. She'd invested more than money into it over the years. Everything that was important in her life was based there. She would make Frank understand.

She drew a quick breath. "I won't say anything to Josie but I think it's best if the fling ends once you return home, and I do want my cut."

"The renovations."

Christine smiled. At last they were on the same page.

Bernard shoved back his chair and lurched to his feet. "I think we're done here."

"We could have an after-dinner drink." She wanted to smooth things between them. There were still the logistics of how much and when to be worked out. It would be awkward if they parted in bad spirits.

"I think we've spent enough time together, Christine."

She flopped back in her seat as he strode away, her resolve fading. He would give her the money she wanted but she hoped she hadn't paid a much higher price for it than she'd intended. Still, the cruise wasn't over yet. Plenty of time to make up with her father. He would come round, he always did. She smiled at her success, eager now to tell Frank they could renovate instead of move.

Twenty-six

Ketty hadn't intended to eat the final course tonight but the others had all ordered something so she'd asked for the strawberry pavlova, which had been served with passionfruit coulis and a chocolate cigarette. The sweetness still clung to her tongue. She nestled back against her chair as Phillip cleared her plate. She felt comfortable, content with life, and she knew that was in part due to Leo's presence. Tonight she'd allowed her outer shell to slip away.

Leo sat on her right, relaxed against his chair, listening to something Jim was explaining, the fingers of his left hand tracing slow circles on the table between them. She was acutely aware of the movement, her eyes drawn to his long fingers, his neatly clipped nails. How long ago it seemed that those hands had held her, loved her. The skin was wrinkled now like hers, the tendons like ropes criss-crossed with deep blue veins. Now it seemed each moment she spent in his company reminded her of the good times they'd had, rather than the bad. She lifted her hand, wanting to place it on his, to feel his touch, but another hand tapped her left arm.

"Ketty, you'd give Celia one of your fabulous makeovers, wouldn't you?"

Josie looked at her expectantly while across the table Celia's expression was wary.

"Celia already looks lovely." Ketty had been pleased to see her wearing the bright red top again. It gave her such a lift and make-up hid most of the bruise.

"Of course she does," Josie said. "But I've been explaining how you set me up with the best colours and styles to look out for."

"I wouldn't want to put you out," Celia said.

"It wouldn't put me out." Ketty smiled encouragingly.

"Ketty loves it." Josie leaned back towards Celia. "You saw that wardrobe of hers. It's full of treasures."

"I do love to make suggestions and share some of my collection," Ketty said. "But I wouldn't want you to think I was somehow casting judgement on your dress sense, Celia."

"I'd be happy of the help. I've always kept my wardrobe simple."

"It still can be," Ketty said. "As long as what's in it suits you. That beige dress is the perfect cut for you but the colour washes you out. Not many people can get away with beige. It's a case of right style, wrong colour."

"Trouble is, when you find a style you like you can't always get the colour you want."

"That's where Ketty Clift Couture comes in," Josie spoke grandly.

"What's Ketty Clift Couture doing now?" Leo asked from her other side.

"Nothing really." Ketty smiled at him. "Just a ladies get-together."

"You're famous, my love." His warm hand gripped hers and the look in his eyes rolled back the years yet again.

"How about we have an afternoon, on one of the cruising-home days?" Josie's grin was wide.

Ketty suspected her delight was as much about the way Leo was watching Ketty as about the fun to be had with a makeover.

"You'll love it, Celia," Josie went on. "And I can show you the eyeliner tricks I was telling you about."

Leo squeezed Ketty's hand. "Ready to go to the show?"

"Yes." Ketty glanced at the others. "Are we all going?"

"I'm meeting Bernie there." Josie stood. "Do you have plans, Celia?"

"No!" Celia's response was emphatic. "Yes." She ducked her head. "At least…I'm meeting Maude for a nightcap. We haven't seen much of each other today."

"What about you, Jim?" Ketty had laid her earlier glum thoughts about grandchildren to rest. She felt gloriously happy tonight and wanted Jim and Celia to feel the same.

"I'll do my usual deck walk." Jim glanced at Celia but she was rummaging in her bag. "Not sure if I'm in the right frame of mind for a comedy show."

Celia leaped to her feet. "I must go."

Jim rose slowly from the table.

Ketty felt a pang of disappointment. She'd thought the two of them had been getting on so well and now they were stiff with each other. She watched as they walked away, together but apart. Then Leo's arm went around her waist and she drew her thoughts back to her own re-blooming relationship.

"Off to the show?" He offered his other arm to his sister and behind his back, Josie gave Ketty a wink.

⚓

Celia made her way purposefully towards the lounge at the rear of the ship. She wanted to give Jim time to get out on deck and the others time to reach the theatre before she ducked back downstairs to her room. She'd made no plans to meet Maude. In fact they'd only seen each other briefly today, for which Celia was thankful. She didn't want Maude quizzing her about Jim again.

It had been so difficult being with him today and trying to hide her feelings. It reminded her of when she'd first fallen in love. She'd been a late bloomer but at sixteen she'd fallen for the brother of her best friend. He was older and not at all interested in her and Celia had twisted herself in knots trying not to show how she felt, but her friend had worked it out. Celia still remembered the embarrassment of her friend teasing her and then telling her brother. Needless to say they hadn't remained friends but Celia's cheeks still burned at the recollection.

She slowed when she reached the photography area. Photos from each event or port were on display and she stopped in front of today's Lifou photos and couldn't help but search for the one of her with Ketty and Jim. Her heart leaped at the sight of it. Jim was in the middle, pulling them close. Celia looked startled, Ketty's head was tipped back laughing and Jim was looking directly at the camera, which had caught his brilliant smile. Ketty was right, he was a handsome man. She bent closer. Particularly when he smiled. It had been hellish sitting next to him at dinner, with her feelings for him so strong but knowing she had to keep them at bay. A walk on the deck with him tonight would have been wonderful but terrible all at the same time.

She turned away from the image and slowly made her way back to her cabin. When she opened the door she was surprised to see Maude was inside.

"Oh, Celia, thank goodness." Maude grabbed her arm and tugged her into the middle of the room. "I was wondering how I was going to find you."

"What's wrong?"

Maude's face was flushed and her eyes had a wild look. "Nothing, exactly. Not for me anyway." She sat on the edge of her bed. "Sit down."

Celia sat, their knees almost touching. She looked at Maude and a bad feeling churned inside her. Surely Maude wasn't going to try to set her up with Nigel again or someone else. "What is it?"

"Can you stay out of our cabin for a few hours?"

"Now?"

"Yes." Maude gave her a nudge with her knees. "I need the cabin to myself."

"Why?" Celia saw the look on Maude's face and felt the heat rise in her own. "You're not bringing a man in here."

"Please, Celia." Maude gripped her hands. "Just for a few hours. Pete and I want to be together and—"

Celia whipped her hands away. "He's married, Maude."

"His wife doesn't meet his needs." Maude lifted her chin, her look defiant. "And I'm taking the opportunity."

Celia had a sudden image of Ed. Is this how he had been? When he left her, it was her body that had missed him most. Not purely sex but the intimacy. It had hurt deeply to think he'd been with another woman when she'd believed they were happy. She thought of Pete, his hands on Maude, and then Anne with her bad leg, tucked up in bed alone.

Maude's brusque laugh cut into her thoughts. "I've embarrassed you."

"No." Celia eased herself up into the space beyond the bed. "You've simply reminded me how fickle men can be." She crossed to the door.

"Just a few hours, Celia," Maude called behind her. "He'll be gone by midnight."

Celia didn't look back. She let herself out into the corridor and strode back towards the stairs.

The theatre lights went up. All around Jim people stood, laughing and talking. He'd ended up going to the comedy show after all and he'd enjoyed it, had found himself laughing hard at times, but now as he watched people leaving he felt the familiar pain of loss: no Jane at his side to enjoy it with. He probably should have gone with Ketty's group but once Bernard joined them Jim would have felt on the outer. Josie and Bernard were very taken with each other and he could see Ketty was becoming more and more entranced with Leo.

Jim remained in his seat towards the side of the theatre as the last of the other patrons moved out. Both Ketty and Celia had been easy company these last few days. He could relax with them and it was a pleasant feeling. He did wonder about Celia though. She'd been jittery all day. He'd enjoyed their dinner together the previous evening and he thought she had too. Perhaps he'd talked too much about Jane, but then Celia had told him about her marriage break-up. Something had definitely changed between them though, and just when he thought they were getting on rather well. Then he'd pulled her close for the photo up at the lookout. She'd flinched and he'd realised straight away he'd done the wrong thing. He'd felt awkward and had berated himself for being so forward. After that he'd tried desperately to keep a cool distance between them. Tonight he'd done his best to keep things casual but there was something he'd wanted to ask her.

When he'd arrived back on board this afternoon there'd been a message for him from his son. Anthony had expected to be finished in time to fly to Noumea and meet him as a surprise but it hadn't been possible. He'd organised two tickets on a catamaran cruise for the next day so he hoped his father would be able to take someone else along instead. It had been on the tip of Jim's tongue to ask Celia over dinner but he didn't like to in front of the others and then she'd rushed off before he could mention it. He'd been puzzled to hear she was meeting Maude for a nightcap. Perhaps it was an excuse. The only entertainment he offered was a walk on the deck. She'd been kind enough to keep him company but how dull that must have been for her. After the first night and his incident on the railing he'd probably become her 'someone in need' project. He couldn't expect anything more than that from her.

Jim stood, worked his way along the row and turned up the aisle. Most of the crowd had filtered out now but in the middle of the theatre in the back row a lone figure remained seated. As he drew nearer he was surprised to see it was Celia. Her eyes were closed. He paused wondering if he should speak to her. Perhaps she was waiting for Maude.

Her eyelids flicked up and she looked at him, startled.

"Jim?"

"Enjoy the show?"

"Yes...I hadn't planned to come but...well, Maude...she's—" Celia's cheeks coloured. "It's difficult to explain."

"Well, it's late." Jim went to move on. She'd made it clear earlier she wasn't looking for his company.

She glanced at her watch. "Oh, it's not midnight yet."

She looked so anxious he felt suddenly protective.

"Are you turning back into the scullery maid?"

She frowned.

His try at lightening the mood had fallen on deaf ears. Celia was very distracted.

"Are you all right?" he asked.

She huffed and stood up. "I'm perfectly fine but I can't turn in yet. Do you fancy a drink?"

"Certainly." He didn't feel like one but he sensed Celia needed company after all.

They walked out to the bar where they both chose a brandy and settled in to the comfortable lounge chairs. Celia glanced at her watch as the waiter set their drinks in front of them.

He raised his glass. "Cheers."

She leaned forward and tapped hers against his. They took a sip each and settled back. She stifled a yawn.

"It's been a long day," he said.

"Yes, we did a lot of walking. I'm feeling quite tired."

"We should drink up then, let you get off."

She glanced at her watch again. "Oh, no. It's not time yet…at least I'm not…" She put her hand to her head and let out a sigh. "Damn, I'm not good at this sort of thing."

"What sort of thing?"

She glanced up and discomfort was written all over her face. "Subterfuge."

"What's going on?" He was intrigued now. Celia was squirming in her chair.

"I can't go back to the cabin till after midnight."

He studied her, waiting for her to continue.

She looked around. There were only a few other people in the bar and they were nowhere near. She leaned in closer.

"Maude's entertaining…in our cabin…a man."

Jim was stunned. It was the last thing he'd expected Celia to say. He wanted to laugh but she was too distressed. "I guess she's made a close friend."

"Very."

"But you don't approve?"

"I wouldn't care what she did but…" Once more Celia glanced around. "He's a married man."

"Oh, I see."

Celia sat back and took another sip of her drink.

Jim was not surprised, upset or shocked like Celia clearly was. He'd known several men, and women for that matter, who'd found a willing colleague or local on work trips. Still, it was hard on her having to give up her room.

He checked his watch. It was only a little after eleven. "What do you plan to do until then?"

"I don't know." She waved her glass in the direction of a dark corner of the bar where there was a small couch. "Do you suppose anyone would notice if I curled up in a chair?"

"I could keep you company."

"That's so kind of you Jim, but it's late. And the thought of returning to my cabin after Maude's been…" She wrinkled her nose. "You know."

"You can't stay out all night." Jim was worried for her now, but also concerned what he was about to suggest might only upset her more. "I hope you won't take this the wrong way but I have an idea."

She put her head to one side watching him. She looked so trusting in that moment he was overwhelmed with a feeling of protectiveness for her.

"I have quite a large suite. It has a couch in the living room."

Her eyes widened. "You're offering me your couch?"

"Not exactly. My son was supposed to travel with me so the bedroom has two single beds. You could use the fresh one and I could sleep on the couch."

"Oh, Jim." She was back to looking agitated again. "That's very kind of you but I couldn't."

"Why not? You can't spend the night sleeping in the bar. I have a spare bed and you are without a room." He gave her an encouraging smile to mask the disbelief that he felt at his suggestion. "I realise you don't know me all that well but I assure you my intentions are honourable."

"Oh, Jim," she said again. "That is so sweet but I couldn't..." She stifled another yawn.

"That's it. Of course you can, even if it's just to put your feet up for a couple of hours until you can return to your own room."

Her look was still full of indecision.

"Please accept, Celia, otherwise I'll feel obliged to stay here with you and then neither of us will get any sleep."

"Are you blackmailing me?"

He was relieved to see a small smile on her lips.

"If needs be."

"All right. Just for an hour or so and then I'll go back to my cabin."

"Whichever, it's fine by me."

They drained their glasses and made their way out of the bar. Jim welcomed the sense of anticipation now, it was a warm feeling and he understood he looked forward to Celia's company – even if it was in slightly awkward circumstances.

Twenty-seven

"What a lovely night." Ketty leaned on the rail and looked out into the inky sky sprinkled with a million glittering stars. The waves rolled and splashed against the hull below her and the steady thrum of the motors was constant and reassuring.

"I think I could put up with more of this." Leo's voice was close but she didn't turn. "Especially being alone with you. I thought my sister would never leave us. Strange that Bernard didn't turn up."

"He must have been with his daughter longer than he'd thought."

"Let's not waste precious time pondering others."

Ketty turned and his face was only a short distance from hers. It startled her. His arms stretched to the rail either side of her and he leaned in. She drew in a quick breath then his lips brushed her ear, she breathed out, slightly disappointed.

"I've been wanting to kiss you since the first night we had drinks on your balcony." His breath in her ear sent a warm shudder through her. She felt like a girl again. "May I kiss you, Kathy?"

Did she want to kiss him? She reached up and put her fingers to his cheek, gently turning his face to hers and before she could speak his lips were on hers, soft at first then hungry, devouring her as he pressed her back against the rail. She felt heat sweep through her, his arms circled her, holding her close. She gasped as a jolt of pain jabbed at her elbow.

"Sorry." He pulled away, leaving her face tingling from the prickle of his beard.

"Blasted arm, it's such a nuisance. I'm fine." She looked into his eyes and fell silent. There was passion in his look, like she'd seen all those years ago. Inside she was a jumble of nerves. She'd gone along with getting to know Leo again, planning to take things as they came, but that kiss had been neither brief nor chaste. He'd demanded her attention with it and her body had responded. Now Leo was leaning in again; this time he kept his hands on the rail, and brushed her lips gently with his.

"Kathy, we could make this work. You and me. You've got your business, I could move to Sydney."

Ketty shook her head. "We've only just found each other again. Let's not rush things. There's still so much we don't know about each other."

"Does that matter? The past is the past. I don't want to lose you again."

"I'm not going to jump overboard."

He took a deep breath, let it out slowly. "I've never forgotten you, Kathy."

"I was a young woman when we knew each other." She imagined them being together now, intimate, lovers. Her scar would be revealed, he'd want to know more then. "You don't know the woman I've become, Leo. You might not like what you get."

He gripped her hand in his. Lifted it to his lips. "Don't run away again."

"I won't." The words came out in a croak, lacking conviction. The past was still between them. A shadow that discoloured every moment with him no matter how hard she tried to ignore it.

He leaned in again. She had to tell him or she'd never be able to fully relax with him, but not tonight. It had been such a lovely evening.

A rowdy group erupted from the door and made their way to the rail a little further along. Ketty straightened. "We'll be in Noumea tomorrow," she said a little too brightly. "Have you ever been?"

"No." He shook his head but his gaze didn't falter from hers.

"We can spend the day together. I can be your guide. Show you the sights."

"Just the two of us this time? Bernard and my sister are beginning to annoy me."

"It can be just the two of us." Ketty was happy with that. They could explore Noumea as well as talk. The time had come for her to tell him the whole reason she'd left Adelaide. It would mean unpacking a lot of hurt she'd buried deep but it needed to be said if they were to have any future together. The air was still warm but a little shiver wriggled down her spine. "Time for me to call it a night, I think."

There was sadness in his expression but he didn't argue, simply offered his arm and they went back inside together.

Christine smiled at Frank as he slipped into the warm bubbles of the spa, beside her. It had taken her some time to track him down once she'd left the restaurant. Eventually she'd found him playing the pokies in the casino. Just as she walked up he'd won a nice bucket of cash. He was happy and she suggested a spa so that they could relax while she told him her good news. It was late and once more they had one of the spas to themselves.

She leaned back and closed her eyes. It was as heavenly as the cocktail he'd bought her, a Dirty Banana.

"I'm glad you suggested this," he said. "I want us to talk, Chrissie. To have a calm and peaceful discussion."

She opened her eyes. "About?"

Frank took a sip of his drink, sat it carefully back on the edge of the spa. She held on to hers, licking the chocolate sprinkles from her lips.

"It's about our future," he said.

She smiled. "That's what I want to talk to you about too." This spa idea was working well. It was the perfect place to talk. She was feeling much better after the rather abrupt end to dinner with her father. She'd kept an eye out for him too when she'd been looking for Frank but had seen no sign. No doubt he'd gone to cuddle up to Josie somewhere. "You start, Frank."

He swept his hair back from his face. "We're not exactly winning the happy couple stakes at the moment."

She sat forward.

"Stop." He put his hand up. "I'm not blaming you, and it's not what I want to talk about anyway." He shrugged his shoulders. "Although who knows, my idea might help."

She flopped back and took another sip of her cocktail, savouring the mix of chocolate and coffee. "Just talk, Frank."

"It's about this job I want to apply for."

She opened her mouth. He put up his hand again.

"Hear me out."

She nodded. She owed him that much. She waved her glass at him. “You have the floor.”

“I’m sorry I didn’t tell you about the job earlier, before we left home. The position is for a director of engineering and horticulture and if I get it, at bare minimum it will have little impact on you and the kids. I would have longer hours so we will need to look at how we manage getting Lucca and Anna to various sports, etcetera.”

“So it will impact me. One of us has to drive them, feed them, wash their clothes.”

He frowned. “I take Lucca to soccer and I cook meals.”

“Pizza,” she scoffed.

“What does that matter once in a while? Anyway I can cook a barbecue, toss a salad.”

“The kids don’t like salad.”

“Then they can just eat the meat. It won’t hurt. You fuss over their food too much.”

“I do not fuss.”

Frank dragged his fingers through his hair. She could see he was struggling to remain calm.

“If we stay in our current house I will have to commute,” he said.

“And if we move I will,” she snapped.

“Perhaps you could talk to your boss about working in the suburban office. That’s the area we could look at buying in.”

“I like where I am.”

“The pay rise is significant. A leap from what I’m getting now.”

Christine sat forward. That was more interesting. “So if you brought home more money we could stay where we are, maybe get someone to help ferry the kids, and we could look at renovating. That ties in with my news.”

"What news?" He took a slug of his drink and glared at her over the glass.

"Dad's going to give us the money for the renovations."

"What?"

"Keep calm, Frank." It was easy to say but she was excited herself. "Just think about it. You could still apply for this new job if that's what you want but we wouldn't have to move."

"Or we could move further out to a bigger place with a decent yard, maybe a pool or a spa, keep the mortgage around the same."

"Our mortgage will stay the same with Dad paying for the renovations."

He shook his head. "I don't like your father paying for this cruise let alone the cost of the renovations you want."

"He's not paying for the whole cruise, only our upgrade, and he's got plenty of money. I'm his only child."

"I don't like being in debt to your father."

"But you're happy to owe the bank." She snorted. "Anyway, Dad's money is a gift. We don't have to pay it back."

"Renovations of the scale you're talking will mean living in a mess for months. Wouldn't you rather look for something that's already what we want?"

"Moving is a bigger upheaval. You want to uproot us, leave behind everything we've put into that house, both sentimental and financial. It's where my heart is and I thought yours too, but you want to change everything for another council job that pays a bit more money."

Frank put his head back on the edge of the spa staring into the distance.

"Please, Frank." She blinked back a tear. "It would break my heart to move."

Frank's head tilted slightly in her direction. His dark eyes were filled with such sadness it made her pause. He stood up. "I'm going back to the room."

"I haven't finished my drink." She lifted the glass of creamy liquid in the air.

He climbed out of the spa and dragged his damp hair back from his face. The water ran in rivulets down his buff torso, dripped from his swimmers to his tanned legs. He wrapped himself in a towel.

"Frank?"

"Goodnight." He walked away.

Christine felt as if he'd slapped her, his departure had been so brusque. She glanced around. No one else appeared to be taking much notice. The group in the other spa were chatting, their voices peppered with the tinkle of laughter.

She swallowed the last of her drink and climbed out. The tropical night was warm around her as she towelled herself dry then made her way down to the back of the ship where the only sound was the constant churning of water and the drone from the giant propellers below. She let herself inside, suddenly chilled by the air conditioning across her damp skin, and walked along the short corridor. It was the first time she'd been this way to her room. She reached the T junction, realised she'd come the wrong way, then paused at the sound of voices. Two people were entering one of the rooms at the far end and she was gobsmacked to see that it was Jim and Celia. The door closed on them and Christine turned away. Tonight she'd planned the big bedroom scene for her and Frank and now he was in a mood. Bloody hell, all the oldies were getting lucky and once again she was missing out.

Celia stood in the middle of Jim's lounge and looked around. There was the couch Jim had mentioned, two other chairs, a desk, a polished-wood wall cabinet with drawers below and glass doors above. Double doors opened into the bedroom beyond. The room was spacious. She turned back to Jim.

"I had no idea cabins could be like this."

"Neither did I. My son made the booking. I think we had a smaller balcony cabin but he was offered an upgrade to this suite."

"What a shame he couldn't enjoy it."

"He has a demanding job." Jim waved to the couch. "Please sit down. Can I get you something to drink; water, wine, cup of tea?"

Celia sank onto the couch. "I'd love a cup of tea. I take it black, not too strong."

Jim busied himself making it and she nestled further into the couch. The last place she had imagined herself being was Jim's room. After Maude's innuendo, it seemed comical to find herself here. Perhaps she would see the funny side if she wasn't so nervous. Maude was the one having an affair, if that's what you could call it. Celia's feelings were running rampant, torn between the embarrassment of being in Jim's room to overwhelming tiredness. She yawned and decided the tiredness was winning.

"Kick off your shoes if you like, make yourself at home."

Celia did as he suggested. It was a relief to slip them off. Jim placed the tea on the coffee table in front of her, took his own and sat in a chair.

"This is kind of you, Jim." She tucked her feet up behind her on the couch.

"I couldn't leave you wandering the ship looking for somewhere to sleep."

The hint of a smile played on his lips. He was such a handsome man when he smiled. What was she thinking? Jim was still getting over the loss of his wife. She hadn't planned to like him this much but when he smiled...She pulled herself up straighter and set her cup on the table.

"You must be tired yourself. You don't have to sit up with me." She gave a brief nod towards the bedroom. "You can go to bed, shut the door. I won't disturb you. I can let myself out."

He looked startled. "Do you mind if I finish my tea?"

"Of course not, it's your suite after all."

They both sipped. The act of drinking tea had a calming effect.

Jim stretched out his legs, crossing his ankles. "It's good to have company. Jane and I would always have a cuppa together in the evening, talk about the day. I miss it." He stared off into space.

The silence dragged out so long she was startled when he spoke again.

"She would have loved this cruise."

Celia nodded.

"It was something she'd always wanted to do. Before she got sick she'd started leaving brochures about the place..." He tapered off into silence again.

Celia felt the need to say something. "Cruising had never been on Ed's agenda so we never went. Then I found out he was taking his new wife on a cruise and I got angry. Stupid really. And now here I am without a cabin." Once more she chewed on her lip. The thought of returning to her room was not a pleasant one. "I think I will stay on your couch, Jim, if you don't mind."

"I wish you'd take the bed."

"It's very kind of you but I'm half asleep now. I'm sure I will be fine on the couch."

"It's one of those sofa bed things." He stood up. "I'll get the sheets from the other bed. They won't fit but at least you'll have something."

Celia staggered to her feet and inspected the couch, which did indeed appear to be a fold-out bed.

Jim came back, his arms loaded with sheets and pillows. Together they opened out the bed and made it up as best they could. Jim placed a t-shirt on the end.

"I thought you might like to change into this. You'd be more comfortable."

Celia looked at the shirt. She couldn't imagine anything would make her comfortable the way her emotions were whirling around inside her but it was a kind thought.

"Thank you."

"Would you like to use the bathroom? There's spare towels but I don't have an extra toothbrush or anything else."

"Oh, that's all right." Celia couldn't look at him. This was all so intimate. She wished she'd stayed in the bar. "I will use the bathroom though, thank you."

She crossed through the bedroom which was about the size of her entire cabin and stepped into the brightly lit bathroom. She washed her face and stared at herself in the mirror. How on earth did she find herself in this situation? It was so far removed from any Celebrity Celia scenario. She shuddered at the recollection of the other persona she'd tried to be.

Back in the living room they said a polite but awkward goodnight, then Jim had entered his bedroom and closed the doors. Celia turned out the light, undressed in the dark and slipped between the sheets. She'd been so tired before but now she was wide awake, aware of Jim moving around in the other room beyond the closed door, then the light that filtered around the edges of the door faded and all went quiet. Celia lay stiffly on the slightly lumpy sofa bed with its ill-fitting sheets rumpled around her. A jumble of thoughts went round and round in her head and all of them ended up back at Jim. Kind, generous Jim and his engaging smile. Celia tossed and turned a long time before she eventually fell asleep.

Twenty-eight

Day Seven – Alongside, Noumea, New Caledonia

Celia jolted awake. The room had been dark when she'd last closed her eyes. Now it was bright from the light filtering around the edge of the curtains. It took her an instant to get her bearings. She was in Jim's suite. It was so different to the pitch black of her interior cabin. She'd tossed and turned through the early hours and felt as if she'd hardly slept. Now she was groggy. She must have gone into a deep sleep.

She lay still, trying to detect the movement of the ship. She'd been more conscious of it in Jim's rear-situated suite than in her mid-section cabin but now she could feel nothing. Perhaps the ship had docked already. She reached for her watch. It was nearly seven o'clock. She sat up carefully and dressed in the clothes she'd worn the night before. Dear Lord, she prayed she would not see anyone when she left Jim's cabin.

She paused in the middle of the room listening for stirrings beyond the bedroom door but there was nothing. It would only add to her embarrassment to see Jim before she'd had a chance to shower and change. She folded the sheets and his t-shirt. There was no way she could put the couch back together without making a noise so she left it and started for the door.

There was a knock. Celia froze. Then she realised the knock came from behind not in front. She glanced back.

The knock came again.

"Celia, is it all right for me to come in?"

She let out the breath she'd been holding. It was Jim.

"Yes."

He opened the door. His hair was damp from the shower and he wore a fresh set of clothes. She hadn't heard him moving about.

"You're ready to go?" he asked.

"I was just leaving." She felt foolish standing there in the clothes she'd been wearing the night before.

"I thought perhaps I could check the corridor first. I wouldn't like to put you in a compromising situation."

She was speechless. How chivalrous of Jim to even think of her reputation.

"I feel silly, but that is kind of you."

Jim hesitated at the door. "Would you like to have breakfast with me…later…once you're refreshed?"

Her heart thudded an extra beat. She was pleased he wanted her company even though he was still so caught up in memories of his wife.

"All right, yes."

"Meet you in half an hour?" He scratched at his temple. "Oh, that's probably not long enough is it? Jane always said I hurried her."

"Half an hour is fine, Jim." She waited for him to open the door.

He was staring at her. "Oh, the door, yes." He opened it and peered out. "Coast clear."

She stepped briskly passed him and heard the door close behind her. It was as if she was being propelled along the corridor, she moved so fast, anxious to put as much space between her and Jim's room before she ran into anyone. Her next hope was that Maude might already be up and gone. She didn't want to face her. Not just because of Maude's own indiscreet behaviour but neither did she want to explain to her roommate about her own compromising night.

Maude was fast asleep when Celia crept in. She managed to gather some fresh clothes and shut herself in the bathroom, hopeful of escaping again before Maude woke. That hope was short-lived. Maude was waiting when she re-opened the door.

"Where were you all night?" Still dishevelled from sleep, hands on hips, she was a forbidding sight. "You're making a habit of staying out."

Celia gripped her discarded clothes to her chest and lifted her chin. "A friend offered me a spare bed. I didn't want to spend my night in the corridor."

"So you stayed all night." Maude wiggled her eyebrows. "With who?"

"I wasn't *with* anyone. I was on the couch."

Maude's look soured. "Humph. You didn't have to. Pete and I—" She looked down. "We—"

Celia held up her hand. "Stop please. I don't want to know."

Maude gave Celia a steely look and sniffed. "Do you have plans for today?"

"Not as yet."

"I'm going with Pete and Anne and co again."

"Anne?" Celia didn't know how Maude could have the front to look the woman in the eye.

"She's a lot more active now." Once more Maude's look was sour. "You know you're welcome to join us."

"Thank you but I don't think I will."

Maude opened her mouth, obviously changed her mind about what she was going to say, and shrugged her shoulders instead. "Please yourself. Have you finished with the bathroom?"

"Yes."

Celia stepped out and Maude took her place, shutting the door without a backward glance.

"Do you mind if I join you, Miss Clift?"

Ketty looked across the table where she'd been enjoying a late breakfast to find Carlos studying her.

"I'd be delighted, if you have time."

"You are not going ashore today?" he asked. He positioned himself at the head of the six-person table where he would have a good view of the dining room.

"I am but not for a while yet. It would be lovely to chat." She leaned in a little. "We still haven't managed a catch-up."

A waiter came with the coffee pot and poured a cup for Carlos, who watched the procedure with his maître d' face on.

"Thank you, Terry," Carlos said. "Would you like a cup, Miss Clift?"

"I think I might, thank you." She smiled up at the waiter, who departed quickly to get a fresh cup. Ketty took the opportunity to lean even closer across the table. "You must call me Ketty if we are to coffee together."

"Once the staff are out of earshot." Carlos poured milk into his coffee. "I am already breaking the rules."

"We've dined together before."

"A quick bite at the end of a shift is hardly dining, Ket— Miss Clift."

The waiter was back. He carefully placed the cup and saucer in front of her and poured.

Ketty studied her friend while she waited for the waiter to leave. "How are you, Carlos?"

"Feeling rather old these days."

"I see a little silver sprinkling that dark hair of yours but you look the same as the fine young head waiter I met all those years ago."

"Ha." Carlos laughed and smoothed the perfectly flat tablecloth with his fingers. "I think you may need to put on those glasses I've seen you wear for reading the menu."

Ketty sensed something more serious lurked beneath her friend's jovial exterior. "We've plenty of life left in us yet, Carlos."

"You are quite right. I am thinking now the time has come to retire."

"Retire?" Ketty felt a pang of sadness to think she'd never come across her friend aboard ship again. Given her financial situation may not allow her the opportunity to cruise anymore, it was possibly going to be the last she'd see of Carlos anyway. Then another thought hit her. It was the last cruise of the *Duchess* too. The end of an era for all of them.

"Have you thought about what you will do? Will you stay in Spain?" She knew his marriage had floundered years ago, one of the downsides of the job he loved, there had been no children and the last she'd heard, his aging parents were becoming very frail.

"I'm not sure."

"You're not too old to try new things."

"I know." He clasped his large hands together on the table. "I think I'll travel. Not cruise," he added quickly. "I've seen a lot of what the world has to offer from many ports but I'd like to visit places cruise ships can't take me. Australia of course. My cousin is keen for me to come and stay."

"Then you must visit me again."

"I will." He met her look with an equally steady one.

They fell silent a moment, perhaps both pondering the uncertain future.

"So how is your table of eight going?" he asked.

Ketty found herself faltering under his keen stare. She lifted her chin. "I haven't had a chance to reprimand you."

"Ah, Ketty." He put his hand across his heart. "Why on earth should you wish to do that?"

"You have given me too many people to sort out."

"But that makes it all the more interesting."

"Bernard has fallen for Josie. It was he who brought the Kellers to our table."

"I know, and the brother, Leo, is very taken with you."

Ketty glanced up to meet Carlos's penetrating stare again. "We knew each other a long time ago."

He nodded. "This morning they dined separately."

"All of them?"

"No. Bernard came early, ate alone and left. The Kellers came later, you barely missed them but they appeared to be arguing when they left."

"Oh?"

"Something about Leo not wanting his sister to…tag along, was how I think he put it."

Ketty frowned at that. "I wonder what's happened? Bernard and Josie were having such a good time. Last night he had dinner alone with his daughter and didn't arrive to meet us to go to the show. Josie was pretending it didn't matter but I could see it did.

Now you say they dined separately this morning when they've been practically in each other's pockets."

"Perhaps a lover's tiff?"

"Perhaps." Ketty pondered that. Both Josie and Bernard had been so happy, so well suited. "I hope Christine hasn't been meddling."

"Bernard's daughter?"

Ketty nodded. "She has her father wrapped around her finger so tightly. And her relationship with her husband is rocky. They are struggling to be civil to each other. And then there's Jim who's a widower, desperately sad and mired in guilt."

"Even on this beautiful ship." Carlos spread his hands wide in amazement.

"Even here, but I think Celia is the woman who could change that." Ketty wriggled forward and lowered her voice. "She came on this cruise to make her ex-husband jealous."

Carlos raised his eyebrows.

"The night she fell outside the dining room she was trying to avoid him. It's all rather complicated."

Ketty was about to start explaining further when Carlos drew a small parcel from inside his jacket.

"Happy birthday, Ketty."

"Oh," she tutted. "Nothing gets past you. Don't you tell anyone else."

"You should celebrate."

"I don't like fuss, Carlos, you know that." Ketty tapped the table lightly with her fingers. She'd forgotten it was her birthday this morning when her waking thoughts had gone straight to Leo. It wasn't until after her shower while she was choosing what to wear that she remembered she turned sixty-five today.

"But surely you came on this cruise as a treat for yourself." He waved at the gift he'd put in front of her. "Open the parcel."

She did as he bid and pulled back the gold paper to reveal a small, flat velvet case. It was stiff to open and she paused as she did. Nestled inside were a pair of dainty scissors, the metal around the finger holes decorated with an intricate flower pattern. The scissors were attached to a chain to enable them to hang around her neck. There was also a needle holder, a thimble and a retractable tape measure, its outer covering fashioned in the same design as the scissors. "Oh, Carlos, they're beautiful. How kind of you. Wherever did you find them?"

"On one of my trips to the Mediterranean. They reminded me of you. I've been sailing with them ever since."

She looked up quickly. His deep brown eyes bored steadily into hers but gave nothing away. She glanced down at the gift again, overcome at the thoughtfulness of it. Cruising had brought some of the happiest times of her life and Carlos, if he had been aboard on her trip, was part of that – but he would come across so many other passengers.

"That looks like Madam Keller now. Would you rather avoid her?"

Ketty glanced up to see Josie peering around the dining room. Her hands were gripped together and she was obviously evading the waiter who was trying to turn her away. "I should find out what's going on but it's getting late. Breakfast is finished, I suppose."

"For you, my friend, we can always make an exception."

Once more Ketty looked into his eyes, and this time she could see they twinkled with friendship. "Thank you, Carlos."

He stood, looking grand as always in his uniform, and waved a hand at the waiter who ushered Josie in their direction.

"You haven't finished your coffee." Ketty felt torn between her two friends but she knew he wouldn't stay once Josie joined them.

"Another time." He pulled out a chair as Josie reached them.

"Oh, Ketty." Josie slid onto the seat with barely a nod at Carlos. "I'm glad I've found you. I'm not sure what to do."

Over Josie's head Ketty saw Carlos's assessing look before he turned and walked away. She watched him a moment then gave her attention to Josie.

"What's happened?"

"I think I've misread Bernie."

"In what way? He's totally beguiled by you."

"I looked everywhere for him last night."

"He was probably caught up with his daughter."

"I don't think so." A waiter appeared with coffee and pastries. Josie chose one with custard and fruit and waited for him to leave before she spoke again. "When I got back to the cabin last night, Bernie had left me a note to say he'd been out late with Christine."

"There you are then."

"But I went back to my room a couple of times between searches, the note wasn't there until quite late and I'd seen Christine and Frank in the spa together an hour before. I'd stuck my head in there because Bernie and I had been to the bar there several times." She popped a piece of pastry in her mouth and washed it down with coffee. "The note also said he couldn't meet this morning and for me to enjoy Noumea and he'd probably see me at dinner."

Ketty wasn't sure what to think about that.

Josie lurched back in her seat. "I've been such a fool."

"I don't think so."

"I do." Josie lunged forward this time.

"You're going to have to stop this lurching about or it will bring on seasickness." Ketty smiled but Josie still looked anxious and lowered her voice even though there were no passengers besides them in the dining room and the waiters were busy across the other side. "The night before last I shared his bed."

Ketty was not surprised. "Good for you."

"But now...oh, this is ridiculous, I feel like I'm sixteen again instead of sixty, waiting for a boy to notice me." Josie took another slurp of coffee. She sat the cup carefully back on its saucer and looked at Ketty. "It's just that I can't help feeling now that we've..." she twirled her hand in the air. "Now that Bernie's got what he wanted, he's going to avoid me for the rest of the trip."

Ketty shook her head in disbelief. Josie had always struck her as self-assured and carefree, especially where men were concerned. She had a vague recollection of Leo saying his sister had made some poor choices with men but surely Bernard wasn't a poor choice. "I'm certain that's not what this is about."

"We had such a good night. He made me feel..." Josie's shoulders slumped. "Very special." Her last words came out in a whisper and her face crumpled. "I know it sounds ridiculous after such a short time but it's more than a flirtation. Bernie and I like the same things, laugh together, we're a good fit...we both mentioned love."

Josie looked straight at Ketty and her face, although made up as usual, was stripped bare of confidence, replaced by a vulnerability she'd rarely shown before. How could it be that at this stage of their lives, when both she and Josie had experienced so much, that they could become so insecure over relationships? Ketty was still unsure of her own feelings for Leo, one minute excited at the prospect of taking things further and the next wanting to back away.

"Let's not talk about Bernie," Josie said. "I'm glad you and my brother are getting along. I owe Leo so much. He was such a help when I left my first husband. Carl was a drinker and prone to lashing out. He was getting worse and I feared for the boys as much as myself. Our father was a…well, a hard man and our mother was in poor health. I couldn't go to them for help. Leo got the boys and I away and helped me financially until I found work." Josie snatched up the last of the pastry and popped it in her mouth.

Ketty studied her friend. Her only other experience of domestic violence had been with Judith, and she was grateful Leo had been able to support his sister to leave the troubled marriage as Ketty had done for Judith.

"Leo mentioned he'd helped you."

"Did he? I've paid him back of course. In fact I was able to help him financially only recently but that's what family's for, isn't it?"

Ketty was puzzled by that. She felt sure Leo had said he'd been the one to help Josie out on several occasions, not the other way around.

Josie clapped a hand to her forehead and groaned. "I can't believe I've been such a fool."

Ketty had no time to worry about who'd said what. Josie needed her support. She reached out a hand and gripped her friend's. "You're no fool, Josie. There will be a reasonable explanation for his absence and I'm betting it will have something to do with Christine. Today you're sightseeing with Leo and me until we come across Bernard and get to the bottom of this."

"Oh no." Josie snatched her hand away. "Leo and I have already had words over my 'tagging along' with you two, as he put it. I can amuse myself."

"Nonsense." Josie was Leo's sister and Ketty's friend. They couldn't just abandon her. "Noumea is an experience and we shall see it together."

Twenty-nine

Christine sat in the coffee lounge waiting for Frank. By the time she'd returned to their cabin last night he was in bed, his back to her. She'd done a lot of thinking before sleep had claimed her and this morning she'd resolved that today she'd get his assurance they would stay in their home but she'd not mention extensions. Rather, she'd do her best to be fun, make sure they had a terrific day and when they got back to the ship, well, it was day seven and she was determined to finally seduce her husband. And in the afterglow, she would slowly work him around.

He could take his new job if he so badly wanted it but they would stay in their current house. After all they'd done to make their home a special place for their family, she was not giving it up to start again.

"Good morning, Christine."

She looked up, startled from her thoughts. Ketty was looking down at her, a sugary-sweet smile on her face. "Hello."

"The tropics are so moisturising for the skin aren't they?" The older woman peered closely at her. "You're positively glowing this morning."

Christine's smile remained on her face but she didn't know whether to be offended or not. Had she looked so terrible before?

"And your back? It's not troubling you anymore?"

"No. How is your arm?"

"Much better, thank you. I'm on my way to have the bandage replaced and I hope I'll be able to rid myself of the sling. It's rather a nuisance."

But good for the sympathy vote, Christine thought. Ketty seemed to like being the centre of attention. Right now she wished she'd move on. They had too little in common to keep up a conversation.

"Have you seen your father this morning?"

"No, why?"

"No reason. I'd hoped to catch up before we went ashore, that's all. Have you got your day planned?"

Ketty's piercing look made Christine shift in her seat. She wished Frank would hurry up. "We're going to do the tourist train tour."

"That's a good way to have a look around. Perhaps your father will do the same." Ketty smiled benignly. "He and Josie seem well suited and they obviously get along."

Christine seethed. Her good mood was disappearing fast. Ketty was such a busybody. What did she know about Bernard and what suited?

"He thought he liked the previous women he got along with and he thought he knew them but that didn't turn out well."

Ketty's smile remained. "It must be worrying for you but I'm sure you realise he's an adult of sound mind who can make his own decisions."

"And when it all falls to pieces and he's penniless, what will become of him then? I'm his only child and I'll have to carry the financial burden."

"Do you really believe it would come to that?"

Christine faltered under Ketty's scrutiny, desperately searching for an answer. "He's so easily led by a good-looking woman," she blustered. "He could waste it all on Josie."

Ketty tilted her head to one side as if she was pondering Christine's words. "You need to decide if your concerns are truly for your father's wellbeing or about your own."

Christine's mouth fell open.

"Hello." Frank stepped past Ketty into the coffee shop.

"Hello, Frank." Ketty's smile returned. "Time is getting on. It's been lovely chatting but I'd better go down for my medical appointment or I'll be late." She leaned down and patted Christine's shoulder. "I'm sure you'll come to the right decision. See you at dinner."

Christine glared after her. She could strangle the woman! Was she suggesting Christine only cared about Bernard for his money?

"What decision?" Frank squeezed in beside her, his long legs bent up so that his knees touched the coffee table.

"Nothing important. That Ketty is the most abominable woman."

Frank looked across the room. "I thought she was quite sweet. She's usually so caring of everyone. Maybe her arm is giving her trouble. Pain can upset people."

"There's hardly anything wrong with her arm. I suspect it was never that bad to start with."

Frank gave her an odd look. "I saw your dad in the corridor but he was ahead of me and by the time I reached the lifts he'd disappeared."

"No doubt scurrying off to meet Josie." Christine wasn't worried about her father now that he'd committed to the renovation money. She'd pin him down for the details before the cruise was over but if he wanted to have a final fling with his floozy, she wouldn't deny him that. Christine had made it perfectly clear she knew what he was up to, and she knew he wouldn't take his dalliance with Josie any further than this cruise. She had her own relationship to work on. She turned her smile on her husband. "What shall we do in Noumea?"

Celia looked out over the blue water of the bay sparkling in the sunshine. There was a gentle breeze but inside the waiting room of the tour office only a lazy ceiling fan ruffled the air. She was still feeling a little nervous that she had committed to a half-day of sailing. When Jim had invited her to go with him on the tour his son had booked, she had been surprised he wouldn't go on his own, and then she'd felt a little glimmer of hope that perhaps he truly wanted her company. Finally the nerves had kicked in. She wasn't sure how she'd go for several hours on a small boat. It was something she'd never done before. She'd taken a tablet for seasickness just in case.

She glanced across at Jim seated nearby, peering at his phone. They'd both been taking advantage of the free wi-fi. Celia had discovered emails from her sons and sent quick replies. There'd been another message from a friend at home who was looking after her unit and several junk emails she'd deleted. Jim appeared to be studying something closely; there was a crease across his forehead and he was intent on the screen. He shook his head, muttered *that's it* and then looked up.

"Is something wrong?"

"I knew I'd seen him somewhere before." He shuffled across into the empty chair between them and held his phone out.

Celia studied the face on the small screen and realised he was familiar. She took the phone from Jim so she could scroll and read the print below the photo. It was a lot of ins and outs of a court case but she sucked in a breath when she read the part about women having some of their money siphoned away. When she looked up Jim was studying her closely. "Should we be concerned?" She handed the phone back.

"I don't know." Jim tucked his phone into the waterproof bag at his feet. "It was a while ago now."

"Perhaps we could talk to Josie, or maybe it should be Ketty."

"I don't feel as if I know either of them well enough to broach it." Jim pursed his lips.

"I don't either. I'd hate to spoil someone's happiness by casting doubt that may not be warranted."

"Bonjour everyone, hello."

They both looked up at the man standing in the middle of the waiting area. He wore a battered captain's hat and a colourful shirt as bright as his smile.

"I am your guide today, Captain Enzo." He tapped the clipboard he held. "Let me check I have everyone and then we can set off for your day in paradise."

Celia was already enchanted by his smile but the French accent was what really took her interest, her concern over Jim's discovery and her fears about sailing dissipating with every word Captain Enzo spoke.

Bernard sat at one of the little cafes with a view across the bay beyond but he was oblivious to the soft blues of the water lapping gently against the white beach and the hazy sky dotted with puffs of cloud. Around him other customers chatted, but Bernard remained intent on the coffee mug he gripped tightly between his hands, staring into it as if the solutions he sought would magically appear in the swirls of milk.

Ever since his dinner with Christine he'd been in turmoil. He hadn't been able to face Josie. He hadn't trusted himself to be able to act normally. Instead of meeting her as he'd planned, he'd bought two whiskys and headed to the small deck at the front of the ship on his cabin level, fairly sure it was a place where no one would look for him. He'd leaned on the rail, the breeze much stronger there. It had helped cool his anger but not his thoughts. He'd steadily worked his way through the two drinks then he'd slipped back to his cabin and lain on his bed in the dark, unable to sleep.

He'd pictured Della's excitement matching his own the day their daughter was born. They had both been besotted with the little human being they had made together. He was shocked to think that Christine imagined her own mother hadn't loved her enough, but a little part of him knew there was an element of truth in it. Della hadn't fallen pregnant again after Christine, perhaps an early complication of the cancer that ultimately claimed her, he wondered now, but whatever the reason there were no more children.

Della compensated by throwing herself into creating a comfortable home environment while perhaps holding Christine a little at arm's length. Bernard knew that was because she had been frightened of losing her only child. They were both responsible for the woman Christine had become. Della not giving enough love and Bernard trying to make up by giving too much. He'd fallen asleep with moisture in his eyes recalling the loss of his wife and woken early feeling as if he hadn't slept at all.

This morning he'd come ashore in Noumea as soon as he could, hoping to avoid anyone he knew, and taken a taxi to this more distant part of the island where once again he felt sure no one would find him. He drained the remains of the coffee and drank a glass of water. He'd had three cups of coffee since arriving at the cafe and knew he should have no more. Perhaps an early lunch so that the staff didn't want to move him on.

He caught the waiter's attention and ordered a croissant, not feeling hungry but knowing he needed some food in his stomach to absorb the coffee that sloshed there. The scrap of paper he'd been writing on fluttered with the breeze but the pen held it in place. It hadn't been until after the second cup of coffee that he had decided to jot down his thoughts and possible solutions. *Christine* was written at the top with several exclamation marks.

Last night at dinner she had surprised him, angered him, and now all he felt was overwhelming sadness for their relationship that had gone so horribly wrong. And yet she was his daughter. He may not like her right now but deep down he knew he could never stop loving her, this person who was the result of his and Della's love.

The next name on his list was Josie and then he'd written *money and investments* followed by a roughly drawn love heart. What he'd thought might be merely a holiday fling had turned into something more. He loved Josie. He knew she would be wondering where he was. She'd be hurt, upset by his avoidance of her but he had to make sure there would be no loose ends before he explained everything and put himself in her hands. He hoped she would still want to be with him but there were no guarantees.

Underneath her name was that of his broker Jack and the words *post office* with a question mark. He stared at his rough writing, and as he did, his thoughts began to make more sense and a resolution formed. He wasn't going to give up on Josie without a fight.

The waiter returned with the food and Bernard asked him where the main post office was. The young man marked it on the tourist map for him.

Bernard studied the map a moment then took up the pen and wrote the name of his lawyer, underlined it and took out his phone. The untouched croissant sat cooling beside him as he dialled the first number.

Thirty

Ketty smiled brightly at her two companions as they alighted from the little train that had toured them around Noumea. Poor Josie's usual spark was still missing and Leo had done little more than murmur at the grand design of the cathedral or the historic architecture of the colonial houses – a particular interest of Ketty's – and he'd barely glanced at the magnificent views across the city to the many bays and nearby islands.

"Come on," she said with forced cheer. "Time to find the patisserie I promised." She strode ahead of them across the road as the lights turned to green and on up the narrow street to a little place she'd visited on previous trips to Noumea.

Josie exclaimed behind her as they stepped inside and even Leo became interested at the sight of the glass cabinets filled with cakes and slices of every description; from chocolate eclairs and mousse and cream-filled cakes, to fruit tarts and colourful macarons, there was something to tempt everyone. Small round tables and wooden chairs furnished the eating section, which was broken up into separate areas by plants, low walls, room dividers and statues, making each table setting a little apart from its neighbour.

The patisserie was busy with customers, some tourists like them, and others locals, placing their orders in rapid French. It took Ketty's little group a while to choose. Once they were happy with their orders, she found them a table tucked between a large potted palm on one side and a room divider on the other.

"I hope their coffee's good," Leo said as he brushed at the tabletop that had looked perfectly clean to Ketty.

"It was when I was here last."

"I do envy you your travels, Ketty." Josie settled herself on her chair. "I'm going to cruise more, I've decided."

"Humph." Leo's snort was soft but disapproving nonetheless.

"You're enjoying yourself," Josie countered.

He turned his gaze to Ketty. "That's because I've found the woman I loved and thought I'd lost. It's because of Kathy, nothing to do with the cruise."

A warm flush swept over Ketty. He'd hardly spoken a word all morning and here he was professing his pleasure at being with her.

"You're very lucky." Josie glanced sideways as the door opened letting in another group of customers. She'd been flinging that searching look about all morning and Ketty knew she hoped to find Bernard but they hadn't caught a glimpse of him. Josie turned back. "Tell me how you two met. I've heard nothing about your young days together. Was it love at first sight?"

"It was for me." Leo looked steadily at Ketty.

Most people were sceptical that such a feeling could truly exist but she had felt the thrill of love and been captivated by Leo from their very first meeting. "And me." The words croaked from her mouth and Ketty cleared her throat.

Their coffee and cake arrived, interrupting the conversation that was far too personal for Ketty's comfort but no sooner had the waitress left than Josie began again. "And when was this? Before you met Marjorie obviously, Leo."

Ketty stabbed her small fork into her strawberry-covered tart, wondering how she would possibly get the food past the lump that had formed in her throat. From the corner of her eye she could see Leo trying to tackle his chocolate eclair.

"You're both very reticent to speak up. Surely you didn't have an affair."

Ketty and Leo looked at each other. She knew her face must mirror the guilt she still felt but his look was brooding.

"Oh no," Josie gasped. "That's it, isn't it. That's why you've been so secretive about your relationship. You had an affair."

"Keep your voice down, Josie," Leo growled.

The sounds of the patisserie floated around them but at their table there was silence. Leo's jaw was clenched and he turned a glowering look to his sister. Ketty tried to shrug off the guilt that flooded her. After all, she hadn't been the one to knowingly have an affair.

"None of it matters now," Leo said. "It's in the past and there's no need to rake it all up."

"And there's no need to be so defensive," Josie muttered. "I always knew you weren't a saint."

"That's rich coming from you."

Brother and sister were so busy sparring they didn't see the couple emerge from behind the screen beside them but Ketty did, and the tiny piece of tart she had swallowed soured in her stomach. Christine and Frank had obviously been enjoying the wares of the patisserie as well. Frank said hello as they passed and Christine gave only the briefest nod of acknowledgement but there was a gleam in her eye and a smug look on her face. Ketty wasn't sure if it was from seeing Josie without Bernard at her side or because she'd been eavesdropping on their conversation. Either way it left her feeling cold.

Josie sat back, her delicate cake untouched. "I'd like to wipe the smile off that young woman's face," she said once they were gone.

"What young woman?" Leo had barely given the Romanos more than the slightest acknowledgement.

"Christine Romano."

"She's not that young."

"She's nearly half your age, Leo," Josie said.

Ketty took a sip of her coffee. Her perfectly planned day out in Noumea was going from bad to worse.

"Anyway, where were we?" Josie leaned in again, her voice lower this time. "I want to know more about your relationship. You two met when Leo was still married to Marjorie?" She winked at Ketty. "I can't imagine you as the other woman."

It was all too much for Ketty. "I didn't know your brother was married." She felt the need to defend herself even though that put Leo in a poor light.

He grasped her hand and squeezed it. "It's true. I didn't tell Kathy anything about my life with Marjorie. I had fallen out of love with my wife by then but...well, I didn't want to lose Kathy. It was weak of me, I know."

His voice was full of remorse but his eyes held a different emotion, perhaps annoyance. Ketty didn't want to be having this conversation either, not while Josie was with them.

"I know it's not caring to say it but I'm glad to hear you're not perfect, Leo." Josie put her head to one side, locking her eyes on her brother. "You always made me feel I was the only one to stuff up relationships."

Leo shook his head and Ketty extracted her hand. This was all too much. Her life was not one that she allowed to be inspected in the open by other people. Not here with Josie eagerly taking it all in. She shifted in her seat but felt no more comfortable. "It was a difficult time for both of us."

"Ketty lost our baby."

Josie gasped. This time her eyes were full of sorrow when she looked at Ketty. "That's so sad. How far gone were you?"

Ketty opened her mouth but no words came. It was as if Josie's concern had opened the lid on the grief she'd thought was dealt with and she was lost as the desolation consumed her all over again.

"It was only a miscarriage," Leo huffed. "Marjorie had one after our three kids were born."

Josie frowned. "Those little babies that died were your children too, Leo."

"Hardly. They weren't even human at that stage. Besides Marjorie had three healthy kids who needed looking after but she went on and on about the—" he held up his hands in disgust "—baby we lost as if it was real."

The knife that was stabbing inside Ketty twisted. She took a gulp of water, her coffee and tart untouched.

"Poor Marjorie," Josie said. "You were away a lot for work then, weren't you?"

"I had to build my business to pay for all these children. As it was, Marjorie ended up with the house and most of the money. Child support nearly killed me."

Ketty stared at Leo. She'd never seen this cold side of him when they'd been together, not a sign of it. Now his good looks appeared harsh; his jaw jutting, his eyes narrowed, his cheeks a ruddy red. Had she been naive or had the years changed him?

Josie shook her head. "You won't get any sympathy from me. I got no support from Carl. I raised my boys on my own."

"I helped."

"In the early days, yes, and I'm grateful for that, but I've paid you back many times over."

He glared at her, opened his mouth then took a slurp of his coffee instead of speaking, as if he'd thought better of it.

Josie turned a sympathetic gaze to Ketty. "Obviously my brother was no help. Did you have support through the miscarriage and getting over it?"

Ketty glanced at Leo but he stared steadily into his coffee cup. She had planned to tell him the whole story but when they were alone and the time had felt right. "I didn't think my parents would understand, although in hindsight I probably misjudged them, didn't give them a chance to help. My brother was overseas but I had a very good friend who supported me."

Ketty jumped as Leo's hand hit the table. They all looked around but no one appeared to be taking any notice.

"Settle, Leo," Josie said. "You accused me of being too loud."

"I know I was a married man," he huffed. "But I wouldn't have remained so for much longer if you'd stayed, Kathy. I would have left Marjorie much sooner."

He glared at her and the pain that had been twisting inside her abated, replaced with a simmering heat.

"You act aloof," he went on, "so not needing of anyone. We were in love. I thought when I met you again we could rekindle something of what we felt. I have, but you won't let me past that exterior you've built around yourself. What's happened to you, Kathy?"

The rage inside her boiled over and she could contain herself no longer. "You happened to me, Leo. You all but destroyed me. I had to work so hard to rebuild myself, to enjoy life again."

"Now you're sounding like Marjorie. Surely it's not my fault you had a miscarriage."

"That's so insensitive, Leo," Josie said. "I can't believe—"

"No, it wasn't your fault I lost our baby." Ketty's quiet words cut Josie off. "But let me tell you how it went, Leo." His disdainful look strengthened her resolve. The words bubbled up her throat, wanting escape from the prison she'd boxed them in for thirty-five years. "I didn't know I was even pregnant. Once again I blame my own stupidity for not recognising the signs. I'd been nauseous on the cruise with my friend, Felicity, but I put it down to seasickness. It remained when I returned home, got worse. Then the pain began, it was terrible. I was writhing in agony, burning up with fever when I managed to attract my neighbour's attention to call an ambulance."

Ketty took a steadying breath, well aware of the two sets of similar eyes watching her, Josie's pretty blue brimming with tears and Leo's pale green and cold.

"At the hospital the doctors said I had lost the baby. That was the first shock. I didn't even know I was pregnant. I'd had an ectopic pregnancy that had ruptured and become infected. They asked if there was someone I should call." Ketty paused, willing herself to go on. "I called you, Leo, on the only contact number I had, your work number."

"I never got the call," he blustered.

"No. When I asked to speak to you, your secretary was very excited to tell me you'd been called away to the hospital…to be with your wife who'd gone into labour with your first child."

Josie gasped beside her but Ketty didn't look away from Leo's face. She watched the surprise and then the shock register.

"She said she'd take a message." Ketty gripped her hands together in her lap. Now that she'd come this far she had to say the rest. Her words tumbled out. "While you were at your wife's side rejoicing in a new child, our baby was lost."

Ketty swallowed, still staring at Leo who had said nothing but at least looked contrite. "I had emergency surgery and woke up with tubes and drains and equipment connected all over me. I was a mess inside. They'd thought I was going to die, and at the time I wished I had."

"Oh Ketty, how awful."

It was Josie's quiet words and the feel of her warm hand sliding over to grip Ketty's that almost undid her. She bit hard on her lip to hold back the tears.

"But you recovered." Leo found his voice at last, a smile that was more like a wince on his face. "I wish I'd known, Kathy, I would have come to you."

"And left your wife when she'd just had a baby?" She glared steadily at him and saw the faintest hint of remorse in his look. Josie's fingers wrapped tighter over hers. "You and I both know that wouldn't have happened, Leo. My life course changed from then on. No babies for me." She was running on empty now; the words that had flowed like lava from her mouth had taken her energy with them.

"I know you felt I was lost to you, Kathy, but…" Leo shrugged his shoulders. "You could have had children with someone else."

Ketty sucked in a breath. "No, Leo. They had to remove my womb to save my life."

"You had a hysterectomy. Oh Ketty, I'm so sorry." Josie slid an arm around Ketty's shoulders but there was no consolation from Leo. He remained rigid in his chair, his expression changing to anger.

"Are you blaming me?" he growled.

Ketty took in his unyielding stare, the stiffness of his jaw, searching for some trace of the man she'd loved.

"When it happened…yes, I admit I did. I felt guilt, shame, despair and I had to put the cause somewhere so it was you. But over time, my body healed and I came to understand it for what it was. I accepted you could not be with me and that I would have no more children. I discovered living wasn't so bad once I'd done that. I'll never forget the child that didn't survive, the lost opportunity for more, but I've found a life fulfilled in other ways."

"There you are then." Leo took up his eclair and bit into it.

"My God, Leo." Josie's words came out in a harsh rasp. "Ketty's poured her heart out and while the final result was not your fault, you did deceive her and you were the father of the baby she lost."

"What is it you want from me?" He looked from Josie to Ketty, genuine puzzlement on his face.

"Have you not one ounce of empathy in your body?" Josie said.

Leo dropped the half-eaten eclair back to his plate and wiped his fingers on the napkin. "Why is it that women get so emotional over babies, especially those that never lived?"

"Leo, I can't believe I'm seeing this side of you." Josie gaped at her brother.

"I'm who I've always been." This time he reached out and brushed a wisp of hair back from where it had fallen forward over Ketty's cheek.

She tensed but there was nothing intimate in the touch. He was purely tidying up something he saw as out of place, she understood that now.

Leo shrugged his shoulders, took a sip of his coffee and wrinkled his nose. "It's gone cold."

Nausea roiled in the pit of Ketty's stomach. She didn't know what reaction she'd expected from Leo but this was not it. She hadn't wanted sympathy, just some understanding, perhaps a tiny bit of sorrow for what they'd both lost. Hearing him speak of his wife's loss so dismissively made Ketty think that perhaps he'd always had that cold streak in him. She hadn't known him long enough to discover it, too mesmerised by his charismatic looks and imposing presence, but now she suspected it had always been there.

"I think Kathy and I should have some time to ourselves." Leo turned to his sister. "Surely you understand, Josie. You can find your way around from here and back to the ship."

Ketty was shaken from her inward thoughts. "I'm not going to abandon Josie."

"But we have had so little time together, Kathy. How about we go somewhere else? One of those nice little restaurants overlooking the bay and have a drink. Talk about happier things."

This time he tried to take her hand. She moved it out of his reach.

"I've run out of words." Ketty felt exhausted now. She'd like nothing better than to go back to her cabin and sleep for the rest of the day.

Leo stood up and held his hand towards her, the commanding look back on his face. "Fresh air and a glass of wine will do you good."

Ketty looked away. She was relieved that his gaze had no effect on her at all except perhaps regret.

"Off you go then, Leo." Josie's tone was matter-of-fact. "We'll see you back at the ship."

Ketty heard his snort of disbelief but she didn't look up.

"We'll talk later, Kathy."

She sensed his movement, a pause then heard the door behind her.

"He's actually left," Josie said. "I'm so sorry, Ketty. I'm embarrassed to think my own brother could act in such a callous way. I thought I knew him. No wonder his relationships haven't lasted if that's how he's treated women."

"This has nothing to do with you, Josie. You can't be responsible for another person's behaviour even if they are family. I'm sorry you got caught up in it."

"I'm not, but I feel so bad about prying now."

"I'd planned to tell Leo today anyway."

Josie gave a weak smile. "At least I could be here for you."

"Perhaps it wasn't the best way to tell him." Ketty couldn't help but think if it had been just her and Leo she could have explained it differently, not sounded so accusing.

"Don't you dare blame yourself for my brother's poor behaviour." Josie wagged a finger at her. "I can see by the look on your face you're feeling sorry and you mustn't. You lived through so much sorrow on your own and yet you've come through it, remained true and honest and kind."

Ketty felt her cheeks warm at Josie's praise. "I'm no saint."

"That clearly means you're human, but now I wonder about my brother. He doesn't appear to have learned anything from his mistakes. After watching him today his past indiscretions all make more sense now."

"He's still your brother."

"Humph. Wait till I catch up with him back in the cabin. He's going to get an earful." Josie picked up her cup, put it to her mouth and wrinkled her nose. "He's right about one thing though, that coffee's gone cold. How about I get us a nice pot of tea instead?"

Ketty nodded and sat unmoving while Josie went to place her order. A heavy feeling washed over her. She recognised the sensation as the grief that had overwhelmed her for so long after her baby had died and her battle to survive the infection that had ravaged her body. It had taken time but she'd come to terms with no Leo and no more children. She'd thought it was all behind her but now, as the prickling sensation wriggled across her shoulders and down her arms, she felt like perhaps she could at last, after thirty-five years, let it go. She would never forget the love – whoever did their first? – nor deny she once carried a tiny human being inside her, a result of that love, but even though it had been awful, telling Leo had been cathartic. She no longer wondered *what if?*

Josie returned and then froze at the sight of something behind Ketty.

"Hello, ladies. I'm so glad I've found you."

Ketty turned at the sound of Bernard's voice. The hesitant look on his face didn't match his cheerful words.

"I don't think we were lost were we, Ketty?" Josie sat back in her chair, pretending she wasn't delighted that Bernard had turned up at last.

"We did wonder what had become of you though." Ketty smiled at him, so glad to feel the muscles of her face turn up all of their own accord. Other people's lives were still so much more interesting than her own and she liked it that way.

Bernard came to stand beside them. "Josie, I was hoping we could talk. Would you excuse us a moment, Ketty?"

"Of course."

"I've just ordered a fresh pot of tea," Josie said.

"It's only tea. I think you should go with Bernard," Ketty said. "I'm going to drink mine then head back to the ship. I've had enough excitement for one day." Ketty took in the prevaricating look on Josie's face. "I think you two should have more of a look around…on your own."

"It really is important, Josie," Bernard said.

She glanced from him back to Ketty. "Are you sure you're okay?"

"Perfectly," Ketty said. "I'm even going to eat this tart now. I'll see you at dinner." She waved them away and settled back in her chair. The prickling feeling had passed and she felt a sense of peace she hadn't realised had been missing since – she put her head to one side revelling in the lightness she felt at that moment – since she'd stepped aboard the *Diamond Duchess*.

She would always hold her child in her heart but the part of her that had ached for Leo was finally healed of its pain. That was a surprising result of meeting him again after all these years. Even though she'd been hurt by him she'd still kept their love on a kind of pedestal that no other man had ever lived up to. Now she was released from that memory. She didn't love Leo, nor did she hate him. There was no real feeling at all now for the man who had once been the centre of her world. It was a surprise to realise she had perhaps wasted other opportunities because of it. She'd fallen for a few men since Leo. Now she knew it was quite likely more her fault those relationships had not come to anything more. A small wave of regret swept her but just as quickly she shook it off. No point in pondering things from the past she couldn't change.

Ketty picked up the teapot and poured, then closed her eyes, savouring the aromatic smell of the tea. Every day was a new beginning and today marked a fresh new year of her life. She straightened her shoulders, took up the little cake fork and broke off a piece of the strawberry tart.

"Happy birthday to me," she muttered under her breath and slipped the morsel into her mouth.

Thirty-one

"That was the most amazing experience." Celia lifted her hand to wave to Captain Enzo then turned to walk beside Jim along the little jetty. Her skin felt tight from the sun and the salt but she still revelled in the exhilaration she'd felt as they'd skipped across the ocean on the catamaran. "I can't believe how much I enjoyed it."

"Are you sure that wasn't because of Captain Enzo?" Jim gave her a soft poke in the ribs with his elbow.

"No." She responded a little too emphatically and a girlish giggle escaped her lips. "Although he certainly was charming." She paused and glanced away out over the bay. Captain Enzo had been entertaining but it was Jim who'd topped the day. She'd seen a whole new side of him. On the water he'd been self-assured, at ease and had taken delight in everything – and from his manner, that included her. She'd been careful to keep her own feelings for him hidden but now… "It was you who made it special, Jim."

"Me?"

They'd reached the end of the jetty and Jim stopped. Celia did too. She put down her bag and studied him.

"If you hadn't convinced me to go in the water again I wouldn't have swum with the turtles. Weren't they amazing creatures? And the dolphins! And not a sea snake in sight." She grinned, covering the fact that she had still been anxiously looking for them every time she went into the water. "And then on the way back when it got windy and I was feeling a bit nervous, you were so reassuring about everything and explaining what Enzo was doing. It was like we were flying over the water. I loved it."

Jim glanced back along the jetty. "It's quite a while since I've been out. Sailing used to give me a lot of pleasure."

"You should take it up again. It seems like an invigorating pastime."

He didn't say anything more but his look was reflective. Celia picked up her bag and they set off towards the market hall where they were to catch the bus back to the ship. "Do you have enough energy for a quick look at the souvenirs?"

"Sure." His smile was warm.

They went inside and wandered between the stalls. Celia sensed a calmness about Jim she'd only glimpsed before. He'd been so kind, coaxing her into the water and staying with her so she'd felt truly safe. He'd relished the sailing part of the day, full of questions about local conditions for Captain Enzo who let him help with some of the sail work.

"What do you think of this?" Jim picked up a funny little turtle from the souvenir stall.

Celia laughed. "Very cute." It had a wobbling head and New Caledonia printed on its back. He jiggled it and she laughed again then stopped when she realised he was watching her intently. Just for a few hours she'd forgotten he was a grieving widower. She thought perhaps he had too.

"Do you have someone in mind for that?" she asked.

"I do actually." He took out his wallet and paid for the turtle but said no more. They strolled on past more stalls and Celia made several purchases.

After one final look she raised her hand in which she clutched several small shopping bags. "I've beaten you in the souvenir stakes."

"I did my shopping in Port Vila."

"What did you get?"

"A pearl necklace for my daughter, Tamara, and a bottle of Glenfiddich whisky for my son, Anthony."

"That's so thoughtful, Jim. My sons are only getting t-shirts." She jiggled her bag again. "And a pack of cards from the ship. Wish I'd thought to buy booze. They'd probably have liked that more."

Jim looked around. "I wouldn't mind an ice cream. Would you like one?"

"I would, but you know I think I'd rather have it on the ship. I can take my shoes off and sit back on one of those sun lounges and eat it."

"Sounds good to me."

Christine and Frank sat side by side on a bench in the leafy park in the centre of Noumea. They'd made use of the free town wi-fi and facetimed the kids. It was late afternoon and the clouds were building, trapping the heat and lifting the air temperature. Christine's hair was damp against the back of her neck and little dribbles of perspiration ran down her cheeks and between her breasts. She marvelled at Frank's cool appearance. The heat didn't bother him at all.

"Do you think the kids looked okay?" She patted at her neck with a tissue.

"Fine."

"I thought Anna was a bit quiet."

"They were both full of what they'd been up to. Lucca is louder that's all." Frank took the iPad from her. "Only a couple of days and we'll be home. You can bet they'll be more interested in the truckload of souvenirs we've bought them than they will be in seeing us."

Christine's thoughts slipped from her children back to Ketty. The exchange she'd had with her that morning at the coffee shop on the ship still smarted. It had been gratifying to overhear the conversation at the patisserie and discover the older woman wasn't so perfect as she made out.

"Fancy Ketty having an affair with Leo when he was married."

"Let it go, Chrissie. We weren't meant to hear about it."

"Well, we did. She acts so superior as if she's perfect and she's not at all." Christine pouted at Frank. "Do you know she lectured me this morning?"

He gave a snort. "I can't imagine sweet Ketty lecturing anybody."

"Sweet Ketty, my eye. She has everyone fooled but not me."

"Let it go, Chrissie." Frank looked back at the iPad on his lap.

Her gaze drifted over the grassy park to the statues and then to the buildings across the road. She was glad she'd convinced Frank to have cake and coffee in that little patisserie. They'd actually talked without arguing. Christine had been on her best behaviour and Frank had responded, easy to get along with as he usually was. At first she'd been annoyed when she'd realised who had taken over the table behind her. When she hadn't heard her father's voice she'd been happy. Perhaps he'd given Josie the flick as she'd hoped, but the icing on the cake had been the conversation about Ketty and Leo's affair.

"What do you think about this place?" Frank interrupted her thoughts.

Christine dragged her gaze to the iPad screen. "It's a house."

"It's got four bedrooms, a study, two-car garage and a pool."

"Why are you showing me?"

"It's in our price range and close to my new work."

She glanced from the screen to Frank. He looked so pleased she chose her words carefully. "I thought we'd agreed to stay where we are?"

Frank put the iPad on the seat between them and took both her hands in his. "I've emailed my application, Chrissie. I really want this job."

She swallowed her annoyance and tried to smile. "If you get the job, we don't have to move. I told you Dad will fund the renovations."

Frank squeezed her hands gently and jiggled them up and down in his. "And I told you I'm not accepting any more money from Bernie. We don't need his help."

"Let's not worry about it now." Christine felt the low burn of anger in her belly but she congratulated herself in keeping her voice casual. "I think it's time we went back to the ship. I fancy a spa." She leaned in and brushed her lips across his cheek.

Frank's eyes widened and before she could move away he kissed her, his lips warm and urgent against hers. "Good idea." His words were almost a groan.

She smiled as she stood and slipped her hand into his. "Let's go."

⚓

Bernard raised his glass to Josie's. "Cheers."

They both took a sip of their champagne cocktails and Bernard glanced around. The late afternoon sun shone through a gap in the clouds and reflected off the pool. The splashing of swimmers and chatting from others stretched out on sun lounges on the deck below them was obscured by the lively music coming from the speakers. He'd picked this spot on an upper deck out of sight of the general crowd in the hope that, while they were a little out of the way, there was also enough noise for them not to be overheard. He'd wanted to take Josie to his balcony but by the time they'd walked back to the terminal and caught the bus back to the ship, she'd lost patience with him and demanded he say what he needed to say.

"So?" Josie placed her glass firmly on the table between them, sat back and folded her arms. "Tell me what's going on."

She was still cross with him. He just hoped she'd be prepared to hear him out.

"I'm sorry I didn't find you last night and again this morning."

"You've apologised several times already, Bernie. Get to the point."

He took another quick sip of his drink. "Dinner with Christine last night was quite a revelation."

She gave a slight shake of her head but she said nothing.

"I have to go back in time to explain. Christine was our only child and...we...I treated her like a princess. She took her mother's death badly. She was only twenty when Della died. Still at uni. It was a terrible time for her."

"For both of you, I'm sure."

He nodded. "I loved my wife but I was so lonely. I began looking for someone to fill the void in my life, someone to replace what I had with Della. I met Gloria and she was just what I needed. I sold the house and bought another so I could make a fresh start. When I look back maybe it was too soon for Christine. She hated Gloria, made her life miserable when I wasn't around. Gloria suggested we move to Brisbane. That was a few years on and Chrissie was living with Frank by then. They were engaged and bought their house. I had acquired some investment properties in Brisbane so I sold up again and moved, but when we got there our relationship waned. I thought maybe Chrissie had been right."

"Right about what?"

"She'd said Gloria didn't love me and was only after my money."

"How to boost a man's ego." Josie gave a wry smile. "And was that true?"

Bernard shook his head. "Gloria had been doing it tough when I met her. I knew that. I didn't mind looking after her financially. When we eventually parted I thought the relationship had run its course and it was because we were wanting to go in different directions. What I hadn't realised until years later was Chrissie had been meddling. She'd chipped away at poor Gloria's confidence until she'd had enough. Our break-up had nothing to do with finances."

"Do you think Christine's behaviour is purely about the money?"

"A few days ago I would have said no but now..." Bernard felt the hurt all over again for his daughter's scheming and callous behaviour.

"Perhaps she's being protective of you."

"She takes it too far."

"I agree but I have to warn you, I have three sons you haven't met yet. I can assure you if we continue to see each other they'll want to meet you, check your intentions."

Bernard reached for her hand and was relieved she let him put it to his lips. "I look forward to it."

Josie continued to regard him with a serious look. "I'm not prepared to show Christine my financials but I am more than capable of looking after myself in that department. She can rest assured I don't want you for your money, Bernie."

He lowered her hand to the table. "I'm afraid there's more to it than that."

Once more Josie's gaze met his but she no longer held her jaw rigid as she had when they'd first sat down. She took the strawberry from the top of her glass and paused with it halfway to her lips.

"Go on," she said.

Christine stepped away from the rail and her view of the layers of decks below and made her way slowly back to the interior doors. There was a sick feeling in her stomach and an ache in her chest. She'd been watching her father and Josie together. She had come looking for her father in the hope of catching him alone and had discovered them seated further along the deck. She'd stopped, leaned on the rail as if watching the people below but kept her eyes on her father and his girlfriend. Their backs were slightly turned to her but they were so intent on each other they hadn't once glanced up.

The warm glow that had enveloped her when she'd left her cabin, where she and Frank had finally consummated their holiday, dissipated.

Ketty opened her eyes and took a minute to remember where she was. Slowly she sat up from her bed and looked towards the window. A dull half-light filtered through the sheer curtains. The sun must have recently set. She reached for her watch. She'd been tired after she'd returned from her trip ashore, exhausted from the emotion of the talk with Leo and Josie, and had planned to eat in her room.

Now she felt well rested and the thought of eating alone in her cabin no longer held its appeal. It was her birthday after all, even if the only other person aboard who knew was Carlos. She glanced at her watch again. There was still an hour until dinner and more than enough time to shower and change. She sat on the edge of the bed a moment and wondered how she would deal with being seated at the same table as Leo after today's disclosures.

But there were more people than Leo at her table and she wanted to see them all, hear about their day. She'd grown fond of them all, except maybe Christine. That poor woman made herself difficult to like. Nonetheless Ketty had to keep trying. She lowered her feet to the floor and crossed the room to her wardrobe. Company would be the best thing for her tonight.

Thirty-two

Night Seven – At Sea

Carlos wasn't at the door when Ketty arrived a little late to the dining room. She glanced around and saw him at a distant table. She smiled as she watched him discussing something with great enthusiasm, his hands dancing in the air. It was strange to think that she should regard him as a constant in her life. She would miss Carlos and their catch-ups, no matter how irregular they'd been over the years.

She moved on, making her way to the table, and only hesitated briefly when she saw Christine and Frank already seated, Christine in Ketty's preferred place at the other end of the table.

"Good evening, Ketty." Christine beamed at her.

She felt a little chill slither down her spine. The other woman's look was meaningful, almost malevolent.

"Hello." Ketty looked from Christine to Frank, whose smile was welcoming as usual.

Ketty chose to sit beside him. She pulled her shoulders back as Phillip placed her napkin across her lap.

"Gin and tonic, Miss Clift?"

"Thank you, Phillip." She smiled up at him.

"Hello everyone." Celia's greeting was effusive.

She sat next to Ketty with Jim on her other side. Phillip had just organised them when Bernard arrived with Josie on his arm.

"Good evening, all." Bernard glanced around the table.

There were murmurs of greeting from everyone except Christine who was glaring at Josie, looking as if she'd swallowed something unpalatable. Bernard barely acknowledged his daughter. Josie was the one to take a seat next to Christine.

"Is it our turn to buy the wine?" Frank asked. "I've lost track."

"We've had a turn." Christine's tone was dismissive.

"Must be me," Josie said.

Ketty saw the look she gave to Bernard. Whatever had been bothering them must be sorted and yet, as the drinks were ordered, Ketty felt tension in the air. Perhaps it was just her. She glanced at the one remaining empty chair and wondered if she wasn't projecting her own feelings regarding Leo's arrival but she pushed that thought aside. Bernard told Phillip a joke and soon the cheeky waiter had everyone smiling. Except for Christine.

Ketty noticed her narrowed gaze was fixed on Josie. A chill settled on Ketty. Something was turning in Christine's brain and she had the feeling it wasn't pleasantries.

"That's a beautiful bracelet." Christine wiggled a finger towards Josie's wrist. "Is it new?"

"Thank you. Yes it is."

Josie clasped her hands together on the edge of the table. The bracelet was gold with several different coloured stones that sparkled as they caught the light when she moved.

"Did it come from the boutique on board?" Christine asked.

"Yes." Josie smiled at Bernard. "Your father—"

"Good heavens, Dad," Christine cut in. "We looked at those. They were very expensive."

This time Ketty saw the flash in Josie's eyes as she turned to Christine. "I was going to say your father kindly helped me pick it out. My sons gave me some money to buy something special for my birthday and I treated myself with the difference."

"A beautiful bracelet for a beautiful lady." Bernard gave Josie a dreamy look.

Ketty was surprised how much she was reminded of Leo. They were not dissimilar. Both good-looking men, although Leo had not been the flirt that Bernard liked to be. He'd seduced her with much more subtlety...Oh damn! She wasn't as comfortable with her feelings as she'd thought. Here she was thinking of Leo when she'd believed she'd firmly put him to rest. She glanced around but there was no sign of him heading their way.

"It certainly is very pretty," Celia said. "Is your birthday during the cruise? They seem to be singing someone 'Happy Birthday' every night here."

"No, it was a few months back," Josie said. "My boys were very generous."

The conversation halted as the waiters arrived with their drinks.

"Here's to you all, my dears." Bernard raised his glass of red to a chorus of cheers from around the table. "I don't believe Leo is joining us tonight so we can order."

Ketty glanced down at her menu but not before she saw the gentle smile Josie sent her way. Perhaps it would be easier if he wasn't here, for tonight at least.

Over dinner the talk flowed as they shared what they'd all done in Noumea. No one wanted sweets but Bernard ordered another bottle of champagne and one of the red wine. Ketty noticed Christine had changed to red during the main meal, downing two glasses and was back on the champagne again now despite her husband's concerned look.

The younger woman had gone quiet since the dessert menus had been whisked away. Ketty had also noticed Frank's arm was draped around his wife's shoulders between courses or his hand was on hers. They were both being more tactile than she'd seen them before. Josie and Bernard appeared to be back on track. She was also pleased that Celia and Jim were more relaxed tonight as well. Ketty hoped the cruise was finally working its magic on all of them. Her thoughts strayed again to Leo.

"Tonight's show is supposed to be good," Celia said. "Is anyone going?"

"I'd like to." Jim smiled at her.

"Look at you two," Christine said. "What could have put a smile on your faces, I wonder?" She waved her glass in the air.

Ketty felt a sense of foreboding.

Christine swirled her glass so the contents swished precariously close to the top. "Let's see, maybe spending the night together must have done it."

Celia gasped. She glanced from Jim to Ketty then looked down at her lap. Her cheeks glowed red.

Jim stiffened. "Why would you take delight in besmirching Celia's reputation?"

"Why worry about reputations at your age?" Christine raised her glass. "You two should go for it. That's what Dad would say, wouldn't you, Dad?"

Bernard stared at his daughter, giving the slightest shake of his head. No one spoke.

"Mum wasn't even gone twelve months before he moved someone into her bed."

"Chrissie." Frank put a hand on her arm but she ignored it.

She shifted her look from her father back to Josie. "You want to watch out. He'll be looking for a new model before long."

"I think you've said enough." Josie shot back. "You're embarrassing everyone along with yourself."

"Not you, I'm sure. You're as tough as they come." The spite in her words bit hard. "Taking your last husband to court for everything he was worth."

Josie's eyes narrowed. "You know nothing about it."

"Oh, but I do. It's amazing what you can find on the internet." Christine leaned forward, staring at her father. "She took him to the cleaners, Dad. You'd better be careful."

"What's got into you, Chrissie?" Frank's shocked tone mirrored the faces around the table.

"Lighten up, all of you." She took another big mouthful of champagne. "I just think you should all be honest. You're all keeping secrets, pretending to be people you're not."

Josie's eyes flashed with anger. "You'd best be very careful."

"Or what?" Christine laughed. It was a hollow sound. She peered at her empty glass and Phillip promptly refilled it.

"Please, Christine." Frank tried to stop her from drinking more but she pulled away from him.

"They all think they're better than us, Frank, but none of them are that special."

"What are you talking about?" Bernard's tone was tinged with anger.

Ketty watched as Christine's dark eyes flicked from her father to Josie and then came to settle on her. She knew as certain as night turned to day that she was next on Christine's hit list.

"I think we should all call it a night," Ketty said.

There was a glint in Christine's eyes. "Ah yes, the lonely busybody. I wondered how long it would take for you to stick your nose in. I thought you minded other people's business because you had none of your own but that's not true is it, *Ms Clift*?"

Ketty held her gaze knowing there was nothing she could do to stop Christine now.

"It seems our sweet Ketty is not so sweet after all."

"Chrissie." Frank's warning fell on deaf ears.

"She had an affair with our missing table-mate. Where is your Leo tonight? Don't tell me you've had a falling out after rekindling your affair. Although now that he's no longer married I suppose it's technically not an affair."

Ketty felt the combined scrutiny of the rest of the table shift to her but she didn't look away from Christine's triumphant smile. She lifted her chin. "I'm sorry you feel the need to share conversation that was not meant for your ears."

"What's this all about, Princess?" Bernard asked.

"Ha," Josie spat. "The perfect title. How dare you smear Ketty and Leo? But it's what you're good at isn't it – making up stories about other people. You always have to be the centre of attention—"

"You bitch." Christine flung the remaining contents of her glass. The pale liquid splashed down Josie's white silk shirt.

There was the tiniest pause then the gasps and exclamations all came at once. Ketty saw it all implode around the table as if she was watching a stage show. Josie rose to her feet. Bernard quickly did the same, putting a protective arm around her. Phillip appeared with a cloth. While they were all talking at once and the commotion centred on Christine and Josie, Ketty quietly slipped away.

"Good evening, everyone. Is everything all right?"

Celia looked up to see the maître d' standing at the end of the table, his hands resting on the back of a chair. His question was dropped lightly but his face was serious. She glanced around at the others. They had all turned their attention to him, even Christine.

Phillip fussed around them, straightening cutlery, picking up napkins that had slipped in the ruckus.

"Bit of an accident with the champagne," Frank offered.

The maître d' turned his steely stare on Phillip who ducked his head.

"It wasn't Phillip's fault," Celia said and attracted a glare from Christine.

"Where is Miss Clift?" Carlos asked.

Collectively they looked at the chair where Ketty had been seated between Frank and Celia.

"She must have left." Celia looked around. She hadn't noticed Ketty leave.

"But it is her birthday." Carlos lifted his hands in the air. "I have arranged a special dessert for your table."

They were silent, glancing in embarrassment at each other. Even Christine looked contrite. Josie and Bernard both sank back into their chairs.

Celia felt terrible. "We didn't know it was her birthday."

"She wouldn't want a fuss," Josie said.

Carlos raised his eyebrows higher, looked at each of them in turn then left them to their mortification. In the distance the staff sang 'Happy Birthday' at another table. Celia chewed her lip. She felt she'd let her friend Ketty down badly.

Thirty-three

"Celia, please don't let it upset you." Jim would have liked to put his arm around her shoulders but he wasn't certain how she'd react.

Once they'd left the dining room she had wanted to go see Ketty but he'd thought it best to leave Ketty to herself for the moment. He did believe that's what she would prefer, but truth be told he also felt a little guilty. He wanted to spend the rest of the evening with Celia. He'd convinced her to come out on the deck first and take a stroll. They hadn't moved far before they'd slowed and been drawn to the rail, both of them standing still, looking out into the dark night beyond the ship.

"I'm not sure how I'm feeling, Jim." Celia turned to face him. "I can't believe Christine said what she did and I don't understand why. I was embarrassed at first. After all that business with Maude then to have Christine make what happened between you and me…or didn't actually happen, into something that sounded sordid."

She gave him a weak smile. He was pleased to see that at least.

"We know the truth," he said. "What does it matter what Princess Christine says?"

Celia chuckled then just as quickly she frowned.

"I felt worse for you than for myself." She rested her hand on the arm he had propped on the rail. "Having your kindness made to look like something seedy."

The touch of her hand on his arm sent a thrill through him. They both fell silent, both looking into the darkness.

"Poor Ketty," Celia said at last. "She looked rather upset and then she disappeared without saying anything, and to think today was her birthday."

"You're such a kind-hearted person, Celia."

"It's good of you to say so but right now I'd like nothing better than to slap Christine's smug face."

"I'd say you'd have to stand in line. I can't imagine how Frank puts up with her."

"And to think Ketty was concerned for her."

"Was she?"

"Remember when we both said we weren't too fond of Christine and Ketty said she was troubled and needed help?"

"Oh yes, vaguely."

Celia's eyes sparkled in the glow from the overhead lights. A small piece of hair had floated in the breeze to rest on her cheek. He resisted the urge to tuck it back.

"Maybe she's done us a favour," he said.

"Christine?"

He reached for her other hand and shuffled the smallest distance closer. Celia's eyes widened a little but her gaze remained firmly on his.

"I enjoy your company. I think you enjoy mine," he said.

"I do."

"Today out sailing…well, I'm happy when I'm with you, Celia."

He bent his head towards her, paused. She was looking at him with such trust, admiration even. Instead of kissing her he gently pulled her towards him and wrapped her in his arms. Perhaps kissing might come later. This was all so foreign to him, holding a woman who wasn't Jane. Celia nestled there a moment then slid her arms around him. She moulded against him, her cheek pressed to his chest. His chin rested on her head, and he breathed in the sweet scent of her hair.

They stayed that way for several minutes. Below them the waves hissed and frothed against the hull of the ship. Somewhere nearby a door banged, and he heard footsteps on the deck moving away from them. He wasn't sure what he should do next.

It was Celia who pulled away first. She bent her head back to look up at him. Her face was lit by the soft yellow of the deck lights and a smile played on her lips.

"Maybe you're right." She smiled. "If Christine hadn't made her little speech we might still be dancing around each other. Neither of us brave enough to tell the other how they feel."

How did he feel? Jim didn't know. A mixture of emotions tumbled inside him. He needed more time to process them but he wanted to spend that time with Celia. That at least he was sure about.

"Do you still want to see tonight's show?" he asked.

"I'd love it."

She slid her arm through his. He gripped her hand tightly, suddenly feeling like a man who had found a foothold on a slippery deck.

Bernard sat on the balcony waiting for Josie to arrive. She'd gone to her room to change and rinse out her top. She said she'd come to his cabin again tonight but part of him didn't believe it. He hunched forward, his head in his hands, his elbows on his knees. Why had he ever thought going on a holiday with Christine was a good idea? If he'd come alone he would have met Josie, been settled in a relationship with her back in Brisbane, and Christine would have been none the wiser until he and Josie had had a chance to— To what, he wasn't quite sure. Know each other better, cement their relationship. He already felt as if he knew Josie very well, and after his explanations today she still wanted to be with him. He hadn't had a chance to tell her everything. Leo had found them before he'd told his whole story but that had probably been just as well. There was only so much of one's past that could be revealed at a time.

There was a knock on the door. Bernard was on his feet quickly and flung it open. Josie stood before him, a bag over her shoulder and a glass of red in each hand. Her smile was wary.

"I hope I'm still welcome."

He took the glasses from her and stepped back to let her pass. No sooner was the door shut and he had placed the glasses on the bench than he took her in his arms and kissed her, long and slow.

She was the one to ease away first with a hand to his chest. "I'll take that as a yes."

"I'm so sorry about tonight."

"Stop apologising for your daughter's behaviour, Bernie."

"She made it sound as if I didn't care about her mother."

"That must hurt." She brushed her lips lightly over his cheek. "Let's sit out on your lovely balcony. I want to explain what she said about me."

"You don't have to."

"I don't mind. You've been honest with me."

She looked away to put down her bag. Bernard was relieved, sure he must have a guilty look on his face.

"Since your confession this afternoon I've wanted to explain. Leo's arrival up on the deck put paid to our personal conversation but I'd like to tell you now."

He turned away quickly to hide his discomfort, picked up the glasses and they settled themselves on the balcony; a chair each and their bare feet resting on the little table. He reached out and trailed a finger down her arm. Even though the light was dim he could see pain etched in her face. He reached for her hand, drew it to him, kissed her fingers.

"You're a lovely man, Bernie. I wish I had met you a long time ago."

"Not that lovely. I've failed my daughter. I didn't realise how badly until tonight."

"I get she's being protective. My boys are like that but perhaps not to the same degree. I tried to shield them from their dad's violence but I couldn't in the end. As they got older he didn't care that they saw him hit me. It was probably his way of keeping them in line. When we left it was with only a couple of bags and the clothes on our backs.

"I worked hard to make a new life for us. It took me a long time to trust a man again and I made another mistake. The boys were in high school when I met Terry, who became my second husband. We had several good years. He was a nice guy, he was a good father to my boys, but he strayed even though he vowed he still loved me. I wasn't prepared to turn a blind eye. We had combined our finances, built a house together by then, I worked part-time in his office, had his kids over every second weekend, but he wasn't going to give me my share. I had to get a lawyer to be awarded what I was owed from our assets. I won't deny I did better out of it than I'd thought I would, but I could have ended up with nothing and I wasn't prepared to go back there." She paused, took a deep breath, looked him in the eye. "That's all there is. That's me, all warts exposed."

"I'd be the last person to judge." He shook his head slowly. "My story is quite different to yours. I missed the closeness I'd had with my wife Della and maybe I did make some bad choices at looking for a replacement but no one was hurt in the process."

"Except perhaps Christine." Josie gave him a wry smile.

Bernie saw a glimpse of what Christine might have seen when he'd first brought Gloria home. It had been Chrissie's twenty-first. Her mother hadn't been dead quite a year. He'd been full of excitement to have some romance in his life again. Perhaps it hadn't been the best time to introduce Gloria. He put his head in his hands. "I never meant Chrissie to be hurt."

"I'm sure you didn't."

"Bloody hell, this mess is all my fault."

This time Josie reached out, put a gentle hand on his. "I used to think it was my fault my first husband hit me."

He lifted his head. "That's ridiculous."

"I know that now." She smiled at him. "Maybe you could have handled things differently or maybe Christine was always going to resent anyone who you took up with. There's no way of knowing but she's an adult now, responsible for her own choices."

Bernard's stomach roiled. "I've made a mess of my daughter's life."

"Hardly. She's got a good job, a roof over her head, two lovely kids by all accounts, and a husband who adores her, although I think even he was shocked tonight. All you can do is reassure her that you love her." Josie gave a dry laugh. "And let her know I'm not after your money. I've learned a few things in my time. I own my apartment, have a comfortable allowance, but my finances are all locked up and my sons the beneficiaries of anything that will be left after I've enjoyed my life as much as I can."

"Likewise." That was almost the truth, Bernard thought, but there was no need for Josie to know those details.

"You've explained your reasons for not wanting to advise me on real estate and I can accept that."

He hadn't told her the real reason for that either but she'd happily accepted that he didn't want to be advising her if they were in a relationship. It wasn't a lie, just not the whole truth.

"I'm not looking for a meal ticket, Bernie." She leaned across, her lips only a short gap from his. "I'm after a man to enjoy life with."

Bernard pushed thoughts of further talk from his mind. Right now he had a warm-blooded woman in his arms and he was going to make the most of it.

Jim walked Celia to her door.

"Thanks, Jim." She gave him a shy glance.

He felt a bit on edge. They'd had a busy evening and now there were no more excuses to be together and they were lingering outside her door.

"Are you still planning on breakfast in the dining room?" It was all he could think of to say.

"Yes."

"Shall I meet you there? Eight-thirty?"

"I'll look forward to it."

He smiled. "The last part of the evening was certainly much more enjoyable than the first."

Celia's face remained solemn.

"You won't let Christine's bad behaviour bother you, will you?" he asked.

She shook her head. "Not even thinking about her."

"Or worry about Ketty?"

"She'd be asleep now. I'll call in on her first thing."

She tilted forward, hovered a moment a few inches from his face then brushed her lips across his cheek. It was a simple gesture. He stood stock still.

"Goodnight, Jim." Celia held his gaze a moment then turned away, fumbled with her card and let herself into her cabin.

He stayed there, solid like a statue, for a few minutes before he turned and made his way to the end of the corridor and along to his own room. What a fool he was. He should have responded, kissed her back. She probably thought he was rejecting her but he'd been startled, that's all. Wished he'd thought to kiss her, on the lips not the cheek. She had warm lips, soft like Jane's.

The familiar wave of pain swept down his chest and settled in his stomach. It took him by surprise. He hadn't felt it for days. He staggered to a chair and sat. How could he possibly have forgotten Jane? He put his head in his hands. He'd brought her on this cruise with him in the same way he'd kept her close at home, and yet these last few days he'd hardly thought of her and today barely at all.

He tried to picture her, couldn't see her clearly, panicked and pulled out his phone. The screen didn't respond. It had gone flat.

"Jane, Jane," he murmured. "I'm so sorry."

He'd held her hand as she'd died and had wanted nothing more than to go with her. He'd kept her memory close these last two years, not letting go of the pain. He'd forgiven her for leaving him, she'd suffered so much, but he could never forgive himself for not being able to help her, and now he'd betrayed her. He'd found himself enjoying Celia's company. He would have kissed her tonight if he hadn't been so inept.

"Jane." He tugged at his hair with his fingers. "My darling Jane."

The pain still gnawed at him. He couldn't bear it. He leaped to his feet, strode to the sliding doors and pushed them apart. He was met by a blast of warmer air and the sound of the sea churning below. He hesitated a moment, his hands pressed to the frame, then he stepped out into the black night.

Ketty gave up trying to sleep and got out of her bed. As much as she'd tried to forget Christine's words, the whole dining room scene kept playing over and over in her head. She dragged her fingers through her hair, pulling it back from her face. She was glad Leo hadn't been there. Goodness knows how he would have reacted. Josie had told her over dinner that Leo had decided to dine alone in one of the other restaurants. There had been no mention of how he was feeling about Ketty's revelations and she hadn't asked. She could see Josie was torn between supporting her friend and remaining true to her brother but Ketty had decided she would rather not set eyes on Leo again if she could help it.

There had been pain in telling him what had happened, then release followed by a sense of calm. She didn't feel bitter towards him; she just…no longer felt anything.

Ketty wandered her cabin, straightening a book, tidying her already tidy dressing table. She was totally out of kilter. This holiday had not gone as she had thought it would. Cruising had become her escape; the one place where she was simply Ketty Clift, a woman who enjoyed travel, dressing up and the company of others. And, when she was on a ship where Carlos was maître d', he made sure she had an interesting group, people who might need a nudge towards love, or healing, or a change of direction. There had never been any harm in it and it had given her great joy to see people take on new possibilities. Did that make her a – what had Christine called her – a busybody?

Ketty slumped to the bed. A small tweak of pain shot along her arm to her elbow. Is that what she'd become; nothing but a lonely busybody? She dabbed at the moisture on her cheeks. Ketty was rarely one for tears but now that they'd started they rolled freely down her face. That was twice this cruise. She mopped at the moisture with her handkerchief. Feeling sorry for herself wouldn't set things straight.

Thirty-four

Christine paced the cabin. Her fingers pressed to her temples, which meant she occasionally jarred her elbow on the wall but she didn't care. If she took her fingers from her head she felt as if her brain would explode out of it, and if she stopped pacing, the room would start to spin again and then she felt sick.

She paused briefly in front of her reflection in the glass of the sliding door then turned and paced again. Had she really said all those things, made such a scene? She groaned. Where was Frank? He'd brought her back to their room, insisting she stay put, and said he'd bring back a big bottle of water but he'd been gone a long time. She knew he was ashamed of her. Perhaps he wouldn't come back. She groaned again. Then her thoughts went to her father, the horrified look on his face, his arm around Josie as he'd guided her away.

Christine had got some satisfaction from wiping the smug look off Josie's face when she flung the champagne at her but it had been short-lived. She would still get his money but she was sure her father was lost to her now.

"Arrgh!" Her cry startled her. It sounded loud in the empty room. From behind her came the sound of the card in the door. She turned as Frank came in with two big bottles of water tucked under his arm.

He glanced at her then moved on past to the desk. He put one bottle in the fridge, opened the other and poured two glasses.

He didn't offer her one, simply waved a hand at it. "You should drink lots of water." Then he slid open the balcony door. Christine felt the tremor inside her ears as the outside air fought against the air conditioning. She crossed to the desk as Frank stepped out into the inky night. She swallowed the glass full of water, poured another and drank half. She looked longingly at the bed. She'd love to crawl in and slip into the oblivion of sleep but she knew if she lay flat the room would spin worse than it did when she stood still. She began to pace again. Each time she reached the open balcony door she glimpsed the still figure of her husband sitting in a chair. He was positioned side-on to her with his face turned away so she didn't know if his eyes were shut or if he was staring out into the blackness. Either way he certainly wasn't talking. A part of her wished he would, wanted him to berate her for her poor behaviour, but that wasn't Frank's nature.

She did another circuit of the room. After the others had all left the table, loyal, kind Frank had walked her silently back to their cabin. The only thing he'd said since her outburst had been to do with drinking water. She moved to the open door. His silence had cut through her more than any words could.

"Frank?"

She thought perhaps he hadn't heard her then he shifted slightly in the chair.

"I don't want to talk, Christine."

The light from the cabin cast a glow across the profile of his face. Her heart ached for him. Only a few hours ago they'd made love. They'd been a proper couple again. She'd accepted he wanted this new job, she hadn't mentioned renovations, deciding to let that slide till they got home. They had been so happy in each other's arms, and then had come the dinner from hell. They had all looked so pleased with themselves, those older couples, and her father was all over Josie even after Christine had warned him off. She'd had too many drinks and the poison inside her had bubbled up and overflowed. Now probably no one would talk to her for the rest of the cruise. She chomped hard on her lip so she wouldn't cry. She hated Frank's silence. One of the reasons for this holiday had been to rekindle her marriage. She couldn't lose Frank. A shock of realisation hit her like a brick – nothing was worth that.

She refilled her glass and moved out onto the balcony where she lowered herself carefully onto the other chair. Her head remained steady and even though her stomach was churning she felt she could sit without feeling like she would lose her balance.

"Thanks for the water," she said.

Frank continued to stare out into the night.

She eased herself lower until her head rested against the back of the chair. "I thought perhaps you might find somewhere else to sleep."

This time his head turned a little sideways so he was looking at her. "I thought about it."

She felt a stab of dread at the disdain in his stare.

"I'm sorry, Frank."

"What for?"

She flung up her hands. The movement made her head pound. "Drinking too much, talking too much, everything." She finished limply, putting a hand to her head.

Frank shoved his chair around to face her and lurched forward. The force of the movement startled her. Anger had replaced the disdain on his face.

"Are you, Christine? Are you really?"

"Of course."

"I don't understand why. I get you've got a beef with your father every time he so much as looks like he might find a woman whose company he enjoys."

"That's not true. I want him to be happy but he always picks the wrong ones." Christine wasn't sure who would be right but certainly not any of the women her father had entertained over the years.

Frank shook his head. "Bernie and Josie aside, what did the others at our table do that hurt you so much you'd want to humiliate them?"

"They were all so superior. Celia acts detached but she's just like Josie, after a man, and she's got her claws into poor old Jim. He's in a fancy suite so he must have money. And Ketty, she acts so high and mighty as if she's in charge of the bloody cruise. Asking us about our day, telling us what we should do, how we should act. They were all being judgemental in one way or another and none of them are squeaky clean."

Frank's mouth fell open. "Listen to yourself, Christine. You're not this person. I want my wife back."

He got up and went inside. She heard the bathroom door close.

Christine rested her head back again and closed her eyes. She watched the colours swirl behind her eyelids. It made her feel sick. She opened them and drank more water.

She pictured her father and the way he'd guided Josie away. It wounded her so much to see him choose another woman over his relationship with her. She should be used to it by now but it hurt every time. Even worse was Frank's scorn. He was usually so non-judgemental. She thought about the things she'd said tonight to the others. Had she overstepped the mark? There had been nothing that wasn't true, she was sure but...when she thought about it, maybe the way she'd said it had been hurtful. She'd only meant to stop them from interfering.

There was movement in the cabin behind her. A couple of lights went out.

"I'm going to bed."

She twisted slightly. Frank was framed in the doorway, a dark silhouette against the remaining light from the room. He was wearing boxers. He rarely wore anything to bed. How different tonight was from this afternoon. Was this really all her doing?

"Don't leave me out here alone." She knew lying horizontal was still not an option. "Please, Frank."

He let out a sigh.

"My head hurts." She closed her eyes and put a hand to her forehead.

"Drink some more water."

She heard the chair creak beside her. She took a deep breath and opened her eyes again.

"I am sorry, Frank. I spoiled the evening. This afternoon was so good between us. I felt like we'd got our mojo back."

She risked a glimpse in his direction. His face was in shadow and he was looking out to sea.

"I only wanted to save Dad from another bad decision," she continued. "He's the only dad I've got."

"He's an adult, not a child."

"I know. I'll go to his room first thing and apologise. Then I'll find out where Josie's room is and...beg her forgiveness." She wouldn't quite go that far but she could at least show remorse for the scene she'd caused.

Frank leaned in. "We could well be dining alone tomorrow night."

"We can always go to the buffet."

"Or I can leave you in the room for the rest of the cruise."

Christine assumed he was joking but it was hard to tell. She took a large swallow of water, gritted her teeth and hoped her face looked suitably contrite.

"I'll find the others and apologise to them too."

"They're nice people, Chrissie." He reached across and took her hand, gave it a gentle shake. "You're a much better person than the one who was in the dining room tonight."

Tears brimmed in her eyes. "I only want everything to—"

"Go your way?" He leaned across and took her other hand. "It can't. The world's not like that. Your dad has survived all these years. You have no idea what he does when he's on his own. Maybe wild orgies every night."

"Frank!" It made her cringe to think about it.

"Point is, it's up to him what he does with his time…and his money. We can stand on our own four feet."

She gave him a wobbly smile. There was no point in mentioning she would still get her father's money. She didn't want to mess up this bridge-building she'd worked so hard on.

"Things will be better in the morning." Frank smiled back, with that gorgeous look that still had the ability to make her toes curl. "How are you feeling?"

"Okay." At least the spinning wasn't as bad now.

"I didn't think we'd lost it."

Christine frowned. "Lost what?"

"Our mojo."

She sighed. "We've been so busy with work and the kids. We should make more time for each other."

"That's why we're here but you've been occupied chasing after your dad."

"I know."

He stood, helped her to her feet and pulled her into a hug. "Let's make the most of the few days we've still got." He wiggled his hips against her.

"Oh," she groaned. "I couldn't lie down yet."

He trailed his lips down her neck. "Who said we had to lie down?"

Thirty-five

Day Eight – At Sea

There was a knock at Bernard's door. Room service had brought breakfast earlier than he'd booked it for but they were both up so it didn't matter. Josie was already wearing the dressing gown she'd brought with her. He pulled on some shorts and a t-shirt as he crossed the room. He opened the door and felt his jaw drop. Christine stood in the corridor.

"Hello, Dad." She was pale with dark shadows under her eyes.

"You're up early." Bernard blocked the space left by the partly open door and resisted the urge to glance over his shoulder to the balcony.

"I obviously didn't wake you. I need to talk, can I come in?"

"That will depend on whether you want privacy or not."

Bernard's heart sank at the sound of Josie's voice right behind him.

Christine's shoulders went back and her expression hardened. "I'm glad you're both here." She tried to look past Bernard. "I'd like to apologise."

He was surprised and wary.

"Let the woman in, Bernie." Josie gave him a gentle pat on the behind. "You can't make her talk from the corridor."

He opened the door wider. Christine gave him a weak smile then stepped past him into the room and followed Josie towards the balcony. She paused as she took in the unmade bed. She didn't speak or look back but continued after Josie.

"Can you squeeze another chair out here, Bernie?" Josie called. "The air is so fresh this morning."

He did as she asked. They shuffled the three chairs, Bernard squeezing his between the two women.

"We're waiting for breakfast," he said. "I thought you were room service."

"That was lucky." Christine glanced from him to Josie and back. "I don't suppose you would have opened the door if you'd realised it was me."

She was quite right about that, he thought. He should have checked the peephole first.

"I don't want to interrupt your breakfast so I'll be quick." Christine sat stiffly. "I want to apologise for my unfortunate behaviour last night." Once more she transferred her gaze from him to Josie and back again. "To both of you."

There was a pause filled only by the sound of the ocean far below them.

Josie sat up. "I accept."

"I am happy to pay for your shirt to be cleaned," Christine said.

"No need. I rinsed it out straight away. It will be fine, I'm sure."

Once more there was a pause. Christine looked at him and Josie gave him a small nudge.

"I'm sorry you feel I can't have room for you in my life as well as Josie," Bernard said. He searched his daughter's face wondering if she was here to apologise or to do more damage. She'd not repeated her threat to expose his real-estate ventures but he assumed that was because she thought he was still going to give her the money she wanted for her renovations. He reached out and squeezed her hand. It was cool and soft beneath his big paw. "You know I'll always love you, Princess. No matter what."

"I do know, Dad. Thank you for saying it though."

There was a knock at the door.

"Room service," came a call.

Christine rose and squeezed behind her chair. "I'll leave you to enjoy your meal in peace."

Bernard followed her into the cabin.

"What are you planning for today?"

She stopped at the door and looked back. "I've got a few more people to track down and apologise to, then I plan to do as little as possible." She gave him a wary smile. "See you at dinner?"

Celia had completed a full circuit of the promenade deck and was about to go inside when a familiar woman stepped though the heavy glass doors. She spun away.

"Celia," Christine called from behind. "Wait, please."

Celia stopped. The dread in her chest deepened. Christine was the last person she wanted to talk to right now. She turned as the younger woman drew level with her.

"You've been hard to find. I've searched the ship top to bottom looking for you and Jim and Ketty. I kept a watch on the dining room until it closed, I've been up to the buffet, the casino, pool deck—"

"Did you see Jim?"

Christine shook her head and glanced down at the hand Celia had placed on her arm.

Celia's arm dropped to her side. "Oh."

"I wanted to apologise for last night. I shouldn't have said what I did."

Celia flapped her hand. Christine's apology was the last thing she'd expected and wanted to hear. "I'm worried about Jim."

"Why?"

"He said he'd meet me for breakfast and he didn't come."

"Maybe he didn't feel like breakfast."

Christine's words were slow and deliberate. Celia could tell she was trying to be tactful now even though she'd shown little evidence of it in the past.

"He would have let me know."

"Did you check his room?"

"I knocked. He didn't answer."

"The steward was cleaning it when I was there. He said Jim wasn't in."

"I've been to all the usual places he goes."

"Maybe he's with Ketty. They're friendly, aren't they?"

"Yes, but I haven't seen her."

"Have you tried her cabin?"

"No." Celia's spirits lifted a little. Ketty would know what to do.

"I don't know where it is," Christine said.

"I do."

"Mind if I come with you then? I need to speak with her as well."

Celia looked closely at Christine. She imagined Ketty wouldn't be so keen to see her either.

Christine held up her hands. "I want to apologise, that's all."

"All right."

Celia led the way to Ketty's deck and knocked on her door. A couple came from further along the corridor. Celia and Christine moved over to let them pass.

Christine looked back at the door and knocked with more strength than Celia had. She pressed her ear to the door then straightened. "She's either not answering or she's not in."

"I don't know what to do." Celia gripped her hands together.

Christine gave her a wary look. "I know this is a risky question given what I said last night but…well, Jim wouldn't be avoiding you, would he?"

Celia was too worried to be offended. "It was him who suggested we eat at eight-thirty in the dining room."

"Maybe he slept in."

"He could have but Jim is such a gentleman, I'm sure he'd have left a message at my door if he couldn't find me." Celia looked at her watch. "I'm going to try the coffee lounge."

"Good idea. Mind if I stay with you for the moment? I could do with a strong coffee."

Celia shook her head and they set off together again.

Christine bought her a coffee and they sat on the outer edge of the lounge. Celia had already scanned those seated and the line of passengers at the information desk, and now she was watching the people passing by. She'd thought Jim had been much happier these last few days and last night she'd felt they'd crossed some kind of invisible line between them, but now she kept having the image of him slipping on the rail the first night at sea. They'd not spoken about it again so she still had no idea if it had truly been an accident or something more sinister.

Frank strolled in, looked around and came over at Christine's wave.

"I thought I might find you here," he said.

"Get a coffee and join us," Christine said. "Celia and I are looking for Jim." She gave Celia a cheery smile. "He's got to be somewhere on this ship. There's nowhere else to go."

Celia felt tears form in her eyes. It was hard to match the reassuring woman sitting opposite her to the one Celia had eaten dinner with last night.

Christine leaned closer. "You're not really that worried, are you?"

"He was so sad those first few days and then…we…I did spend the night in his room but I was on the couch." Celia fanned her face with her hands. "It's a long story. Anyway, I thought Jim was beginning to feel a lot happier."

"What's happened?" Frank arrived back with his coffee, a frown on his face. "You haven't upset Celia again, Christine?"

"She's been very kind," Celia said quickly. "It's just me. I'm being ridiculous."

She tugged a tissue from her pocket and blew her nose. Christine filled Frank in on what had happened so far.

"I don't think he'd do anything silly," Celia said. "But I don't know him that well."

"Christine and I could do another sweep of the boat," Frank said.

"You've only just got your coffee." Celia sniffed and dabbed at her eyes.

"Why don't you tell us the places you think Jim might be while we drink," Christine said. "Then we can coordinate our efforts and you can stay here in case he comes past."

Celia listed the places she thought Jim liked to visit. Christine and Frank listened carefully then made a plan between them.

Celia chewed her lip as the tears threatened again. She felt so helpless.

Frank placed a hand on her shoulder and gave it a firm squeeze. "Don't worry, Celia. I'm sure there will be a reasonable explanation. Jim's a good bloke. He'll turn up."

Christine gave her an encouraging smile and the two of them set off.

Every time someone came down the stairs or through one of the entrances Celia's hopes rose then dipped when Jim didn't appear. She watched the glass elevator and the information desk but there was no sign of him. She looked at her watch. Fifteen minutes went by and then thirty. Where could Jim be? Her heart thumped faster and her hands ached from gripping them so tightly. She took a deep breath, trying to remain calm. He didn't have to meet up with her if he'd changed his mind. But then, as she'd told Christine, he had been the one to make the arrangement and she was sure he would have got word to her if things were different.

She ordered another coffee even though she didn't feel like it, and had just finished it when Frank came back.

"No luck, I'm afraid. Chrissie's gone to try his room again."

Celia closed her eyes and pressed her fingers to her cheeks. Once more she felt Frank's gentle hand on her shoulder.

"Christine's back."

Celia's eyelids shot up. She searched the space between her and the door but there was no Jim, only Christine walking over to where they sat.

"No luck anywhere," she said as she slipped onto the low couch beside Frank. "I even tried Ketty's room again."

"He'll turn up." Frank gave Celia another of his warm smiles.

"I don't want to be an alarmist," Christine said. "But if we can't find him and Celia's worried perhaps we should let someone else know."

"You're not going up to speak to the captain I hope." Frank gave her a nudge.

"Don't be silly, Frank, of course not, but someone at the information desk might let us know what we should do."

"You really think we need to go that far?" Celia asked.

"I do." Christine nodded firmly.

Celia felt a mix of relief and panic. Relief that they were going to get some help but panic that they were making a terrible mistake and Jim was probably sitting in a corner somewhere reading a book.

"It's getting on for lunchtime," Frank said. "You two go and talk to the people at the desk about what to do and I'll check out the eating areas."

Christine stood and waited for Celia to walk with her across the atrium floor to the information desk. It felt like a marathon rather than several steps. They waited for someone to be free to talk with them.

It was a smiling young man with *Jesse* on his gleaming gold name badge who called them forward. "How can I help?"

Celia opened her mouth to speak and croaked.

"My friend is concerned that someone is missing," Christine said.

Jesse nodded wisely at Celia and asked her a couple of questions before directing them to wait. He left the desk and came back with another man in a white ship's uniform. He introduced himself as Alfred, the ship's purser. He came out from behind the desk and ushered them into the empty dining room. Christine sat beside her and held her hand while Celia explained how they'd planned to meet for breakfast and the big search she, and then the Romanos, had conducted.

Alfred asked lots of questions and noted the answers on the paper clipped to a board he carried. Celia was distressed when it came to a question about Jim's state of mind. How did she answer that? In the end she said she thought he had appeared sad when she'd first met him, he had been a widower for two years, but she thought he'd been much happier the last few days and Christine backed her up.

Alfred suggested they stay in the dining room while he put plans into motion but Celia wanted to go back to the coffee shop. At least she could see people coming and going from there.

Christine offered to buy her another coffee.

"No thanks," she said. "I'm already jittery. Another coffee would do me no good."

"Tea then, or something cold?"

"No, I'm fine really." But she didn't feel it. It had been a relief to have Alfred take charge but now she was terrified. Her breaths came faster. He'd either find Jim or he wouldn't, in either case she'd be wrecked.

They sat without talking, both of them watching the information desk for any sign of things happening, but the staff behind the counter continued to serve the passengers who popped by. There were no worried looks, flashing lights or sirens. Celia wasn't sure what to expect but she thought she'd notice something different.

Alfred came from the door behind the desk and began to walk in their direction. At the same time, a man strode through the entrance to the atrium.

Celia leaped to her feet. "Jim!"

Alfred turned to look. "Mr Fraser?"

"Yes." Jim only gave him a cursory glance. He waved at Celia and hurried towards her. "I've been rather worried," he said and then looked embarrassed. "I was late going to bed and then I slept in. Breakfast was done by the time I came downstairs. I ran into Maude on the pool deck and she said you were up and gone before she woke up this morning. I've been looking—"

"Jim." Celia said.

He stopped talking and looked at her then over at Christine, a small frown creased his brow. "What's going on?"

"We thought you were lost."

"Are you Mr Jim Fraser?" Alfred had joined them.

"Yes." Jim's frown deepened. "Is something wrong?"

"No, sir, but can you please all wait here?"

They watched as Alfred crossed to the desk and leaned in to talk with Jesse, then he came back to them.

"I've called off the search," he said. "Let's go into the dining room."

It took Jim a while to explain what had happened. He was thankful Christine hadn't stayed with them. He felt mortified that Celia had reported him missing. "I've been here all the time," he kept saying. He'd explained how he hadn't gone to sleep until the early hours of the morning and then he'd slept deeply, not waking until nine o'clock. By the time he'd reached the dining room there were no guests there and they were closing the doors. He'd tried her room with no luck and stupidly hadn't left a note, thinking he'd find her somewhere around the ship.

And Celia, who was a constant shade of pink, kept apologising to him and to Alfred who was very good about it.

"These things happen from time to time," he said, and when he was satisfied all was well he left them alone.

"I'm sorry."

Jim took a breath. They'd both spoken at once.

"I'm glad you were looking out for me, Celia, but where did you think I would be?"

"I knew you'd be at breakfast if you could. I looked everywhere for you."

"I spent a bit of time in the coffee lounge thinking you might go there, then I went up to the front deck on our level to watch for a while, then I took a walk on the promenade deck."

"I looked in all those places."

"We must have kept missing each other."

"Everyone will think I'm crazy now." Celia put her head in her hands.

Jim took her hands in his and gently eased them away. "Who's everyone?"

"The purser, the staff who went searching, Frank, Christine..."

"I'm sure they admire you for being such a caring person." He paused. "Was Christine looking for me too?"

Celia nodded.

"I saw her at one point up on the pool deck. I went the other way to avoid having to speak to her." He shook her hands gently. "Anyway, it doesn't matter now and surely we don't care what Christine thinks?"

Celia looked up. Her face was blotchy and the strand of hair was stuck to her cheek again. "She apologised for her outburst and she was such a help to me when I thought...well, when I was looking—"

"It's all right, Celia. I know you thought I'd jumped."

"I didn't." Her eyes widened then her face crumpled. "Well, there was that first night but..."

"I'll admit I was pretty miserable those first few days on my own but I was never going to throw myself overboard. I truly did slip. It scared the life out of me."

She looked at him with such distress he reached forward and hugged her to him.

"I'm here," he said. "Not in the Coral Sea."

"This is all my fault." Her words were muffled against his chest.

He held her back a little so he could look at her. "How is this your fault?"

"I truly like you, Jim but I understand you're still grieving. I've been expecting too much of you."

"You're not expecting too much. Last night I did a lot of thinking." He couldn't resist tucking back that wayward strand of her hair. "Jane's gone. She went so quickly in the end. The doctors told us we might have a year. It was barely four months. I felt so guilty." He took a deep breath, about to admit something he'd never told anyone. "I promised I'd help her, you see…if it all got too much. It did, but the reality of helping her to die was beyond me." He sagged, his arms dropping to his sides. "It's taken me a long time to forgive myself."

The old familiar pain niggled and he took a calming breath. "We had a wonderful life together and my memories of her will always be with me, but being with you made me realise I'm ready to let her physical presence go. Last night I walked, I talked." He grimaced. "To myself. I was exhausted by the time I fell into bed but I believe I've turned a corner. I slept deeply and woke refreshed for the first time in a long time. I've accepted Jane's gone. I'll always have the memories but this cruise has allowed me to make new ones. So many people have told me I've got to look forward instead of back. I wasn't ready to listen, but something Ketty said on the beach at Port Vila has helped. She told me it was all right to grieve, to feel the hurt, and it was the hurting that brought the healing. I think she's right. Grief is a terrible burden but eventually you have to set it down. I know it will never truly leave me but I'm ready to move on."

Celia was looking at him with such trepidation he leaned forward and kissed her. Not for long but it was the warm touch of one person's lips against another's.

"Jim." She cupped his cheek in her hand. "Thank you for trusting me. You've been through a terrible time and I don't want to rush you. I'm happy that we're friends. This cruise has been extra special because of you."

"Ditto," he said, and took her hand in his.

Thirty-six

Ketty made a final inspection of her stateroom. It now resembled the closest thing to a ladies' boudoir as she could make it. She had cleared the desk of everything but the phone and hidden that behind a bowl of fruit. Plenty of room there for Josie to lay out her make-up. The top of the mirror was swathed in sheer fabric and inside that she had secured a small string of battery-operated fairy lights that were part of her cruising luggage. The stool and the chair were set up in front of the desk, each draped in one of her sarongs. Out on the balcony, room service had set up a small trolley for her, with champagne on ice and a selection of canapes. All around the room, wherever she could find a place, she'd hung gowns and draped wraps.

She looked down at the small shelf that perched beneath a second mirror outside the bathroom door. Here she had set out several strings of pearls in varying lengths, a variety of sparkling necklaces and a velvet box full of earrings. Nothing especially valuable but she'd acquired the jewellery on her travels, a reminder of special times. The scene was set for a happy few hours with Josie and Celia. She let out a contented sigh. This was what she loved to do: play with fabric, dress styles, colours and accessories. The soft sensation of silk between her fingers or the textured feel of lace, draping colours to find the perfect hue to highlight a complexion; it was all about inspiring the best in other women and gave her great delight.

She glanced at her watch. There was still time before the other two arrived to duck down and buy some chocolates to add to their afternoon nibbles.

Bernard sat opposite his daughter on the balcony of his cabin. Below and beyond the ocean stretched in every direction. It was deep blue today and ruffled by a strong sea breeze creating little white caps, reflecting his own unrest at the conversation he was about to have. He found the endless movement of the sea mesmerising but not today. He had decided he needed to sort things out with Christine or he would not be able to move forward with Josie, and he wanted that more than anything. He looked back at his daughter now. She was watching him steadily.

"Josie and I are good together. I'm tired of being on my own."

"You don't have to be, Dad. You could move back to Melbourne."

Christine reached for his hand but he pulled away and he saw the surprise register in her eyes.

"When we get back to Brisbane Josie and I plan to keep seeing each other. We both need to find out if this is more than a holiday attraction. I want us to be able to do that on our own terms without your interference."

Christine stiffened. He could tell she was about to speak but he got in first.

"You can say something to Josie but it will not be based on truth. I've told her everything so—"

"Have you included your dodgy dealings?"

He sighed. There was no easy way to silence his daughter. "I made a few mistakes but I didn't do anything illegal."

"Is that so? I saw the paperwork, Dad."

"You may have seen the original document for that sale. I wanted Kath to be in on the deal but things were a bit rocky between us by then, and then when I found out—" His eyes narrowed as he looked at his daughter. "When you provided the information that Kath was already married…"

Her mouth dropped open. "Surely you don't think I enjoyed that. You had to know."

Once more he sighed. She was right but she had relished in the telling, knowing that he'd end the relationship. He'd have preferred to have found out for himself. Kept it quiet between him and Kath.

"Anyway," he continued, "Kath reneged even though it was good business and nothing to do with our relationship. That document was never signed. Whatever you think you discovered, there was no substance to it. I put up my own money to buy the house you're referring to and borrowed the rest. It did make a miraculous turnover but the profits were all mine. I didn't diddle Kath out of anything because she didn't invest in it."

"You've done very well since."

"Not by siphoning money off from wealthy women as you've suggested. It's been through my own hard work and with my own money. I studied the markets, bought and sold at the right time, made practical improvements to properties, and I was lucky enough to reap the rewards. You can try to cause trouble between

Josie and I like you did with Gloria and me, but you won't succeed this time."

Christine looked away.

"I know all about your meddling. I found out later how you wore Gloria down. You always rang when you knew I wouldn't be home, filling her head with hints that I wasn't being faithful, couched in concern for her. In the end she saw the scenes you painted even though there was no basis to them. That's what broke us up. It wasn't until a few years later after I'd been through a similar scenario with Kath that I ran into Gloria and discovered what you'd been saying to her."

"She's lying, Dad."

He propped his fingers together and looked at her over the top. "I don't think so. What would she have to gain from it?"

"To make me look bad in your eyes."

A deep sadness thudded in his chest. "You've managed to do that all by yourself." He was glad now he'd finally told Josie the whole story Christine had come up with. He'd explained about the proposed joint venture with Kath that had never gone ahead, and from that time he'd learned his lesson: never to advise or make joint purchases with the women he dated. He warned Josie it was possible Christine might try to make it sound as if he was being dishonest with his financial dealings but there was no substance to it and he had offered to let her accountant talk to his. Josie had dismissed the idea but forewarned was forearmed. "I've told Josie about your accusations. She believes my side of the story."

Tears rolled down her cheeks. "I love you, Dad."

"I know. And I love you. So did your mother, maybe not in the way you wanted her to, but she did love you."

Christine dabbed at her eyes with a tissue. Bernard was unmoved by her tears. Usually they would be enough to sway his resolve but not this time.

"And it's because of that love that I spoiled you. I see it now. The more I gave, the more you wanted. It's got to stop, Chrissie. You keep wanting more and more and none of it's necessary. You've got Frank and the kids, good jobs, a home. Frank's a dependable bloke and if he gets this new job I think you should follow up his suggestion of buying somewhere else. I might be able to help with advice."

She opened her mouth but he held up his hand. "There will be no money from me for your renovations."

"Dad." The tears fell faster now, making dark mascara lines down her cheeks.

"I've thought about this a lot. If I were to drop dead tomorrow you would inherit a considerable sum of money and I'm worried you'd fritter it away."

"*Fritter*?" Her eyes widened and she gaped at him.

"Because of that I'm changing my will. When I go, and I am truly hoping that's a long way off, my remaining funds are to be split three ways."

"Between who?"

"You and Lucca and Anna. Their share will be held in trust until they're thirty. I know how tough the real estate market is for young ones now. I want them to have something, and I'm not sure there'd be anything left if you got it all."

Christine was silent. She sagged back as if she'd been pricked by a pin and all the air had left her.

Bernard had said all there was to say. He wanted no further discussion about money. He reached for the bottle of white wine he had chilling in an ice bucket at his feet.

"I think we should have a quick drink, then I have to go." He gave a small sigh. "I promised Josie I'd go with her brother to the horse race event in the sports bar."

He was aware of Christine watching him closely as he poured. He handed her a glass. "All will be well, Princess." He raised his own glass in the air and winked. Her lips turned up in a watery smile. "Cheers, big ears," he said.

Celia flung open the door to her cabin and went straight to the wardrobe. She and Jim had talked for ages over lunch and now she'd be late for her girls' afternoon with Josie and Ketty if she didn't get her skates on. The bathroom door opened behind her and she put her hand to her chest.

"Maude! You startled me. I didn't realise you were here."

"I wondered if you'd moved out." Maude's voice was sharp in the little room.

Celia felt an immediate pang of remorse. She'd hardly seen Maude but for a quick hello or goodnight for days. "Of course I haven't." She turned back to the wardrobe and took out a plain white shirt that buttoned down the front. She hadn't much of a clue what Ketty had planned but she knew there would be some trying on of clothes and thought it best to wear something that was easy to remove.

"I thought we could have the afternoon together." Maude stacked up some brochures that had been spread across her bed. "Since we haven't seen that much of each other these last few days."

Celia concentrated on the buttons of her shirt. If the truth be told she was pleased they'd not seen much of each other but then she felt mean.

"I can't right now, Maude." She glanced at her face in the mirror and decided against reapplying her lipstick. Josie was bringing her make-up case to Ketty's. "I'm meeting Josie and Ketty."

"Oh, well if you have plans…"

Celia looked at Maude's reflection in the mirror. Her expression was unusually contrite.

She turned around. "Is something wrong?"

"I was looking for some company, that's all."

"What about Pete?"

Maude sagged to the bed. "Anne's feeling a lot better and they're making up for lost time."

"I see."

"No you don't, Celia." There was a spark of anger in Maude's eyes. "I know I shouldn't have encouraged Pete but in the end nothing came of it."

"What about the night you asked me to stay out of our room?"

"Pete called it off. Anne had been given some special invitation to a fancy invite-only cocktail party and they went to that. It was in the Diamond Lounge or somewhere. I went looking but couldn't find it."

Celia felt a surge of relief but then remorse at the miserable look on Maude's face.

"In Noumea they ended up taking a different tour to the rest of us." Maude plucked at the hem of her dress. "The others are nice people but it isn't as much fun when Pete's not there."

Celia couldn't bear to see her friend so sad.

"What about pre-dinner drinks?" she said. "It's formal night again. We have to glam up. We should get our photo taken." Celia put a hand to her cheek remembering the last formal night. Her bruise had faded but she must ask Josie to take special care to cover up any remaining discolouration.

"You didn't want to last time."

"I wasn't feeling up to it but tonight I will be." Celia smiled. "A memento of our cruise."

"What time?"

"For drinks? Six-thirty in the club bar above the atrium." Celia threw a few items of jewellery and some cosmetics in a bag. She wanted Josie to show her how to make the best of the make-up she owned. She plucked the dress she planned to wear tonight from the wardrobe.

"Where are you going with all that?"

"To Ketty's."

"Oh. She seems to be flavour of the month now. I didn't think you went for her much."

Celia opened her mouth, closed it again. "I was wrong about her. She's actually very warm and generous, and she's going to show me a few style tricks."

It was on the tip of Celia's tongue to invite Maude but a girls' afternoon wasn't something she imagined Maude enjoying and Celia didn't want to spoil the fun she knew would be happening in Ketty's room.

"I'll see you at six-thirty." She opened the door and the last she saw of Maude was her sitting rather forlornly on the end of her bed.

Ketty made her way back up the stairs with her box of chocolates and as she rounded the corner nearly ran straight into a woman coming down.

It was Christine. She looked at Ketty, no doubt as surprised to run into her as Ketty was. Ketty had no desire to lock horns with that young woman again but she looked as if she'd been crying and that tugged at Ketty's heartstrings.

"Is something wrong?" she asked.

"No." Christine shook her head and smoothed the hair on the top of her head with her hands. "I looked for you earlier today actually."

"I was in the day spa most of the morning." Ketty glanced down at her nails. The young technician had talked her into a deep red colour. She still wasn't sure it was right but she'd had a delightful morning indulging herself with a massage and facial and manicure, another part of her birthday treat.

"That would have been lovely." Christine smiled.

Ketty thought she should do that more often, she looked so much more attractive.

"Ketty, I want to apologise."

A group of people trooped down the stairs and Christine drew Ketty to one side.

"For what I said at dinner last night. My behaviour was unacceptable and I'm sorry." Christine tugged at the shoulders of the singlet top that she looked dangerously close to falling out of. She glanced at the floor then around as if she was looking for inspiration.

"Thank you," Ketty said.

"I've caught up with everyone else and apologised."

"That's good."

"Did you hear about Jim's drama?"

"No." Ketty had a sudden flash of concern. She hadn't seen any of her fellow diners since last night. "What's happened?"

"Nothing really but Celia thought he was missing and we had to tell the purser and—"

Another woman came puffing up the stairs, almost bumping into Ketty.

"Hello, Maude."

"Oh, Ketty, hello." Maude looked from Ketty to Christine. "Sorry, had my head down and my bum up, so to speak. These stairs will be the death of me."

"I'm sure the exercise keeps us from rolling off at the end of the cruise." Ketty chuckled. "They spoil us with all the good food, don't they? Have you met Christine? She's one of my fellow evening diners. This is Celia's roommate, Maude."

The two women gave each other cursory hellos.

"Celia said you were having a get-together to get ready for tonight," Maude said.

"That's right. I love to play with clothing, see what suits best, tizz it up a bit with jewellery."

Maude sniffed. "Well, I won't keep you."

Ketty thought her face was positively maudlin. "Are you off to meet your friends?" Ketty studied Maude closely, wondering if her ploy to send Anne and Pete off for some special together-time had worked.

"No, not today." Maude sighed. "Just back to my cabin."

"Me too." Christine took a step away. "Now that I've seen you, Ketty, I can go and stick my head under a pillow."

Maude gave her a quizzical look.

Ketty thought both women in need of some cheering up. "Why don't you two come and join Celia, Josie and me?"

Maude's face lifted in a smile and then dropped. "I'm not much of a one for tizzing things up, as you say."

"Doesn't matter. The more the merrier. It'll be fun. Please join us. What do you say Christine?" Ketty hoped Celia and Josie wouldn't mind. "There's champagne."

Maude's face lit up fully this time. "If you insist."

"Perhaps for a while," Christine said. "Frank's gone with Dad to do some horse race thing."

"Good, I'm up on the next deck," Ketty said. There was a soft groan from Maude as they set off.

Both women stopped in awe as she opened the door to her cabin.

"I didn't know there were rooms like this," Maude said.

"This is amazing." Christine walked straight to the pearls and picked up a strand.

Ketty had just poured the champagne and rung room service for more glasses and another bottle when there was a knock on her door. She opened it to welcome Josie and Celia. They both stopped short at the sight of Ketty's extra guests as she ushered them inside. The looks on their faces were too precious for words.

Thirty-seven

Celia hadn't been able to believe her eyes when Ketty had revealed Maude and Christine already inside her cabin. Now with a few champagnes each and Ketty in full swing suggesting styles and colours, everyone was laughing and talking like old friends. Maude had cheered up and was in a detailed conversation with Josie about the pros and cons of foundation application and Ketty was draping Christine in vibrant colours as alternatives to the black she was so fond of wearing.

Celia put her empty champagne glass firmly on the bench. She'd had two already and was feeling light-headed. She poured herself some water, popped a caramel-filled chocolate into her mouth and watched Christine's reflection in the mirror. Ketty was swapping the midnight blue scarf she'd draped below Christine's chin for a softer blue blouse to show the difference the colours made to Christine's complexion.

"The darker colour looks so much better." Celia couldn't help but join in.

Ketty swapped back to the deeper blue. "You could wear an ice blue if you wanted something lighter but I don't have an example of the shade with me."

"I like the midnight. It does make a change from my usual black." Christine turned her head from side to side, admiring herself in the mirror. "If I'd known I would be doing this I would have washed my hair." She fluffed it with her fingers. "It's so thick and heavy and getting ratty."

Celia noticed Ketty give Josie a questioning look. Maude had stopped talking and was working her way through Ketty's collection of necklaces. Josie came around the bed to the desk where Christine was seated. She reached out tentatively and took a lock of Christine's hair. "Can I suggest something?"

There was hesitation on Christine's face, then she nodded.

"You've got beautiful hair and you're lucky it's so thick but I think it could do with some layering. I also think it would lend itself to putting up in a style. Take it away from your face." She swirled sections of Christine's hair and piled them on her head. With the deep blue scarf still draped across her chest, Christine looked suddenly younger.

"Perfect." Ketty clapped her hands. "Did you know Josie's a talented hairdresser?"

"Are you?" Celia and Christine spoke at once.

"Not professionally any longer but I trained in my younger days. It was my first job and I've worked in salons at various stages in my life, although not for a long time now." Once more she made eye contact with Christine. "I could cut it for you if you like. Just a tidy up, nothing major."

Celia barely caught Christine's nodded response because Ketty had thrown an arm around her and was guiding her to the wardrobe where articles of clothing hung from the open doors.

"I'm so excited you're my size, Celia. I've brought so many things with me I'd love you to choose something to wear tonight. Which colour is your favourite?" Ketty pulled out two dresses.

One was cornflower blue satin with tiny sprigs of white flowers in the sheath style she preferred but with more shape to it. The other was a pale shade she would describe as lavender or even blue, with tiny beads that glinted in the sunlight coming through the open door. Celia's heart skipped a beat.

"What colour do you call that?"

"Periwinkle." Ketty held it under Celia's chin.

"Can I try it on?"

"Of course. Try several." Ketty took out a softly draping dress in carnation pink and a floaty chiffon in pale green.

"Humph!" Maude snorted and nodded at the clothing. "Nothing there would go on my big toe."

"But I have plenty of accessories, Maude," Ketty said. "I'm sure I can find you something. What will you be wearing tonight?"

The two women drew together leaving Celia holding the periwinkle gown Ketty had thrust at her. She ran her hands over the sheer fabric feeling the roughness of the tiny beads beneath her fingers. Now that she had a closer look, the neckline would be revealing. She clutched it to her trying to imagine herself in such a glamorous dress.

"I think that's the one."

Celia spun at the sound of Ketty's voice low in her ear. Beyond her Maude was swapping between a long strand of pearls and a set of glittering beads.

"You can try the others but the periwinkle is the perfect colour for you. It's organza, a remarkable fabric on its own, but I love the subtle embroidery on this." She lifted the hem and touched it to Celia's cheek, her penetrating look pinning Celia to the spot. "The beads will highlight the sparkle in your eyes."

"Did you get a chance to talk with your dad? I know he wanted to catch up with you."

Josie's hands rested gently on Christine's shoulders as she looked up at the older woman's reflection in the mirror.

She could see no hint of hostility in Josie's look.

"I did."

"That's good. I hope you had a chance to clear the air properly."

Christine wondered how much Josie really knew. Bernard had said he'd explained everything to Josie but did she know Christine had asked him for money? Did she know about Christine's undermining of his early relationships after her mother had died?

"We had a long talk," she said.

"Good. It's early days yet between your dad and me."

Josie began to play with Christine's hair while she talked. It was surprising she was being so gentle after the previous evening's confrontation but Christine soon relaxed. Warmth flowed from Josie's hands, as she gently massaged her scalp and swirled strands of her hair in different ways.

"I like your dad a lot, Christine. I hope we'll keep seeing each other back in Brisbane and I'd like to get to know you better too." She piled Christine's hair on top of her head again and tugged out some tendrils to fall softly down her neck. "I don't have a daughter. My boys would barely sit still long enough for me to brush their hair let alone cut it. I promise I won't do anything you don't approve of."

"Why don't you pop back to your cabin." Ketty said. "Wash your hair, get the clothes you're wearing tonight and come back for a proper makeover?"

Christine glanced across at Ketty then back at Josie who was smiling at her in the mirror. "I would love to have something done with my hair. I haven't had time to get to the hairdresser since…well, I can't remember when my last appointment was."

"Off you go then," Ketty said.

The door shut behind Christine. She moved along the corridor a little way then could go no further. She slumped against the wall, fighting back the tears. Her nose began to run. She dug in her pocket for a tissue but couldn't find one. She straightened as a couple came round the corner towards her, wiped her nose with the back of her hand and blinked hard. She couldn't believe how kind the other women were being after her tirade. Celia was still a bit reluctant to get too close and Josie had been cool at first but everyone had eventually relaxed. Ketty was everywhere, offering suggestions for clothes and colours, lining them up for make-up advice with Josie and keeping their glasses filled. Christine had stuck to water.

Josie had been so nice about her hair and was doing her best to be kind but Christine was still aching with hurt over her father's decision not to give her any money. And when he'd told her he'd changed his will as if Christine was a conniving money-grabber, she'd crumpled inside. Is that what he honestly thought of her?

She waited for the couple to pass then moved on down the corridor. The excitement generated in Ketty's room had helped ease the shock of her father's news. Alone with her troubled thoughts the sorrow returned.

Maude and Celia were trying on some of the jewellery Ketty had set out so she took the opportunity to draw Josie onto the balcony.

"Thank you for being so kind to Christine." Ketty kept her voice low, not wanting the other two women to hear. "I know it can't be easy for you."

"I'm doing my best," Josie said. "I want this to work with Bernie and I don't want to come between father and daughter in the process."

"That's very wise." Ketty moved to the rail and drew in a deep breath of Coral Sea air. "That young woman needs mothering and you're the perfect person."

"Now hang on, Ketty." Josie came to stand beside her.

"She needs some nurturing, that's all. Her mother's been gone a long time and I think Bernard's way of dealing with his daughter's grief was to throw money at it. She's come to expect it. What she needs is the interest of an older woman. Someone to chat to about her children, let off steam about her husband if she needs to, a confidante."

"Surely she's got friends for that."

"She probably has but I think she'd like her dad to be there for her more." Ketty turned and smiled her sweetest smile at Josie. "You could be the bridge between them. Add the feminine touch to the relationship. Perhaps even give Bernard some guidance with how to deal with his daughter."

"You've got to be kidding."

"I'm not. I think Christine needs the counselling of an older woman in her life. If you and Bernard work out together, that role could be yours."

Josie gaped at Ketty who grinned wider. "More champagne?"

Celia popped her head through the door. "Sorry, am I interrupting?"

"Not at all," Josie said.

"Could I have a word, Ketty." Celia glanced apologetically at Josie. "In private?"

"Do you have a clutch, Maude?" Ketty burrowed in her wardrobe, looking for the bags. Maude had tried on nearly every piece of jewellery Ketty had brought with her and she wanted something else to distract her with. After Celia's revelation, Ketty's head was buzzing with questions and she needed to clear her thoughts and concentrate on her ladies. Her hands found the soft pouch with several clutches inside. She lay them on the bed and once more Maude pounced.

"I've also got some shimmering gold nail polish," Ketty said, eyeing Maude's bright pink nails.

"That sounds perfect," Maude gushed.

"Why don't we do them now?" Ketty settled Maude on a chair.

Josie was blow-drying Christine's hair at the make-up station she'd created, leaving the bathroom free. She made eye contact with Celia who was once again looking longingly at the periwinkle dress.

Ketty smiled and nodded towards the empty bathroom. "You actually have to put it on to know what it will look like."

Everyone had exclaimed in delight when Celia had stepped out of the bathroom. Now Ketty had gone back to painting Maude's toenails – Maude had wanted them done after she'd admired the shimmering gold on her fingernails – and Josie was brushing up

Christine's hair. Celia stole another look at herself side-on in the mirror. The periwinkle dress glistened as if it had its own party lights. It fitted her snugly to the waist where it flared slightly and hung in soft folds. She was used to the lower neckline now, which was studded with diamantés and showed just a small amount of cleavage. She wore no jewellery except a pair of sparkling earrings dangling from her ears.

"Sometimes less is more," Ketty had murmured in her ear when she'd first put the earrings on and they'd both glanced at Maude, who once again sported her sequined gold dress but this time she'd added several pieces of Ketty's jewellery to her outfit.

Celia was happy with what she saw in the mirror. Josie had totally concealed the remnants of the bruise and fluffed her hair out so it had more bulk around her face. Celia thought she looked younger than the woman she'd seen in the mirror at the start of the cruise.

Ketty came to stand beside her, smiling. "You look..."

"Like a celebrity?" Celia cringed at the memory of her early days aboard when she'd been practising her moves in the bathroom. Thank goodness Ketty didn't know about that.

Maude began to laugh from her seat on the edge of Ketty's bed, her feet stretched out drying the polish. "You called yourself that one night. I think you must have been talking in your sleep but you were almost singing it out. Celebrity Celia. You said it several times." Maude's stuttering cackle faded as she turned her attention back to a second container of earrings Ketty had dug out.

Celia felt the heat in her cheeks.

Ketty met her gaze in the mirror. "I think *enchanting* a much better description," she murmured.

"I wish we lived closer, Ketty. I'd love to visit your shop."

"Do you shop online?" Josie asked. "Ketty has a website."

"Oh, it's terrible and not set up for online shopping," Ketty said.

"Your website is very good," Josie said. "Leo was looking at it. He was impressed so I took a look too."

Ketty frowned. "He did say something about it."

"Where did I put my phone?" Josie glanced around. "I don't have the ship's wi-fi but I took advantage of the free connection while we were ashore. I snapped some screen shots of a dress I liked. I was going to ask you if you could make it in another fabric. I'd forgotten about it."

She plucked her phone from among her make-up then began to scroll. "There." She held the phone out to Ketty, who had put on her glasses.

"For goodness sake," Ketty exclaimed then she laughed. "I certainly recognise the fabric." She peered closer.

Celia looked over her shoulder. The dummy in the picture wore a loose-fitting dress in a bright paisley-patterned fabric with a band of contrast colour across the bottom. Maude and Christine squeezed in for a look too.

"The fabric's a bit out there, isn't it?" Christine said.

"Mmm," Celia said. "But I agree with Josie, I like the style."

"I'd look like a bag of lollies in something like that," Maude said.

Josie took back her phone. "I was surprised. I know your shop has lots of one-offs but I didn't think you had an actual line of ready-made, Ketty."

"I don't." Ketty's face was a picture of puzzlement.

Josie selected another screen and enlarged the picture. "It says *easy wash-and-wear dresses to suit travellers. Buy in store or online.*"

She held out the phone for Ketty again.

"Well, I never." Ketty shook her head. "That fabric was bought in error. I didn't have a clue what I was going to do with it but it's certainly easy wash-and-wear, and it looks like my ladies have turned it in to a new fashion line." She looked up, her lips lifted in a smile. "And my young assistant, Lacey, has been true to her word and come up with a new website. And...an online shop! She was talking about it before I left but..." She glanced back at the phone again. "I can't believe what an impressive job she's done."

"Looks like your staff have been busy while you've been away."

"It does indeed."

Ketty hung the last of her dresses back in the wardrobe and Josie had packed up her make-up. Apart from the fairy lights and scattered scarves and jewellery her cabin was almost back to normal. She was a little saddened by that. This could well be her last cruise and so the last time she hosted one of her cabin makeover sessions. They had given her so many happy memories.

Tonight was not the time for backward glances. Not that she allowed herself too many of those but this cruise had certainly conjured up a large number.

Ketty glanced at her watch. "Nearly time to meet the men for drinks,' she said. "How's that hairdo coming along, Josie?"

"One more pin and we're done." Josie poked a clip into Christine's hair and the younger woman turned so they could all see.

There were delighted comments from everyone. Ketty squeezed her hands together in pleasure. Brooding Christine had been replaced. Her hairstyle gave her elegance and the soft make-up, not so thick around the eyes, made them look larger, bringing out the chocolate brown. She was glamorous, radiant even.

"You're sure this dress is all right?" Christine asked as she stood and tugged at the skimpy neckline. "It's the one I bought in the boutique but I didn't realise how much boob shows."

"You look perfectly lovely but may I make a suggestion?" Ketty plucked something from the bed and went to Christine. She swept the black lace wrap around Christine's shoulders and pinned it in place with a small diamanté brooch, then she stepped back.

"I remember this." Josie lifted a corner of the wrap.

"So do I." Celia had a faraway look in her eye.

"It suits Christine so well, don't you think?" Ketty said pointedly and they both agreed. She smiled at Christine. "Still showing off your creamy shoulders and the perfect amount of cleavage. I always think the trick is to hint at the beautiful bosom below, not bare it for the whole world to see."

Christine looked back at the mirror. "I feel like Cinderella."

"So do I." Celia sashayed from side to side, her dress swishing with her. "This has been so much fun," she said.

"Yes, thanks for having us, Ketty." Maude's smile was wide. "It's been all right doing this girlie stuff."

"It has," Josie said. "Last time I did this with Ketty there were only three of us but we managed to laugh and drink our way through a pleasant afternoon. What was the other woman's name?"

"Mary," Ketty said.

"She was interesting. She took two cruises every year. Used to take the odd cruise with her husband and after he died she decided to do it more often. I wonder how she is?"

"Mary's well," Ketty said. "We drop each other a line from time to time. She sent me a postcard from the Mediterranean this year."

"We should do that," Celia said.

"I'd be in for a Mediterranean cruise," Maude said.

"It would be nice." Celia's response held a hint of hesitation. "But I meant we should keep in touch. You and I will of course, Maude, but we should all swap email addresses."

"I'm not much of a user of email," Ketty said. "Mostly it's only for work."

"I think you might have to improve," Josie said. "And I think your young assistant…what's her name?"

"Lacey."

Maude gave a snort. "Did you make that up?"

Ketty shook her head.

"I think Lacey will be the one to help you with that," Josie continued.

"Perhaps you're right." Ketty still hadn't had her appointment at the internet cafe. After seeing the glimpses of her site on Josie's phone she was keen to find out more.

"What are you wearing, Ketty?" Celia asked. "You're the only one not changed."

"I thought I'd wear my red shantung tonight with the wide neck and buttons at the back. It's part of my Jackie O–inspired collection and I haven't worn it yet."

"Come on then," Josie picked up her make-up case. "I'll take this to my room and come back."

"I have to make sure Frank's found the right clothes," Christine said.

Celia linked arms with Maude. "We'll meet you down there. Maude and I are off to have our photo taken together." She glanced at each of them. "We should have a group photo. A memento of our girls' makeover day."

"Great idea," Josie said.

The door shut on them and Ketty paused for the briefest moment. The sparkle of friendship and good times lingered on, a warm presence in her room.

She reached back with her good arm and slid the zip part way down her back then lifted the hem of her dress. She got it over her head, her injured arm still a little awkward since it didn't go as high as the other, and felt a sharp tug in her hair.

"Blast," she muttered. The zip had caught.

There was a light tap on her door. "Ketty."

With relief at the sound of Josie's voice, Ketty managed to lower her hand enough to open the door.

Josie stepped in. "What on earth are you doing?"

"The blasted zip has caught my hair."

She felt Josie's hands at work and then the sweet release of the zip and the dress was over her head and off.

"Thank goodness you came back. I thought I was going to lose a chunk of my hair." Ketty rubbed at the spot on her head.

Josie gave her a weak smile.

"Is something wrong?"

"No...it's...well, your stomach."

Ketty looked down. Her favourite French knickers had slid a little in all the kerfuffle and revealed the unsightly scar that went from one side of her abdomen to the other. She quickly pulled her underwear back into place and stepped into her dress.

"I'll need your help with the buttons as well." She turned her back to Josie and felt her fingers go to work.

"Is that from the hysterectomy?" Josie's voice was so soft it was almost lost in the hum of the air conditioner.

"Yes."

"I'm so sorry, Ketty."

"Why? It's not your fault. Not anyone's. The doctors did what they had to do, to save my life. I grieved for a long time then I knew I had to get on with living. That scar reminds me every day how lucky I am to be here."

Two hands gripped her shoulders and turned her towards the mirror where Josie's look was one of admiration.

"You are one amazing woman, Ketty Clift," she said.

Ketty swallowed the lump in her throat. She didn't feel amazing. She felt quite ordinary. She'd had to learn to deal with that scar and she had. "Nonsense." Ketty patted one of Josie's hands then slipped away. "We all just do what we can."

"I am sorry though," Josie said. "Leo says he's coming to dinner tonight and he hasn't had the chance to talk to you alone first. He badly wants to apologise."

"He must come. He's your brother and he's part of our table." Ketty found she didn't mind if he was there or not. "But perhaps I won't sit next to him."

Josie smiled. "Of course not. Thank you for being so gracious. He doesn't deserve it but I'm sure he'll make it up to you before the cruise is over."

Ketty preferred not to think about that. She glanced at her watch. There was something she wanted to do before dinner. "I'd love your help with make-up please, Josie."

"I've taken my case away."

"Let's make do with what I've got." Ketty sat herself in front of the mirror.

Josie was soon absorbed in her work, leaving Ketty to reflect. In her younger days the scar had been the reminder of no more children and had been like a flashing neon sign saying 'barren woman' to any man she'd become intimate with. The first man after Leo, she'd thought, could have possibly replaced the hurt in her heart, but he'd badly wanted his own children. It had driven them apart. Later it was of no consequence, as she chose partners who were simply relieved there was no possibility of children, and while she'd been happy, she'd liked none of them enough to make a permanent commitment. Now she realised she'd never let them get close enough. Meeting Leo again had been revealing.

His actions, along with the information Celia had shared earlier in the day out on the balcony, had destroyed the myth Ketty had created. Now he'd been knocked firmly from the lofty heights where she'd enshrined his memory. Tonight at dinner he would be simply another diner at her table for eight.

"There."

Ketty opened her eyes and studied her reflection. "Thank you."

She saw a woman of mature years who looked like she was ready for a night out. She stood up. But before she joined the others she was hopeful the young man at the internet cafe would have time to give her some help.

Thirty-eight

Night Eight – At Sea

"I'm sorry we weren't seated together over dinner."

"Leo." Ketty turned in surprise at the sound of his voice. She glanced around the atrium and saw no one else she knew. "I've said my goodnights, as you know. I'm heading off to my room."

"Couldn't we have one final drink together?" He put a firm hand on her arm. "Please Kathy. I need to apologise."

It was the last thing she wanted to do but Josie had said he badly wanted to make amends. She didn't want to talk to him at all but to refuse would be churlish. "Just for a few minutes."

They took the curved marble stairs. Leo offered his arm but Ketty preferred to hold the polished rail as they ascended. From a podium beside the bar two men, one on piano and one on sax, played jazz music and a young woman in a sparkling dress sang. Ketty sighed. Of all nights and places it would be jazz.

"Remember this song?" Leo murmured in her ear.

"'How High the Moon'." Of course she remembered it. So many times she'd been in his arms when it was played and so many times she'd wished she still was, whenever she'd heard it since. But not tonight.

Leo sang softly along with the words.

They'd reached the top of the stairs and a waiter greeted them. "I'll have a Scotch on the rocks, thank you." Ketty showed her card.

"I can get it, Kathy."

"Thank you, Leo, but I pay my own way." She nodded at the waiter and moved to take a seat, making sure she had a single chair rather than one of the cosy couches available.

She sat and watched as Leo spoke to the waiter and she saw him hold his card out. After her day spa treatment this morning she'd visited one of the self-serve passenger stations and printed a copy of her onboard expenses so far. It had surprised her to notice that whenever she and Leo had been together for drinks she had ended up with most of them on her bill. He had paid for very little since their first pre-dinner drink together.

"Are you sure you wouldn't prefer the couch?" Leo looked down at her, the charm of his smile completely lost on her now.

"I'm fine here," she said.

He gave the slightest shrug of his shoulders and took the closest chair to hers.

"Kathy, I'm sorry."

He looked at her expectantly but she gave him no response.

"Josie pointed out that I may have appeared uncaring."

Still Ketty remained silent.

"It was a shock to have you fling all that information at me in the cafe. It took me by surprise."

"I'm sure it did, Leo."

"I really am sorry you've had such a tough life, Kathy, but mine hasn't been easy either."

The waiter arrived with their drinks. Ketty took a hasty gulp fearing she might scream if she didn't have something else to distract her.

Leo raised his whisky tumbler in her direction. "To us, Kathy."

She put her glass carefully back on the table and sat up straight. "There is no us, Leo."

"We can put the past behind us and start again. I'd move to Sydney, I can help with your business." He leaned in. "We'd be good together."

Ketty shook her head. He was confident even now. How had she been so blind?

"What would you be bringing to this…" She rolled her hands. "Arrangement?"

"Myself, my expertise. I find myself starting all over again financially as I said, but I'll be back on my feet soon."

"How exactly?"

"Investments. I know where the smart money is."

"And whose money would you be investing?"

His looked away, took a sip of his drink then licked his lips. "Yours to begin with but—"

She put up her hand. "Please stop, Leo. I know about your previous investments, as you call them." She'd been late for the pre-dinner drinks because she'd been at the internet cafe. The assistant there had been very helpful. He'd found her website straight away and left her to scroll through. The opening page had left her awe-struck. It was a photograph of the front room of the shop and she'd had to look closely to recognise it. There were now only two racks, ranging along the internal wall. The front rack held a few gowns and day dresses, the colours graded. The second rack was harder to see but she recognised the bright patterned fabric of the front dress. Instead of the centre rack there was one shop model, draped in palest peach chiffon and silk. Even though the pictures were small, she immediately recognised the beauty that the changes to the space had brought. She should have decluttered years ago for this more svelte look. A few clicks on the other pages revealed some of the dresses Josie had shown her. She'd been delighted and humbled by the new web presence Lacey and her friend had achieved. Sadly she hadn't had time to dwell on that. She'd gone on to do a different search.

During the makeover afternoon when they'd had a few minutes on the balcony alone, Celia had told her how Jim had thought he'd remembered Leo and had done some internet searching while they'd been in Noumea. It had been all over the media in South Australia a year ago but perhaps not so prominent everywhere else. Christine had been right. It wasn't difficult to find information on the internet.

Ketty looked Leo squarely in the eye now. "I believe your last business partner accused you of skimming funds from your financial planning business."

His smile was replaced by a dark look. "She was lying."

"Your business partner was also your lover, wasn't she, Leo?"

"She didn't mean anything to me. It was a business arrangement."

"Did she know that?"

"It's in the past." He shifted in his seat, took another sip of his whisky. "Anyway, nothing ended up going to court."

"The money was miraculously found." Ketty wondered if Josie knew the money she had given her brother had gone to saving his bacon. Perhaps she did. Ketty knew Josie felt she owed him a great debt.

"What's the point of raking that up now. It has nothing to do with us, Kathy."

Ketty drained the remains of her drink and stood looking down at him. "Goodnight, Leo."

As she walked away the singer's voice drifted after her. Ketty felt a wave of sadness as she recognised the song – 'As Time Goes By'. She wondered if Leo had ever genuinely loved her as she had loved him.

"Do you think Ketty will be all right?" Celia watched her friend walk away from Leo. She and Jim had seen him speak to Ketty and they'd followed, taking seats out of sight on the other side of the bar. "Perhaps I shouldn't have told her."

"I think Ketty is more than capable of looking after herself."

"Leo certainly didn't look too happy." From where Celia sat she could only see the back of Ketty but she had a clear view of Leo. "He's thrown himself back in the chair like a petulant child."

"I don't think we need to worry." Jim reached for her hand. "People are dancing. Would you care to?"

"I'd love it." Celia stood and took the hand he offered. The heels she'd chosen weren't practical for dancing but she was sure he would keep her upright. She wobbled a bit, leaned too far and bumped against Jim who was only half out of his seat. He fell back, dragging her with him, and she sat with a plop on his lap.

They looked at each other, stunned for a moment, then laughed.

"Celia?"

She looked up. Ed was staring down at her, Debbie beside him.

"It is you," he said.

Celia struggled up and readjusted the shoulders of her dress. "Hello, Ed. Fancy running in to you on a cruise."

"I thought I saw you several nights ago. There was this woman, obviously drunk, who fell down the stairs and—"

"I'm Celia's friend, Jim." Jim had managed to get to his feet. She felt the press of his body against hers in the confined space between chair and table.

"This is my wife, Debbie." Ed's face was composed again, his manners always impeccable. "This is Celia, my—"

"Your ex-wife, Ed, yes I know." Debbie held out her hand. "I have seen photos."

Celia barely took the other woman's hand.

"Debbie and I thought it time we tried cruising," Ed said, his look appraising Celia now.

"Oh, Ed, you fibber." Debbie gave him a playful pat. "You know very well I had to work hard to convince you to come. How are you enjoying it, Celia? Isn't cruising a lot of fun?" She gave a quirky grin. "I said I'd come on my own, that sealed it."

Celia opened her mouth but no words came out. She felt Jim's arm slip around her waist.

"We were about to take to the dance floor," he said.

"Oh, I'd love to do that too but Ed says he's had enough for today." Debbie gave a pout.

"Goodnight then." Jim steered Celia away, turned her to face him and held her close.

"Fancy your ex being on this cruise," he murmured in her ear.

Over his shoulder Celia saw Ed reach the door arch. He turned back, stared a moment then left. Celia began to laugh. Jim stopped dancing and looked at her and he was laughing too.

No sooner had she arrived back in her cabin than Ketty's legs went to jelly. She'd been holding herself together and now she was exhausted from the effort.

She moved to the bed and fell back against the pillows, almost squashing the chocolate Peter had left. It all made sense. Poor Celia had been so worried telling her about what Jim had found out. When Ketty had searched, there'd been a few other instances of Leo possibly mismanaging funds but nothing that ever stuck or was proven. That and the discovery of her ship's account with his additions explained so much more about Leo than she'd ever understood. He was an opportunist and he'd had her firmly in his sights. She'd been flattered by his attention and the appeal of his body had awakened feelings she hadn't felt for some time. Thankfully she'd seen him for what he truly was before he had the chance to break her heart again.

The buttons on her dress dug into her back and she sat up. She reached around but her injured arm was still stiff and she couldn't manage the buttons.

"Blast!"

There was a tap on her door.

"Miss Clift, a message for you," called a female voice with a distinctive Indian accent.

Ketty opened the door. A waitress she recognised from the dining room held out a small envelope.

"Thank you," Ketty said.

She let the door close and stared at the writing, then she ripped open the envelope. There was a short note inside written on ship's letterhead. It was from Carlos asking her to join him at eleven pm in the dining room. It wasn't something he'd ever done before. Their catch-ups had usually been somewhere private. Ketty tapped the paper against her brightly coloured nails.

"What are you up to, Carlos?"

Ketty had done a quick scan of the bar where she'd last seen Leo but there was no sign of him so she stepped off down the marble stairs, enjoying the experience one more time. Piano music filtered down from the bar above – no sax or singer now.

The doors to the dining room were firmly shut but a waiter almost leaped to attention as she approached.

"Miss Clift?" he asked.

She smiled, anticipation building. "I am."

"Please come this way." He unlocked the door and held it open for her to enter the dimly lit space. As soon as the door closed behind them the music and rumble of voices was silenced. Ketty looked around. The dining room appeared to be empty.

"Please follow me." The waiter led her slowly along one aisle between tables to a secluded corner of the room that was subtly lit by lamps.

She stopped at the sight of Carlos waiting beside the table. He was out of uniform and wearing a white dinner jacket and black pants.

"Welcome, Miss Clift," he said then looked at the waiter. "Thank you, Benjamin. Please pour the champagne."

"Carlos?" Ketty gave him a wary glance. "What's going on?"

"Our last chance for a get-together on the *Diamond Duchess*." He pulled out a chair for her. "Please sit."

She did as he bid. He flicked out the napkin and placed it across her lap.

"I've had dinner, Carlos."

"This is not dinner. We are having champagne and cake." Carlos took a seat opposite her and raised his glass. "To the *Diamond Duchess* and all who have sailed on her."

Ketty was a little bemused but also touched that he had gone to all this trouble. "To the *Duchess*."

Benjamin was back with a small cake with coffee icing, decorated with shards of chocolate. He placed it in the centre of the table and stepped back.

"We can manage now, Benjamin." Carlos gave a nod. "Thank you for your help this evening."

"Yes, thank you," Ketty said and, as he moved away, she looked back at Carlos.

"The champagne is for the *Duchess*," he said. "And the cake is for you. You left before I could deliver it the other night."

"What a lovely surprise but I do hope there's nothing more."

"No, this is it."

"So I am not going to be surrounded by waiters singing me 'Happy Birthday'?"

"I could arrange it."

She shook her head. "Don't you dare, it's enough that poor Benjamin has been kept back."

"He was happy to earn a few extra dollars."

They both took sips of their champagne.

Carlos looked over his glass at her. "I wasn't sure that you would come."

Ketty chuckled. "When one is summoned by the maître d', one doesn't refuse."

"I am so sorry your fellow diners have caused you a lot of grief this time. It was not my intention to spoil your cruise."

"You didn't. It's turned out all right."

"Really?"

"Yes, really. On the whole it's been a lot of fun and I've made several new friends."

"And caught up with some old ones?"

She ignored the question in his eyes and took a small forkful of cake. It was chocolate; dark, rich and creamy. "Mmmm!"

She rested the fork back on the plate and patted at her lips with her napkin. "I think I've laid a few skeletons I didn't know still lived in my closet to rest on this holiday, and I think a few of my table companions have more to look forward to when they return home."

"Good." Carlos raised his glass. "We should toast your success then. Perhaps it hasn't been quite the cruise you planned but it has not been a total failure."

Ketty tapped her glass gently against his. "And here's to retirement, Carlos. I wish you happy days in the sun. Who knows, perhaps we will meet up on a cruise one day where you will be a passenger."

Carlos nearly choked on his champagne. "Oh Ketty, you are a funny woman. I have loved this life but once I leave it, I never want to set foot on a cruise ship again. I think I'll become a train traveller. There are some intriguing journeys to be had around the world. Several in Australia that interest me. Do you like the idea of train travel, Ketty?"

She met his questioning look across the table. Cocooned in the glow of the lamplight, it was as if she and Carlos were the only two on the whole ship.

"Carlos," she said. "Anything is possible."

Thirty-nine

Day Nine – At Sea

Christine pressed against the back of the deckchair and relished the warmth and the invigorating fresh air. It was their last morning at sea and she'd be sad to leave this cabin and even the luxury of Maria whipping in to clean and tidy after them, although Christine would only admit that to herself. Frank had surprised her with room service for breakfast and she was feeling pleasantly sated and even a little light-headed from the champagne they'd shared. It was the first drink she'd had since the night of her outburst. She was very lucky to have a man like Frank. She wasn't sure she appreciated him enough and she was determined to do better.

She poured another coffee. "Tell me about this job. What exactly does a Director of Engineering and Horticulture do?"

He glanced up, put the last piece of his bacon and toast in his mouth and sat back. "Is there coffee left?"

She poured him a cup.

"They want someone with bigger picture ideas who could oversee a variety of projects from design through construction to maintenance. My department—"

"Your department?"

He nodded. "If I were to get the job I would have to oversee a large staff. It would be much more demanding than my last role. Different hours, some travel."

Christine sat up. "How are we going to manage, Frank? The kids have so many commitments."

"We might have to look at that."

"It's not fair to curtail what they do because of our work."

"Why not? We have to work, Christine. Lucca and Anna are older now, maybe they need to make some choices about what they want to do outside school. They've done so much, it might be time for them to decide on their favourite interests and stick to those instead of trying every new thing that comes along."

"I want them to have lots of experiences."

"They are, but life is getting busier. Anna's going to be in year eight, Lucca's study will be more demanding. We have to build in some downtime."

Christine felt the weight of life at home settle on her shoulders. She'd managed to shrug it off these last few days. Cruising, being on holiday, was such a release. She missed her kids but she didn't want to think about going home.

Frank leaned forward, took her hand. "You get so tired, Chrissie. I thought with my new job you could maybe change to part-time."

"Part-time, so I can do more for everyone at home?"

"No." He shook his head slowly. "I was thinking you could have more time for yourself."

"More time to cook and clean?"

"To do what you want. Cook and clean if that's what you want to do, take up a hobby, go to the gym, walk the dog, anything. You're always saying you don't have any you-time."

She frowned. She'd worked full-time since Anna had started school and part-time before that. There had never been the luxury of time to herself.

"We have to sit down and look at the finances, Chrissie, but maybe we could get a cleaner."

She put her coffee back on the table. "Are you really saying this job is going to earn you so much that I can cut back hours and we can run to getting a cleaner?"

"I told you it's a bigger responsibility and it's significant money. The cleaner might only be a once a month thing for the bigger jobs but we can look into it." He moved his chair closer so their knees were touching and he was looking directly into her eyes. "This is a chance to make a few changes in our lives."

The feel of his bare legs against hers sent a little shiver of desire through her but she tried to remain focused. "I don't want to leave our house, Frank."

He leaned closer, his hand on her thigh. "We don't have to move if that's what you really want."

She nodded. The thought of packing up and moving house was beyond her.

"But we can't renovate. Even if we had the money, construction on the scale you are thinking would mean living out of one corner of the house for months, in fact we'd probably have to pack up and move out while it was done."

She stared steadily into Frank's deep brown eyes. It was as if he'd read her mind. It was hard to concentrate as his hand slid further up her leg.

"I'm excited about this job, Chrissie."

He leaned in and kissed her, soft at first then firmer, deeper. When he stopped she opened her eyes. His face was only centimetres from hers.

"I'm sure we can find a house you'll love."

A lock of his hair had fallen forward over his cheek. She reached up and caressed it back into place. He kissed her wrist. She slid her arm around his neck and drew him closer till their lips almost touched.

"Okay. Let's discuss it later. But for now..." She wrapped her other arm around his neck. "Take me back to bed, Frank," she murmured.

Bernard stepped carefully down into the spa and handed Josie a long tall glass of orange-coloured cocktail with a cheerful cherry on top. They tapped the glasses together.

"Cheers, my dear," he said and before she could take a sip, he kissed her.

Her spare hand pushed on his chest. "Down, boy."

They both took a mouthful of cocktail.

Josie licked her lips. "That is delicious. What is it this time?"

"Mucho Mango. It's blended with Bacardi and Malibu."

Josie raised her eyebrows. "Drinking in the middle of the day can be treacherous. I will need to have lunch soon."

"I've booked a table at the Italian place."

"Perfect." She took another sip then rested her head on the edge of the spa. "This is divine."

Bernard took in her bare shoulders then his gaze drifted down to the top of her bikini. "I'd say so."

She looked at him, a cheeky smile playing on her lips. "You're not bad eye candy yourself."

"We are going to keep seeing each other when we get back to Brisbane, aren't we?" He didn't want this time with Josie to end.

She sat forward, her face close to his. "You said you had a pool and a spa?"

"Yes."

"Then I'll need to check it out." She trickled her fingers down his chest. "And you, on a regular basis."

Bernard smiled and put one arm around her shoulders, drawing her closer. "What do you say after lunch we book our next cruise?"

"Seriously?"

"No time like the present."

"I did like the look of that one to South-East Asia."

"Let's do it."

"I'd have to check the dates and my diary."

"Fair enough." He leaned down and nibbled her ear. "We can share a cabin."

"Wouldn't that be nice?" She twisted under his arm and lifted her sunglasses to look him straight in the eyes. "I'd be paying my own way though. Wouldn't want anyone to think I was sponging off you."

"Of course." He laughed. "That's the only reason I asked. Makes it cheaper for me."

She gave him a nudge and settled back into the nook of his arm again. "This is the life."

"It was the best decision I've made in a long time to come on this cruise." He kissed the top of her head.

"I'll drink to that." Josie tapped her glass to his.

Celia smiled at Jim across the table. "I hope you don't mind Maude having lunch with us." She glanced in the direction her friend had gone towards the sweets buffet.

"Of course not." He looked in Maude's direction too. "She seems rather sad."

"Things have fallen apart a bit. Pete's wife is much improved and she's wanting to do lots of things to make up for lost time. Maude's feeling a bit the odd one out. I'm not sure what's gone on but from what I can gather it seems since the night of the planned meeting in our cabin that didn't happen, Pete has backed off and spends most of his time with his wife."

"As it should be."

"If I didn't know better I'd think Ketty had something to do with it but I can't see how."

Jim lowered his voice. "Maybe Ketty could steer Maude in Nigel's direction?" He knew it was being a bit unkind to both Nigel and Maude but poor Celia had had a tough time because of both of them.

"I don't think Maude would appreciate it. Or Nigel, who got over me and has found the perfect partner, *apparently*."

"I'm glad. I can't imagine how dull this cruise would have been without you."

"You would have made other friends."

"Maybe." He studied her closely. "But none as nice as you."

She met his look, glanced away, chewed her lip.

"We haven't discussed what happens tomorrow," he said.

"I don't want to think about it."

"You'll disappear back to rural South Australia."

"I've a couple of days in Sydney first."

"That's great." His spirits soared then dropped. "With Maude?"

"No. On my own. Maude has to get back but I have a ticket for a show."

Jim leaned forward a little. "My son booked us into a hotel in the city for a couple of nights. I had planned to cancel and change my flight home but now...well, perhaps I'll stay on."

"We could go sightseeing together. My last trip to Sydney didn't end well. I'd like to make some new memories."

"You two look pleased with yourselves." Maude placed a plate loaded with several desserts on the table.

Jim sat back and retracted his hand. "Making plans for tomorrow."

Maude gave a shrug and resumed her seat next to Celia. "My flight leaves around one so I'm taking the shuttle from the terminal to the airport. Then that's it. Party over. Back to reality." She took a bite of a mini pavlova loaded with strawberries and cream.

"You'll be back in time for the bowls carnival. That's what you decided when we booked."

"Only because Beryl convinced me to be her partner."

"You'll enjoy it once you get there."

"Home will be dull after this."

"I'll be back in a few days," Celia said. "I'll be able to show you how to make that online photo album we talked about."

Both Celia and Jim watched Maude stuff the last piece of pavlova into her mouth. Jim turned to Celia. She was smiling at Maude. It was a kind and reassuring look, then she shifted it to him and he smiled back with a new warm feeling he was coming to enjoy. Anyone Celia Braxton called friend was a very lucky person indeed.

Forty

Night Nine – At Sea

"Ah, Miss Clift, you are very prompt this evening."

Ketty smiled at Carlos. She was at the head of the line of diners waiting to enter as the doors opened.

"Good evening, Carlos. I would rather like to sit at the top end of the table on my last night."

"Of course." He inclined his head as she moved on.

As anticipated the table was empty, and Ketty edged around the outside to the chair at the other end with its back to the column.

"Good evening, Phillip, Rupert." She smiled at both waiters and drew two envelopes from the small clutch bag she'd brought with her. "Thank you both for your excellent service." She slipped an envelope to each of them.

"Thank you, Miss Clift." Their smiles were wide as they slid her gift discreetly into their pockets.

"It has been our pleasure to serve you." Phillip laid the napkin across her lap.

"Gin and tonic?" Rupert asked with a grin.

"Thank you, yes, and can you also bring a bottle of the white wine we've been having for later please?"

"Certainly, Miss Clift."

Ketty glanced around the dining room while she waited for the others to arrive. Josie had called in to return a necklace during the afternoon and told her that Leo was planning to eat elsewhere. She had looked a bit sad about it but Ketty had been relieved. Tonight she selfishly wanted only happy memories of the final dinner aboard the *Diamond Duchess.*

For her the last night of a cruise was usually a happy one, tinged with a little sorrow that she would be going home tomorrow; the sign of a good holiday, she thought. Now when she imagined returning home, it was with optimism. Obviously, things had been happening at Ketty Clift Couture while she'd been away and she was impatient to see them for herself.

"Hello, Ketty." Frank grinned broadly.

She smiled as the Romanos filled the seats to her right, Frank beside her and then his wife. Christine handed her a small bag. "Thank you for letting me wear your lace wrap."

"You know, it was perfect for your dress, why don't you keep it."

"Are you sure?"

"Of course. A memento from me of your holiday."

"But won't you want to lend it to someone else?"

"Sometimes my bits and pieces find new homes. I think the black wrap will do very well with you."

Christine blinked back tears. "That's very kind."

Jim and Celia arrived next and sat on Ketty's left. The two of them had a glow on their faces and a sparkle in their eyes that warmed Ketty's heart to see.

Bernard and Josie were only a few minutes behind them, leaving one last empty seat that Ketty avoided looking at. Phillip and

Rupert moved around, distributing napkins, filling water glasses, telling a new set of jokes.

Drink and food orders were taken and no sooner were the waiters away than Bernard leaned in and looked directly at Ketty.

"When should you give them the tip?"

"Whenever you like," Ketty said. "Although with everyone here perhaps as you leave."

"Tip?" Frank looked to Christine. "We didn't organise anything."

"Part of the cost of our cruise is shared to the staff in gratuities." Christine sniffed. "I'm certainly not giving our room steward anything extra."

"My chap was excellent," Jim said.

"And mine," Celia said. "And our waiters have been very efficient and good humoured. I'm happy to give them something extra."

"So am I," Bernard said. "These two young blokes have families, Chrissie, and they don't get a huge wage. I am sure any extra bit helps."

"I think we should," Frank added.

Christine looked a little contrite. "We can leave some money on the table when we go. Although it won't be much if they don't hurry up with our drinks. I'm parched."

In only a few minutes everyone had a drink and Bernard raised his glass towards Ketty.

"We need to make a special toast tonight," he said. "For your belated birthday."

"Oh yes, happy birthday, Ketty." Celia smiled from down the table and the others echoed the sentiment.

Once they were done Ketty wagged a finger. "Now, no more fuss about birthdays," she said. "I have been very spoiled."

"Chrissie," Bernard said. "You're wearing the necklace. Where was it?"

Christine and Frank glanced at each other and she put her hand to the heart-shaped pendant.

"In one of my shoes," Frank said. "I'd left them under the bench and we think the necklace must have dropped in. I found it tonight when we were packing our bags."

"So not stolen then," Bernard said.

Christine shook her head. There was extra pink in her cheeks.

"I hope there won't be any delays tomorrow," she said. "We'll be cutting it fine to make our flight to Melbourne."

"Are you taking the cruise ship shuttle?" Ketty asked.

"Yes."

"They'll have it in hand. You don't need to worry."

"Jim and I had both arranged to stay on in Sydney for a few days," Celia said. "We wondered if anyone would like to catch up for a meal."

"I'm flying back to Brisbane after lunch tomorrow," Bernard said.

"I can go for a meal," Josie said. "But Leo's going straight home." She looked a little sad.

"Would you join us, Ketty?" Jim asked.

"I'd love to."

Their waiters whisked away the entrée plates and began setting out the main course.

"It's a pity you're going straight back to Brisbane, Dad," Christine said. "The kids are on holidays and I have to go back to work in a few days. You could have come to Melbourne and looked after them and spent some time together."

Bernard scratched at his chin. "You didn't mention it before."

"It might not work out this time," Josie said. "But I do hope Bernie and I can come and visit. If it's helpful we could coincide with the next school holidays."

"The kids would love it and so would we, wouldn't we, Chrissie?" Frank said.

Christine was staring at Josie across the table in surprise. "Yes, we would, thank you."

"Anyway, I'm still on holidays this week," Frank said. "And if I get this new job I might be able to take leave until my notice." He smiled around table. "We're going house hunting."

"Great," Bernard said.

"Let's not jump ahead too far," Christine said. "I can't see how we'll have time to look for a new house, get uniforms and books sorted for the new year. If we're putting our place on the market there will be so much to do. You'll have to clean out the shed, Frank, and Anna and Lucca will have to get rid of the stuff they've been hoarding in their bedrooms. I'm not going to do everything by myself."

Frank frowned and shook his head. "You won't be."

"Humph!" Christine picked up her empty wine glass. "Is the bottle empty? Where are those waiters?"

Ketty smiled down at her hands. It was probably too much to expect Christine to totally change her ways.

Celia sensed something different about Jim. He'd asked her to go on a walk around the promenade deck as they'd done on several nights, but this time he was almost twitchy.

"You'll need to slow down a little, Jim. I don't have my proper walking shoes on. These are only suitable for strolling."

"Sorry." He gripped the arm that she had hooked through his, then he stopped.

Celia halted beside him. "Is something wrong?"

"No." Jim shook his head. "Not at all." He looked away.

Celia glanced in the direction he was. There was nothing but inky blackness out there and the sound of the sea as it rushed past the side of the ship.

"All right." He spoke loudly, startling Celia. He was studying her intently but said nothing more.

"All right what?" she asked.

"I have to ask you something. You can say no. I don't want to pressure you."

"What is it, Jim?"

"It's probably presumptuous of me but..."

Butterflies were galumphing around inside her again. "Perhaps if you just ask."

"I'm so out of practice at this." He gripped both of her hands in his.

"Whatever *this* is, I think I might be too."

"Celia, you are the nicest person. I feel foolish now."

"Please don't feel foolish, Jim." She extricated one hand from his tight grip and rested it against his chest. "I think my heart is beating as fast as yours."

"I've ordered supper and some champagne in my room...for the two of us, if you'd like to join me. Only it's such a nice suite and I've had it all to myself, except the night you stayed, and I thought perhaps we could enjoy a drink and some nibbles and sit on the balcony and—"

"I'd love to." It was such a relief to find out what he was asking. It was their last night aboard ship and she wasn't ready for it to end.

"Oh, great. Yes, that's good. Shall we go there now?"

"Why not?"

Inside the suite, room service had already been and everything was set out waiting for them.

"I shouldn't feel hungry after that beautiful dinner," Celia said. "But those canapes look good."

"Try them." Jim popped the champagne cork and poured.

Celia picked up a bite-sized salmon cake and dipped it in the saffron sauce before slipping it into her mouth. The flavours merged in a pop of savoury and sweet.

Jim passed Celia a glass. "What should we drink to?" he asked.

"More happy days ahead?"

"Happy days." He smiled then his eyes widened. "Wait."

Celia had her glass nearly to her mouth. He put his down.

"I have something for you." He went to the wooden wall cabinet and then was back in front of her holding out a small coloured box, his eyes alight with barely controlled mirth.

"A gift? Jim what are you up to?"

"Open it."

Celia put down her glass and slid the top from the box. Nestled inside was a turtle. She could see New Caledonia written on its back.

"Oh, Jim."

She laughed as she lifted the turtle from its box and its head began to jiggle. She gave a brief thought to the expensive turtle still in its wrapping that Nigel had given her and knew that she'd treasure this quirky little souvenir far more. She sat it on the low table and glanced up. Jim was watching her closely, his look slightly amused. He was a handsome man, funny and kind. He made her feel happy too and perhaps a little bit daring.

"That would have to be the second-best souvenir of the cruise," she said.

"What was the first?"

"You."

Celia swallowed and leaned forward, finding his lips with hers. Slowly his arms slid around her and pulled her closer, and he kissed her back. Snuggled against Jim's chest, Celia let out a small sigh.

"Thanks, Celia," he murmured.

She tilted her head to look at him. "What for? I don't have a gift for you."

"Making me laugh again. For me that's enough."

Forty-one

Alongside, White Bay Cruise Terminal, Sydney

The sun shone on the harbour and glinted off the glass of the terminal as Ketty made her way along, towing her overnight bag. She couldn't resist one last look back at the *Duchess* to try to work out which balcony had been hers.

She'd sat out on it first thing this morning as the ship had quietly entered Sydney Harbour. She loved the view of the little bays and islands that dotted the harbour, the Opera House, dull under the early morning cloud cover, and the sight of the Manly Ferry leaving Circular Quay. The ship had cruised under the bridge without the fanfare of its departure and then on up to its mooring in White Bay. She was home.

Before she'd closed her door on her cabin one last time, she'd wandered through it, tracing the surfaces with her fingers, saying goodbye. After her first cruise on the *Duchess* her life had fallen apart, there had been challenges, still would be ahead, but she felt after this final cruise on the grand old dame of the sea that her life was firmly back together and she had much to look forward to.

There was a pinging sound from her bag, another text message. This morning when she'd put her phone on to charge in her cabin, several texts and a missed call had registered. The call had been from her brother and when she had listened to the message, he'd said, "It's your brother, call me when you can." It frustrated her that he could never leave a hint as to what his call might be about.

The texts were a series sent by Judith and a couple from an unknown number that she discovered was Lacey's. Judith's had been sent daily with the total takings for each day and what was banked. Ketty's eyes widened as the totals steadily grew larger. Except for the first few days, her business had been taking in much bigger amounts in her absence. Lacey's texts were to do with her website and now that Ketty had seen it for herself she understood they'd opened online and picked up business immediately.

Now, as she entered the terminal, her excitement was building but the new messages would have to wait. She'd stuffed the phone in her bag and she wasn't going to be bothered to stop here and rummage for it.

She made her way through customs, found her case then stepped out into the open expanse of the terminal hall.

"Ketty?"

She looked up to see Greg striding towards her. Her eyes drank in his slightly dishevelled dark curls, his warm smile. It was unexpected but delightful to see her adored nephew.

"Welcome back." He drew her into his arms, wrapping her in a bear-like hug. "Crikey!" he stepped back. "I thought they were supposed to fatten you up on those cruise ships. You're as thin as ever."

Ketty smiled. Greg was tall and rather well filled out. Many people would seem thin to him. "I ate my fair share."

"I like your hair. What a great cut."

"Thank you, Greg, but what are you doing here in Sydney?"

"I told Dad I'd meet you."

"Is your father in town?"

"And Mum. We're hoping you feel up to having lunch with us. Let me take your case. I'll drive you home first and you can freshen up."

She opened her mouth to protest.

"For your birthday."

"You don't need to fuss."

"I'm not. Mum and Dad were in town anyway and…well, there's someone I'd like you to meet. I have a bit of news."

"I would love to see everyone. I've got gifts."

Greg opened the door and they stepped out of the air conditioning into a muggy Sydney morning. Ketty loosened the scarf she'd draped around her neck.

"Dad tried to ring you before you left and I've sent a few texts." He gave her a sideways glance. "Is your phone turned on?"

"It is now. There was a message from your father but as usual there was no information."

They reached Greg's car. He opened the door for her, put her bags in the boot then climbed in beside her.

"Good cruise?" he asked as he turned on the ignition and cranked up the air con. A chocolatey smooth voice blared from the speakers. He turned it down.

She smiled. She'd taught him about jazz as a teenager.

"It was lovely."

"Made a new lot of friends?"

"Going to have dinner with a couple in a day or so."

Ketty studied Greg. He hadn't started the car but sat sideways looking at her. A little niggle of concern chipped at her excitement. Perhaps her brother's call wasn't good news and that's why he hadn't left a message.

"How's everything here?" she asked.

"Fine. Everyone's well." He rattled the keys in the ignition.

"You said you had news."

"I'm getting married."

"Good heavens." She reached out to hug him. "How wonderful. Who to? Will I approve?"

"Cass. I love her."

"Then I'm sure I will too."

"Aunt Ketty, there's something else."

"Uh oh." She studied him closely. "You only call me 'Aunt' when you're in trouble. What's happened?"

"I want to tell you the rest before you meet Cass. We're having a low-key wedding very soon."

"How eminently sensible. Weddings are getting out of hand these days."

Once more the keys jangled. She waited.

"Like I said, I love Cass."

Ketty nodded.

"And, she's pregnant. We're having a baby." His face split in a huge grin.

Ketty threw her arms around him again. "Oh, Greg, that's terrific news. A wedding and a baby."

"You'll be its surrogate grandma."

She let him go. "I'm having none of that. Your mother can be Grandma. I'll be plain Ketty."

Greg laughed. "There's absolutely nothing plain about you, Ketty."

He started the car and they drove out of the carpark and past the taxi rank where Jim was helping Celia into a taxi. Ketty waved and they waved back. She looked beyond them to the cruise ship towering high above the wharf. Was Carlos still on board or would he have gone ashore already? She felt a moment of sadness at the thought she'd probably never see him again. Her phone pinged and this time she dug it out of her bag.

She smiled when she saw the latest text was from Carlos, as if thinking about him had conjured him up. She had to find her glasses to read it. It simply said *look at this* and was followed by a long line of blue text that she knew indicated a link to a website. Something to do with the Ghan rail journey. She put the phone down again. Ahead of them Sydney sparkled under a brilliant blue sky and her spirits sparkled with it. Not only was she blessed with dear family and good friends but she had Ketty Clift Couture and she was eager to find out more about the changes that had taken place in her absence. She peered at the phone in her lap, thinking about the photos she'd seen on her new website depicting a much more modern-looking shopfront. She'd like to look at them again but she had no idea how to do that on her phone.

"Greg, dear."

He glanced at her. "Now it's my turn to 'uh oh'. I know that tone."

"Nothing you can't handle. I've already had a bit of a lesson on the ship but I think you are going to have to help me get up to speed with emails and websites and things."

"Sure Ketty. Any time."

He accelerated, opened the sun roof and turned up the music. Ketty watched the harbour and caught her last glimpse of the *Diamond Duchess* as it disappeared behind sheds and fences.

The breeze flicked her scarf as she settled back in her seat. The sun was warm on her face and the wind ruffled her hair. Jazzy piano blared from the speakers and Bryan Ferry sang 'As Time Goes By'. Greg began to sing along. She joined in and flung her hands in the air through the open roof. They looked at each other and laughed.

Ketty had no regrets now. She sang louder as the car accelerated over the bridge. She was going home and looking forward to what the future would bring, both for her and for Ketty Clift Couture.

Acknowledgements

My husband and I have been lucky enough to take several short cruises, both with friends and as a couple; either way, we've made many more friends and enjoyed the experience immensely. Exceptional staff did their best to look after our every need with a smile. We visited other countries, dipped into other cultures and met many friendly fellow travellers, none of whom are the characters in this story.

There are a couple of small exceptions, of course. I did sit next to a woman one night at dinner whose love of cruising inspired me to create Ketty. And I would like to thank Jan Fenell and her daughter Sally, whose company we enjoyed on a trip to the South Pacific and who allowed me to embellish their real-life water snake experience.

My thanks also to Jesse, a customer support officer, who, after my reassurance that I was asking purely for research for my next book, very kindly answered questions about the process that is followed if someone is suspected missing on a cruise ship.

Other than that the rest is fiction. Cruising set my imagination cogs turning and whether you've cruised or not, I hope you enjoy the result.

A lot of work goes into bringing a book to you and I am so grateful to be part of the Harlequin and now HarperCollins family. This is our tenth book together, a place I never imagined myself being. Thank you to my fabulous publisher, Jo Mackay, who kept me focused on Ketty's story when it seemed too challenging, and to editor extraordinaire Annabel Blay, who helped me, sometimes with the jab of a blunt pencil, to draw out the best in the tale. I am grateful to the rest of the dedicated people who've had a hand in bringing this book to life from proofer Alex Craig, to the design team and cover designer Michelle Zaiter – I love the cover – sales director Darren Kelly, marketing and publicity team Adam van Rooijen and Natika Palka, and the many others involved. It's been a real team effort and I look forward to the next.

Big cheers to my local community who sustain my writing in many ways – your words of encouragement and support for events are much appreciated. New publicity photos were taken for this book and I want to thank locals Selina at Tangles for her cut and style of my wayward hair and Kym from Kym Gregory Photography for his photographic expertise. And thank you to Sandra Paddick and her team from Kadina Travel who always make sure our holiday plans run smoothly. I am very lucky to live where I do.

I appreciate the support of writing buddies, ever at the end of an email or the phone or happy to chat over a drink, ready to share ideas and reassurance in this sometimes isolated writer's life. In particular, thanks to Meredith Appleyard and Rachael Johns for the many chats that helped keep me going.

As ever I am grateful to my dear friends and family whose encouragement is boundless. I am so lucky to have my children and their partners, who look out for me and help me in many ways. This book is dedicated to my wonderful daughter-in-law Sian, who is always there for me when it comes to tweaking and proofing. And thank you to Daryl, who is cooking me a gourmet meal as I write this. How blessed am I?

And a big hello and thank you to all the booksellers and librarians who champion my books, and to you dear readers. It's my delight to bring *Table for Eight* to life for you.

Finally, this story has touched on different aspects of the grieving process, something that everyone has to deal with at some point in their life. If this has raised issues for you, please remember no one needs to face their problems alone. Help is always available from family and friends and further afield. Two of the groups who offer support are:

Lifeline, a national charity providing all Australians experiencing a personal crisis with access to 24-hour crisis support and suicide prevention services. Call 13 11 14.

Beyondblue, providing information and support to help everyone in Australia achieve their best possible mental health, whatever their age and wherever they live. Call 1300 22 4636.

One

Felicity

Felicity Lewis paused a minute to take it all in.

It was a balmy night in Adelaide; the temperature had dropped just enough after a hot March day for perfect outdoor entertaining. At number seventeen Herbert Street, West Beach, two streets back from the ocean, a party was in progress. Behind Felicity the carefully selected mood music resonated from the curved teak speaker, enough to be heard but not so loud people couldn't hear themselves speak. It had been a birthday gift from Ian and Greta, not a total surprise, not any kind of surprise. She'd dropped several hints, which included leaving shop brochures lying around opened to pages with the desired gift circled.

The speaker sat on the polished shelf below their wall-mounted television in the big open-plan family room that stretched almost the full width of the back of the house. The glass doors to the deck were all thrown open. Around her milled friends and family enjoying the food she'd cooked and the drinks she'd selected.

Light spilled across the freshly oiled deck and out onto the back lawn where strands of festoon lights, hung in precise loops across the garden, added their glow to the glorious spectacle of a million stars twinkling overhead. It was a perfect autumn evening.

An arm slipped around her waist. "Everything looks fabulous, Mum."

"As do you." Felicity beamed at her daughter.

"I've taken lots of photos of the guests." Greta lifted her phone and leaned her head against Felicity's. "Selfie."

Felicity blinked at the flash. "I haven't had a chance to tell you how good you look in that outfit." She adjusted the soft bow pulling Greta's drapey pants in.

Greta batted her hand away and readjusted the bow. "I don't know that cream is a good colour for me."

"It's perfect against your tan."

"I was thinking more that I'm likely to spill something down it." She glanced around. "Where's Suzie? I haven't seen her yet."

"I told you Paul took her to America for her birthday."

"No you didn't." Greta frowned.

"They'll be gone for two months."

"How will you manage not seeing her for that long?"

"Technology."

"Dad should have taken you away, instead of you doing all this work."

"I've enjoyed it—"

"Oh, look there're the Gilberts. Thank goodness there's someone more my age. I'll get a photo of them too." Greta dashed away.

Once more Felicity stood alone. She'd organised this special night to the last detail, a combined celebration for her fiftieth birthday and the completion of the renovations. She'd been planning, styling, cooking for weeks. The only downside was her best friend Suzie couldn't be there.

Suzie and Paul had only been gone for two weeks and were having the best time. Felicity had already seen the photos of their Caribbean cruise and now they were driving themselves up the coast to New York. Suzie had rung this morning via WhatsApp to sing her happy birthday all the way from Jacksonville, Florida. Her brilliant smile and animated words had filled the room. Felicity had sat for a long time after the call had ended trying to swallow her glum mood and lack of enthusiasm for a party without her best friend. Suzie had provided all the energy for both of them during the call.

"Happy birthday, Felicity." Humphrey from next door drew her into a bear hug and planted one of his sloppy kisses on her cheek.

She adjusted her new glasses firmly back in place as his wife Melody also wrapped her in a hug.

"Perfect night for a party," Melody said.

"Thanks for coming. What would you like to drink?" Felicity waved over one of the young uni students Greta had organised to act as waiters for the night.

"Feliciteee, I love what you've done with the house." Pam, her social tennis friend, air kissed her cheeks. "I haven't seen it since you did this back extension, and the deck is fabulous. I can picture us having a few post tennis sessions here." Pam clutched a glass of champagne and as her arm swept out in a dramatic arc it connected with a man just stepping up onto the deck.

"Oh, I'm so sorry." She dabbed at his wet sleeve.

"No problem."

"Pam, I don't think you've met Tony," Felicity said. "He's been overseeing the renovations."

"Has he now?" Pam looked him up and down. "Well, there's a secret you've been keeping to yourself."

"Nice to meet you, Pam." Tony smiled, offered his hand.

Pam's return look was vampish.

"Let me get you another drink," he said.

The bar was an old table Felicity had scrubbed to create a rustic look, adorned with ice buckets and glasses and one large bowl of flowers in soft pinks and mauves. She'd canned Greta's suggestion of balloons but had allowed the banner, which looped across the sheer curtain she'd hung on the wall behind. In cursive letters cut from sparkly gold it said 'Cheers to fifty years'.

Tony set off towards it. Pam stared after him.

"Did you knock into him on purpose?" Felicity said.

"Moi?"

"He's married." Felicity didn't actually know what Tony's marital status was but he was too nice a man to get tangled up with Pam. Every one of her relationships since her last divorce had ended in drama.

"Really? No ring on his finger."

"You've checked already? He's too young for you."

"Past the age of consent."

"Hi Felicity, Pam." More hugs all round, this time from Tansie, another of their tennis group, and her husband Charles.

"This is Tony," Pam said as he came back with several glasses of sparkling gripped between his two large hands. "He's responsible for Felicity's fabulous renovation."

Tony shrugged. "Felicity was the driving force, I just made sure the structural stuff was legit."

"You're very modest, Tony," Felicity said.

Tansie and Charles were planning a new bathroom and when Felicity could see Tony was safely in a discussion with Charles she edged away.

At the other end of the deck her own husband, Ian, was deep in conversation with their across-the-road neighbours, Sal and Les. Like Ian, they were bike riders. Along with several others from their neighbourhood, they rode regularly. Not Felicity, of course. She didn't own a bike and never wanted to. Getting hot and sweaty in lycra had never been her thing. Nor Ian's until they'd moved here. Two years older than her, the approach of his fiftieth birthday had seen him turn into some kind of fitness freak. Not that Felicity minded. She was a homebody and the renovations had kept her busy, first in the planning, then in the construction and the refurbishing. Her workout was her weekly social tennis match and that was more about the company than the exercise.

After they'd moved they'd started taking regular walks to the beach but hadn't in ages. These days Ian power walked everywhere on his own or with his walking group, training for more arduous treks, while she'd been filling her time with colour charts and fabric swatches. Ian had been involved in the renovations when they were deciding on the structural changes to the house but after that he'd been happy to let her make decisions about the finishing touches.

This party was a birthday celebration but also the official end to the whole house renovation, a project that had consumed her since the moment they'd made the decision to buy the fixer-upper more than five years ago. She'd given up her job as practice manager at a doctor's office when they'd moved. Now she'd have to find something else to fill her time. It wasn't until she'd been dressing for the party that she'd realised she had no idea what that would be.

"Have you seen our parents yet?"

Felicity gave her sister a quick look then shook her head. Tall and lanky like their father, June was wearing a grass-green all-in-one jumpsuit. It reminded Felicity of a praying mantis. For two sisters born less than a year apart they were chalk and cheese.

"Not like them to be late," June said.

"Dad's hard to get moving these days."

"We did offer to collect them."

"I'm sure they'll be here soon," Felicity said. It was possible her father had pulled another of his tantrums and they wouldn't turn up at all but she kept that to herself. He could do no wrong in June's eyes but there had been so many times over the years when he'd spoiled celebrations or social occasions.

Her wedding day had been mortifying. Most dads were proud and happy on their daughter's wedding day but not her father. Felicity had caused a ruckus by daring to find a husband before June. Not that June minded but their father did. She was always first in his eyes and Felicity had stolen her position this time.

On the day of the wedding he'd been grumpy, oozing disapproval of the goings-on, as he'd called it, as Felicity and her bridesmaids were getting ready. Just before they'd been due to leave for the church he'd gone out for a walk – to clear his head, he'd declared. They hadn't been bothered until the photographer was tapping his toes waiting to take the standard father–daughter photos. June had been the one to track him down and drag him home to walk his daughter down the aisle. Their mother had been upset and so had Felicity. They'd arrived fifteen minutes late to the church and for the rest of the day her father had told anyone who'd listen it was because Felicity had been disorganised with her preparations and the household carrying on like a bunch of chooks.

"Perhaps I should ring Mum." June cut into her thoughts.

"Let's leave it for a while. They'll turn up."

Hazel Gifford was a saint to have put up with her husband all these years and if her father was in one of his moods Felicity would rather he didn't come.

"Oh, isn't that your old neighbour?" June waved in the direction of a man towering over the crowd. "The one that lived down the road and sold up and bought a caravan."

"Yes."

"Such a lovely couple. Can't see her, what were their names, but then she's so short, isn't she." June set off towards the new arrivals without waiting for an answer.

Instead of following her Felicity stepped down off the deck, fanning her face with her hand. The air was slightly cooler out from under the verandah and she relished it. Hormone replacement tablets ensured the hot flushes of menopause didn't affect her too terribly but just at that moment she felt as if her internal thermostat was ready to boil over. She moved further away and took the path to a corner of the yard that wasn't lit. From her vantage point she had time to let her body cool down, to take a breath and observe. She'd been on her feet since she got out of bed this morning and she needed a few minutes to regroup.

She enjoyed creating special dinners for friends, loved parties and entertaining, but she was far better at the preparation, the cooking and the serving than the conversation. If it wasn't for Ian insisting they go out for dinner, see an exhibition, travel, she'd simply stay home in her comfy clothes and slippers.

It had been more her idea to move than his but he'd gone along with it, liking their proximity to the beach and the walking and bike trails. His income was a good one and even though they'd extended their small mortgage to do the renovations they were comfortable these days. Felicity had been careful to stick to the budget they'd allocated and they hadn't overcapitalised.

She took in the sleek lines of the back of the house, the glass, the deck and the party now in full swing. Someone had turned up the music and the voices carried loudly on the still night. All their neighbours were here so the noise shouldn't bother anyone. They'd been lucky with the people in their small street. Ian had made it his business to get to know them all as soon as they'd moved in and they'd proved to be a friendly lot. She was glad they could all come. Even a few who'd moved away were here.

"What's the birthday girl doing out here on her own?" Ian came towards her, a glass of champagne in each hand. He offered her one, brushed a kiss across her forehead and tapped his glass against hers. "Happy birthday, Lissie." She smiled, took a sip and watched as he did the same.

"Thanks," she said. Ian rarely drank these days so she was pleased by the sentiment and that it was just the two of them.

"I should make a speech soon and you should cut the cake before our friends drink too much more of this champagne."

"One more minute," she said. Butterflies flapped inside her at the thought of being the centre of attention and she took another sip.

"You wanted this party." Ian's words were accusatory and yet his tone gentle.

"I love parties, just not being the main event."

"Remember my fiftieth? I wanted us to go away but you insisted on a big party instead."

"Hiking the Inca trail to Machu Picchu wouldn't have been a holiday."

"But it was what I wanted."

She looked away from the yearning in his eyes back to the party. "We've been so lucky," she said.

His yes was barely more than a whisper.

"I worry one day it's all going to come crashing down."

He took a sip of his drink before he responded. "That's a morbid thought on your birthday."

"We've had a trouble-free life."

"Not always." This time his reply was quick and sharp then he drew in a long breath and let it out again, slowly. "Remember when we first married. We had nothing."

"Everyone started that way. We lived on love." She smiled at him but he was looking at the crowd.

"You were laid up with that broken ankle and we nearly lost the house."

"That was so long ago it's hard to imagine now." They'd not had loss of income insurance in those days – a combination of thinking they were bulletproof and not being able to afford it. She'd asked her father for a loan. He'd refused. Ian came from a big family with not much money to go round but his parents had lent them a bit to get them by. They'd paid them back of course, but it had been a terrible struggle.

"Then the babies we lost." Ian was still staring at the crowd. He was usually a cup-half-full kind of guy. This melancholic side of him was rare.

"I wish I hadn't said anything now." She sipped some champagne then tried a light laugh but the liquid caught in her throat and the laugh came out as a series of clucks.

"There were three little ones we never got to know," he said.

She gripped the stem of her glass. She knew how many babies they'd lost as well as he did. It wasn't something she was ever likely to forget but there was no point bringing it up now. "You really are going down the sad old memory lane. The miscarriages were tough but we've got our beautiful Greta."

"She's a wonderful young woman," he said.

Happy to banish any further maudlin thoughts, Felicity tapped her glass to his. "I'll drink to that."

"We should go back to our guests, get the formalities over then you can relax." He started to walk away, his look distracted. She'd hardly seen him these last few days. She'd been so caught up in party preparations, and now that she thought about it they'd not said more than two words to each other for...she couldn't think how long. Weeks?

"Ian?"

He stopped, turned back. The frown he'd worn changed to a smile but she could tell it was forced. He reached out a hand. "Come on, Lissie. This is your night. Time to face the music and have your friends sing 'Happy Birthday'."

"Mum?" Greta came towards them across the lawn, the brightly lit house glowing behind her. "What are you doing out here? I've been looking everywhere for you." She held her mobile phone towards Felicity. "It's Nan. She sounds upset."

Damn Dad, Felicity thought as she pressed the warm phone to her ear. He's kicked up a fuss and decided not to come. "Hello, Mum."

"Felicity, I tried June's phone."

"She never has it on her."

"Then I tried yours."

"Mum, take a breath. Why aren't you here? Is everything all right?" She hated asking that question knowing everything wouldn't be all right. Not that she really cared but for her mum's sake...

"It's your father."

Felicity pursed her lips. Of course it was her father. "What's he up to this time?" She raised her shoulders and gave a slight shake of her head at Greta and Ian who were both standing by.

"Is June there?" Hazel's voice had an edginess to it. Felicity hoped she wasn't going to have one of her dizzy attacks.

"Not right beside me but she's here."

Ian began to tap his foot.

"I'll call you back, Mum, we're about to cut the cake."

"Oh, I've ruined your lovely party."

"No, you haven't. I'll bring you some cake and leftovers tomorrow." Damn her dad for his moods. For the zillionth time in her life she wondered how her mother put up with him. Tomorrow there'd be the aftermath of the party to clean up and Felicity would be tired but now she'd be stuck in the car for nearly two hours going to and from her parents when they could have come tonight.

"You'll have to be strong for June," Hazel said.

Ian was tapping his watch now and pointing back to the party.

"Mum, I have to go – can you tell me tomo—"

"Felicity, brace yourself." There was a sharp intake of breath. "Your father's dead."